sheer pressure

sheer pressure

a novel by

Greg Abbott

Dale,

Enjoy the ride.

Greg

iUniverse, Inc.
New York Lincoln Shanghai

SHEER PRESSURE

iUniverse books may be ordered through booksellers or by contacting:

iUniverse
2021 Pine Lake Road, Suite 100
Lincoln, NE 68512
www.iuniverse.com
1-800-Authors (1-800-288-4677)

This is a work of fiction. All of the characters, names, incidents, organizations and dialogue in this novel are either the products of the author's imagination or are used fictitiously.

ISBN-13: 978-0-595-38653-6 (pbk)
ISBN-13: 978-0-595-67631-6 (cloth)
ISBN-13: 978-0-595-83034-3 (ebk)
ISBN-10: 0-595-38653-9 (pbk)
ISBN-10: 0-595-67631-6 (cloth)
ISBN-10: 0-595-83034-X (ebk)

Printed in the United States of America

To my saviors: Ian, Malcolm, Helena, Janice, George, Chris, and especially Marcia, my guardian angel. Thanks for putting up with me.

1

The Great Escape

With mounting nervousness, Alex Halaby chained his new Harley to the stoop of his parents' townhouse. Given the posh Manhattan location, between Madison and Fifth on well-lit East Seventy-Third Street, he could have safely parked the bike on the curb. *This* motorcycle, however, was too magnificent and too recently acquired to subject even to the slightest risk. It was his thirtieth birthday gift to himself, and a thing of beauty: six hundred fifty pounds of gleaming chrome and psychedelic paint, complete with large "retro" fenders like the bikes of the sixties and leather streamers dangling from the handlebars. The saddle and saddlebags were hand-stitched and trimmed with fringe, as was his motorcycle jacket.

The Harley salesman in Long Island City had been emphatic: "A Harley is more than a bike," he had told Alex during his spiel. "It's an attitude. A Harley says power. It says danger. It cannot be ignored. A Harley, my friend, is the ultimate ticket to adventure!"

Blowhard as the salesman was, Alex needed all the adventure he could get. Rather than buy one of the ready-made bikes off the showroom floor, he began poring over photos in biker magazines, picking out elements he liked about dozens of bikes to incorporate into his own customized invention. It took the dealer's mechanic four months to build the rip-roaring sex machine to its buyer's specifications. After much anticipation, and with nothing pressing on his work calendar, Alex had chosen today, his birthday, to take possession of his toy and ride it all around the city. Rather than satisfy his recent restlessness, however, it only fueled his wanderlust. Only when he was riding atop the splendid machine was he the master of his fate.

He lingered on the stoop, admiring his creation, which sparkled even in the early evening shadows. With May sweetening the air and Central Park in bloom, the temptation to take off to parts unknown was almost unbearable. He saw himself speeding west through the New Jersey countryside, pointed toward the sunset, streamers flying, not caring where he was going, responsible to no one. The

1

Harley was his first step toward autonomy, as his shrink had pointed out. His shrink: another new acquisition that his parents were sure to condemn.

He entered the six-story limestone townhouse, which served not only as his parents' residence but also as the headquarters for the family business. Alex found the setup smothering. Family obligations and business obligations beckoned together from one black hole on the Upper East Side.

"You should live here and save money," his mother had carped the other day. "You never know when you'll need it."

"I'm thirty years old, Mom," Alex gently reminded her, shutting himself off from her intrusive gaze while at the same time not wanting to hurt her feelings.

"We'll give you all the privacy you need. You can come and go as you please. Consider it like a family compound."

"Isn't it enough that I show up here every weekday morning at eight-thirty?"

"But always from a different direction," joked his father.

Having tonight's milestone birthday dinner in the townhouse annoyed him; he would have rather taken a private room at a restaurant and invited the people he wanted. However, his suggestions, as always, had fallen on deaf ears, and arguing with his parents was never worth the aggravation. They always bludgeoned him into submission.

Business was conducted on the first floor, though a casual observer would have no way of telling what kind of business it was. The place looked more like a consulate than the offices of a pantyhose company. There was no showroom, and no freestanding plastic legs graced the reproduction Chippendale furniture. The venerable, century-old residence, adorned with high ceilings and ornate woodworking, gave the illusion of an older, more solid fortune than actually existed. Buying the townhouse had strained the company's balance sheet, but Alex's father insisted that an opulent facade was good for business. It was his calling card, proof of his success.

Even with a shaky economy, the mass exodus of apparel companies offshore in the wake of NAFTA, and women in droves forsaking skirts for pants, his father had kept his North Carolina plant humming by focusing his talents on the fastest-growing trend in America—obesity—and by pledging his undying fealty to R. Havemeyer Company, America's second-largest retail chain. His control-top and support pantyhose, with their unique contoured features and high gross margins, had enabled him to gobble up a greater and greater share of Havemeyer's business. By refusing to sell his patented products elsewhere, or to build his own Halaby brand, Harry Halaby had remained anonymous, squeezing out his private-label competitors to become Havemeyer's sole supplier. He knew the R.

Havemeyer Company and everyone in it inside and out, which was paramount given that it accounted for 100 percent of his company's $100-plus million in annual revenues. With more than three thousand soft-goods outlets in malls throughout America's heartland, Havemeyer was a prized plum.

The exclusive arrangement had always struck the prodigal son as suicidal; the wrong Havemeyer buyer could prove fatal. Alex had offered ideas for sprucing up the product line and increasing the customer base, but his father, focused single-mindedly on servicing Havemeyer and making the relationship work in spite of inherent strains, never took him seriously. Having a single customer may be a risky proposition, but it suited Harry Halaby's autocratic personality, enabling him to conduct business at home like a pasha and write off virtually all of his living expenses. Within such narrow confines, Alex was a glorified clerk, with no room to demonstrate his abilities or discover his talents. The pay was better—a lot better—than he could earn anywhere else, and someday he would probably inherit the business. But was the price of all the inner rot in the meantime worth it?

Flora, Harry's indefatigable secretary and company receptionist, was still buried in paperwork at six-thirty. With her gray hair cropped short and her gabardine-clad spine straight as a filing cabinet, she perfectly represented the company's no-nonsense, no-frills image. Much like the pantyhose the company produced, Flora was sturdy, utilitarian, and prudish. In theory, she was also Alex's secretary, though Harry monopolized her. There was not enough room for Alex to have an office of his own; he had to make do in the conference room in back. Working at one end of the large oval table, he sat within shouting distance of his father, who besides micro-managing the company monitored his son's phone calls to ensure they weren't personal. If Harry needed the conference room for a meeting, Alex had to remove his papers—and himself, when he wasn't invited to attend.

If Flora was taken aback by Alex's motorcycle attire she gave no sign. "Your mother's been asking for you. Guests are coming in half an hour. And oh," she added, as if crossing another item off her list, "happy birthday." Alex placed his helmet on a chair, and as he started for his father's office in back, Flora issued a stern warning: "I wouldn't. He's meeting with Jack Larkin, the new buyer."

"I *know* he's the new buyer. He's our *only* buyer. You'd think the exec VP of sales would be notified of such a meeting, no? Surely an oversight."

"It's pretty tense in there," cautioned Flora, to deaf ears.

Without knocking, Alex opened the mahogany double doors to the company's inner sanctum, just in time to see his father pat the perky, nylon-clad derriere of a fit-model as she scurried off to the bathroom to change. Harry was nothing if he wasn't a hands-on operator. *Fresh meat*, Alex thought, salivating in Pavlovian fashion at the model's disappearing figure. One step into the room refocused his attention on the stench of stale smoke. In Harry's paneled office, cigar smoke was as permanent a feature as the walnut desk and credenza, the kilim rug, and the quilted leather sofa, and this evening the haze was amplified by Jack Larkin's pipe. The office desperately needed airing out; still, Harry, with an agitated wave, ordered Alex to close the door. Alex recognized the tart smoke spewing from his father as the product of a second-rate Dominican rather than the usual mellow Havana, and his spirits sank. Harry made this sacrifice only when business was rotten, and it invariably worsened his mood. Though a non-smoker, Alex had developed the nose for being able to distinguish a Havana from a non-Havana. During business hours, Harry was either too harassed or mired in minutia-laden manufacturing reports to communicate beyond a few grunts, so smoke signals were Alex's tea leaves when it came to deciphering the company's moment-to-moment condition—and with just one customer, "moment-to-moment" was the operative phrase.

Alex offered Larkin his hand, but the ruddy-faced buyer ignored him, uncrossing his ex-Holy Cross basketball-player legs and rising out of his chair. At six-six, with his leonine head a mass of platinum hair, Larkin would have cut a distinguished figure had the pant cuffs of his R. Havemeyer suit not betrayed him by ending an inch above his enormous wingtips.

Harry's hand was stretched inside the nylon of one of his trademark products to demonstrate its strength and durability. Framed on the wall behind him was his favorite customer letter, from a South Dakota woman whose pickup truck had stalled out in the Black Hills due to a broken fan belt. With gratitude, the woman described how she had removed her R. Havemeyer pantyhose and constructed a makeshift fan belt, enabling her to make it to the nearest gas station thirty miles away.

"Look," Harry exhaled, "nobody can match our quality. We're the best in the business. Everyone knows that, even our competitors."

"The product isn't moving, Harry," said Larkin. "That's why they brought me in as buyer, to jazz up the line. Maybe you could get the last guy to rubberstamp everything, but I know all the tricks. You rotate the same old styles like crops."

As Larkin stretched his arms to the ceiling and yawned, Harry rose to his feet. The top of his head came only up to Larkin's lapels, and his tangerine Hermès tie clashed with his pink-pinstriped Turnbull and Asser shirt. Manhattan living had afforded Harry a taste for the finer things in life, but not the talent for combining them. Of greater concern to Alex was that his father was breathing laboriously and looked pale and out of sorts. He never took proper care of himself. A lifelong workaholic, Harry wore his stress like a badge of honor and refused to exercise beyond an occasional round of cart golf. His weight fluctuated wildly between 200 and 250 pounds, depending on whether he was gorging or crash-dieting that month, and these days he was pushing the upper end of the range, belly sagging over belt. Despite these signs, Alex continued to see his father through a rose-colored lens of invincibility. In truth, he was in awe of his father and wanted nothing more than to earn his respect. Though Harry's once-thick, jet-black hair had dwindled to fragile strands of silver, he still oozed with vitality, gruff charm, and substance. One look at this entrepreneurial warrior and you knew he was the Real Deal. His intense brown eyes warned people not to cross him, conveying the message that he would make mincemeat of anyone who did. His strong, expressive hands, which had in earlier days done everything from fixing knitting machines to sweeping floors to patenting yarns and the pantyhose products that would make his fortune, were perpetually in motion, as if they were still searching for a lever to pull or a tool to hold. This evening, Alex got the distinct feeling that they were itching to close tight around the throat of his only buyer.

"I gotta go," said Larkin. "Wright-Fit's taking me to dinner."

"You're selling us out to those cheap, cut-rate bastards!" Harry squawked. For years the multi-billion-dollar Wright-Fit Stockings had been trying to invade his turf. "They peddle crap and you know it. Crap made in China and Honduras."

"Sexy, fashionable crap, Harry. Not the clunky crap you've been peddling since the eighties."

"Look beyond the Hudson River, where your stores are, Jack! Women's legs aren't what they used to be. They're too muscular from treadmills, or too fat from junk food and no treadmills. Nobody's showing off their legs. It's all about the gut. Control tops and support hose will continue to be your mainstays if you expect to have any pantyhose business at all!"

Larkin couldn't help but chuckle at this crusty assessment, but then his gray eyes turned steely. "I can't let the R. Havemeyer Company bank its future on one supplier," he said, jabbing the air with his pipe.

During the ensuing cold silence, Alex was tempted to ask how a goliath whose pants didn't cover his ankles was qualified to make fashion decisions for the women of America. But he remained mum as Larkin continued:

"You shouldn't be so dependent on us. Get some new customers, Harry. Oh, and while you're at it"—Larkin pulled a glossy brochure from his briefcase and brandished it under Harry's nose—"check out this Mercedes two-seater."

Harry recoiled. "Is this what I think it is?"

Larkin flashed his shiny gold Rolex. "Wright-Fit thought I needed a new watch, so I'd be on time for all the strategy sessions we're planning together." He tapped his watch and then the brochure. "They both go from zero to sixty, but imagine what I could do for you with a new Mercedes."

Despite the disaster mushrooming in front of him, Alex found himself stifling a yawn, one that wasn't just the product of his habitual nocturnal carousing. Nothing drained him faster than attending these business meetings as a mute. It made him feel invisible, nonexistent. However, today was his thirtieth birthday, and suddenly—maybe because of the Harley—he found himself speaking up.

"Hold on. Jack, you're right," he said. "We should expand our customer base. It'll be healthier for both of us." Despite the ominous sight of Larkin glaring down at him, Alex took a breath and forged on. "But it takes time. You can't expect us to diversify overnight. Let's work together to…"

"Who asked daddy's little ass-wipe?" Larkin snarled.

"How *dare* you insult my family! You lousy son of a bitch! Get out!" Harry exploded, all before Alex had a chance to defend himself. "Take your watch and your car, or I'll cram them up your *ass* in 'zero to sixty!'"

The fit model emerged fully clothed from the bathroom, flattening herself against the doorframe as Larkin backed away from the advancing Harry. "You know the problem with your company?" the buyer sputtered on his way out the door. "It's spoiled rotten." The man's cold eyes reflected his mental hunt for the retort most likely to sting his adversary. "Just like your son."

Harry tore after him. The frightened young model edged past Alex as if he were diseased and followed the gladiators at a safe distance. Alex stood numbly for a moment before stepping into the reception area. Flora had finally gone home to whatever life she had, and his father and Larkin had taken their argument outside to the stoop. He thought about going out to join the fight but decided that interjecting himself further would only make things worse. He picked up his helmet and stepped into the elevator.

Peering into the elevator cabin's smoked mirror, Alex tidied his wavy brown hair, which curled like ribbons at his neck. Even after visiting the hair salon, he invariably looked a tad scruffy, and the helmet had disheveled him even more. He knew this would aggravate his mother, especially with guests coming. As the elevator squeaked and groaned upward toward the third floor, he examined himself more closely, not admiring the man he saw but liking his looks. On top of material comfort, his parents had given him their best DNA: from his mother,

Grace, he had received refined Anglo-Saxon features, blue eyes, and musical talent; from his father, Harry, a robust constitution, extroverted personality, and just a smidgen of Syrian ethnicity in the lips and brow to spice up the package.

If anything, Alex had too many blessings for his own good, including a six-figure salary he didn't deserve and a slick one-bedroom apartment in an East Side high-rise. In past years, he had spent summer weekends in the stifling luxury of his parents' Southampton beach house; this summer he would be renting an old hippie cabin on the other side of the tracks from the town's estate section. But that expression of independence hardly changed the fact that everything he possessed—except his degree from Princeton—had been provided for him by his parents. Although his parents had of course paid his tuition, he had gained his Ivy League admission with no connections whatsoever and had graduated magna cum laude with a degree in American history, facts he clung to as evidence that he could be a self-made man. Even when he seduced a woman, it felt counterfeit. He was invariably convinced it was his family money and bogus title, rather than his true self, that did the trick. And the more he carelessly squandered his true self on airheaded party girls, the more it eroded.

In such an eroded state he had met Lorna Foxhall at a mutual friend's Super Bowl party. Like most of the socialites and Eurotrash in attendance, Lorna had not a clue as to which teams were playing. However, she did possess a Spence—Yale—Locust Valley pedigree and a vast family banking fortune, as well as a certain stately beauty and poise beyond her years that served her equally well on a tennis court as at a dinner party. In the same way that a conscientious child eats his lima beans, Alex began seeing her, assuming that blue blood was good for him. His more mercenary male acquaintances punched his shoulder and flashed thumbs-up signs; his mother was thrilled to see him finally dating an "adult." The fact that their dates almost always involved other people and charity events, with no intimacy beyond sex, seemed to suit Lorna just fine; and if only to get the whole discouraging process of dating behind him, Alex went along.

Within a month or two they became an item, regulars in the social columns thanks to Lorna's publicist, and Alex began to consider escaping his own semigilded cage by marrying into this uppermost social stratosphere. One night over Drunken Fish at Mr. Chow, he drank like a fish himself and popped the question. Lorna accepted his proposal without hesitation, and his state of inebriation prevented him from concealing his surprise. "Seriously?" he asked in astonishment.

"You have potential," she had informed him, patting his hand.

Instead of contentment in the ensuing days, Alex experienced panic attacks, fueled by the frenzy of wedding planning and by Lorna's insistence that they find a Park Avenue apartment to accommodate three kids. Alex couldn't begin to afford such a spread, even on his inflated nepotistic salary, and the fact that Lorna regarded it a drop in the bucket and was willing to pay for it herself only intensified his sense of being engulfed. Still, he did his best to salvage the situation.

"Why don't we elope?" he suggested one day at lunch. "Fly to the Caribbean and get a ship's captain to marry us at sea."

"Don't be juvenile."

"I'm serious, Lorna. It's romantic, adventurous."

"You *know* I've always dreamed of a big church wedding with lots of people," she groused. "Besides, we have no reason to elope."

"What about our religious differences?" Alex grinned. "I'm Episcopalian; you're Presbyterian."

Over the top of her menu Lorna peered menacingly. "You're a bundle of nerves today. Premarital jitters are normal. Buck up."

"It's just that…I don't know…everything's happening so fast.…"

"You want to break our engagement, don't you?"

"I didn't say that."

"At least have the guts to admit it," Lorna bristled.

"I just want to *talk* about some things for once."

"You sound like a woman," said Lorna, with a look of pure disgust, and the next thing Alex knew she was turning on the charm into her cell phone. "Hello, Kurt? It's Lorna…You too. Listen, sweetie, I know this is short notice, but I was wondering if you were free tomorrow night to take me to the Cancer Society ball…Engaged? Can't talk about it now…Oh, Kurt, that's so sweet of you! Can't wait! Pick me up at eight."

Alex wasn't sure whether to laugh or cry as Lorna walked out of his life. Once again, he was trapped in the vicious cycle of putting pantyhose on women he didn't know by day and removing them from women he didn't love by night.

Stepping off the elevator into the living room, Alex mentally composed his curriculum vitae: Conceived in mid-August and born in mid-May so that Mom could avoid a summer pregnancy; bottle-fed and processed like cheese; a malleable, well-rounded product of Choate and Princeton, with just enough sports not to become an athlete, just enough education not to become a scholar, and just enough piano lessons not to become a musician. A ball designed to roll smoothly through life without taking any odd bounces, groomed for the family business by not being groomed for anything else. Prepackaged and preordained, like a pair of size B, reinforced toe.

His childhood and even adolescence had been marked by neither satisfaction nor dissatisfaction with his lot in life. His apathy had suited his parents' design well. At what point exactly his current malaise had begun, he couldn't pinpoint. All he knew at the moment was that he was churning with discontent, spoiling for a fight, so it was just as well his mother wasn't there to greet him. Instead, a large rectangular present, richly wrapped in red paper and red ribbons, sat on the red sofa. As he made a beeline for the platter of prawns on the red-lacquer coffee table and dipped one into cocktail sauce, he observed that even the hors d'oeuvres and his gift were color-coordinated to the room.

For ages, going back to when the family had lived upstate in Aurora, New York—a tiny agricultural community in the Finger Lakes region—one of Grace's premier ambitions was to decorate a room totally in red. It wasn't until Harry landed the Havemeyer account and moved his manufacturing to North Carolina and his family to Manhattan that she had been able to fulfill her vision. The upholstered outcome, like everything she did, fell well within conventional bounds of good taste. The symphony of reds—geometrics, paisleys, florals—created a sensibly warm ambience, the only exotic touch being the coffee-table book on feng shui, which stated somewhere inside that a red room made people overly excited and nervous. The Halabys had given their decorator carte blanche in selecting the abstract paintings, the one prerequisite being that they harmonize with the fabrics. Alex, hardly an art critic, regarded them as soulless rip-offs, on a par with pre-K finger painting.

"There you are!" his mother startled him, just as he was tossing his helmet onto a crimson needlepoint wingchair, out of her view. Grace entered from the dining room and gave him the same perfunctory hug she had given him for as long as he could remember—a brisk gesture that symbolized rather than expressed motherly affection. Tall, manicured, exquisitely self-controlled—a true lady from her shocked auburn perm to her polished pumps—she was guided in all things by one fervent belief: Anyone who didn't live the way she did and share her Republican values was unstable. Her bibles were *W, Town & Country, Architectural Digest*, and *Martha Stewart Living* (Grace didn't care about her silly legal problems; Martha was still God). Casting a jaundiced eye at his leather jacket and blue jeans, she said, "There's an extra blazer in the hall closet. And you promised me you'd cut your hair."

"I did cut it," he said, drifting into the dining room. He checked a few of the place cards and winced.

"Better hurry up. Your friends will be here in half an hour."

"You mean *your* friends," said Alex, spying the ice bucket of Veuve Clicquot Grande Dame on a side table. He poured himself a flute-full.

"They're family friends. Besides, how can we invite your friends if we don't know who they are? You never bring them over, and the few you have…well, I do hate to say this, but they look like exotic dancers. That last one—red fishnets! Really, Alex." Grace was not looking at him but instead was intent on adjusting the tray on the coffee table, moving it an infinitesimal amount to the left and then to the right.

"Maybe if we made red fishnets we wouldn't be losing…"

"Anyway," his mother interrupted, compulsively fluffing pillows, "the Dennises are sponsoring your father and me for membership at the Southampton Ocean Club, so be nice. They're bringing their lovely daughter Jennifer. She's just back from Italy and is excited to meet you, though after what you did to Lorna I don't know why. The poor thing must still be devastated."

"I've told you a thousand times, Mom, the breakup was mutual."

"Lorna was perfect for you." Still his mother's mantra.

"That's the problem. If she weren't so perfect, she'd be…perfect."

He smiled, proud of his wordplay, which only made Grace seethe. She picked up a framed photo of Alex and Lorna and looked at it nostalgically. "The Foxhalls still won't speak to me."

"They never did," said Alex, leaning over the coffee table and scooping a spoonful of glistening black caviar, there, no doubt, to match the ebony grand piano. One of Grace's numerous rules of thumb was that every room prospered from a touch of black. "Can we lose the photo, please? For my birthday?"

Grace returned the photo to its exact position on the side table. "Quick, Alex," she said, "open your present."

Almost as soon as Alex began tearing away the red paper, he knew it was a briefcase. He ran his hand over the velvety leather and then probed hopefully inside. No luck.

"Better go downstairs and change into something presentable before the guests arrive," Grace ordered. "Chop-chop."

Alex was about to inform his mother that he had no intention of changing, since it was his birthday after all, when his father burst out of the elevator. Ignoring Alex and Grace, he did a hit-and-run on the tray of prawns on his way to the phone.

"I would like to sell this company and retire—*before* I die," Harry roared in Alex's direction, picking up the phone and punching in a number. "So do me a favor: When I'm talking to the buyer, zip it."

"Oh please, not tonight," Grace pleaded, raising her hands in front of her face as if to divert the conversation.

"Sell this company?" Alex scoffed. "Who the hell's going to buy a company that makes geriatric products and has only one customer? How do you sleep nights?"

"Don't tell me my business," Harry commanded. "I've been doing this since you were born, and you're not exactly starving."

"There are many forms of starvation. What exactly *is* my job as executive VP of sales anyway? I joined the company to contribute something, not be referred to as 'daddy's little ass-wipe.'" He gave his father a long look. "Is that how you want people to see your son?"

"If you think working for me is tough," Harry retorted, "try finding a job that pays you half what I pay you, that..."

"Then let me earn my salary and go out and get some new customers."

"And let Larkin off the hook? No way! I need you right here attending to R. Havemeyer, following up on all the nuts and bolts details, not off chasing rainbows." Harry shifted his attention to the phone. "Hello, police?"

"Police?" said Grace, but Harry kept talking into the phone.

"Yeah, officer, some idiot chained a motorcycle to our stoop."

"Oh, good Lord!" Grace moaned. "We have to get someone to tow it away before people..."

"Dad, wait!"

Spotting the helmet on the wingchair and taking another gander at Alex's leather jacket, Grace suddenly caught on. She went to the phone and pressed her finger on the cradle, disconnecting the call. Once Harry realized the phone was dead, he glowered at his wife, who in turn poked an accusing finger in the direction of their son.

"He's the idiot," she said.

"I sold the Porsche to pay for it," Alex said defensively, expecting them to attack him out of the box for being a spendthrift.

His mother seemed to regard this as a theft. "You sold your graduation present?"

"I graduated eight years ago, Mom."

"You had no right to *sell* it!" she brayed.

"It was *mine*, wasn't it?"

"How do you plan to get to Southampton and back on weekends?" Grace wanted to know. "Not on the motorcycle, I hope."

"Of course on the motorcycle. It's all I've got."

"Alex, are you insane!" Grace began to pace. "The Long Island Expressway is treacherous! The traffic! The thunderstorms! The reckless drivers! Truckers will run you off the road!" She stopped pacing and faced him squarely. "You know we're up for membership at the Ocean Club!"

"Well, *I'm* not. So what's the big deal?"

"The big deal," Harry growled, relighting his cigar with his gold lighter, "is that there are a few tight-asses at the club who'd love to use something like this to blackball us. Half of them already think I'm Jewish, for Chrissake. God knows what'll happen if they find out my people hail from a country next-door to Iraq. The least you could do is not act like a hoodlum."

"Why do you want to join that mausoleum anyway?" Alex implored, thinking how grounded and accessible his parents had been during his boyhood in Aurora, before moving to the city and getting caught up in the social frenzy necessary to establish themselves in Manhattan's upper tier, a daunting task at their ages, starting as they had from scratch. "A bunch of self-important jerks trying to pre-serve their self-important way of life."

"It's not only for us," urged Grace. "It's for you. You'll be able to use the facil-ities, go to the parties, and meet some nice young women."

"All of them named Muffy, I'm sure," Alex drawled. Underneath his scorn, he felt compassion. Neither of his parents had been able to afford a college educa-tion, and he admired them for having come so far in life, for working themselves to the bone to give him opportunities they never had. It had taken courage to uproot in their fifties and settle in Manhattan without knowing a soul. Even Alex, tempered by Choate and Princeton and with far less to worry about, had found the urban adjustment difficult. He had often felt lonely growing up, alien-ated in prep school, an only child shouldering high expectations, and he empa-thized with his parents' desire to be accepted into higher social circles. Still, falling all over themselves to join a club full of stiffs was beneath them. A sudden wave of love for them washed over him. "Mom, Dad. Don't you realize? You two are better than the whole lot of them."

Unmoved, Grace went over to the French window and cranked her head to view the evil object. "Heavens, look at that monstrosity! Alex, how could you do this? Tonight of all nights! You knew people were coming! Now go down there and move it—now!"

Alex was willing to accommodate her, but only after he had asserted his principles. "Just because I work for the company doesn't give you the right to control every aspect of my life."

"Control!" blustered the inventor of the Total Control Top. "You don't know the meaning of control! We leave you totally alone."

"Oh, yeah? Who threatened to fire me if I moved to the Village? Who threatened to fire me if I didn't dump the girl in red fishnets?"

"She was a tart!" cried Grace. "Her name was Tammy!"

"And who said, just last week, 'As long as you work for me, your hair is company property'?"

"If you married Lorna," his mother reminded him, "you wouldn't have to worry about the business ever again."

Alex addressed the ceiling. "Jesus, no wonder I'm in therapy."

"Therapy? You're in therapy? But why?" gasped Grace, with a look of worry.

The shrink had asked the same question, and Alex's response had been a jumble of psychobabble, because he wasn't exactly sure himself. Now, however, the answer flashed before him in neon: to pluck up the courage to quit the family business and do something he really loved, whatever *that* was.

"Does this have something to do with Lorna?" His mother's voice neared panic. "Oh, Jesus, don't tell me you're gay."

"Jesus, Grace," Harry shuddered, "that was uncalled for."

"Is there something *wrong* with you?"

Had Alex not been so stunned by his own insight, he would have laughed at Grace's shrieked questions. At that moment, though, he simply tried to answer her. His revelation proved too overwhelming to put into words, so he gave his mother the same vague reply he had given his shrink: "My life's going nowhere. I'm depressed."

"You're depressed?" Grace exhaled in relief, cheeks regaining their color. "Why didn't you tell me? Go up to my medicine chest. There's Prozac, Paxil…"

"Hard work," Harry barked, "is the only cure. How do you expect me to take you seriously when you look like a Hell's Angel? No employee of mine is going to be driving around on a frickin' motorcycle, and that's that!"

"Well, that's what I'm driving," Alex dug in. "There's more to life than pantyhose—or so they tell me."

"Pantyhose fed and clothed you! Pantyhose paid for Choate and Princeton!" Harry snorted. "Your life would be nothing without pantyhose."

"Sending him to those schools was a mistake—they warped his sense of reality," Grace interjected, and piled on from there. "I don't understand why you need a psychiatrist. Why can't you figure things out on your own? I have. I'm happy." She lit a cigarette. Thanks to the patch, hypnosis, and an assortment of antidepressant medications, Alex's mother rarely smoked anymore—it had become too socially unacceptable. She gave into it only when she was really rattled. "All a shrink does is blame your parents for everything."

Alex shook his head. "It's not about you. Can't you see I'm searching?"

"Good grief," Grace stomped. "What on earth are you searching for?"

"For myself—you know, inside?"

"Oh, Alex, don't be so impressionable! There's nothing inside!"

This rendered him momentarily speechless. Then he smiled at her, not without bitterness. "Nothing but liver and kidneys and nicotine, you think?"

Harry, fed up with all the family bickering after another hard day, expelled a cloud of Dominican smoke in his son's direction. But the playful gesture, far from restoring male rapport, only inflamed Alex. They never listened to him or respected his feelings. It was always their way or the highway, and now, with his Harley parked outside, the highway was beckoning. He snatched the photo of Lorna and himself and took it to the dining room, where he set it on the plate marked by his place card. "There, no one will know the difference," he said, returning to the living room and grabbing his helmet.

"What the hell are you doing?" said Harry.

"Leaving."

"Don't be absurd!" Grace said. "I have nineteen people coming to celebrate your birthday!"

"No, Mom, you have nineteen of *your* friends coming to have dinner with *you*. But don't worry; the bike will be gone by the time they arrive."

"Harry, say something to him," Grace demanded.

With his wife's eyes promising to make his life unbearable if he didn't take a hard line, Harry said emphatically, "It's one thing to give me grief, but to humiliate your mother is unforgivable!"

Alex hesitated as a wave of quiet washed over him. He had joined the company to use his brain and make a difference, not to be pigeonholed as the boss's ineffectual son who couldn't make it in the outside world. If he backed down now, he might never be his own man. How many times had his father said that a man isn't a man until he stares into the abyss and sees what he's made of? Still, beneath the intoxicating flood of anger he could feel the insistent drumbeat of doubt. What the hell was he doing hurting his parents like this? Sure, they were woefully overprotective and had their blind spots, but weren't such flaws relatively benign? They didn't necessarily know what was good for him at this stage of his life, or what he needed, but they certainly cared. Compared to 99 percent of the parents out there, they were exceptional, of the highest character; they deserved his honor and respect. And to throw away his fat salary and cushy life without the slightest idea of what he might do next, to start life over from scratch—was he completely crazy?

"Find another water boy," he said, plunging into the abyss. "I quit."

Minutes later, as the streetlights blinked on, he was speeding down Fifth Avenue on his outrageous Harley, completely terrified and happier than he had ever been in his life.

2

Family Portrait

Abigail Lukes, in her pattern-on-pattern mauve damask gown, peered down at her son, Charles, as he made love to his wife, Emily. Though it was only a portrait, the sight of her mother-in-law hanging majestically over the king-size bed made Emily feel eerily spied upon, as if the stout woman were taking a dim view of their uninspired coupling. The painter had faithfully reproduced the famous Lukes eyes—piercing, intelligent, as dark and cold as the eyes of a dead peacock—and had combined them with a cryptic Mona Lisa smile. The result was a facial expression that could change from disapproving to amused, depending on from what angle or with what mood the viewer observed it. However, what never changed, even after her death four years ago, was the emotional and fiscal stranglehold Abigail Lukes exerted over her two sons.

A fossil-fuel heiress, Abigail had died one of America's richest women, and from what Emily could glean, she had also been one of America's most miserable. Her vast fortune and domineering nature attracted sycophants who simply wanted to be taken care of, and she had married and divorced three gigolos, and married and annulled a fourth. Whether her lack of respect for the male species stemmed from these marital experiences, or whether her innate contempt for men had sabotaged her marriages, was hard to say. Each one of her husbands had received a million or so for his trouble. Charles, who liked to make jokes about everything, but especially about his mother, always referred to these settlements as "Mummy's 401K."

Emily closed her eyes and tried to concentrate on her body's sensations. It was obvious to her that her husband was more intent on producing an heir than on pleasing her, and she was irritated that after three years of marriage he still had no clue about what satisfied her in bed. No matter how she tried to guide him, he remained confident that vigorous thrusting was the only essential. She focused on relaxing her muscles, trying to enjoy her husband's ice cream–smooth skin under her fingers; yet even with her eyes shut she could see Abigail's visage looming. At first Emily had thought the placement of the ancestral portrait amusing; she and Charles would sometimes joke about it after a night of champagne and dancing, draping it gaily with a robe before falling into bed. When she began to find the picture oppressive, she had cajoled Charles into moving it to one of the guest rooms, where it had remained for almost a year. One day, without warning, Abigail appeared back in her old peeping Tom position in the master bedroom. When Emily protested, Charles had arched an eyebrow and said, "Is that any way to talk about my Mommy Warbucks, my pet? After all, she goes so darn well with the upholstery in here."

Charles took great delight in telling new visitors to his lavish homes, or first-time passengers on his Citation X jet, that he was born into poverty. Once he got his guests' undivided attention, he would recite his Horatio Alger success story: "My biological mother put me up for adoption, and I hit the parent Lotto jackpot," whereupon he would, with a droll smile, raise his glass of champagne and toast the American Dream. Abigail, thinking herself infertile after three childless marriages, had adopted Charles and raised him alone for ten years, focusing all her doting attention on him. The one fly in Charles's ointment came when she capriciously remarried and to everyone's shock conceived on her honeymoon. When a month later she caught her new husband pleasuring the pool boy in their Palm Beach cabana, she had the marriage annulled and bore their son alone. The Palm Beach episode caused her to resent her biological son, whom she named William but called Billy, and it was hardly surprising that he grew up rebellious and difficult. Charles, who did everything in his power to crush his sibling rival, remained Abigail's favorite right up to the day of her death, an inequity that was formalized in her will.

In a crowning act of spite, Abigail bequeathed a staggering $300 million in muni-bonds and T-bills to Charles, $100 million to the Episcopal Church, and a token $2 million to Billy, whose mortifying six-month prison sentence for petty cocaine dealing had nearly persuaded his mother to disinherit her bloodline entirely. Charles was also given the crown jewels of Abigail's real estate: her sprawling Fifth Avenue duplex, with its distinguished modern art collection, and her Stanford White estate in Southampton, Long Island. Billy got the one house his mother had come to hate: the Spanish Colonial in Palm Beach, site of the infamous cabana buggering. He immediately sold the place to Charles to cover his legal fees and debts, using what was left to open a nightclub in the up-and-coming Williamsburg section of Brooklyn.

Considering how well Charles had fared in life, it was ironic that he himself was categorically against adopting a child. His insistence on a biological heir was also a somewhat unrealistic point of view, given how rarely he and Emily made love. After her first year of marriage to Charles, Emily had more or less accepted the fact that the physical part of their union was not going to be stellar. She couldn't help wondering if she would have married him at all had they not waited to have sex until their wedding night. Charles had made a game out of this quaint marital tradition. "An old-fashioned courtship," he persuaded his dazzled bride-to-be, "is the ultimate in good taste and will only make our honeymoon saucier." In Cary Grant fashion, he gave her slow, tender kisses, nuzzled the back of her neck, and promised he would spend his life catering to her every desire. When, after a spectacular sunset wedding on the Seine, the long-awaited carnal denouement finally took place, she was so giddy with Paris and the glamour of marrying the dashing Charles Lukes that she hardly minded when all he did was enter briefly and promptly fall asleep. Charles apologized for his inadequacy charmingly the next day, complete with the finest chocolate and flowers Paris had to offer. But when rockets failed to go off for her the next time, and the next after that, Emily began to realize that her husband, who on the dance floor could tango better than any man she had ever met, was oblivious—or uninterested—in the bedroom.

Emily was startled out of her reverie by a halt in the proceedings. Charles had slipped out and was offering her an apologetic smile. "Ahem, ladies and gentlemen," he said, using his best Amtrak voice, "sorry, but we seem to be experiencing mechanical difficulties." After some fumbling and positional adjustment, he then resumed, dashing his wife's faint hope that he would give up and call it a night.

Emily's sexual self-esteem had never been overly high. She had spent her elementary and high school years at the all-girl Academy of the Sacred Heart in Manhattan, subliminally learning that women were either virgins or sluts. Throughout her teens she remained a shy, gangly towhead, inspiring her father to dub her "Q-Tip." Her figure finally blossomed, but her confidence lagged. She was convinced that her luxurious ash-blond hair looked washed out, her pale skin sickly, her willowy body anemic, her green eyes peculiar. Later, at Columbia, she was surprised to discover how attractive she was to the opposite sex. By the end of her sophomore year she had acquired an on-and-off serious boyfriend—a brilliant Yale philosophy major who was a considerate, if somewhat phlegmatic, lover. Meanwhile, she spent most of her time secretly and desperately pining after her lanky sculpture professor, who sadly was interested only in her terracotta.

Emily graduated from Columbia with a degree in fine arts, winning a college prize for her oils, and was eager to continue her studies at the Sorbonne, of course.…Her father, however, considered art inappropriate for all but the most gifted and hungry. Convinced that his beautiful daughter would end up haunting dilapidated neighborhoods and hanging out with all the wrong people, he denied her even modest financial support and forced her to get a "real" job. In retrospect, it wasn't entirely his fault; Emily never quite forgave herself for towing his line. She could have followed her instincts to Paris rather than her father's threats and her own strangely childish fear of poverty, a malady that hits most of those born with the birth defect of rich parents. Through his connections, her well-meaning but essentially selfish father procured a sales position for her at Sotheby's, where she could be of the art world but not smack dab in it, dealing with rich collectors rather than artists.

There she had met the tall, suave Charles Lukes, who had taken one look at her and quipped, "What's an angel like you doing in this den of equity?" He was ten years her senior, one of the country's most ostentatious collectors of modern art and, according to *Town & Country*, one of New York's "Top Ten Best Catches"—despite his divorce and his well-publicized drunken escapades, and the fact that, technically speaking, he still lived with his mother. When, a month into their courtship, Abigail choked to death on a lamb chop, leaving Charles alone and squalidly rich, he began to see Emily exclusively, with an eye toward marrying her. "You're better than a puppy dog as a playmate," he once marveled, while she flirted with him shamelessly, emboldened by their sexless romance, never questioning her own motives. "I've never met any woman who has your remarkable quality of being suitably impressed by my money without actually coveting it."

Indeed, pre-Charles, Emily had rejected the advances of several rich men of various ages. Charles seemed to exist on a loftier plateau from the cutthroat business types and brooding, self-absorbed artists who used to pursue her. Most notably, he gave Emily every indication that he believed in her as a painter. He took her to art openings all over the globe and made sweeping promises: "I will leverage my art world contacts, my sweet, and find just the perfect gallery to represent you." He bought her the finest sable brushes and oils from Italy and France and discussed art with her until the wee hours. There were trips on his jet to Palm Beach, St. Bart's, and her beloved Paris; weekends at quaint New England country inns; baubles from Harry Winston and Fred Leighton when she least expected them. Their flamboyant courtship was celebrated in the society pages, applauded by family and friends, and so engulfed her that she never fully comprehended Charles's fundamental emptiness.

This evening's sexual encounter was their first in two months and was inspired solely by her husband's obsession with procreation. Being adopted, Charles harbored a deep yearning for a real blood family of his own, and since 9/11 he had been almost frantic to father an "heir to the Lukes throne." However, his actual attempts at conceiving hadn't matched his rhetoric. Fertility doctors blamed Charles's low sperm count and poor motility and had told him he needed to drastically alter his diet of rich food and alcohol—to which Charles had protested in feigned horror, "What are you fellows trying to do, kill me?" Emily could have offered the professionals a simpler diagnosis: lack of passion in their marriage—to be blunt, not enough exchange of bodily fluids. In any case, she was not sure she even wanted to have children with Charles. Certainly Lukes offspring would have everything money could buy, every material advantage. But what kind of father would her husband make? Would their children drink champagne with breakfast while making witty, self-deprecating jibes about their own poor performance on the playground? At the thought of this, she shuddered and opened her eyes, a movement which Charles, reaching the end of his endeavors, mistook for an expression of pleasure. He actually winked at her. "Oh, how lovely. Good job, my pet."

Hoisting himself up against the quilted headboard, Charles smoothed the buttery yellow Pratesi sheets neatly over the lower half of his body, took a sip from the ubiquitous champagne flute on the bedside table, and then picked up the *New York Observer*. He liked to read aloud to his wife in bed, interjecting his own sarcastic asides between paragraphs.

"Ah, here it is…Listen to this unbelievable drivel, my dear." When Charles addressed her it was never without the possessive pronoun: it was always "my dear" or "my sweet." He finger-combed his sleek black hair away from his face, took a sip, and prepared to entertain her.

"If you don't mind, Charles, not right now," she said, grabbing Hemingway's *A Moveable Feast* off her bedside table and sitting up. In the beginning she had found Charles's sharp wit exciting, exotic. Being with someone who could laugh at life and at himself was a novelty to her. While Charles had a scathingly critical sensibility—skewering everybody from national politicians to his own household servants—he was never as hard on anyone as he was on himself. "Must be some grand joke of the universe that I ended up with so much money and yet so little talent for anything but spending it," he had waxed one late night when into his cups. "Though you must admit, I do spend with unparalleled panache." No one could shop, travel, or order food like Charles. He had turned extravagance into an art form, and for a time Emily thought her life with him was going to be nothing but laughter, excitement, and beauty.

Exactly when her respect for him started fading Emily couldn't remember; the decline had been gradual. What she had seen as a devil-may-care attitude she now realized was nothing but posing; her husband never followed through on anything he started. And as much as Emily had admired his insouciant ability for self-mockery, eventually it was the thing that separated them. She couldn't sustain the cynicism necessary for the sport.

"I can certainly understand your aversion to the *Observer*," said Charles, with a sad glint in his eye. She caught his double meaning; he was referring not only to the peach-colored newspaper but also to himself. "But shouldn't you remain horizontal a bit longer and give my tadpoles a chance? I'm not sure how well they can swim upstream."

"I don't see how it makes much difference," she said, "as long as you're going to drink every minute of the day. Your sperm is probably too tipsy to swim."

She had meant it as a joke, but it had come out as meanness. Nevertheless, Charles chuckled. "You're probably right, my darling. Perhaps you should stand on your head so they can fall gently into your womb."

Allowing him the final word, Emily opened *A Moveable Feast*, hoping to escape to Paris, to her dream world of painting and wild amours. The memoir had inspired her art in college, and she was revisiting it now in the hope of rekindling her creative spark. Recently she had begun to feel as if she were in a shrinking box, the walls of which were made of cocktail parties and charity balls—the same old people, the same banal conversation. The smaller her world became, the less she wanted to paint, which suited Charles just fine. His interest in her painting had flagged shortly after they were married, and had gradually morphed into passive-aggressive opposition. He denied her request to rent a studio downtown ("Too bohemian, my dumpling") and only grudgingly allowed her to convert one of their three fallow guest rooms into a work space when he couldn't come up with a compelling argument against it and Emily had coolly put her foot down. Still, she found it difficult to sustain enthusiasm for her art while under the same roof with him and his million-dollar paintings. The air was much too heavy for creative endeavors. The one thing that kept her from going completely bonkers was her volunteer work for C-SAW, the nonprofit Children's School Arts Workshop. At least there she felt as if she were making a difference in the world.

"Any chance I got you pregnant today, my darling?"

"I told you, I'm not ovulating," she said, planting the book in front of her face, pretending to read but absorbing nothing.

"You'd think," said Charles, "that with all my money they could make you ovulate upon demand."

Annoyed by his chatter and craving solitude, Emily glanced at the rococo clock on the mantel and slipped away from the bed. "We better get moving or we'll be late," she said.

"I can't think of a worse way to spend the evening. I should just send my checkbook. That's all Billy wants."

"Be nice," she said, "he's your brother."

"Not by blood. Let's cancel and go to Coco Pazzo instead. Ring up dear old Billy and tell him we're too tired."

"We can't cancel—not again! Plus, I want to go. Aren't you curious to see what he's done?"

"Knowing Billy, the silverware will consist entirely of tiny cocaine spoons," Charles drawled.

"Maybe those six months in prison changed him."

"Don't be naive, my darling. People don't change."

"Who told you that? Your shrink?" she asked pointedly.

Charles looked up at his mother. "Who else?"

"If people can't change, why have you spent your entire adult life in therapy?"

Charles stretched, leaned his head back, and offered a satisfied smile. "Because it's so amusing to see the therapists try to change me."

Therapy for Charles was like most people's tennis game: He considered it a lifelong recreation; he loved to talk about it; and he was always looking for a new instructor. He chose his shrinks according to who charged the most. Psychotherapy was perhaps the only project Charles had ever undertaken in which he hadn't lost interest.

Emily escaped to the bathroom, flicking the lock and expelling a heavy sigh. She dimmed the lights, lit candles, and drew a bath. Charles's ex-wife, befriending her like a sister, had warned her early on that she would inevitably be driven "into the arms of a vibrator." Something about a buzzing plastic phallus offended Emily's sensibilities; she considered it vulgar, degrading, preferring more organic means of self-pleasure: like the soothing scent of lavender bubble bath and the rush of warm water from her European hand shower. While cleansing her body with a large sponge and trying to get into the mood, a nagging little voice in her head wouldn't stop reminding that this was no way to go through life. How she wished she could talk freely with Charles about sex. Once, frustrated after months of abstinence, she had summoned the temerity to suggest they see a sex therapist, but Charles dismissed her request out of hand with his usual verbal aplomb: "Too close to the bone, my love." For him, therapy was a game with very strict boundaries. Taking the porcelain hand shower, Emily teased her breasts and nipples with the undulating current, experimenting with the various settings, moving the pulsing plaything underwater, fondling herself with her free hand, closing her eyes, fantasizing feverishly. But this evening nothing was working.

"Finally!" Charles sighed, when his wife reappeared in her silk robe—semi-refreshed, blown dry, squeaky clean. "What took you so long in there? Have you got a lover stashed away under the Turkish towels?"

He sat on the edge of the chaise struggling with one of his shoe trees, clad in gray flannels and a baby blue cashmere turtleneck, as informal as he ever got in the city. A bottle of champagne sat on the table beside him, and tonight he had brought an extra glass in honor of Emily's birthday, even though the milestone was tomorrow. A mere birth*day* was not enough for any wife of his; nothing less than a Birthday Week would suffice. His puffy face had a convivial glow; it was the face of someone who knew that whatever he wanted would instantly be granted to him. "How about a festive glass of bubbly?" he offered.

"No thanks," said Emily, moving to the dresser. Studying herself in the sixteenth-century Venetian mirror, she began brushing the tangles out of her hair, which fell to the middle of her back. Almost everyone of both sexes found her mane glorious—especially Charles, who for the first several months of their marriage spent a full hour every morning combing it as if she were his own personal Barbie. She disappeared into her enormous closet to dress, opting for a black turtleneck, black leggings, and over-the-knee black suede boots, which made her long legs look even longer. Billy had once dubbed this ensemble "Puss n' Boots," an insolence that had provoked a loaded barb from Charles: "Ah, dear, dear Billy. Such a class act. Mother would be so proud." Tonight, Emily knew she would derive a perverse pleasure from wearing this particular outfit again in front of black sheep Billy.

She returned to the bedroom just in time to see Charles draining his glass bottoms-up, then immediately refilling it. Like a soufflé, the foam rose an inch above the rim without overflowing; Charles had acquired a daredevil mastery of this ritual, seldom spilling a drop before midnight. "So, my sweet," he asked, "what would you like me to bring you back from Japan?"

"Oh, Charles, are you really going to invest in that goat cloning thing?" Even as she protested, her heart leapt at the prospect of being alone for three weeks—of having him gone.

"By that 'goat cloning thing,' I assume you mean Spidex. The Spidex process is the biotechnology of the future, my little Luddite. It happens to be the hottest invention since aluminum."

"That's what you said about the valve company and the peacock farm," she reminded him. "But crossing a spider with a goat? I think this time you've really lost your mind."

"Don't be boorish, my darling." With a glint of unease, Charles took another swig of champagne, as if trying to convince himself. "The resulting goats are only one-seventy-thousandth part spider. But the amazing thing is that even that small amount of arachnid genetics is enough to put spider web capability in the goats' milk! By harvesting the milk we can make a thread that is five times stronger than steel…"

Emily began applying eye-shadow, only half listening, and the more Charles rambled on about his newest project, making it all sound so pat, the more she tuned out. Since graduating from Harvard twenty years ago and falling into Phase I of his trust fund, he had never held a job or earned a dime beyond clipping coupons. He hadn't even been interested in venture capital until a couple of years ago. When she met him he had been pursuing documentary film making; then he dropped that, claiming, "Too many dolts to deal with, my love," and had taken up writing. He wanted to be a theater critic. But somehow he never found a place to publish his pieces, and soon he was working on a collection of his reviews of the year's best plays. After that it was a crime novel, which now lay unsolved in a drawer in his study. This latest hobby of his was the wildest, however. He remained coy about how much he had sunk into research, though she suspected that the amount had reached mid seven-figures. When Emily thought about how she had to beg and plead to get him to make even a modest donation to C-SAW—money that would mean so much to learning-starved kids—it enraged her. No one wanted to give money to charities these days, particularly charities that weren't high-profile and didn't confer social prestige on the donor. Everyone was cutting back, trying to survive the economic downturn—everyone, that is, but Charles. With the bulk of his capital invested in ultra-safe municipal bonds and T-bills that churned out more tax-free income than even he could spend, he was untouched. She knew she should be grateful for the security his money provided her, but his immunity and smugness about it only made her angry.

"Come to Tokyo," he pleaded, "and meet my new partners. First class is more luxurious than flying private. The hotel has a world-class spa. We can pamper ourselves, eat sushi…"

"We pamper ourselves and eat sushi here. Besides, a few quiet days in Southampton may help me rekindle my creative fire."

This literally made Charles wince. "Won't you be ovulating?"

"Please stop pressuring me," she said, as gently as she could muster. "I'll never get pregnant unless I'm relaxed."

"All right, never mind. We don't want a nervous Nemily around the house." He came up behind her and gave her neck and shoulders a ten-second massage. "Who knows," he joked, "maybe they can mate me with a spider or a goat." He took her hand and kissed her fingers one by one. "Love you badly, madly, my sweet," he murmured, then, humming cheerfully, turned away to call down for the car.

3

The Princess and the Piano Player

Across the East River, in a wholly different universe, Alex Halaby and Billy Lukes were celebrating the one-week anniversary of Alex's liberty. So far, Alex's wanderlust had taken him to the End of the World, which in this case happened to be a nightclub in the Williamsburg section of Brooklyn. Strangely, he was no less paralyzed now than he had been in the family business, still dizzy from the rootlessness of having abandoned his old family stronghold and unsure where to direct his energies.

Seated at the long stainless steel bar while Winnie the leggy bartender made them "Dirty Bombs"—Bombay martinis garnished with the dregs of the olive jar—he was helping Billy assess the babe factor for the evening. The pickings were slim, though camped out at the far end of the bar was a kinky-looking trio in suggestive leather. June was approaching, and the burly, six-two Billy was in search of a new diversion. Gazing narcissistically into the tilted, fractured mirror that ran the length of the bar, he fussed with his slicked-back chestnut hair. For Alex's benefit, he pulled the lavender silk handkerchief from his breast pocket, which as he shook it out proved to be, upon closer inspection, a pair of women's silk panties left over from his last exploit. Billy reeked of teddy bear charm, but the cuddly exterior camouflaged a truly wolfish nature—a philandering instinct Alex tried to admire as a kind of JFK thing.

The younger Lukes brother had spent everything he had turning five thousand square feet of empty space in Williamsburg into a theme bar, designing into the cavernous place an Armageddon ambience that was part army bunker, part sci-fi movie set. Gas masks and K-rations adorned the walls; "jungle bridge" walkways arched over meandering mini-canals of black water; a dry ice machine continually blew smoke into the air, producing an eerie, dank haze. Several video monitors suspended from the ceiling showed a continuous loop of disaster scenarios—nuclear explosions, earthquakes, landslides, volcanic eruptions, missile launches....Occasionally a still image of an elderly woman in a white dress holding a croquet mallet would appear on the screen for several seconds, in between crumbling bridges and tidal waves. Billy had explained with an evil smile that this was a photo of his mother, "the truly deadly Abigail Lukes." The waitresses wore weird, sexy outfits made from skimpy cut-offs, ripped-up fatigues, and army boots over torn Halaby stockings donated by Alex. World music, fusion, and death rock issued from hidden speakers; cracked frameless mirrors hung on dingy gray walls; and the light level was that of an opium den.

Billy was particularly proud of his drink menu, a product of his own feverish brain. House libations included the Doomsday Daiquiri (made with prune juice instead of lime); the Mass Murder Martini (two parts vodka, one part gin, a dash of Vermouth, three black olives); the Jonestown Julep (bourbon, Kool-Aid, and fresh mint); the Pearly Gate (blue Curacao, vodka, and cream); and for the truly reckless drinker, the Four Horseman Line-Up (which consisted of four shots of different kinds of Tequila).

Unfortunately, only four months after an auspicious start, and a very cool opening that brought in Robert De Niro, Paris Hilton, and a couple of fairly famous gangsta rappers, 9/11 occurred. What had been considered a campy theme bar was now a theme bar in extremely bad taste. Business collapsed overnight; just how Billy had managed to keep it alive on fumes for two years Alex wasn't sure. With his inheritance eaten up—not only by the abrupt downturn in his business, but also by legal fees stemming from his cocaine conviction and by his sybaritic excesses—Billy desperately needed investors, but nobody reputable would invest with a drug felon.

"Live music's where it's at right now in this business," Billy said, rolling his eyes derisively at the End of the World's sole capacity for live music, a rickety upright piano. "Once I scrap the doomsday décor and build a proper sound stage, with state-of-the-art lights and effects, I guarantee you this place'll be rockin' again." Despite Alex's family-outcast status, Billy couldn't help himself from making a pitch for money any more than a scorpion could help himself from biting. "Don't you want to be part owner of a nightclub? Think of the perks." His absurd appeal fizzled like a dud firecracker, whereupon he slid a key in front of Alex. "When I was locked up in Danbury, you were the only one who visited. Not even big brother Charles bothered to make the trek, what with all his precious social engagements. Upstairs, second door on the right. Nothing much. Just a ratty futon and some dirty sheets. There's a laundry-mat down the block."

"Thanks. I'll only be here a couple of days."

"Hey, nobody knows more about family dysfunction than *moi*," said Billy, "though personally I think you're a fool for passing up all that easy money. Why be a family outcast like me if you don't have to?"

"I gave nepotism my best shot," Alex sighed. "What I need now is a complete break—starting with a whole new persona. Thanks for the room. I'll make this up to you."

"How about tonight?" said Billy. "My piano player bailed. We need entertainment." With no more warning than that, he began forcibly hustling Alex to the piano.

"C'mon, Billy! You know I don't play in public."

"You want a new persona—here's your chance."

Alex was in a sweat, doubting he could establish any sort of musical rapport with the club's patrons. Besides the leather trio, there was a smattering of neighborhood "regulars": two or three local shop owners; a few dazed-looking artists with specks of paint on their glasses; a gaggle of extremely thin teenage girls in ultra-tight retro-wear; a couple of dark-lidded Gothish females; some pierced-and-tattooed androgynous waifs in black; and, Alex was relieved to see, three or four newly arrived cuties of the linen-and-chinos variety who had obviously come over to Brooklyn to check out the scene.

"Relax, Sahib. Who cares what those dolts think," said Billy, pushing him down on the bench and signaling Winnie to kill the music tape. "Just pretend you're in your apartment, wearing your flowing robes, playing for your coked-up harem."

Ever since learning of Alex's half-Syrian roots back in prep school, Billy had peppered him with puerile Arab jokes, and with various monikers like "Sahib" and "Ahmed," notwithstanding the fact that Alex's ancestors were Maronite Christian and that he looked more like his WASPy mother. The jokes had never been amusing, but given the existing level of anti-Arab sentiment Alex now found them particularly unfunny.

"Wonder if I could survive as a saloon piano player," Alex wondered aloud.

"Hey, it's *my* survival we're talking about." Billy placed a large framed photo on the piano, featuring himself and another man posing stiffly together in tuxedos. "Brother Big Bucks is on his way over."

"Finally I get to meet the fabled billionaire brother."

"He loves Porter, Gershwin, Broadway show tunes, so pretend you're a queen and keep it sappy. A few old-fashioned love songs and he might open his wallet and redistribute some of his ill-gotten inheritance. Otherwise it's the end of the world for the End of the World." Billy expelled a contemptuous little snort. "I've been open over two years and this is his first visit. Shit, I bet he's never been to Brooklyn in his whole life....Now play, Mohammed."

Billy departed in a flash to greet some new arrivals, a pair of slouching simians in gold chains who looked conspicuously out of place, but whom Billy welcomed as if they were visiting dignitaries. After handing out cigars and obsequiously lighting each one, Billy led them upstairs to his private living quarters. Something shady was going down, sensed Alex, escaping to the piano.

He could play almost anything by ear—preferring to improvise jazzy melodies—and while he had always had fun entertaining dates and friends in the privacy of his living room, he had never performed in any professional capacity or really worked with any diligence to hone his God-given talents into something distinctive. He felt ridiculous, moreover, conforming to Billy's request to play Fred-and-Ginger music for the End of the World's clientele. He warmed up with something easy, "It Had to Be You," which under normal circumstances he could have played blindfolded. Tonight, conscious of curious looks from the oddball patrons, he started thinking about what his hands were doing, causing a few initial blunders.

Despite this stage fright, Alex was feeling footloose, having just that morning sublet his bachelor flat. He had also unloaded his furniture for $5,000, a fire-sale price that only a fugitive would have accepted. However, it was a bargain as far as he was concerned; he had never felt so wonderfully unencumbered. All he owned now were his clothes—mostly comprised of useless suits in mothballs—his Harley, and a just few thousand in savings over and above the furniture sale, having squandered the preponderance of his former salary on bon vivant pleasures in the assumption that the gravy train would never end. He didn't bother to count the Halaby Hosiery stock his parents had given him when he was a child as part of their estate planning. After all, it was illiquid, unmarketable, worthless paper for all practical purposes. He owned 10 percent of nothing. Just how far his meager cash would carry him was anybody's guess; he had no experience at being frugal. The plan was to spend the summer in monastic solitude, figuring out his life and waiting for an inspirational jolt.

His shack on the distant outskirts of Southampton, rented from Memorial Day Weekend through Labor Day, was already paid for in full courtesy of his former salary. The prospect of spending three months in the country without any family obligations buoyed him to the brink of tears, though he still considered his week-old freedom to be precarious, knowing how adept his parents were at bending him to their will. He had been screening calls to avoid talking to them, afraid he might cave in if they caught him at a vulnerable moment. Were it not for the fifty-dollar fee involved, he would have changed his number—and yet when he received his Halaby Hosiery paycheck in the mail as if nothing had happened, he tore it up and mailed back the pieces. He had also given his shrink the heave-ho: "I can no longer afford to be sane," were his parting words. And so, for the first time in his life, he was completely on his own, with just enough money to keep from starving and no family support system to disguise his spurious image.

Fortified by gin and vermouth, Alex began to warm to his new role as saloon piano man. The sparse applause was gratifying—a far better reception than being pelted with rotten fruit like the old vaudevillians, he mused. After about thirty minutes, Billy and his unsavory visitors descended from upstairs. Billy saw them out and returned to Alex at the piano.

"Who were those goodfellas?" Alex asked, slipping into a super slow version of "Someone to Watch Over Me."

"My business partners, Warren Buffetino and Bill Gatesaroni," said Billy with a crooked grin. "How else do you suppose a drug felon like me could manage to procure a liquor license?" He changed the subject. "What are you going to do with your life, Ahmed?"

Alex feigned nonchalance. "Well, to start, get the hell out of Dodge and go lie on the beach. You, of all people, should know what inspiration can come out of a little quality solitary confinement. Didn't you get the idea for this bar in prison, when you had all that time to think?"

"If you're comparing a Southampton shack to a prison cell, you're more sheltered than I thought," said Billy. "And if you think you're going to turn into some self-made man by getting in touch with your fucking inner child, you are totally whacked. Do you realize that other than being fairly decent at tickling ivories—good job, by the way—you have zero marketable skills?"

"Thanks. And just what skills did you acquire from the Danbury Correctional Facility?"

"Hey, man, I'm in the company of the Reverend Sun Myung Moon, the Berrigan brothers, G. Gordon Liddy, Clifford Irving, just to name a few cult-hero Danbury alums. Who went to Princeton besides Brooke Shields?"

Alex had never been sure whether Billy Lukes was a good friend for him to have or a bad one. They had met at Choate, in Wallingford, Connecticut—as different as two lily-white Choaties could be—and had spent their entire four years there hating each other's guts. Alex, sheltered almost to the point of no return, had never been away from his parents, not even to summer camp. Billy, a precocious urbanite who had never met his own father and was pawned off on boarding schools as soon as he was old enough, was the class charismatic leader and malcontent, breaking school rules with impunity, following in JFK's hallowed footsteps at Choate. Whenever Billy was about to be expelled, his mother bailed him (and the family name) out by donating a building, setting up a scholarship fund, arranging for a famous speaker to address the school.

Alex's social fate at Choate was sealed in his very first week, when he confided to a few classmates that he had never kissed a girl. Led by pied piper Billy, these fourteen-year-old roués teased him viciously, and Alex soon discovered that being the butt of his classmates' jokes was like floundering in quicksand: the harder he tried to climb out of the muck, the deeper he sank. When clever ripostes were called for, the rube from Aurora would lapse instead into lame and sputtering profanity, which only made him a more gratifying target. By junior year he had retired into a shell, striving for good grades and varsity letters in basketball and baseball, convinced that being accepted by an Ivy League college was the only thing that would make enduring Choate worth it.

Graduation day brought his catharsis. Not only did it mark the end of his agony, but when Billy called him a "camel jockey," Alex exploded with both fists, unleashing four years of pent-up anger and bloodying the larger boy's nose before some masters broke up the fight. Both boys received their diplomas in torn gowns, but exhilarated and probably, as Alex looked back, already on their way to friendship. Their paths parted then. Billy went off to Harvard—the only university in America secure enough to overlook his bad behavior and B-minus average, and which also happened to have a Lukes Modern Art Center.

Six years later the antagonists met again by chance at an Upper East Side cocktail party. All vestiges of bad feeling between them were wiped away when Billy whipped out a plastic vial and introduced Alex to the wonders of toot. Inclusion in the ritual meant Alex was now on even footing and gave him something far more potent than sports to fill his emotional void. A shared infatuation with the white powder soon made them inseparable chums, dedicated to partying and to bedding babes whenever and wherever they could. Alex felt privileged to run in such fast company, though the bacchanalia of loose women, cocaine binges, and occasional all-night Ecstasy raves suited Billy's temperament far more than his own. When Billy got busted for selling two grams to an undercover cop, Alex regarded it as a wake-up call. He was becoming dangerously dependent on the soul-robbing drug and had even started snorting at work. The more he used it the more he needed it, and the more it ruled him. So on the day they sent Billy to Danbury, Alex summoned all his willpower and flushed his stash down the toilet.

Thereafter he spent a couple of months of private agony, with a nasty regression or two, until he was able to wean himself for good. Twice he visited his buddy in prison, a pilgrimage he deemed his fraternal duty, but illegal drugs were from that point banished from his life—to date his greatest accomplishment.

Alex was startled out of his thoughts by the sound of coins rattling in his glass atop the piano. Annoyed that the remains of his martini were spoiled, he glanced up to see a sultry redhead smiling at him; looking like Cat Woman in her skin-tight bodysuit.

"Forget it, doll," said Billy, shooing her away. "His father cut his nuts off years ago. And recently he's been disowned." As the abashed temptress slunk back to the bar, Billy preempted Alex's protest. "You can't afford groupies. Better get used to living like a monk."

"Monkhood can only be an improvement. Who knows—maybe it'll be the best thing that ever happened to me," Alex said, trilling some notes for emphasis. There were now, in fact, a few tasty dishes among the human smorgasbord at the End of the World bar, but he was barely tempted. He had come to distrust his own instincts when it came to women, having habitually chosen beautiful bodies with not much inside them—hard-boiled ice queens like Lorna Foxhall or thin-skinned chicks with unceasing emotional issues. Shell-shocked by the attitude, entitlement, avarice, toughness, and meltdowns displayed by his female prospects, he had briefly dabbled with a much younger crop, only to discover that innocence these days found its expression in pan sexuality, studded tongues, pierced pussies, and monarch butterfly tattoos. These self-mutilators were the future, and his outlook was bleak. Women were mutating faster than insects! Instead of poetry and flowers, they either wanted impersonal threesomes or your most recent financial statement. Romance, along with communism, had been relegated to the ash heap of history.

In the middle of his lament, a blond phoenix rose from the ash heap. She was chicly clad in black, but all Alex saw was pixie dust. As her willowy figure glided into the club and glanced skittishly about the bar, looking too refined for the venue, his heart experienced an almost unbearable surge of desire. Something was bothering her; her fruity mouth contorted and her eyes squinted with concern. He found himself trembling, clammy. Rather than rush over willy-nilly to assist her, he observed her from a safe distance, afraid that she would wither from too strong an approach, or worse, reject him out of hand. Paradoxically, she seemed both approachable and unapproachable.... His former shrink would surely have a field day, he thought; clearly he was projecting his own needs onto this total stranger. Still, this was no assembly-line beauty; already he was less interested in her looks than in the mysteries that lay beneath.

When she spotted Billy and began heading in their direction, his mouth went dry, his heart raced. He braced for her first utterance, hoping it wouldn't contain a bubble-bursting twang or an outer-borough accent.

"Billy, can you please help us?" Her dulcet lilt rocked Alex's solar plexus. "Our limo accidentally knocked over a motorcycle."

Alex ran out of the club to find his cherished creation lying on its side, behind an idling black limousine. When he saw the dent in his front fender he suffered a small death. He circled the bike, carefully surveying the damage, then bent down and tried to lift it. However, the thing wouldn't budge, and so he simply knelt there beside it.

"I'm terribly sorry," came a concerned female voice. He straightened up and his eyes met the spring-green eyes of Emily Lukes. She quickly dropped her gaze. "Our driver didn't see it. Can I help?"

"Can you bench-press six-fifty?" Alex smiled.

Billy, emerging from the club, waltzed up and rapped on the limo's back window. But the man inside gave an agitated wave and returned to his cell phone.

"Please don't worry," Emily said, "we'll pay for the damage."

"It's a custom bike, with restoration parts," Alex pouted.

"What does that mean?"

"It means," Alex said, milking her for sympathy, figuring that sympathy was a good start, "that I designed it myself, and that some of the parts, like the fender you just dented, aren't readily available."

The chauffeur opened the limo's cabin door and out stepped a lank-haired, vaguely effete man in gray slacks and a turtleneck sweater, still talking on his cell phone. Alex recognized him from the picture that Billy had placed on the piano. Closing his cell phone, Charles said in a singsong cadence, "Billy, oh Billy, bring out the champers, oh silly, Billy boy!"

"No champagne," Emily chided, "until we pick up this motorcycle."

"It's too heavy, my love," Charles said, with a slight slur. "And anyhoo, I do believe, if one owns a motorcycle, one probably has to get used to certain inconveniences, like having one's motorcycle knocked over."

"Those who knock motorcycles over," Emily quickly intervened, "must get used to certain inconveniences, like picking them up."

While Charles would not exert himself personally, and under no circumstances would he allow his wife to help ("You'll strain something, my darling"), he did contribute by holding Billy's martini glass and by allowing his chauffeur to pitch in. Luckily a muscular passerby offered his assistance; it took all four of them to get the bike back up on its wheels. Charles tried to minimize the extent of the damage, pointing out that aside from the dented fender and some minor scratches on the chrome—all of which, he hinted, might have been there before the accident, for all he knew—the bike was in fine working order.

"No one's hurt, right?" said Charles jovially, thrusting a hundred-dollar bill into Alex's hand, "so let's just keep it between us, hmm?"

Alex stared incredulously at the paltry sum, but was prevented from saying anything by Billy, who shot him a grim look and began herding Charles and Emily back into the bar. At the doorway, Emily broke away and came back.

"If you need more money, please let me know," she said. "It's a beautiful motorcycle—though to be honest they scare the life out of me."

Her willingness to take responsibility for the accident was enough to soothe Alex. In the face of such loveliness, his dented motorcycle fender faded into oblivion. Her marital status notwithstanding, he found himself driven to impress her, almost desperately so. Endeavoring to erase all vestiges of the stifled boss's son and start life afresh as a free spirit, he introduced himself with first alias that came to mind, "Alex Monk."

"Emily Lukes."

As her hand melted into his for a blissful second, he noticed her enormous diamond and her wedding band. That she wore these tokens on her right hand told him she was left-handed, and from that tiny bit of evidence he wondered a bit flakily if she was a touch off-beat and creative.

Patting the gas tank, he said, "You don't know what you're missing."

"Well, Mr. Monk," she said, seemingly unnerved by his gaze, "I'd better get back." With that she waved bye-bye and returned inside.

Emily's "HindenBurger" was unappetizingly gray inside, and her mouth revolted at the amount of salt and paprika on the "Atomic Fries." She hated to think what the "O-Zone Layer Cake" or the "Three-Mile Floating Island" she had seen on the menu tasted like. She was, however, enjoying listening to the piano music, an odd mix of old Broadway and new jazz. Next to her, Charles and Billy, feasting on blackened "Waco Mako Shark" and a French Cabernet Sauvignon called "Fat Bastard," pretended to bond. Billy, eager for investors, was full of bonhomie; Charles took a certain satisfaction both in his magnanimous decision to visit his brother's club and in his camp in braving Brooklyn. Neither man made much of an effort to include Emily in the conversation, though every so often Charles would reach out and squeeze her arm, like a person making sure he hadn't misplaced his coat.

She tuned in and out, relieved that Billy hadn't invited one of his bimbos to join them. Try as she might to be a good sport, she had yet to meet one she could relate to or didn't pity. Much as she welcomed the relative peace between the brothers, their rudeness irked her on principle. She sat numbly between them, reminding herself uncomfortably of her mother, who had silently endured one business dinner after another until she couldn't take it anymore and became a closet drinker and prescription drug abuser. Coming from such genes, Emily considered herself fortunate that she didn't have an addictive personality.

Srill, Alex Monk's chords were going to her head, her most critical erogenous zone. With the exception of heavy metal (it was for the brain-dead, in her opinion), she appreciated almost any kind of music, from classical to rock to even hip-hop. Her musical tastes were certainly wider-ranging than those of her husband's, who, with the exception of the Beatles and Broadway, had no use for any music recorded in his lifetime. Emily and Charles did share, however, a fondness for love songs that hearkened back to an era when men and women actually sought fulfillment in each other—songs that took your heart for a whirl, to which you could dance cheek to cheek, that didn't hit you over the head with modern-day vulgarity, that her own generation had all but forgotten. Elegant, wistful songs like "The Very Thought of You," "He Loves, She Loves," and "The Nearness of You"—all of which the fellow in the *Easy Rider* get-up had played with, if not professional polish, a soulful touch. The incongruity intrigued her, made her curious.

Moreover, his eyes kept seeking her out. He had penetrating blue eyes, like an Alaskan husky's, which made her self-conscious and a bit nervous—though the disaster videos on the wall behind him served as a constant reminder that any friend of Billy was suspect. She forced herself to look at her plate, at the other customers, at the videos—anywhere but at the piano player—even as his music kept transporting her to a Jazz Age Parisian boîte filled with writers, artists, and expatriates, and his hypnotic glances kept drawing her back to him.

As a waitress clad in skimpy camouflage rags began clearing, Billy pitched Charles on his plans to renovate. Much as Emily likened investing in such a venture to pouring gasoline over money and torching it, she pitied Billy, knowing that her husband was stringing him along and had no intention of giving him a dime. She wished their mother's will had been more equitable; she had always felt uneasy benefiting more from the Lukes fortune than Billy did. Certainly there was enough lucre to go around and make everybody comfortable. What a buzzard Abigail Lukes must have been!

In the middle of Billy's hard-sell, Charles, bored and sloshed, suddenly noticed the still of Abigail playing croquet flashing by on the monitor behind Billy's head. "Hullo! It's Abigail Lukes herself! What, no poolside pictures of Mumsie in Palm Beach? No photos of dear old Dad on his knees in the cabana?"

He chuckled delightedly at the not-so-inside joke. Emily rolled her eyes just as Alex threw her another intense look. Mortified, she furrowed her brow and feigned interest in her husband as he began to favor Billy with an unsolicited treatise on the financial aspects of his Spidex deal.

"Stronger than steel, at a fraction of the cost," warbled Charles. "And the glory of it, the topper, is that it's *renewable.*"

"Yes, yes," Billy squirmed, obviously eager to change the subject back to his bar renovation, "it's the constant changes you must keep your eye on."

"Always think long-term," Charles continued.

This type of business talk bored Emily to tears, especially at social occasions; she had been overexposed to it while she was growing up and appreciated more than most people the value of frivolity. Her father placed his corporate career above everything. During dinners and any other time together, he discussed his business nonstop, instructing his family in the finer points of his work. It was his way of teaching them about life, but such early training had the opposite effect he had intended. Both of Emily's older twin brothers had escaped to Montana (where they taught fly-fishing) and wanted nothing to do with him. Her mother had come unglued as soon as all three children left the nest. Her father had no patience for weakness, and his wobbly wife marred his image, hampered his momentum. He barely kept up the facade, commuting to his Greenwich home as little as possible and living primarily in his Manhattan *pied-à-terre*, where he could more easily gratify his libido. His very public affair three years ago with a former beauty queen, whose most notable traits were silicone breasts and cash-register eyes, would have torn most marriages apart, but Emily's parents were devout Catholics. As her father loved to say when addressing business groups, "You can't climb Everest without a base camp."

"Just imagine," she overheard Charles say, "bulletproof armor as lightweight as my wife's nylon nightie. Isn't that right, dear? Darling?"

"Oh, um, I don't know," murmured Emily, snapping out of her musically induced reverie. "The whole concept seems crazy."

With an air of self-importance, Charles declared, "Call me crazy, but I leave for Japan the day after your birthday."

"Happy Three-O, by the way," Billy toasted her.

"Guess what I'm giving her," Charles said, picking up his wife's hand and kissing it in proprietary fashion.

"A bullet-proof nightie?" said Billy.

Before Charles could tell him, the entire club was startled by the familiar descending octave chords of Grieg's A-minor Concerto, slammed with violent fury. Once the piano player had everyone's attention, he blew into the microphone like a Las Vegas lounge singer and tickled out a flowery intro reminiscent of the Gay '90s. Then he began to sing:

> All the world seems in tune,
> On a spring afternoon,
> When we're poisoning pigeons in the park.
> Every Sunday you'll see,
> My sweetheart and me,
> When we poison the pigeons in the park…

Emily glanced at Billy and noticed his bilious expression, which seemed to suggest that he had hired Alex Monk to provide background music, not put on a show. She sensed that Alex was showboating for her, reaching out to her in a strange if not frenzied way.

> When they see us coming,
> The birdies all try and hide,
> But they still go for peanuts
> When coated with cyanide…

Charles leaned across her and clasped his brother on the arm. "The guy's actually quite hilarious! I love high-brow humor." He listened a bit longer. "How's his comedic repertoire?"

"Extensive, wicked, loaded with social commentary," said Billy, eyes shifting. "No other club in the city offers this kind of thing."

> We'll murder them all
> Amid laughter and merriment,
> Except for the few
> We take home to experiment.
> My pulse will be quickenin'

> With each drop of strychnine
> We feed to a pigeon—
> It just takes a smidgeon—
> To poison a pigeon in the park.

As Alex basked in applause at the end, Charles asked his wife a question he would come to regret: "Why don't we hire him for tomorrow night, my darling? He could liven things up—maybe sing a ditty or two satirizing the rich."

"What's happening tomorrow night?" Billy asked.

While Emily cringed, Charles covered smoothly. "Oh, it's just a little impromptu thingamajig I'm slapping together for Emily's birthday."

"You're coming, aren't you?" said Emily, appalled by her husband's insensitivity. "I assumed Charles had invited you."

"Of course you're invited! And bring along your piano player to entertain us," Charles added, with an imperious gesture toward the piano.

If Billy was offended, he kept it to himself. Apparently his need for funds was acute. "Anything for you, *mon frère!*"

"Considering that we dented his bike, wouldn't it be nice to invite him for dinner?" Emily offered, enthralled by Alex's smooth, brainy wit and feeling a bit irreverent as Alex responded to cries of "Encore!" by launching into another zany song.

> First you get down on your knees,
> Fiddle with your rosaries,
> Bow your head with great respect, and
> Genuflect, genuflect, genuflect!

Emily, who hadn't attended Mass in years and blamed Catholic hypocrisy in part for her family's dysfunction, took delight in the lyrics, even as Charles denied her request.

"Let's not go overboard, my pet. I've gone to great pains to achieve even numbers. Besides, he'd only be out of his element."

4

Melodies and Madness

The whole point of a Harley, rued Alex, was having a special someone like Emily clutching him from behind as he zoomed down a country road. Inching eighty blocks from the Williamsburg Bridge to uptown Manhattan, through fume-laden traffic, with two-hundred-pound Billy Lukes on the back, was, short of a fatal or maiming accident, the closest thing imaginable to Harley Hell. Billy's bulk, along with his inability to go five seconds without whipping out his cell phone, made the journey twice as harrowing. After the Queensboro Bridge they were finally able to pick up speed, though dressed in his evening clothes Alex felt more ridiculous than emancipated.

He was, however, looking forward to this evening's party. The prospect of seeing Emily again exhilarated him, but there was something else: He had attended his share of chic soirees but never as hired help. Tonight he would be an anonymous observer, the Invisible Man, released from the pressure of having to live up to expectations that his former life had always placed on him. In his mind's eye he saw a candlelit room filled with New York's social elite applauding his performance at the piano, tossing envious compliments at him, while he, ever the man of mystery, would not allow himself more than a hint of a smile and maybe a small nod at their adulation.

Loath to leave his dented bike on the street inviting another catastrophe, Alex flirted with the idea of checking it into a parking garage. However, for financial reasons he declined. Such a matter he wouldn't have bothered to debate back when he was an overpaid boss's son. During the short cross-town walk toward Fifth Avenue, Billy prepped him.

"Remember, Charles actually thinks you wrote those songs. Thank god no one remembers Tom Lehrer anymore. Let's not shatter anyone's illusions tonight, eh? They think you're hilarious. We must preserve your mystique until Charles bankrolls my new club." Billy honored Alex with several I-am-not-worthy bows. "You did a great job, Ahmed, and I'm grateful. So much for your stage fright anyhow."

Alex didn't want Billy to know that it was near insanity level desperation that had been the cause of his success as a performer. Completely taken by Emily, craving her attention and irritated by her apparent interest in her husband, he had started performing "Poisoning Pigeons in the Park" without really knowing what he was doing. "So," he casually asked Billy now, figuring that there was no love lost between the Lukes brothers, "what's the story with Emily?"

Billy grabbed his arm, spinning him around and almost knocking him off his feet. "Out of bounds," he warned, juggling the gift he was carrying so he could give Alex's sternum a hard poke. "I don't need complications. Besides," he tossed off, as they resumed walking, "if she's going to stray, it had better be with me. Such things must be kept in the family."

"Are they happily married?"

"People that rich don't concern themselves with pesky matters like whether or not they're happily married," Billy snorted. "Watch yourself, Sahib. My big brother may seem like an over-groomed pussycat, but he'll show his claws fast enough if you get anywhere near something that belongs to him. Not that *you* would ever stand a chance with her." Suddenly he stopped. "Well, here it is—the sweet little cottage I grew up in."

The Lukeses' apartment building stood directly across from the Central Park Zoo on the most expensive residential real estate in Manhattan. The baroque granite façade of the pre-war edifice looked almost white compared to adjacent buildings, suggesting a recent power-wash. Billy greeted the ancient, epauletted doorman as if the two of them were old friends, offering him an exaggerated military salute as he passed. The doorman, showing not the slightest flicker of recognition, eyed them suspiciously before collaring them long enough to make sure their names were on the guest list, which clearly offended Billy. "I grew up here, you toad," he said. The enormous lobby, with its Tudor-style linen-fold paneling and stiff furniture, was dimly lit, as befit a lair of the aged rich. The two bedraggled bikers spent a few moments in front of the mirror dusting off their tuxes and ruffling their helmet-matted hair. Billy then led Alex through the gloom into an elevator and pressed "P" for the penthouse.

Moments later they were delivered into a very spacious and bright gallery with fifteen-foot arched ceilings. The sound that greeted them was more suggestive of a reception than a party, less of a festive buzz than a bored, impersonal murmur. Glistening marble floors and ivory walls set off equally well Charles Lukes's collection of exquisite modern paintings and exquisitely clad guests. Alex and Billy were accosted almost immediately by an elderly English butler—looking straight out of central casting, with plastered hair, pale complexion, and impassive demeanor—who took the gift from Billy's hands without visible acknowledgment and waved them over to a guest book on a little marquetry table.

Billy grabbed the pen next to the ostentatiously displayed guest book and scribbled "Rightful Owner," grumbling, "Fucking Riggs used to shine my shoes and pour my fucking Wheaties."

"Cheer up," said Alex. "This is the first time I've ever come to one of these parties as the hired help."

"Yeah, well, I'm only here as your manager."

No sooner had Billy said it than Charles was upon them, his red handkerchief peek-a-booing from the breast pocket of his tuxedo, his black-velvet slippers embroidered with gold pheasants. "Well hullo you two," he boomed, "welcome to Chateau Lukes!" He looked his entertainer up and down and seemed pleasantly surprised at how well he cleaned up. "Well, Maestro! You look tip-top!" Smoothly greasing Alex's palm with a couple of C-notes and then placing a perfectly manicured hand lightly on each man's shoulder, he ushered them in with the nonchalance of a man whose interest earned interest while he got a massage or sipped a cocktail.

Alex had a fleeting desire to tell him that the two hundred bucks he was receiving for entertaining tonight was less than he used to spend on dinner and was not nearly enough to fix his fender, but he was too cowed by the grandeur. Even his relatively untutored eye could identify most of the artists on the wall: Rothko, Warhol, Pollock, Diebenkorn, Stella, Frankenthaler, de Kooning—millions of dollars displayed with understated elegance. "Jesus!" he said, stopping in his tracks. "Is that a Dali?"

"But of course," Charles said smugly. "Do you really think I'd hang something that looked like a Dali, but wasn't?" At this, Billy peeled away in disgust.

"When I studied Dali," came a soft female voice, "we learned that an object that looks like one thing may actually represent another." Alex turned to behold Emily, a mist of gossamer mint-green satin, shimmering black pearls and diamonds, and radiant blond hair. She smiled cordially at him.

"When you studied Dali, my darling," said Charles, "you never realized you'd own one someday."

"To own something implies one has already lost it," she said.

"Nonsense!" Charles blustered, eyebrow cocked. "When you own something you can do with it anything you damned well please."

A tray packed with the largest shrimp Alex had ever seen was presented to them by an unsmiling waiter. Following his host's and hostess's example, Alex politely demurred. He sensed a glimmer of tension between the Lukeses. Not that this was necessarily significant. His own parents invariably fought before throwing parties.

"Did you study art too?" he asked Charles rather stupidly, in an effort to keep himself from gaping at Emily.

"Didn't have to—I grew up immersed in it." As if by some unspoken command, another waiter appeared at Charles's elbow with a glass of champagne, which he accepted without seeming conscious of it. "As my late, great mother, Abigail Lukes, was so fond of saying: 'All you really need to know about a piece of art is how much the insurance company will pay you if someone steals it from you.'"

"So you collect mainly for investment purposes?"

Charles frowned at this gaucherie. "I buy only what I like. But I never let sentiment interfere with judgment."

Alex wondered whether Charles had acquired his wife using the same criteria. "You seem partial to well-known artists."

"I'm partial to well-known everything, actually. Except piano players, of course." He smiled broadly. "The piano's in the living room. Keep it light and simple and save your amusing compositions for when we're having coffee and dessert, ça va?" He gestured to his wife. "Why don't you escort him, darling?"

"Your songs last night were wonderful," she said to Alex. "I haven't laughed so hard in ages."

"We laugh all the time, my dear," Charles said, flashing a strange look at Alex. With that, he turned to greet two silver-haired gentlemen whose identical tuxes, TAG Heuers, and perfect tans made them hard to tell apart.

Emily led Alex into the living room, furnished in eye-popping French Art Deco and offering a breathtaking panorama of Central Park.

"How's your motorcycle?" she asked.

"Still dented and full of character," he grinned. "And your limo?"

"Newly waxed and buffed to perfection," she bantered back, as their shoulders accidentally brushed. "So, were you born with songwriting talent? Or is your genius like Edison's—one percent inspiration and 99 percent perspiration?"

"My genius," he informed her, after a sheepish hesitation, "is one hundred percent imitation."

Her face flickered disappointment. "You didn't write those songs?"

"No, a Harvard professor named Tom Lehrer did, decades ago," he said, forgetting in his giddiness his promise to Billy to maintain his mystique and keep this tidbit a secret. "But I do get a big kick out of singing them, and of having beautiful women like you think I wrote them."

"Ah, an impostor. You'll fit right in," she said, rendered shy by his little compliment as they arrived at a glistening Steinway grand. "Well, Mr. Monk, I look forward to your performance, plagiaristic or not."

"Any requests?" he asked, but she was already gliding back in Charles's direction to greet more guests. Alex gaped after her, until a silver tray filled with champagne flutes went by. He helped himself to one and sat down at the formidable piano. The party's mortuary atmosphere and the apartment's formality gave him pause. Only a few bold souls dared to settle on the museum-quality furniture. This opulence went far beyond anything in his experience and made his parents' townhouse and reproduction antiques look like a college dorm by comparison.

For courage, he downed most of his champagne in a single gulp before tentatively beginning to play what was becoming his opening mainstay, "It Had to Be You." Across the living room, under a Kenneth Noland target, Billy was targeting a social X-ray. As Alex's music wafted unnoticed through the living room against the competing drone of conversation, several stunning women caught his eye, but their gowns and stiff coifs had all the welcoming aspects of barbed wire.

"Alex? My God, is that you?"

He jerked his head in the direction of the voice. Standing over him was his ex-fiancée Lorna Foxhall, sheathed in the most tasteful of black dresses and attached to a tall, clean-cut blond man. The man's arm was draped possessively around her, his fingertips tapping against her bare shoulder. Suddenly a nonentity, little more than a servant, Alex felt stripped naked in Lorna's condescending gaze. He had never considered the possibility that she might be among the Lukeses' guests, though it made perfect sense. He wondered why over the course of their three-month relationship she had never unveiled him to the Lukeses, but for the moment he was afraid to ask why.

"Moonlighting? How quaint," Lorna drawled. "Do your parents approve?" Her jaw barely moved when she spoke. Had she not been so hyper-conventional she might have made an excellent ventriloquist, Alex mused.

"I'm a free agent now," he said, sounding sophomoric even to himself.

"Alex," she said, smiling up at her beau, "meet Kurt Oberling."

In the process of extending his hand, Kurt knocked Alex's flute with his forearm. Champagne splashed everywhere, dousing Alex's lap and the piano keys.

"So sorry, old boy. How clumsy of me," said Kurt in a clipped German accent, looking neither clumsy nor sorry. Neither he nor Lorna lifted a finger as Alex set his empty glass back on the piano and blotted his pants and the ivories with a cocktail napkin.

As if nothing had happened, Lorna informed him, "Kurt's a partner at Deutsche Bank."

Putting down his napkin, Alex responded by playing in a slow, jazzy cadence and singing: "*Deutschland, Deutschland über alles…*"

"*Scheisse*, Lorna, did *you* ever dodge a bullet!" Kurt snickered.

"*Über alles in der Welt…*"

They left, shaking their perfect heads.

A nightmarish feeling began to steal over Alex as he finished one song after another, with no applause and not even a glance in his direction. He had thought it would be great fun to entertain here, that he would be the center of attention. He had even imagined Emily leaning languidly against the piano as he played. Instead he felt as if he had ceased to exist. The ghost of Alex Halaby. What in God's name had he done walking out on his life? Most of the world would give anything to have what he had recklessly thrown away.

Suddenly he was joined on the bench by Billy, who pulled his hands off the keys and shut the piano cover. "I'm taking you off the bench and putting you in the game."

"I'm thirty minutes into my new career—my first payday from someone other than my father," said Alex, watching Emily and Charles work the party from opposite ends of the room, imagining that they also slept on opposite sides of a king-size bed, like North and South Korea. Already he had come to the self-serving conclusion—based in large part on the delicacy in her eyes and the vague flicker of meanness in his—that they were intrinsically ill-suited. "As my manager, don't you think I should keep playing?"

"Hey, nobody's listening," said Billy, tugging on Alex's arm. "The beauty of black tie is that a minstrel looks the same as a mogul." He led Alex away from the piano and into the crowd, and Alex's eyes gravitated to a high-style blonde lounging on a settee. Her platinum hair was done in ringlets and she wore a short, pouffy canary-yellow dress that showed her slender legs to splendid effect. All her effervescent attention was lavished on a dusty, dried-out sausage in a burgundy velvet smoking jacket.

"The Baron de Lapalisse," said Billy of the sausage. "Lives to shoot small game and stuff wild fowl. The wild fowl sitting next to him is Her Royal Horniness, the Baroness de Lapalisse—by way of outer Atlanta."

"I don't suppose she's his granddaughter."

"Wife. A retired international runway model who continues to ply her trade as an international nympho. Claire and I were once like this," Billy boasted, crossing his fingers, "until she found out Charles was like this." He rubbed his thumb and index finger together to indicate big bucks, a gesture that quickly became a phony little finger wave as the baroness noticed them staring at her and blew Billy a kiss.

"She dated Charles?" Alex asked.

"All the way to the altar. Marriage lasted a year."

"And she's invited to Emily's birthday party?"

"Just one big happy incestuous family," Billy said, as another tall, expensive blonde began sashaying in their direction. She possessed enough silicone to raise the Titanic; the only things that jiggled were her diamond drop earrings.

"Oh, Billy," the bombshell sighed, planting a kiss on Billy's mouth and smearing him with lipstick, "I didn't know *you* were coming."

"Nor did I," said Billy. "Vanessa Muss, meet Alex, our ivory tickler." Vanessa's wattage dimmed considerably, until Billy threw in, "Alex is less known for his musical talent than for being the younger brother of Her Royal Highness Queen Noor."

"Queen Noor? Of Jordan?"

"What other Queen Noors are there?" said Billy coolly. He had devised the "Queen Noor Ploy" several years ago after discovering in a magazine article that Queen Noor's maiden name and Alex's surname were identical. While the device proved to be an excellent method of smoking out gold-diggers and causing them to make swooning fools of themselves, Alex, even at the peak of his drug days, had never felt comfortable taking full advantage of it.

As might have been predicted, blood rushed to Vanessa's cheeks. She beamed at Alex, straining toward him like the figurehead at the bow of a ship, shoulders back, chest out, serving up her bosom as if on a tray. "So, how exactly does it work?" she said naively, batting her lashes. "Does being a queen's brother make you royalty?"

"No," Billy interjected, "but the oil royalties make up for it."

Alex's heart was not in the game. Something told him to glance over his shoulder, and as he did he noticed Emily slipping away from the party and escaping up the grand staircase. He felt an irresistible force dragging him in the same direction.

"Excuse me, I must relieve myself," he said.

As he swiftly departed, Vanessa called out, "Just aim between the Rothko and the Warhol. And don't forget to come back."

When Alex reached the foot of the staircase, he found himself face to face with Charles's breathtaking ex-wife, the woman in the pouffy yellow dress whom Billy had pointed out moments ago. After they zigged into each other, then zagged, she thrust out her manicured hand. "Baroness de Lapalisse," she said, with a Continental patois and a commanding presence. "But my friends call me Claire." She immobilized him with her spicy perfume and brilliant smile. "Should I know you?"

"Alex de Monk," Alex replied, with a burlesque bow.

Up close, her manicured beauty inspired more distrust than enchantment; she was as hard and polished as sterling silver. She glanced suggestively up the staircase. "Come to storm the castle, Alex de Monk?"

Alex felt himself flushing red.

"Perhaps when you get to the pillaging and whatnot, you'll call me," she said, and with that Alex went bounding up the stairs. When he reached the top landing, he glanced back down and saw the baroness still smiling at him. Buoyed by that added rush, he blew her a stage kiss and disappeared down a long Oriental runner, poking his head into a couple of pitch-black, unoccupied guest rooms, pretending to look lost, before coming upon a dimly lit room. Emily was standing with her back to him, gazing out the window. When she sensed his presence, she jumped and whirled around.

"God, you scared me! Shouldn't you be downstairs playing music?"

"Sorry," he said, "the union makes me take breaks."

"What are you doing *here*? Why aren't you mingling with all the pretty women?"

"If I may say so, the women are prettier as a group than as individuals. Sorry, I didn't mean to intrude on your privacy." Instead of departing on that note, Alex looked around at what appeared to be an art studio. The space was sparsely appointed—easel, high-tech floodlights, oversized armchair, and a long table against the wall on which brushes, tubes of paint, and sketchbooks were neatly arranged alongside various and sundry computer equipment. He recognized the distinct odor of linseed oil and turpentine, which was the primary sensory impression he had retained from his one painting course at Choate. In college, he had stuck to the appreciation side of art; none of the messy creation stuff for him. "Funny," he said, "I sort of thought you might be an artist."

She made a dubious face. "Everyone, from cook to upholsterer to piano player—no offense—calls himself an artist nowadays. Me: I just paint."

Alex noticed a stack of canvases propped against the wall, covered by a sheet. "May I?"

"I'd rather you didn't."

It was too late; Alex had already lifted the sheet and was looking at the top painting. When she didn't move to stop him, he eyed a few more canvases. Each was about three feet square and featured three female clowns, but the seeming banality of the subject matter evaporated when he examined them more closely. The clowns were grouped together but trapped in their own private worlds: floating upside-down, balancing on a ball, juggling birds, playing a flute, riding a unicorn, hiding in a transparent box, twisting in bizarre yoga positions. Muted colors predominated—amethyst, lavender, mauve—and while all the clowns wore clown suits, frilled bibs, and jester's hats, the mood was dark and un-circuslike. The feeling of isolation of each of the clowns was eerie and disturbing. The expertly rendered expressions were fractured, chaotic, intense but oddly enigmatic: a savage glare full of amusement, a smile about to dissolve into weeping.

"These are wonderful!" he marveled. "They have a real edge. Alienation…longing…turmoil. I was half expecting bowls of fruit."

"At least they're my own," she retorted, nervously twirling a lock of her hair before swallowing the rest of her champagne. Alex was charmed by the little gasp she made at the end, like a child finishing her milk.

"Your version of East Side women?"

"Art should be appreciated, not analyzed."

"I realize I'm no expert," he said, "but you're obviously talented."

"Painting's just my hobby," she said, pacing aimlessly, "and these clowns are not recent. I haven't been inspired lately."

Watching her long legs as they moved beneath her diaphanous dress, Alex felt himself floating on air. "Maybe you need someone to inspire you," he said. This was risky; it was really none of his business, and she would have every right to tell him so.

"And maybe I'm just a dilettante. True painters paint because they have to paint, like they have to breathe."

"This mausoleum could cause anyone to stop breathing. Is that why you escaped up here, to get a little air?" While Emily flung the sheet back over the canvasses, Alex urged, "Why don't you get a studio somewhere else, out of the shadow of your husband's collection? Tap into your true passion. Paint as if your life depended on it! Shake people up!" Advice on artistic living was unfamiliar territory for Alex, but in this woman's presence everything seemed clear. Already he wanted to believe that they were kindred spirits faced with kindred challenges. "Birthdays are good times to make changes."

"Changes? What changes?" came an amused voice from the doorway. Leaning casually against the doorjamb was Charles, inhaling a gold Balkan Sobranie cigarette from a tapered ivory holder. Alex wondered how long he had been standing there.

"Charles!" said a startled Emily, as her husband strolled into the room, one hand in a trouser pocket. "I just came up for a moment of quiet, and…"

Her voice tailed off as Charles peered into Alex's face, as if studying some bizarre form of primitive sculpture. "Ah, our pithy pianist. So sorry, old man, my wife has a terrible habit of distracting the help. It's some kind of stray puppy dog impulse left over from childhood. When you're done with your—break?—our guests are suffering terribly downstairs from the lack of background music." With a bemused smile and a quick glance at each of them, Charles tapped his dead ash casually onto the table of brushes and paints, pivoted on his toes like a flamenco dancer, and strode out, leaving Emily and Alex silent and motionless.

"Guess I better get back to work," Alex said, finally exhaling. He left without waiting for the hostess's answer.

To return to his place at the huge Steinway, Alex had to suffer the indignity of making his way through the milling guests, who were involved in the chaotic process of checking for their place cards in order to seat themselves at the dinner tables that had been set up in the dining room. Feeling swinish for having been so forward with Emily and getting busted by Charles moments ago, he settled on the bench and was about to throw himself back into the role of paid entertainer, when he sensed someone at his ear. It was Emily.

"Here's something to nibble on," she said.

Her face was an unreadable mask as she set a plateful of canapés and a fresh glass of champagne on the piano. Before he could thank her, she was gone to take her seat in the dining room a mere ten feet away. The proximity only magnified Alex's sense of isolation from her; it was as if they were separated by a wall of prison glass.

There were four round tables of ten people each, the one farthest away hosted by Charles, the closest one presided over by Emily. Seated to her right was the craggy Baron de Lapalisse and his hearing aid; to her left, a tiny male pixie whose plummy voice, floral vest, and dainty manner screamed out "decorator!"—causing Alex to wonder if Charles had arranged *le placement* in order to keep any threatening males away from his wife. His suspicions were given added credence when he looked over and noticed that the most stunning females, including the former Mrs. Charles Lukes and Vanessa Muss, were situated decoratively around Charles's table. Had the guests been as carefully arranged as everything else in the apartment?

Watching the guests suck on artichoke leaves, Alex mused that the artichoke and Emily were quite similar: cute little plates of armor on the outside protecting a tenderly delicious core. As leg of lamb and decanted Bordeaux followed, he periodically tried to make eye contact with her, but unlike last night there were no furtive glances. Not even his most haunting of melodies elicited a smidgeon of her attention. She was the birthday girl, in the spotlight. He tried to eavesdrop, but the clinking of silver and crystal and the sharp acoustics left only brief snippets of conversation understandable. He watched his hostess's smile grow stiffer and stiffer and wondered what she really thought of all these people. They chattered on like well-trained chimps; as soon as one finished a sentence, or even paused for a second or two, another leapt in, as if he or she had merely been waiting for the other to finish making noise. They debated the virtues and flaws of the latest book, the trendiest artist, the hottest plays and films, the best restaurants, and of course politics—reveling in the certainty that their own opinions on these topics reigned supreme. They dropped names as if they knew everybody worth knowing. Most of all, they gossiped about money: who really had it ("He's a billionaire, Greek shipping money…Yes, Greek—he dropped the 'populous' years ago…."); who only pretended to have it ("He's a lightweight, worth only fifty, sixty million tops…."); who was prevailing in the divorce ("She's getting the apartment, the house in Milbrook, the car and driver, and the dog; in return, she acknowledges his right to exist…."); and who was secretly seeking greener pastures ("She should've done her research on the Count of No Account before marrying him. Now she sleeps only with Arab sheiks and rich Jews. You think the Middle East is in turmoil *now*…."). How they loved hearing themselves talk, and the more Alex listened to them mercilessly skewer one person after another, the more he regarded his upcoming Tom Lehrer shtick during dessert and coffee as a suicide mission.

Ninety minutes later the lights dimmed and a waiter appeared carrying a huge cake blazing with candles. Everyone began to sing "Happy Birthday," belatedly accompanied by the piano player.

"Make a wish, my darling!" Charles called from across the room, as the cake was set down in front of his wife. "In fact, make thirty of them!"

As Emily closed her eyes presumably to make a wish, Alex was dying to be privy to her inner thoughts, to know what she really wanted. She opened her eyes and blew at the candles, taking an extra breath to extinguish them all. The room applauded; she made the first ceremonial incision; whereupon the droning persiflage resumed as the cake was toted back to the pantry to be cut. Before the waiters had finished pouring champagne, Charles was standing and rapping his spoon against his crystal water goblet, pinky pointed toward the ceiling.

"Do forgive me, now, if I wax a bit sentimental," he began. "You know toasts are inevitable at these things. If any of you start getting bored, please feel free to drink more champagne." This drew some laughter and caused the raising of a few glasses for refills, until Charles loudly and ceremonially cleared his throat. "They say that the ideal gift for a beautiful woman is a book—to make her feel intelligent. And that the ideal gift for an intelligent woman is a hat—to make her feel beautiful. Well, since my wife is *both* beautiful and intelligent, what do I give her?"

Alex looked over at Billy, who was gazing ceiling-ward in disgust.

Ambling over to his wife, Charles reached into his breast pocket and removed what looked to be a cashier's check, which he waved in the air. "As many of you know from Emily, her pet organization is the Children's School Arts Workshop. It funds art instruction for public schools in lower-income areas."

He handed his wife the check. As Emily examined it, her face went from chalk white to beet red.

"A million dollars ought to do the trick, eh, my darling? Art for the disenfranchised! Let them eat paint!"

People stirred in their seats but otherwise remained silent. Jealousy seemed to be the prevailing sentiment—especially among Billy, Claire, and Vanessa, who appeared to be engaging in catty whispers. Into the stilted moment, Emily rose to give her husband a hug of appreciation.

"Thank you, Charles," she said, projecting her voice so that the whole room heard her. "I don't know what to say. This will mean so much to so many kids."

"To my philanthropic wife! A social worker by day, a socialite by night!" As his wordplay fell flat, Charles arched a dark eyebrow and cocked his head slightly, an attempt at comedy made somewhat less effective by the evening's alcohol consumption. Dimly aware that his acerbic wit was somehow failing him, he persevered. "And here's to me as well, for being atypically sensitive and socially conscious."

Finally the company raised their glasses and consummated the toast.

Next to rise was Charles's ex-wife, Claire: "Happy birthday to Emily, who managed to tame the beast, and whom I truly hate for being so happy, well-adjusted, and rich."

This set the runway for similar tributes: "Happy birthday to my dear friend Emily," toasted Vanessa Muss, "whom I truly hate for being so beautiful." Another tipsy female guest teetered to her feet and slurringly threw in, "Here's to Emily, whom I truly hate for being such a goddamn good tennis player."

A discomfiting pall fell over the party. Another toast was obviously called for—something more meaningful, or at least without joking animosity. Brother-in-law Billy, glum, stayed riveted to his seat. Alex glanced over at Emily—standing next to her husband and holding the check as if it were a yoke—and detected a glimmer of dazed anguish beneath her polite smile. He hardly knew her, and the idea of stepping into the breach without a Tom Lehrer lyric to bolster him was terrifying. If there was anything he was dedicated to at this nascent stage of his life, however, it was taking risks. He pushed the piano bench back and stood, brimming with conviction but with no idea of what he was going to say.

Nobody paid attention at first. When he began tapping his glass—rather ineffectively with the only utensil available to him, a shrimp fork—he could hear whispered inquiries about what his role in the festivities might be. As the room slowly quieted, Emily looked at the floor, as if anticipating a disaster; Billy's scowl implied that Alex was overstepping himself. Charles was the only person in the room who looked completely sanguine. After all, he had instructed Alex to entertain during dessert and was probably expecting his hired entertainer to burst into a clever ditty.

"To talented, lovely Emily," Alex began, "whom I truly admire for being able to put up with all of you." Charles's smile collapsed. Urgently trying to get Alex's attention, Billy sliced his hand across his neck. Lorna covered a laugh with a cough and whispered something into Kurt's ear. Contempt took possession of Alex, filling him with a mad resolve. Feeling that his heart was about to pound through the wall of his chest, he looked over at Emily. Her frozen expression told him that she was mortified. He was a dead duck. "Emily," he quacked, "I'd rather have one of the paintings I saw upstairs than any of the paintings down here. Here's to finding the courage to do what you were so obviously meant to do!" He raised his champagne glass high and then guzzled the contents. Placing the empty flute on the piano, he stuffed his night's wages into it. "And now," he concluded, "if you'll all please excuse me, I'm off to find out what *I* was meant to do." With that, he bowed to the astonished assembly and made his less than grand exit from Chateau Lukes.

5

Post Mortems

At clamorous, glamorous Harry Cipriani's on the day after Emily's birthday party, three blondes of slightly different tints nibbled on salads of slightly different greens. Ash, platinum, and honey munched on arugula, endive, and radicchio. The honey, Vanessa Muss, was giving Emily Lukes and Claire de Lapalisse the scoop on her latest romantic prospect, Lester "the Jackal" Ruby.

"Doesn't it bother you that you're dating a guy called 'the Jackal'?" Emily asked, sipping her mineral water.

"I'm dating a jackal who's in the *Fortune* 400," Vanessa retorted.

"They're all jackals," Claire tossed off.

"Just how did he get his nickname?" Emily asked naively.

Her two friends looked at each other in disbelief, until the baroness finally said, "Let's just say that his hostile takeovers are exceedingly hostile." From behind her blue-tinted sunglasses, Claire was expertly scanning the fifteen or so tables in her vicinity, taking social inventory—who was lunching with whom, what they were wearing, who looked newly Botoxed, liposuctioned, or lifted. Emily could practically read her mind.

Vanessa fished a copy of *W* out of her lizard-skin satchel. The cover photograph, captioned "The Jackal at Play," featured the bald, diminutive Ruby and herself, arm in arm, laughing together at something apparently hilarious. "I guess I'm Lester's latest takeover target," she preened.

"Just make sure he doesn't liquidate you and sell off the pieces," warned Claire, demolishing a breadstick with her perfect teeth. "And watch out for private detectives."

"For your information," said Vanessa, nose upturned, "Lester is setting me up in my own couture business—just as soon as his divorce is final."

"Oh, he's setting you up, all right. But not for what you think, darling," said Claire. She took a closer gander at the photo. "Somebody get that midget a toupee!" The baroness paused thoughtfully. "Actually, he's so repulsive he's kind of sexy."

"Billionaire sexy?" posed Emily.

Claire's small Hermès bag started playing "Für Elise." Reaching inside, she fished out her cell phone and glanced at it. "Philippe," she grimaced, pressing the mute button and setting the phone on the table. "My husband is the last person I want to talk to when I'm trying to eat."

The three attractive women, the flashiest window-dressing Harry Cipriani's had to offer that day, were stationed at the center table so that they could be seen by everyone. The chronically stylish Claire wore an azure-blue Gucci blouse to match her eyes and a retro Parisian cloche with fruit salad on the brim to hide them. The only missing accessories were Basil and Babette, her toy poodles, whom Harry Cipriani was barred by city ordinance from allowing on the premises. "No wonder the French despise the Americans!" the Francophile from Atlanta frequently fulminated. Vanessa, who worked as a designer for Carolina Herrera, wore a Herrera linen jacket over her bulging Herrera blouse, while Emily, the only one of the three who didn't require bells and whistles to look beautiful, wore jeans and a blazer, had her hair pulled back into a simple ponytail, and got most of the male stares.

Claire removed her sunglasses for a fast polish with her napkin, revealing bruises around both eyes.

"Oh, my God!" gasped Emily. "Your eyes!"

"Jesus, who did that?" Vanessa's glare was litigious.

Claire plopped back behind the glasses. "It's supposed to go away in a day or so. That's what I get for letting Dr. Bruno up my Botox injections. Philippe started complaining about my wrinkles again."

"Little does the baron know that your face isn't the only body part getting regular injections from the attentive Dr. Bruno," Vanessa gleamed.

"As long as I keep the equipment in good shape, my hubby doesn't mind too much if I loan it out once in awhile."

As Emily sat listening to the banter of her girlfriends, she felt trapped in a world of alien creatures, creatures who were poisoning her air. They had seemed the epitome of sophistication and worldliness—certainly far more entertaining than her own conservative, preppy set or even her art crowd—and in spite of the fact that both were former flames of her husband, lunching with them had become one of her new routines as Mrs. Charles Lukes. Much to her surprise they had sought her out, and she hadn't wanted to be pigeonholed as provincial. People in this world judged you by two things—money and savoir faire—and the former Academy of the Sacred Heart girl felt compelled to prove that she was no slouch when it came to the latter.

It had taken her a carefree year or two to realize that her new friends were less sophisticated than crass, and that their life theories were not so much the products of wisdom and experience as they were of avarice. Both women were focused nonstop on upgrading their situation. It was therefore natural that they would befriend Emily, having no reason to assume that she had done any differently in snagging Charles. Emily believed she had married Charles for love, but whenever she was with this duo for more than an hour she would begin to wonder what her subconscious motives might have been. The thought that she might be like them horrified her so much that she felt like knocking over the lunch table—salads, breadsticks, and all—and running screaming from the restaurant.

Not that she was immune from participating in these harmless strategy sessions, which could on occasion be mildly amusing, but today for some reason this man-trapping talk was irritating her, nagging at her as if a small but persistent gnat were stuck inside her head. Perhaps it was because she had spent the morning at one of the C-SAW centers in Spanish Harlem, working with children on the rudiments of perspective and then stunning Mr. Montoya, C-SAW's managing director, by handing him a check for a million dollars. Mr. Montoya had almost fainted, before falling to one knee and soaking her hand in kisses and tears. Never had he seen such a check—though it wasn't just the money that touched him, but also Emily's giving of her time each week. Philanthropists, he noted, rarely got their fingernails dirty. His gratitude and the affection of the kids, who seemed to regard her as their fairy godmother for tutoring them each week, had moved Emily to tears herself, though she demurred when Montoya suggested that they rename the program after her. That wasn't the point, she explained. Seeing all those wide-eyed, productive faces was enough; it was unlike any pleasure she had ever experienced. How she wished that just once Charles would venture uptown to see all the good she and his financial contribution in her name were doing. Such experiences could be transformational—though knowing Charles, he probably would be squirmy around so much sincerity and make Hispanic jokes on the limo ride home.

Meanwhile, Vanessa was explaining that Lester's divorce was going to be final in six months and that wife-replacement hopefuls were queuing up already. Competition was fierce. "What do you think, Emmy?" she asked, adjusting her implants. "Will a chin tuck close the deal?"

"How about getting your head examined?" Emily teased.

Pinching a flaky piece of bread from the basket in the center of the table, Claire offered her own unique slant: "A nip here, a tuck there, a few strategic implants—those are the best investments a woman can make. Compared to stocks and bonds, the returns can be staggering."

"God, Claire," moaned Emily, "you are such a stereotype."

"Listen to Little Miss Muffet here," clucked Claire, "sitting on her billionaire tuffet. Talk about a stereotype."

Emily knew that she could never out-debate the babbling baroness. "Sometimes I wonder why I even have lunch with you two."

"Because we're so naughty and nice," purred Vanessa. "Oh, Sergio!" she cried a bit too loudly to the maître d', emitting a slight hiccup in the process. "*Encore un Bellini, s'il vous plini.*" Vanessa had a weakness for Cipriani's signature drink of peach juice and champagne and could never stop at just one.

"Maybe you two naughty, nice girls would like to do a good deed and donate a small something to C-SAW," Emily hinted, mainly to see their reaction.

"After your hubby bankrolled the program for the next decade!" Claire shrieked. "Besides, you know the baron takes care of all our tax deductions."

"Don't look at me, I've got my own fundraising to do," said Vanessa, tapping the photo of her and Lester with a long fingernail. "I've never really understood this pet project of yours, Emmy." Vanessa opened her mascara-framed eyes wide and serious. "I mean, what good is giving kids painting lessons if they can't even read and do arithmetic?"

"I've explained this to you both before," Emily sighed. "This program is helping a lot of disadvantaged children develop creatively."

"Graffiti isn't enough?" murmured Claire.

"Why don't you ask your toasting troubadour for a donation?" Vanessa smiled. "He's obviously smitten. And loaded too—Queen Noor's oil-rich baby brother, in case anyone was wondering."

"A Muslim named Monk?" Emily chortled, taking it all in, disappointed in a strange way by his supposed pedigree. Three years as a Lukes made her long for simplicity.

"He's more hunk than monk," Claire observed, astutely adding, "and more poor than Noor. I saw him heading upstairs. So, Emily—tell us all the lurid details."

Emily felt herself blushing. "He looked at some of my paintings."

"Ah, yes," cackled Claire. "He'd rather own one than a Rothko."

"It's nice to have one's work appreciated," Emily parried.

Claire rolled her eyes. "Appreciated indeed! I haven't heard a testimonial like that since my first *cinq-à-sept* with Dr. Bruno."

"He's just enthusiastic, that's all," Emily said dismissively.

"And what did my ex-hubby think about the piano man's enthusiasm?"

Late the previous night after the party, while Emily helped Charles pack his bags for Japan, he had pressed her about Alex.

"Why were you showing off for that piano player?" Charles demanded, teasing but with a steely undertone. "You never show off your paintings. Was he an art dealer in disguise?"

"I didn't invite him to my studio, Charles," she replied. "He just popped in."

"He just followed you around, like a big puppy? Is that what you want as a pet? Here I offered you a top-breed Newfie, and you turned me down? Holding out for something better, my dear?"

"Do you want to take the charcoal Armani or the black?" Emily asked, hoping to divert Charles's sharp tongue.

"I'll allow that owning a piano player might have certain advantages over a pooch," Charles continued, waving his hand at the darker suit. Once he was on a roll, there was no stopping him. "For instance, you'd get better quality noises, no shedding, no pooper-scooper. Though I've seen dogs with far more talent than his on the David Letterman show. He'll go far, no doubt, as an entertainer in downtown circles, pestering the guests while they're eating, making melodramatic toasts—performance art I think they call it?"

"*You* invited him," Emily reminded him, desperate to get him off the subject.

"What a blunder that was," Charles acknowledged. "I thought I was hiring Noel Coward, not Che Guevara. He should stay in the Brooklyn dives Billy favors. I think we've suffered enough Stupid Pet Tricks for a lifetime, don't you agree, my darling?"

"He was definitely out of line," Emily agreed, under the glare of his laser-like gaze.

Once the lights were out, however, she lay awake, thinking about Alex, pondering his candid tribute to her, wondering what had moved him to make such a spectacle of himself.

"Oh, you know, Charles made the expected jokes," she told the girls now. "At the risk of you two cynics jumping to all the wrong conclusions," she ventured, "I found Alex interesting…sort of a charming iconoclast. I'm not sure *what* to make of him."

"Emmy," moaned Claire, "you're so naïve it hurts my teeth. Good-looking I'll grant you, but *interesting?* C'mon—he's got 'Boy-Toy' tattooed all over the chip on his shoulder. If you're bored, take up horseback riding or bungee jumping or something. Charles isn't like my Philippe, who lets me dabble in extracurricular hobbies. Beneath all the bubbles and fluff, he's ruthless."

"Charles is hardly ruthless," Emily shot back in obligatory fashion.

"Take it from his ex-wife, who got hosed in the divorce."

"Hosed!" Emily laughed incredulously. "You were married to him for one year and cheated on him constantly!"

"And got chump change—the same amount he gave to your deprived kiddies, in fact. Though we're still friends. I insist. It's the only civilized way to be."

"I swear, Claire," said Vanessa, "if I had your kind of chump change I'd never get married. What would be the point?"

"Children?" offered Emily.

Claire waved her enameled hand. "You don't need a man anymore for that. Just essence of man. You can get it at the bank—the one bank where I'm afraid Charles has a negative balance. If I were you, my dear Emily, I'd try little harder to give poor adopted Charles and his less-than-mighty sperm that heir he wants so badly. A baby ties you to him for life. Then you can get all the piano lessons you want."

Emily started to protest this invasion into her privacy; it was too much, even for Claire. But Claire waved her off.

"Now, Emily, I'm only saying this because I care about you. My inability to give him a child, not my indiscretions, is what broke Charles and me up." She waved for the check. "If you want to screw around with unbalanced musicians, that's up to you. I'm just saying that if you're going to graze, it's best to stay in your own pasture, where people know what the rules are."

Two hours later, with the East River between her and her lunch companions, Emily stood outside a new art gallery, gazing at the lumpy, drippy brown canvases in the window with a mixture of disgust and macabre fascination. The oeuvre was nothing if not an homage to excrement. If this artist could find a gallery to represent him, she thought, then there was no reason she, with a little dedication, couldn't become the next Picasso. She couldn't believe what masqueraded as art these days. Still, it was a beautiful spring day, and she was glad that instead of depending on their chauffeur she had followed her impulse to hail a cab all the way to Williamsburg to check out the newest crop of up-and-coming artists. Showing up at bohemian art galleries in a limo, whether in the capacity of artist or collector, sent the wrong message and made honest communication with the gallery folks all but impossible.

Those hen lunches drained her a little more every time. Why did she keep agreeing to them? After her uplifting morning at C-SAW, Cipriani's had given her claustrophobia, and the yammering of her girlfriends had driven her almost out of her mind. Maybe Claire was right. Maybe she should get pregnant, if for no other reason than to escape this crowd and acquire a more family-oriented circle of friends.

Absurd as it was to socialize with Charles's exes, she had to admit that for all their barracuda callousness, Vanessa and Claire were probably right about Alex. It was likely he had a crush on her; moreover, she found herself constantly fantasizing about him, thinking an affair with someone exciting might bring her alive again. However, that wasn't who she was, or who she wanted to be. Her father's cheating had caused considerable anguish in her family, a legacy she was determined to break. Claire's nymphomania had rendered her callous, making Emily wonder if she really enjoyed sex as much as she pretended. The last thing Emily wanted was to follow in their footsteps.

When she reviewed the events of her party—especially the conversation with Alex in her studio—she realized that she had merely been moved by a handsome man's flattery, which was probably part of a well-honed seduction technique. She desperately wanted to think of herself as a painter, but who was she kidding? If she were a painter, she would be painting. She had been blaming everything on Charles, just because he didn't rave about her so-called talent, but true painters had it in their blood. She had to accept the fact that was she was no more an artist than Charles was a businessman. This painful truth was where her real unhappiness was founded, and probably why her husband was annoying her so much. The attraction to Alex Monk was just a psychological smokescreen.

Her eyes adjusted from the art in the window to her reflection in the glass. She studied herself and saw a graceful vision of wasted potential. Few women her age could boast such smooth skin, but being a pale blonde's it was also temperamental, a delicate barometer of her inner life. She wondered how long her bloom would last. Charles, noting the intensity of her expressions when she painted, had recently noted, "Darling, you'll grow old before your time if you pursue your art too seriously. That furrow in your brow will become permanent." But wasn't the reverse true? Painting would keep her young, feed her spirit. Denying oneself the basic human needs of love and intimacy—that was what would accelerate the aging process. With that thought, she adjusted her focus once again, this time to behold the flashing reflection of the red neon sign across the street: "End of the World."

Nobody, she reasoned, could fault her for dropping in on her brother-in-law when she was in his neighborhood. And if Billy happened to bring up Alex in conversation, or, better yet, if Alex happened to be there, could that be perceived as anything but a coincidence? She had no preconceived notion as to what she wanted or where it would lead, but she was deeply curious to learn more about Alex, if for no other reason that to get him out of her system. She couldn't stop thinking about him.

Like a moth attracted to the flame-colored neon, she crossed the street and entered the club. The place was empty and looked even more apocalyptic without all the doomsday videos playing. She took a few tentative steps forward, only to jump when she noticed a man standing behind the bar. He was whipping back a shot and smoking a cigar, his face covered in shadows.

"To what do I owe this honor, Mrs. Lukes?"

Recognizing Billy's voice, she crossed a jungle bridge spanning a black canal and stepped up to the smoky bar, but still couldn't see his face. "I was in the neighborhood—gallery hopping."

"The denizens of Brooklyn must feel blessed." Billy emerged from the murk. His right eye sported a fresh shiner.

"My god, Billy! What happened?"

"I owe people some money," he said, grinding his cigar into an ashtray, creating a dense, filthy pyre. He was smiling, but his eyes had a hunted expression. "They don't like it when I'm late paying them back."

"What can I do?"

"Lend me two hundred thou. While Charles is in Japan you could make a wire transfer, and he wouldn't even notice."

"You know I can't do that," she said.

"What about your father?" Billy persisted. "I read somewhere that he invests in creative enterprises. And no one has more connections."

"My father? We don't speak much—certainly not about business. I could never ask him for anything." She was sorry she had ventured here; she had barely said "hello," and already he was hitting her up for money.

Billy poured himself another shot of bourbon. "Jesus, I sell a measly gram of coke to a consenting adult, who turns out to be an undercover cop. What kind of police state have we become? I wasn't hurting anyone. *I'm* the victim: raised without a father by a mother who hated my guts before I left her womb. I don't begrudge Charles—the adopted son, who was left everything, who barely welcomes me into the apartment I grew up in. But being the brother of an only child ain't easy. At least grant me that."

"I've always granted you that," said Emily gently. She knew how painful it was to grow up without nurturing parents; she also knew how vile Billy's temper could turn when he was under the influence.

"Then lend me a hundred grand!" Billy pleaded. "Fifty! You and Charles are the only family I have. How much has Charles pissed away in venture capital? How much is he blowing on these spider-goats? Not to mention what he gave you for your kids program. What about me? Can't you think of me as a disadvantaged kid? Charles is always calling me childish. Aren't I underprivileged—for a Lukes?"

"Oh, Billy. Don't you know anyone who can help?" Into the uneasy silence Emily broached the subject that had really brought her here: "What about your friend Alex Monk?"

"Alex *who*?"

"Alex Monk. Your piano player friend."

Billy pondered this and sniggered, "He has a *stage name*?"

"What are you talking about?"

"His name is Alex Halaby, Emmy, and he's in worse financial straits than I am."

"Halaby?"

"Should be Wannabe." A bitter cast came over Billy's face. "You like him, don't you? It's why you came all the way over to Brooklyn and walked in here, isn't it?"

"Don't be absurd. I always come to the new galleries. I was in the neighborhood."

"You brought him up. First chance you got."

"I was simply trying to help you out of your financial squeeze, Billy," Emily frowned. "Vanessa mentioned at lunch that Alex was Queen Noor's baby brother; that he owns oil wells and is loaded."

Billy smiled up at the rafters. "Ah, the old Queen Noor ploy," he said wistfully. "Alex concocted it years ago to get into girls' knickers. He's your garden-variety charming shit. A lost soul." Billy downed his bourbon in one swoop. "Sorry to disappoint you, but his birthday toast was almost certainly drug-induced. Coke, Ecstasy, pot—Alex is always on something. In fact, he was the one way back when who introduced me to cocaine."

Emily struggled not to appear crestfallen. Other than a few experiments with pot at Wellesley, she knew nothing about recreational drugs, except that they scared her. "Then why do you still spend time with him?"

"Don't you have a few leeches in your life you can't get rid of?" Billy gave her a long look, but Emily retained a blank expression. "He had no place to stay, so I put him up here out of the goodness of my heart. And this is how he thanks me: by making that ridiculous toast and ruining any chance of rapprochement with my brother."

All the negative information was disconcerting. "He lives here?" she asked numbly.

"Not anymore. After the party I threw him out. Just like his father did from the family business. The old man couldn't take the incessant drug use." Observing her carefully, Billy said, "You look like you could use a drink."

"No thanks."

"Sure?"

"Yes, quite."

Slowly he ambled around to her side of the bar. "Look, I understand a woman's need for companionship. Being married to my brother can't be easy."

"What are you talking about?"

"I just hope he appreciates you."

Billy clasped her arm. The smell of bourbon and cigar smoke, mixed with something dark and indefinable, grew stronger as his face lurched to kiss her on the mouth. Horrified, she ripped her arm away and staggered backward. She peered into his glassy, bloodshot eyes: There was nobody home.

"For your sake, Billy," she said, grabbing her bag, "I'm going to forget this ever happened." And with that, she fled.

After a few blocks of fruitless searching, she was able to convince an off-duty cabbie to take her to Manhattan. She was incredulous that Billy had actually tried to kiss her. He was getting sleazier by the minute, which made Alex sleazy by association. Much as Billy's depiction of Alex didn't mesh with her impressions of him and struck her as at least a partial hatchet job, for whatever reason, she couldn't get around the fact that if they were longtime chums it was likely Alex was a drug dabbler at the very least. Befriending an unemployed Hell's Angel musician with an alias suddenly seemed like a completely self-destructive idea. What had she been thinking? She should relish her solitude while Charles was away; use her time for inner reflection and painting. Maybe she should consider therapy. She needed to make her life—and her marriage—work.

As if to confirm her decision, a present from Charles was waiting for her upon her return home. "Miss you terribly, *mon petit chou*," the card read. She tore away the paper and found an inexpensive still-life of a head of cabbage that she had admired a month ago in a Chelsea gallery, and her heart warmed toward her husband. Once again, she felt safe and sound.

6

But Oh (!) That Risotto

Alex awoke in darkness, before the birds. How many times in his life had he just been rolling into bed at this hour? How deeply satisfying to be in sync with the rhythms of nature, he thought wryly, but with some sincerity. He pushed open the warped screen door and stepped onto the splintery deck. Peering into the mist, he saw a deer—a buck with a magnificent rack of antlers—up to its neck in the marsh grass. He moved closer for a better look, only to stub his toe on an exposed nail and cry out an expletive, causing the spooked animal to disappear with a *whoosh* into a thicket. Despite the mishap, the fleeting encounter left him feeling blessed, as if good things were coming his way. He stretched his arms to the sky, sniffed in the salt air, and closed his eyes to meditate on the stillness. A lone bird began to chirp; minutes later the surrounding pines resounded with an avian chorus. The fog and sun lifted, unveiling Peconic Bay, and as the water began to glisten, he went inside to shower and dress.

His tiny rental was several miles north of Southampton's estate section, in a remote wooded area bordering on a nature preserve. Built by a hippie carpenter back in the sixties, according to the real-estate agent, and allowed to degenerate from there into its current dilapidated condition, it was concealed by pine trees and thickets. Local knowledge of back roads was required to find it, and even then you could easily miss the overgrown driveway, as Alex had found when he took possession a week ago. There were just two small, sparsely furnished rooms separated by a kitchenette. The cabin's smoke-stained, rustic bones—wide cherry-plank floors, wood beams, stone fireplace—appealed to him, though the bedroom, with its slumping bed, dingy shag rug, and dusty old curtains, was a little depressing. There was no TV and just one antiquated cordless phone with no answering machine. This former pot palace was all Alex had been able to afford even on his boss's-son salary—such being the state of the Hamptons' real-estate prices. He didn't want to think what lay in store for him when the rental expired three months from now, at the stroke of midnight on Labor Day.

By nine o'clock he was out on his Harley, heading nowhere in particular. He buzzed past windmills, potato farms, and riding stables, stopping now and then to marvel at the bright blue ocean shimmering beyond the dunes. By mid-morning he arrived at the East Hampton village green, which sloped down to a willow-shaded duck pond. After parking, he stretched his body out on the lawn. Euphoria shot to his head like wine as he contemplated his newfound freedom. The warm sunlight made him tingle as he thought about his former existence, his life as an indentured merchant. He would never return to the business, not for all the money in the world!

However, as he remounted and doubled back against the steady flow of weekend traffic—against the grain of humanity—insecurity began to gnaw. He had no source of income, and mundane expenses he had once taken for granted—items to make his cabin barely livable, such as Pledge, Windex, Tidy Bowl, paper towels, and scented candles to cover up the musky odor—had already eaten up a chilling chunk of his savings. For the first time in his sheltered life he felt real empathy for families eking by. It made his gripes, past and present, seem petty by comparison. At this rate he would be broke well before year end. He needed a plan. Limping back to his parents with his tail between his legs was tantamount to death. He figured he was too resourceful to starve, but the possibility that his life would pass by unnoticed filled him with profound terror. Getting rich wasn't the point; when he thought about it, the only reason he had ever cared about money to the extent he did was that everyone around him did. It was how society measured you, but it certainly wasn't how *he* measured people or what motivated him in the deepest sense. Why must he cow-tow to the values of a slave planet? Making a difference, living an exemplary and joyous life, was ultimately what counted. But how? He wasn't nearly talented enough to pursue a serious career in music, and if the party at the Lukeses hadn't completely taken the romantic sheen off the idea of gig-to-gig performing, yesterday's audition at Chauncey's in Sagaponack certainly had. Hoping to lock in a subsistence-level income and defer for at least a while the inevitable fiscal come-to-Jesus, he had shown up there in response to a newspaper ad. Only when he stepped inside and saw the pink baby grand and found himself shaking the soft hand of the aromatic, ascotted proprietor did he realize just what kind of bar it was. If his parents had taught him anything, it was to be courteous at all times, and so he went through the motions—until Chauncey's smarmy gazes proved too much to handle. He aborted his audition mid-riff.

"I can't do this," Alex sighed. He had nothing against gays, had no problem with gay marriage, gay adoption, gays in the military. But he did have a problem with being mistaken as one and being checked out by men. Surely the Thought Police could cut him that much slack. "I'm straight. Sorry—couldn't help it if I tried."

He was almost out the door when Chauncey, arms akimbo, called out, "For heaven's sake, where are you going? Chauncey's is the *only* piano bar in the Hamptons. Aren't you looking for a job? I'm not going to bite you—at least not unless you ask. A hundred a night."

Alex stopped, turned. He did need the money, and why should he care what anyone thought? He was Alex Monk. Despite his weak bargaining position, he took a feeble stab at negotiating: "A hundred a night is chickenfeed."

"Plus tips. I'm sure you'll just clean up." Alex was on the verge of rising above the stigma, when Chauncey made the fatal mistake of trying to manipulate him into it: "What are you afraid of, big boy," he said, with an intrusive stare, "coming face to face with your inner demons? You know what they say about homophobes."

So much for show biz. He still had a few thousand in the bank; poverty wasn't imminent. He wasn't all that passionate about a musical career anyway, certainly not the way Emily was about her painting. She may have claimed she wasn't, but the yearning in her eyes told him otherwise. The plain hard truth was that he was thirty years old and starting at square one, with absolutely no inkling as to how to proceed, or of what he wanted to do.

He came to the Watermill windmill, but instead of heading north toward his shack, he veered south and took a wooded, residential route that eventually led to Southampton's estate section. The sweet smell of honeysuckle cheered him as the road curved around to Gin Lane, which ran parallel to the ocean. Not that he could see the ocean, with the gargantuan estates blocking his view. Breaks in the high privet hedges revealed fleeting glimpses of gambrel roofs, widow's walks, tennis courts, and pool houses. Alex's stomach began to churn knowing that Emily spent her summer weekends in this vicinity, in the Stanford White estate that Charles Lukes had inherited from his mother. Alex had been aware of that much for years, having listened with varying degrees of attention to Billy's griping about Abigail's will. However, he had no clue where the house was, and the phone number was unlisted. Billy, of course, knew it, but Alex wasn't about to call him. Billy's coked-up tantrum at the club following Emily's birthday party had put a serious crimp in their brotherhood. Howling that Alex's theatrical toast and precipitous, unmannerly exit had spooked Charles into a full retreat from investing, Billy spewed so much profanity—he was not merely obnoxious, but dangerously unhinged and high—that Alex, fearful for his own safety, left the

End of the World in the wee hours and drove his hog to Southampton, holing up for two nights in a fleabag motel until his even more fleabag of a rental began.

Now, as he purred through the estate section, a red-winged blackbird shot out from the tall reeds and hovered above him, accosting him with shrill cries—protecting its nesting area but also serving as the neighborhood's cranky gatekeeper. Alex had always been drawn to the elegant trappings—the mansions with their meticulously barbered hedges and lawns and stately old trees, the flashy cars, and especially the beautiful women. For several consecutive summers Southampton had been his playground, but still he felt vaguely alienated here. Just what it would take to feel otherwise—love? money?—he had no idea; he suspected that the whole place was one big illusion, a mirage; that the misery index here was no less than anywhere else. When he puttered past the stuccoed Ocean Club, the familiar whiff of exclusion made his nostrils flare. He revved his engine loudly to create maximum shock effect, turning a couple of indignant heads. It pained him that his parents were so anxious to join this snooty club, where they would be at the mercy of the small-minded, boozing board of governors, most of them either spoiled dilettantes or self-important, hard-boiled moguls.

Minutes later, he arrived at the equally exclusive Meadow Club. Remembering the drunken birthday toast about Emily's tennis prowess, he trespassed in the parking lot long enough to peek through an opening in the hedge and scan the grass courts on the off-chance of spotting her among the slim blond women in their bleached tennis whites. No luck. She hadn't struck him as the clubby type; he was almost relieved not to find her here.

He continued along the ocean, to where Gin Lane became Meadow Lane and a mile or so farther down became Dune Road. On he sped, imagining, as he often did when he covered this stretch, what this sandy spit of land dividing ocean and bay might have looked like thirty years ago. How idyllic it must have been, with a mere smattering of Wuthering Heights-type mansions a mile apart from each other, a sanctuary where families picnicked and lovers lost themselves amongst the giant dunes. That was before the hot breath of status swept through town like a cloud of locusts starting in the 1980s, gobbling up every square inch of property and throwing up eyesores of all descriptions—pretentious, post-modern monstrosities mostly, with no sense of harmony or history or connection with the land. Here the Masters of the Universe and their puffed-up architects had erected second, third, and fourth homes, which rose like middle fingers to taunt the Shinnecock Indian reservation across the bay.

Toward the end of Dune Road he slowed to a stop. On the ocean side stood the "Nuclear Power Plant"—Alex's nickname for his parents' beach house, inspired by its square industrial shape. The house was a hybrid of genteel aspirations and nouveau riche taste. Though covered in shingles like the grand old houses in the area, its structure was contemporary and lacking in architectural vision. Purchased by his parents six years ago from a high-end spec house developer, it was originally a simple cottage with a plethora of deck space; yet with each compulsive renovation by his parents, the indoor square footage got larger, and the deck all but disappeared, until the house lost what little charm it had and earned its moniker from Alex.

After concealing his Harley safely behind some bushes, he looked up the pebbled driveway to make sure his parents' Mercedes wasn't there. Reasonably confident that Harry was out golfing, or that both parents were over at the Ocean Club bolstering their membership prospects, he made his way on foot up the driveway. He hadn't seen either parent since quitting the business, and while he intended to pay an olive branch visit to them at some point, today he had a different mission: to pilfer their *Blue Book*. Rich summer people who refused to be listed in the phone book could often be found in this private directory. Just what he intended to do with Emily's number once he found it, he wasn't sure. The thought of calling her made him more nervous than he had been in years.

He let himself in with his key and was greeted by the familiar combination of piano music and the washing machine, which meant his mother was there. Grace did laundry constantly when in Southampton, fighting a Wasp jihad against her most hated enemy: sand. As with most beach houses, the main living space was on the second floor, and as Alex wavered on the stairs—plotting how to get the *Blue Book* off the telephone table, a mere twenty feet from the piano, without being seen by his mother—he was treated to a medley of "Porgy and Bess." Grace was the real piano player in the family, despite the fact that she had never taken a piano lesson. Her relationship with the instrument was supernatural, her playing as unpredictable as the rest of her was predictable. Family legend had it that the very first time she sat down at a piano, at age four, she played "Tea for Two" like an accomplished pianist. Alex had seen her return from a Broadway musical and duplicate the entire score; she also played a wicked Scott Joplin, strictly by ear. Now, creeping up the stairs, he relived an Aurora childhood memory: lying in bed and being lulled to sleep by the same sultry rendition of "Summertime," played as he imagined a black female jazz pianist might play it. How sad, he thought, that his mother had never taken her spooky talent beyond her own parlor.

The commodious living room had broad views of both ocean and bay but had been rendered lifeless by the decorator's sterile "concept": a beige-and-green color scheme to match the sand and the dune grass outside, with Ultrasuede sofas and lizard-skin tables. Luckily Grace's back was to Alex, though as he quietly crossed the thick pile rug he had a near coronary when she burst into an ear-splitting "God Bless America." She was often given to inexplicable bursts of patriotic fervor. He snatched the *Blue Book* and snuck back down the stairs unnoticed.

Back on Dune Road and riffling through the book for Emily's number, he was trembling—not from the heist but from what he was about to do. His motives were muddled: he had no desire to cause trouble, and yet his need to connect with Emily bordered on desperation almost beyond his control. Family money had always been his lure, and now that he no longer had it he was dying to know if he still had any appeal. Against Charles's stupefying wealth, all he had to offer her was his drifting, penniless self. On the other hand, the worst that could happen was that she would shoo him away like a fly, which wouldn't exactly be fun, but he would live. With that bolstering rationalization he sped a mile or so to the public beach; he sat down on the sand and tried to calm his nerves by listening to the surf, inhaling the salt air. Nature, however, seemed to be against him; the more he communed with it, the more inner chaos ruled. In the churning waves he saw turmoil, not meditative tranquility. The gods clearly weren't pleased at the waves he was about to make. Punching out Emily's number, he was ready to hang up if Charles or the help answered. Even when he heard Emily's soft "Hello," he nearly bailed out in panic.

"Emily? It's Alex Monk." Silence. "Hello?"

"Where did you get our number?" she asked. "Why are you calling?"

Alex hadn't known what to expect but hadn't imagined such an icy reception. Was Charles in the room? "I want to apologize for my behavior the other night," he cordially forged on. "Though for the record, I meant everything I said. If you have any free time, I'd like to see you again under different circumstances and maybe explain myself."

"If you owe anyone an apology, it's Charles," she said. "And I'm afraid he's out of the country."

Out of the country—wow! Had she let that slip on purpose? "Look, I just don't want things awkward between us."

"There's nothing between us. You hardly know me. I hardly know you—not even your real last name apparently. Let's leave it at that."

"I can explain the alias."

"Save your breath."

Alex felt himself sinking into the white sand, so dangerously close to the realm of begging that he began to babble. "I was offered this gig at a local piano bar. A gay bar, believe it or not, called Chauncey's, in Sagaponack."

"A gay bar? You *are* full of surprises."

"I'm not gay—I turned it down. What I'm trying to say is, I'll go back and accept the job if you agree to come and see me play tonight. What could be a safer venue for you than a gay bar?"

"Sorry, but I'm going to an open...I already have plans."

"Open? Open what?"

"Never mind."

"Open house? Open heart surgery? C'mon, Emily—open sesame!"

"I'm hanging up now."

"Just promise," he said, "that if we happen to run into each other you won't scream."

"I never make promises I can't keep." Then a miracle happened: Emily laughed. An involuntary, throaty, wonderful laugh. It was like an iceberg cracking and melting. "Good-bye, Mr. Halaby."

That short exchange left him so drained that for the next few minutes he sat there on the sand, staring at the blue ocean, giving inflated significance to the mixed signals she had given him: telling him that Charles was out of the country, calling him "Halaby." She knew his real name; she'd done research! *Open...The U.S. Open isn't until September—and besides, she said she was going to "an" open, not "the" open....* Trudging toward his bike, it dawned on him how lowly he was behaving. Despite his history of sleeping with almost anything reasonably attractive that moved, he had never even imagined crossing the line with a married woman. It was beneath even *his* principles—the pastime of sneaks and sleazebags. Yet here he was chasing after Mrs. Charles Lukes, who happened to be married to the richest person he knew. Had quitting his job knocked all the judgment neurons out of his brain? He couldn't exorcize her from his mind; no woman had ever altered his molecules like this.

At the edge of the dune grass, a wizened old man in a beret was painting on an easel and like a bolt of lightning the answer came: *Open-ing! Art opening! Duh, obviously! What else could it be!* He spent the next hour calling all the art galleries in Southampton, learning that the Xavier Gallery on Job's Lane was having an opening that night at six.

That little glimmer of hope was all he needed to be galvanized into full-fledged fantasy mode. He was too jumpy to wait until the appointed hour; he needed to *do* something—anything to kill time. And so on the extremely remote chance that he would not only find her at the Xavier Gallery but could somehow lure her back to his cabin for an intimate dinner, he buzzed off to the grocery store to lay in supplies: Italian rice, French bread, raw shrimp, chicken stock, saffron, curry, a red onion, salad greens, a clump of grapes, two bottles of Chianti, and some daffodils. The spree emptied his wallet of all but a few singles. He didn't possess an ATM card and the banks were closed for the long weekend, but what did a little pocket change matter at a time like this? He had learned to make risotto a couple of years ago, courtesy of an Italian playboy who claimed to have made most of his conquests in the kitchen. But apart from risotto, grilling red meat, and popping champagne corks, Alex as a cook was all thumbs, so he decided to play sous-chef now to avoid chaos later. Disregarding the overwhelming probability that his efforts would be for naught, that the whole "spontaneous" evening he was planning was nothing but a feverous delusion on his part, he washed the salad greens; made a vinaigrette dressing; sliced, buttered, and foil-wrapped the French bread; chopped the onion and slid the bits into a plastic container; then crammed everything into the tiny refrigerator before wiping clean two plates, two glasses, and two sets of utensils and laying them out on the counter. No vase could be found, so he arranged the flowers in a pitcher and placed them on the mantel. After making sure he had matches and that the fireplace flue worked, he built a teepee of logs and crumpled newspaper. He opened the doors and windows to air out the place while he cleaned everything in sight, made the bed, showered, and dressed. His last entrepreneurial act before leaving was to arrange the candles around the bedroom.

He timed his arrival at the Xavier Gallery on the early side. A golden-skinned, languid crowd in crisp white linen and khaki milled around the rambling space, oohing and aahing at the Old Master-ish canvases on the walls depicting Indian holy men. While the artist displayed some proficiency in painting turbans, cobras, and torsos, the faces of his gurus were so wooden that Alex's gut told him this was less of an art show than a scam—a cynical appeal to rich, empty patrons that all they needed to attain enlightenment, or to be considered spiritual by their equally empty peers, was to hang one of these formulaic canvases in their living room. A quick scan of the space yielded no Emily; however, as he went farther back into the gallery, he shivered when he spotted her standing next to the cheese buffet. She was conversing with a gothic creature in a Medieval black cape, black tights, and a bowl haircut. Ornate gold on all ten fingers complemented inch-long fingernails. As Alex got within earshot of his effetely superior British accent, he felt literally sick inside. Could she actually be falling for his act? She wasn't, he hoped, a protoplasm who swooned over all things arty and affected, who gushed over any movie with subtitles, who possessed no sword of discernment. How on earth could she give this creepy-crawly moth-man the time of day? Still, he was delighted to see Emily's range. Without Charles casting his shadow on the proceedings, she seemed relaxed and animated—the artichoke heart without the armored leaves. Only on a baby had he seen skin so soft and smooth. Her hair spilled profusely over her safari shirt. An antique silver Celtic cross dangled at her throat, its suggestion of chastity at odds with his imagination. He circled up behind her and waited for a break in the conversation.

"Your work is better than anything here," he said.

She turned around with a scowl. "You! Why am I not surprised?"

"Your clown faces have far more depth." He gestured up at a bearded spiritualist, who was peering down at them with flat eyes. "He looks constipated. Whoever arranged the cheese had more talent."

At this, moth-man arched his nose with snippy disdain and with an ostentatious wave of his cape fluttered away.

"Congratulations," Emily chided, "you just insulted the artist on his opening night."

"Artist? I thought he was a tarot card."

"At least he's not pretending to be a monk."

Alex laughed aloud. "His stuff is awful."

"Maybe that's because you don't understand it."

"What's his medium—snakeoil?"

"Why don't you give it a rest? Go try your BS on someone else." She tried to move away, but Alex cornered her with his bulk.

"Listen," he said, "if I wanted to BS you, I'd tell you I had a fifty-foot yacht, a villa in Spain, and a gallery in Soho desperate to give you a one-woman show. You don't think I have more imagination than, 'Gee, I really like your work'?"

"A one-woman show would be nice," she murmured, before adding harshly, "What are you so ashamed of that you need to change your name? Were you Billy's drug dealer? His prison roommate?"

"I did coke with Billy just once."

"Once! How dumb do you think I am?"

"Once! From the summer of 1998 to the fall of 2001."

Unamused, Emily glanced past him, and her face suddenly furrowed with concern. Alex followed her eye line and saw a tall, dark-haired woman, teetering dangerously on a stool in the corner of the gallery and slurring loudly to the bartender. "Felicity—oh, god," Emily frowned.

"If it looks like shit," Felicity trumpeted, "then it probably izz shit, right? Whazz your name, sweetie?"

"Max."

"Max. What a sexy name." The stool had reached its point of no return. Energized by Emily's presence, Alex dashed over just in time to catch the sloshed brunette in his arms before she hit the floor. She gazed up at him, a horse-faced vision of smeared mascara and smudged lip-liner. "This is the third time I've fallen for someone this week," she said. "Kiss?"

"Let's go home, Felicity," Emily urged, as Alex lifted the tipsy woman up to a vertical position.

"Why?" Felicity howled, ogling Alex as if he were a filet mignon. "I'm having fun."

"Too much fun, I'd say," said Emily.

"Party pooper. Charles is in Japan. What do you want to go home for?" Felicity whooped. She reeked of gin.

Emily's eyes appealed to Alex for help, and together they escorted the giggling Felicity outside to a cherry red Ferrari, where they managed to stuff her into the passenger seat and buckle her up. After rummaging through Felicity's purse for the key, Emily scurried around to the driver's side.

"Where's your car?" Alex asked. Thunder rumbled in the distance.

"At home. Felicity picked me up." Apparently feeling compelled to explain her association with the woman passed out in the passenger seat, Emily said, "She's a contributor to C-SAW. She's going through a vicious custody battle."

"I can see why." Alex felt some raindrops. "Won't you need a ride home after you drop her off?"

"Don't worry. Felicity and I live within walking distance." With that, she climbed into the Ferrari, started the engine, and sped away.

Alex dashed over to his Harley and gave chase, not an easy task given how Emily was driving: whipping around corners and speeding down the straightaway of First Neck Lane like she was eluding the law. Fortunately for Alex, the journey lasted only a couple of minutes, ending at an ultramodern house resembling a large boom box perched on the dunes, a few residences down from the Ocean Club. He swerved up the pebbled driveway and dismounted just in time to help Emily lift Felicity out of the car and practically carry her to the front door. There, he discreetly backed off and let Mrs. Lukes hand the lady of the house over to a uniformed servant.

A steady drizzle fell as they ambled back toward the Harley, leaving Emily no choice but to accept when he gallantly offered her his leather jacket and helmet.

Alex wondered why the gods were suddenly aiding and abetting him. The crescent moon was disappearing behind gathering clouds, and the wind was whipping up as he straddled and steadied his bike.

"Are you fit to drive?" She searched his face.

"Relax, I can do it in my sleep."

"Please keep your eyes open and drive slowly." Warily she climbed on behind him.

He revved the engine. "Just hold on."

She had to shout above the Harley's throaty roar. "Make a left out of the driveway."

Carefully he maneuvered his large bike down the pebbly path, and at the end of the driveway he made a right.

"I said left!"

He accelerated, bracing for her protest, but instead she stiffly clutched his waist and fell silent—loath, he imagined, to distract him while he drove. Avoiding town where they might be recognized, he veered off onto dark back roads toward Watermill, wondering several minutes into the drive why she was remaining so mum. Was she terrified? Ecstatic? Whatever she was, the urge to stop and ask quickly gave way to the realization that nothing good could come of it. Once they crossed the Montauk Highway, the route became wooded and desolate, and the traffic dwindled to practically nothing. As the rain intensified, he drove faster. Each time he leaned the bike into the twisting curves, Emily's fingers dug into his waist sharply; her touch was strictly functional. By the time he turned into his overgrown driveway, gusts rustled the pines and thickets. Thunder crackled as they dismounted and dashed to the cabin to get out of the rain. Only then did Emily, pale as a ghost and trembling like a leaf, express concern over being shanghaied.

"Where are we?" she asked.

"Welcome to Chateau Halaby—at least for the next three months."

"Then what?"

"Who knows? Chateau Homeless?"

He led her inside. As she eyed his humble quarters, her expression narrowed in pity. She removed the helmet and gravitated to the stone fireplace. The ride had chilled them through. Alex lit a match and touched it to several corners of his prepared fire, watching as the news of the outside world went up in flames. For a minute they warmed themselves in front of the hearth, then, without a word, Emily crossed the room, pushed open the creaky door, and stepped outside to the deck. While she took in the view of the choppy bay and a faraway flashing lighthouse, Alex made a beeline for the kitchenette, where he opened a bottle of Chianti and filled two glasses. Hoping to make dinner a fait accompli before she could object, he went to work, removing the chopped onions from the fridge and two pots from the cupboard. Into one pot he dumped the chicken stock and set the burner on high; into the other he dropped a stick of butter and set the burner on low. While things heated, he paused to sip his wine, watching Emily in her contemplation of the bay and its constellation of wind-whipped clouds, her long blond hair blowing every which way. He wondered what she was thinking, until a ferocious crack of thunder and a sudden cloudburst drove her back inside. She balked when he handed her a glass of wine, eyeing his culinary preparations with suspicion.

"When was the last time a guy cooked for you?" he deflected.

"How about never." Avoiding his eyes but accepting the glass, she drifted toward the flames. She began perusing the bookshelves, which contained an eclectic collection of dog-eared paperbacks, the cabin's sole amenity: novels by Tolstoy, F. Scott, Maugham, Hesse; biographies of Mahatma Gandhi and Richard Burton, the British explorer; *Zen and the Art of Motorcycle Maintenance, The Way of I Ching.* She selected *The Quotable Oscar Wilde* before settling on the nest of large pillows arranged in front of the fire. While she sipped her wine and skimmed Wilde's witticisms with flickers of amusement, Alex stirred the sizzling onions into the melting butter. Once the onions were translucent, he poured in the rice and a cup of stock. World-class risotto required vigilance—keeping the rice moist and creamy by adding just the right amount of stock whenever it thickened and stirring nonstop for twenty minutes or so. Normally he found this tedious. Tonight he embraced it; it channeled his nervous energy and probably spared him some awkward moments.

Emily broke the silence from twenty feet: "Just who are you, anyway?"

"I've been asking myself the same question a lot lately."

"And?"

"Well, let's see…I know more about pantyhose than any woman you know."

"Pantyhose?" she laughed. "And how, pray tell, did you come by this great knowledge of yours?"

"It's the family business. And mine, until recently."

"And now you play the piano at apocalyptic venues?"

"Because working for my father was like trying to fit two men into one pair of tights. So I quit." At her dubious look, he added, "I was suffocating. I ran away from a fat salary and an equally obese expense account, by the way. The real quitters are those who just go along and never question things. Ninety-nine percent of Americans just float along doing whatever is in front of them, believing what they're told, succumbing to the hive mentality sweeping the nation."

"Now you sound like a revolutionary," she said.

No one had ever called him that before, and despite her sardonic laugh, her words made him glow inside as he kept stirring. Maybe he *was* revolutionary at heart. There was so much in these times to be rebellious about, yet so few revolutionaries. "Can you really blame me for not wanting to dedicate my life to pantyhose?" he said. "You know, as I think about it, they epitomize my former life: confining, claustrophobic, cramped. Women wear them but hate them. Seriously, don't you hate them?"

"Hate is too strong an emotion to squander on pantyhose."

"That's easy for you to say," he grinned.

Emily resumed reading. Neither of them said anything, and after a time Alex began to wonder if he had said the wrong thing. Maybe she loved pantyhose. Maybe they were her favorite apparel.

"I find it hard to believe that you just threw it all away," she finally said, peering at him like she wasn't totally buying his story. "Isn't turning your back on family and security shortsighted? Maybe you should have stuck it out, faced whatever issues you have with your father, and yourself, instead of running away like a spoiled child."

"You have no idea how I detest being perceived that way. I had no choice but to break away."

"Drifting in resort areas can be insidious. Next thing you know you'll be forty and bitter. A lost soul. I mean, is your father such a bad man?"

The question produced a lump in his throat, and he briefly stopped stirring. "He's a great man. Came from nothing. Built his company from scratch, against tremendous obstacles. His employees and friends love and respect him tremendously."

"How great can he be?" she taunted. "He made a fortune in disposable consumer goods. Did he make the world a better place for anyone other than himself?"

Alex blinked at the force of her words. His answer was nearly a whisper. "Yes. You don't have to be Mahatma Gandhi to make the world a better place."

"I've never had a pair of pantyhose last. I gave up trying to keep them. Don't all pantyhose manufacturers purposely make shoddy products in order to sell more units?"

"That's a myth," he explained. "There's a trade-off between sheerness and wear life; the finer the stocking the more fragile it is."

"Like people," she muttered as an aside.

"Back in the seventies, my father was the first hosiery manufacturer to introduce the cotton crotch—for health reasons, even though he incurred more cost. When NAFTA forced every other hosiery company offshore, he created specialty patented products and found a way to stick by his people and stay. He's principled...sometimes to the point of idiocy." He stirred a cup of broth into the rice. "Never missed a Little League game."

"A saint compared to my father. And you've abandoned him?"

"It's not easy being the son of a man who not only played offense and defense on his high school football team but also changed uniforms at halftime to play the French horn in the marching band. The inventor of the Total Control Top is a total control freak. I could never be my own man working for him."

Emily returned to her book. Several minutes of silence later she placed a log on the ebbing flames and returned to the kitchenette with her empty glass. Alex pivoted to pour her a refill before returning to his pot. The rice was almost done. He added the shrimp, saffron, and curry, and as he stirred the ingredients together, the soupy concoction turned a sumptuous gold. He removed the bread from the oven and spooned the risotto onto plates. Emily pitched in by tossing the salad.

They took their plates and wine to the fire, which, along with the candles, was all that lit the darkening room. They sat on the nest of pillows, a cozy five feet apart, and shyness overcame them. In tongue-tied silence they began to eat, staring at the fire, listening to the downpour pummeling the roof. The storm outside seemed to encase them, cocoon-like, keeping them holed up in the shelter together. Furtively he admired her rosy cheeks and windblown hair shimmering in the firelight, bathed in soft shadows. The pillowy contour of her loose-fitting safari shirt suggested endowments that were rare for her willowy breed. She was ethereal. She was earthy. She was everything! Was this really the same woman who had sold her soul to marry Charles Lukes?

"Why *are* you friends with Billy?" Emily asked, with a quizzical tilt of her head. Alex had popped the cork from the second bottle of Chianti and was refilling their glasses. He was in heaven but couldn't remember much of what they had talked about. Time had flown by and he had been barely in his body. "Don't ask me why—call it female intuition," Emily added, "but something tells me Billy doesn't have your best interests at heart."

"Billy's a piece of work for sure, but underneath he has a good heart. I've known him since prep school. I may be his last friend."

"Still," she gently persisted, "you two seem like total opposites."

"My first compliment from you," he smiled, raising his glass. "Speaking of opposites, how did you and Charles meet?"

"Sometimes opposites attract. I was working in sales at Sotheby's..."

"Sotheby's?" he interrupted. "Isn't that the wrong side of the art counter?"

"My father hated the idea of me becoming an artist; considered it a dead-end path. He thought it would reflect badly on his image as a Master of the Universe. So he cut me off and found me a job in the art world."

"You let daddy call the shots?"

"I'm an art major—not exactly bursting with marketable skills. And besides, I had no funds of my own. You're right though—I can't just blame my father."

"Tell me about him."

"Long story."

"So, you met Charles at Sotheby's and became his trophy wife in order to escape your father?" As soon as it slipped out, he regretted it. He had meant it semi-facetiously. Fortunately, Emily seemed to let it roll off her back.

"I am *not* a trophy wife," she said, with a twinkle in her eye. "Nor do I let men call the shots—they only think they do. Tell me about *your* love life."

"I fell into a catch-and-release practice, like trout. Never found anybody right—probably because things weren't right with me." He tried to gaze into her eyes, but she deftly avoided him.

"Surely you've been in love before."

"No, just engaged," he said. "Broke it off just before I quit Halaby Hosiery."

"Do you ever stick to anything?"

"Sometimes shedding skin is healthier." He wobbled to his feet. The wine rushed to his head as he bent down to pick up their empty plates. Rain was still peppering the roof, and on his way to the kitchenette, he skidded. He was standing in a small puddle. As he peered up at the ceiling, a drop of water went *splat* in the face. He took the plates to the sink and rinsed them off. While removing the grapes from the fridge, he said, "I don't think it's rained this hard since Noah's ark. Just imagine: all those animals on one boat, safe from the deluge—elephants and giraffes, hippos and rhinos, eagles and egrets..."

Idiotic as it sounded, Emily tipsily picked up the slack: "Great Danes and dachshunds, ostriches and peacocks..."

"But everyone else drowned, because God wanted to start over fresh." He carried a basket of grapes back to the fire and collapsed on the pillows, creating a cloud of ancient dust. He grabbed his glass and thrust it aloft.

"Not another toast," she groaned playfully.

"Here's to starting over fresh!" After an awkward clink-and-drink, he popped a grape into her unsuspecting mouth. The brazen gesture appeared to make her uneasy, so he returned to the relative safety of the animal kingdom: "I read recently that if a lion is caged for a long time and then is suddenly offered his freedom, he won't leave the cage. He'll just lie there, fearful of the unknown, accepting the cage as his reality."

"You've left your cage, it seems."

"I heartily recommend it," he said, causing her to look down. "So, why do you paint?"

"I'm good at it." She laughed, like she was taking a mischievous liberty in saying so. "It's an escape—the one thing where I'm in charge, where I can express myself without interference, create my own reality. Everyone should have such an outlet." Contemplatively she sipped her wine. "My college art teacher, who always thought in absolutes, told me that if I wanted to become a great painter I must never have children, never get married, and never do anything that took me away from my work. My father took the same hard-nosed approach with his career; his wife and kids were not much more than props, so I guess that experience soured me on careerist extremes."

A booming thunderclap shook the ground; seconds later a flash of lightning illuminated the cabin, and in the process electrified Alex right out of his inhibitions and into an advanced state of clarity. There was no risk in expressing the feelings in his heart; on the contrary, she was dying for him to do so. Her father was a prick, her husband an ass; she was as desperate for intimacy as he was!

"Do you really want to spend the rest of your life with Charles Lukes?" he said. "I saw you at that party, with his circle of well-mannered-but-catty, well-traveled-but-provincial, well-educated-but-hostile-to-new-ideas so-called friends. Is that really your world? Or your cage?" His words hung in the air like a live hand grenade.

"Well...*that* mouthful certainly came out of left field."

"It's more like the elephant in the parlor, if you ask me."

"You call this a parlor?" she scoffed, with a derisive toss of her blond mane. "At least I *have* a life. What about you? Cruising around on your motorcycle, lurking around galleries trying to pick up married women, taking credit for songs written by other people?"

"You're right—who am I to judge?" Alex conceded. "But it does seem you and I have a lot in common. From the outside we appear to have everything, but inside, deep in our hearts, we ache for something more." He gulped the remainder of his wine, bottoms up. "Don't get mad, Emily, but when you walked into the club the other night, everything in my life changed."

Her eyes fled to the fire. Alex was astounded by what he had just said, but while his stomach leapt like a skydiver's and his head whirled with wine, he felt strangely attuned to his true self. Proposing to Lorna Foxhall had seemed far more reckless.

She held up her finger to show him her wedding band and colossal diamond engagement ring. "Doesn't it bother you that I'm married?"

"As a matter of fact, it bothers me terribly," he sighed.

"Is this a game? One of your life experiments?" Before she could rise, Alex took hold of her arm.

"It's no game, Emily! You..." Words suddenly eluded him.

"I what? You don't even know me."

"You make my socks go up and down."

She laughed, despite herself. "You had to get us both drunk to say that. Which means it isn't real."

"An artist, more than anyone, should know precisely what is real—our moments and phrases outside the norm. Whatever you're going to become with Charles has already taken place. There's no art to it, no drunken soul." He learned toward her; she stiffened but made no effort to stop him as their mouths met inquisitively. The faint spray of wine on her breath proved more intoxicating than the wine itself, adding to his desire to throw all caution to the wind. Despite her boundaries, he sensed a deeper place without any—a nirvana he was driven to pursue. Just when he had the epiphany that he would never want to kiss another pair of lips again, Emily pulled away from him. Looking like she had suddenly come to her senses, she seized her shoulder bag and scrambled to her feet. She marched to the door and thrust it open, but the torrential rain made her balk. Alex, coming up behind her, gestured at the storm, at his Harley sitting forlornly in a giant puddle.

"God obviously wants you to stay," he said, softly addressing the back of her neck.

"Oh, really? You speak to him?"

"No, but I'm praying. Emily, you must stay," he whispered urgently. "We were meant to be together. It's as plain as the stars in the sky."

"You can't see the stars. It's raining."

"But they're still up there. Don't ever forget that. Don't ever forget who you are."

"I'm trying not to forget who I am."

She turned around to face him. As if surrendering to an inexorable fate, she eased her arms around his neck and they fell into a deeper kiss. Moments later they were looking at each other in wide-eyed amazement, like they had just opened a gift, until shyness overtook her. Silently he led her by the hand to the pitch-black bedroom. Clothing fell off of their bodies like dropping petals, as he guided her onto the creaky bed. Needing to see her face, he fumbled through the dark for a match and clumsily lit a candle. As the flame dilated, her pale apparition made him shiver in happiness.

"I need this," she said. "Please don't make me regret it."

As if to bestow the proceedings with a divine blessing, he kissed her Celtic cross where it lay against her neck. With great care, as if handling something breakable, or explosive, he took her in his arms and began kissing her all over, wanting so badly to please, determined to become the impossible standard by which she would measure all men. He sensed that she hadn't enjoyed sex for a very long time. He could barely believe this was happening. While his hands explored every smooth curve and their mouths played titillating little games, her hands slid down his body like feathers and fondled him, timidly at first, but soon her innate artistry took over. Her thighs parted as he felt her moist thatch of hair. Each touch made her tremble.

The moment of penetration proved almost too much for Alex; only a Herculean all-body contraction kept him from becoming a twenty-second wonder. "Don't move," he whispered, and when she immediately complied he felt trust. It wasn't long before he was able to plunge into her with abandon, only to tease her now and then by playfully retreating. These sporadic surprises made her gasp, but eventually they merged into a single heavenly entity and fell into a luxurious cadence, ebbing and flowing in perfect symmetry, losing all sense of self and time and place....

Some time later he felt a thrill when she began whispering his name. He cradled her round, smooth bottom and gently rocked her, kissing her neck. Moving toward ecstasy, her body grew taut. Her vagina clutched him with anxious appetite, cajoling him into a consistent, languorous rhythm that held them both spellbound. She fell limp as she came. Alex had never felt so intimate with anyone, and her vulnerability shattered his self-control. He held off for as long as he could.

As they lay in each other's arms, listening to the rain dripping off the eaves, he only hoped that he had won more than her body. Soon they were kissing again, unable to get enough of each other. All his life he had longed to feel what he was feeling tonight.

Coming up for air, she murmured, "What am I getting myself into?"

"Stay with me, marry me, follow your dreams. We could be Mr. and Mrs. Alex Monk."

"In *your* dreams," she said, throwing herself back into the kiss.

At dawn they were rudely awakened by a ringing sound. Emily quickly sat up and rummaged through her bag for her cell phone; she looked at the caller ID. "It's Charles," she said, her expression offloaded with worry. "He must be going crazy. I'm always reachable by phone. I'm sure he called the help and grilled them on my whereabouts." Uneasily she rested in Alex's arms, nervously twirling his chest hair, the giant diamond on her finger impossible to ignore. "God, what am I going to tell him?"

Alex smoothed a strand of hair around her ear—the ear of an angel. "The truth?"

"I don't know the truth, and neither do you."

Her almost hostile tone silenced him, made him feel precarious as they lay there clinging to each other.

"Take me home," Emily demanded.

"But the bed's so warm and comfortable."

"Then call me a taxi."

"Okay…you're a taxi."

"This isn't funny, Alex. I'm married, and this is wrong."

"Let's skip the decorum. There are no rules about such feelings, and this feels more right to me than anything I've ever done. What's *wrong* is your marriage. It's an unhealthy union." He nuzzled her, but Emily shook him off.

"I swore to God I'd never do this," she said bitterly. "My father cheats constantly on my mother. She's in and out of rehab thanks to him. He ruined her."

"People are seldom ruined by other people. Hurt, sure, but ruining—that we can only do to ourselves. Spend the day with me."

Emily was already flying out of bed and getting dressed. Alex placed his hand on the empty place where she had been lying, trying to absorb the residue of her energy.

Compared to bed, the damp, chilly air outside was like the first slap out of the womb. Emily watched while Alex toweled off the seats of the Harley and struggled to kick-start the cold engine. In their daze they forgot the helmet, so Alex drove extra-slowly and cautiously, creeping over the slick pavement, veering away from puddles. It was a much different ride from the previous night's. She hugged him from behind, seemingly without bones or muscles; a warm, soft presence resting her head against his back as they detoured along the ocean. Once back in her neighborhood, however, she grew stiff again. She directed him to shaded First Neck Lane; moments later his arm received a tug in front of a pair of stone lions. Countless times over the years Alex had jogged or bicycled past these formidable beasts, curious to know who lived beyond their protection, never imagining that their owners could be his contemporaries. The driveway, lined by an allée of mature lindens, was so long that you couldn't see the house from the road. A sense of desperation filled him.

"I'll walk the rest of the way," she said, climbing off the bike. "I don't want the help to see you."

Alex dismounted for a final kiss, but when an approaching police car slowed to a crawl, Emily turned to ice. The rubbernecking cop unnerved her, and as soon as the patrol car disappeared onto Great Plains Road, she started talking fast.

"Before you say anything, last night was spontaneous…and beautiful. Fine. But what's between us is purely physical. Nothing can possibly come of it, so let's just…"

He nodded slowly. "Go inside and pack a bag. Then let's hop back on the bike and go to the Vineyard, Big Sur, anywhere….You and me, right now! I mean it, Emily."

She wriggled away from him. "You don't know what you mean, or who you are! You're a dreamer!"

"Aren't you? What *are* we without our dreams?"

"You're dangerous." She pressed the nose of one of the stone lions and the gates began to open. She turned and began marching up the driveway.

"Emily, wait!" he called after her, but she kept right on walking without looking back. He watched her disappear and continued staring down the empty driveway until the gate closed in his face. Feeling deflated, at loose ends, he climbed back on the bike and made a U-turn toward the ocean.

He hoped that Emily, after appeasing Charles and taking a nap, would agree to a picnic in the dunes—but as he cruised past the regal Hampton estates, his spirits began to flag in the face of reality. The size of the Lukes spread had shaken off his joyful delusions of romance. Who was he kidding? Women never left husbands that rich for guys like him, with no career prospects and no money. He was nothing but her one-night escape, as so many women had been to him. And just like them, he'd been foolish enough to assume the beginning of a relationship. It served him right. Sure, she was emotional, intense—sweetly virginal even—but maybe that was her game.

Back at the cabin, thoughts of her consumed him. The experience had been so different from anything he had known. He longed for her more after sex than before. He spent a restless morning dying to call her but afraid any hint of obsession would only serve to drive her further away. In his earlier blissed-out state he had forgotten to exchange phone numbers and e-mail addresses with her. The cabin was listed but not in his name, so contact was left totally up to him. Finally, by early afternoon, feeling imprisoned and wanting her like crazy, he broke down and called. A housekeeper answered and informed him in a snippy tone that Mrs. Lukes was not taking calls.

His heart fell to the floor. He suddenly saw himself as Emily probably did: not much more than a gigolo, whose only true accomplishments were in the areas of risotto, witty songs and remarks, and lovemaking. A third-rate Renaissance flake. What was he doing here? Searching for direction, or just hanging out like any beach bum? Maybe he would still be doing this when he was sixty: just scraping by, looking ridiculous cruising around on the same has-been Harley. All this passion bubbling inside him and no idea where to channel it. Looking up at the heavens, he beseeched God to give him a sign. What was his mission in life? Churning with inner bedlam, bereft of clarity, he curled up in a fetal position on the bed. He had no zeal for anything—no idea of who the hell he was. How could a woman like Emily take him seriously when he was nothing but a businessman without the suit, a spoiled rich kid without the trust fund?

When evening came, he heated up the leftover risotto and poured a glass of wine, taking his dinner outside to watch the sunset: brilliant reds, yellows, pinks, slowly dwindling to a milky amethyst glimmer on Peconic Bay. Night fell. The horned moon smiled, filling his lonely soul with cautious optimism. He stared at the sky—dark, clear, vast, splashed with stars—mesmerized by the possibilities that a life of complete freedom presented, but void of specifics. He reminded himself that he had been free for less than a month, that he must be patient and trust the process—let the game come to him rather than force things, just as he had learned to do when playing guard on the Choate basketball team. The points and assists would come. A breeze rustled the trees. An owl hooted.

When the phone rang, he jumped. Surging with excitement, he flew inside to answer it. Who else could it be but Emily! How on earth, he wondered, had she found him? Had she called all the real estate agents in town to get his number, just as he had called all the art galleries to find her?

"Hello?" he answered eagerly.

"Oh, Alex! Thank God I found you!"

His spirit plummeted at the tremulous sound of his mother's voice. He immediately braced for some sort of attack on his character.

"We're at New York Hospital," she said. "Your father's had a heart attack."

Alex went numb; the breath was knocked out of him. His shaking hand could barely hold the phone. "Is he okay? Is he alive?"

Grace, normally of iron constitution, began to sob. "He collapsed on the golf course. Dr. Sprinkle insisted we helicopter him here," she managed to say, before uttering something incomprehensible and breaking down.

Filial instinct, deep as buried ancestral treasure, took over. "Mom, don't worry," Alex said, in his most comforting voice. "I'm on my way."

7

Life Interruptus

Guilt consumed Alex as he and his Harley hurtled toward New York City. He had abandoned his father at a critical time, adding to his burden. Keeping the business going with all the pressures was a monumental task; Alex had seen it continue so long that he no longer credited his father with the miracle it was. In his impulsive decision to follow his dreams, he had trampled on his father's, with almost fatal results. His mind kept replaying the last words Harry had heard him say: "I quit!" The thought of losing his father made his own chest unbearably tight, until he was a danger to himself on the highway and had to pull over to the shoulder to compose himself.

There was no man he loved and admired more. He began to see how leaving on a whim had been juvenile, selfish, and shameful. Freedom from responsibility was a luxury Harry Halaby never allowed himself. He had worked full speed since he was a kid and had never stopped. All that mattered to him was his family and his business. Inflexible and maddeningly stubborn as he could be, the man never turned his back on anyone, never abandoned his principles, and never let his family down.

Harry's parents, Maronite Christians fleeing Muslim persecution, had emigrated from Syria in the early 1930s as newlywed teenagers. They opened a small grocery store in Aurora, New York, where relatives had already settled, and went on a breeding spree. Somehow they managed to support their eight children on the store's meager proceeds throughout the Depression and World War II. Harry, the youngest, grew up in the shadow of his seven obstreperous siblings. He was only ten when his father died and had hardly known him. While his brothers and sisters got all the attention, earnestly and loudly setting out to change the world through political activism and academic pursuits, young Harry, with nothing else to hang on to, embraced the American dream. His siblings produced radical-left rhetoric, harping endlessly about the nebulous twin evils of

Zionism and capitalism. Harry was determined to become a business success—in his mind, the sole white sheep in his family. To earn extra money he threw himself into after-school jobs—delivering papers, shining shoes, milking cows. Whether, as he unwaveringly insisted, he actually did change out of his high school football uniform at halftime to play the French horn in the marching band and then change back into his pads again to lead his team to victory, would probably never be known for sure. Alex assumed it to be a self-serving myth, a motivating fairy tale, though if anyone was capable of such a stunt, it was his father. The fact of the matter was almost beside the point.

What Alex knew for sure was that his father had skipped three grades and graduated from Aurora High at sixteen, then immediately began supporting himself. After a stint in the army, stationed in Berlin, he went to work in his uncle's hosiery plant in Elmira, New York, where he met a fetching, no-nonsense Wasp named Grace Murray, a minister's daughter. Alex's parents were always less than forthcoming about personal matters, but according to the snippets of family folklore he had managed to piece together, Grace's parents warned her against marrying the swarthy Middle Easterner: "They have wandering eyes," Grace's father reputedly told her. Young Grace, however, on the rebound from a short marriage that her parents had pushed her into, was disarmed by Harry's generosity and sense of humor, impressed by his ambition and by the fact that he placed her on a pedestal. This time she defied her parents and married the man she wanted.

Armed with a small bank loan, Harry returned to Aurora with his new bride to start his own hosiery company. He had been unimpressed with his uncle's operation and believed he could do better. They parted amicably, the elder Halaby uttering the words of every generation to the next: "You'll see." Like his uncle, Harry initially found himself merely serving as a contract knitter for brand-name hosiery companies, handling their sporadic overflow and vulnerable to precipitous cutbacks. Harry knew he couldn't get fat accepting crumbs at the bottom of the food chain. The way to get ahead was to deal directly with national retailers, to listen to their needs and then respond with innovative products. With Grace pregnant and his company in the red, Harry worked feverishly on weekends in his small manufacturing loft to create products that would distinguish him from the pack. Most notable among these were control-top and support pantyhose with real spandex panties sewn on—as opposed to knitted in—for a contoured fit. Armed with these groundbreaking items, he began commuting to New York to court the R. Havemeyer Company, which was considering a relationship with him but had been unwilling to make a commitment.

A frenetic decade later Halaby Hosiery was the smallest of three pantyhose companies supplying Havemeyer. To compete against his cutthroat rivals like Wright-Fit Stockings, Harry focused the full force of his character and personality on Havemeyer, refusing to pursue other customers. The buyers, preferring dealing with the founder rather than slick, hot-aired salesmen, grew to trust and rely on him, to consider his word gospel. And his products truly made a difference. By playing with yarn textures and creating an optical illusion, he invented and eventually patented a reinforced sandalfoot toe, an innovation that effectively doubled pantyhose wear-life. While other manufacturers treated pantyhose as a disposable commodity, Harry kept developing longer-lasting, better-performing garments for which Ms. Middle America was willing to pay a premium, items exclusive to Havemeyer that increased its market share. When the OPEC oil boycott caused the price of nylon to skyrocket in the Carter years, Harry was the only Havemeyer supplier who held prices, taking a short-term hit in order to gain a bigger slice of the pie. Just when it looked like he was about to become Havemeyer's number one supplier and muscle out his formidable competitors, the union came to Aurora.

It was while watching his favorite team, the Yankees, out-slug his father's beloved Dodgers on TV during spring training that Alex first overheard his parents talking about "the union." He had no idea what a union was. All he understood from his parents' frightening argument in the adjacent bedroom was that some employees were planning to "strike," a word that apparently had nothing to do with baseball.

"This is what you get for hiring your Communist brother!" his mother had yelled. "I warned you! But of course you never listen! Even a blind man could see that Sam had a political agenda, that he resents you and hates me. And you made him the knitting room foreman!"

Prior to hearing his mother's angry outpouring, Alex had assumed his Uncle Sam—his father's oldest sibling—was the stars-and-stripes guy in the army recruiting posters, not a Communist. He had no conscious memory of ever having met Sam. Only years later did he learn that Grace had kept the pariah uncle away, afraid he might brainwash her son with radical ideas and undo her own brainwashing. Whatever the problem now, nine-year-old Alex had no doubt his father would handle it in his usual reliable fashion. At the time, Alex had no room in his heart for anything but baseball, and when his father tucked him into bed that night, Alex asked, "Dad, if the Yankees and the Dodgers win the pennant this year, will you take me to the World Series?"

"If *both* of them win? Sure," Harry qualified with a laugh, ruffling his son's hair. Harry's love of the Dodgers went back to when they were the Brooklyn Dodgers, the team that integrated baseball and epitomized the underdog. Harry identified with the underdog, even after he had achieved success and became a staunch Republican, even after the Dodgers abandoned their hometown fans in 1958 and moved to La-La-Land. His loyalty was unshakable, his love unconditional.

"Promise?" Alex persisted.

"Promise," answered his father.

Prowlers skulked around the house that long, hot, trying summer. Nails appeared on the driveway, puncturing Alex's and his friends' bicycle tires; screen doors were slashed, windows broken; dead Cayuga Lake carp appeared in the swimming pool—scare tactics not of employees but of professional union recruits whom Sam had imported from New York. A sizeable number of employees remained loyal to Harry, but union intimidation resulted in a steady trickle of defections. An employee couldn't enter the plant without passing through a hostile and raucous picket line. Sam arranged for a busload of shaggy Cornell students from down the road in Ithaca to join the pickets. He got the Aurora *Tribune* to print graphic and distorted descriptions of the "sweatshop" conditions in Harry's mill, as well as a vicious exposé centering on Harry's legendary temper. Shipments were vandalized, more employees crossed over, and the PR-conscious R. Havemeyer Company told Harry to forget about doing *any* business with them until he got his act together. Halaby Hosiery was rapidly bleeding to death.

Apart from the nails in the drive and some teasing at school for being the son of a "capitalist pig," Alex was mostly sheltered from the conflagration. He was more concerned about the Major League Baseball strike, which fortunately lasted only a few weeks. When the improbable happened and the Dodgers and the Yankees both survived the playoffs and clinched their respective pennants, Alex reminded his father of his promise to take him to the World Series. Harry was more than reluctant to leave town just then; he had gotten wind that some pros from the International Ladies' Garment Workers Union would be busing up from New York to show their solidarity with the strikers and lay siege to his plant. However, the idea of breaking a promise to his son was unthinkable. He had always purported that a man was no better than his word, and so with Halaby Hosiery on the brink of ruin, he dropped everything against Grace's strenuous objections and drove his family six hours to New York City to see baseball's two most hallowed franchises square off in the World Series. It was perhaps the only truly irresponsible act of his life and done only out of his sense of responsibility to honor his promise to his son.

World Series tickets were not easy to find, unless you were related to George Steinbrenner or Reggie Jackson. Harry was a rube in those days, with no connections whatsoever. To his son, though, he was larger than life; it never occurred to Alex that his dad wouldn't fulfill his promise. "I'm going to the World Series!" he announced to his friends at school as soon as the pennants were determined.

Harry approached the difficult task of obtaining tickets as he approached all difficult tasks: undaunted. He first asked the Hotel St. Moritz concierge, who normally could get any tickets, anytime. No luck. He called one agency after another. They laughed at him. Series tickets? Was he crazy? He called every nylon, spandex, and packaging manufacturer from whom he had ever bought goods, hoping for a favor—but came up empty. While Grace kept Alex occupied at FAO Schwarz, Rumpelmayer's, and the Museum of Natural History, Harry took to the streets, hitting every theater box office in Manhattan—East Side, West Side, even stopping random pedestrians. Weary and dejected, plumb out of options after three days of fruitless searching, he slumped into a Midtown bar just in time to catch a replay of light-hitting Steve Yeager's unlikely home run off Yankee ace Ron Guidry to win Game Five. The Dodgers had swept the heavily favored Yankees in LA and were heading east; if they won at Yankee Stadium tomorrow, the series would be over. Harry had never been a daytime drinker, but that afternoon out of sheer frustration he ordered a beer and struck up a conversation with the bartender, offering him a contraband Havana cigar. Harry told the man about the sacred promise he had made to his son and his sorrow at not being able to keep it. The Sicilian bartender, savoring the taste of the cigar for a long moment, reached into a drawer and handed Harry a dog-eared business card, which contained an address in Trenton, New Jersey.

Harry never fully divulged to his son the details of the ordeal he went through that night, though to this day Alex suspected a mob benefactor. As if it were yesterday, he remembered his mother fretting and pacing in the hotel room all night long and his father absent until breakfast. He vividly recalled the packed subway ride to Yankee Stadium that evening, the endless wait at the ticket window, and the utter stupefaction in his father's face when he was handed two tickets. The seats, incredibly, were two rows behind the Yankee dugout. Joe DiMaggio, seated directly in front of him, autographed his Yankee baseball cap! It was the high point of his nine-and-a-half-year life. When he thought about it now on the highway, that and getting into Princeton were the high points of his first thirty years—until Emily. She was the first woman he had ever really cared about.

Stuffed with hot dogs and peanuts, glorious in his autographed cap and warm-up jacket, Alex didn't even care that his father's favorite team, not his own, won the game 9–2 and became world champions. On the subway back to Manhattan, he slept soundly, cushioned against his father's bulk, unaware until years later of even a fraction of what the man had done to keep his word.

God must have smiled on Harry for this. Two months later, the union, unable to sustain support, folded its tent and left Aurora. Sam slunk off to become a thorn in the side of someone who wasn't a blood relative and R. Havemeyer came back into the fold. Harry moved his plant to North Carolina and hired a German engineer named Gunther Spear to run it. The two men proved to be simpatico teammates, and with Gunther handling production and Harry handling sales, the company prospered. Fifteen years later, when NAFTA forced most apparel and textile companies to lay off their workforces and relocate offshore to compete in the new world economy, Harry found ways to survive and flourish and stick by his people. That was the sort of man he was—the salt of the earth.

Alex parked his Harley in the New York Hospital lot and barreled through the revolving door. A woman at the information booth informed him that his father was in the Cardiac Care Unit on the sixth floor. He flew to the bank of elevators and waited an eternity for one to arrive and another eternity while it stopped at every floor. Every time the bell dinged Alex mentally repeated his mantra: *It's my fault.*

His mother was in the waiting area conferring with Dr. Sprinkle, Harry's personal physician and friend, and from her face he could glean that his father was at least alive. He went over and immediately embraced her, feeling the hot fear pulsing through her brittle body. Her bones were like toothpicks. She had depended on Harry all her life; he was her bulwark between her and the world, and Alex couldn't imagine her handling life as a widow.

"How is he?" Alex asked eagerly, looking first at his mother, then at Dr. Sprinkle.

Tall, with a pointed gray beard—an old-fashioned doc who, like his patient, had nothing but contempt for homeopathy and alternative medicine—Sprinkle peered sternly over his bifocals in a way that magnified Alex's guilt. "He's had a serious heart attack. He's lucky to be alive. The next six months are critical. He needs to follow a strict diet-rest-exercise regimen and lose fifty pounds."

Fifty pounds! Alex experienced chills. His father had lost weight before but never in the steady, disciplined way Sprinkle was no doubt prescribing. Harry's temperament was volatile, and his life revolved around meals. His pattern was to lose ten pounds in two weeks and gain back twelve in the next two. He sought dramatic results, instant gratification in both eating and in dieting, and Alex couldn't imagine him tucking into a bowl of sprouts or sipping carrot juice.

"No rich foods, no cigars, and absolutely no stress. Meaning no work for six months," Sprinkle emphasized, with a knowing glint. "I don't want him even discussing it."

"But he lives for his business," protested Grace weakly, nervously fiddling with the top button of her blouse. Her face was composed, but there was panic in her eyes.

"You want him to die for it?" Sprinkle shot back.

"May I see him?" Alex asked, expecting to be turned down due to the late hour.

"Keep it quiet and short," Sprinkle barked.

Alex couldn't remember the last time he had held his mother's hand, but his grip was resolute as they made their way down the hall. Nothing could have prepared him for the shock he got upon entering Harry's room. His father, oxygen tubes in his nostrils, body wired to an EKG, looked as if he had aged ten years since they had last seen each other a month ago. Hair snow white, skin ashen, eyes glassy and unfocused. In the ghostly silence, Alex gazed horror-struck at his father's shriveled form, unsure what to say.

Harry's eyes briefly acknowledged his son before fading off into space. Silently thanking God for granting him a second chance to make things right, Alex released his mother's hand and approached the bed. Fighting off tears, he leaned over and planted a kiss on his father's pallid cheek. "I'm sorry about everything, Dad," he whispered. "I know I let you down. I...I love you, Dad."

"Larkin's killing us," Harry murmured, barely audible. "We're going under."

"No, we're not," said Alex, not knowing what else to say. The next words flew out of his mouth without any prior consideration: "Don't worry about business, Dad. I'm back." His throat caught as he said it; he felt the world closing in on him.

Slowly Harry's hand reached up toward Alex's tear-stained face. Alex closed his eyes, awaiting a fatherly pat on the cheek, bracing for reconciliation. Instead his neck received a jerk forward. His father had grabbed his shirt collar and was shaking him violently. "You broke my heart!" he growled.

The breath left Alex's body as his father's fist pressed against his Adam's apple.

"You deserted me! In a crisis!" Harry's eyes glared like the devil himself.

"Good *God*, Harry!" shrieked Grace. "You've just had a *heart attack!*"

"I thought I raised a man!" Harry ranted.

"I *am* a man," Alex croaked, nose to nose with his seething father. "Just not the one you had in mind. Jesus, let go!"

Unable to make a dent in the melee, Grace flew out of the room for help.

"Now listen, Mr. Rat-Off-A-Sinking-Ship. I don't need your help. Gunther's in charge." Harry said it as if he had never given any thought to his own succession and was making a snap decision then and there.

Alex might have felt relieved of all responsibility were he not so appalled by his father's behavior and judgment. Yet who else could Harry have chosen but his number two man for the past twenty years? The number one son was a quitter.

"Gunther! Are you nuts?" Alex rasped. "He can't sell. He's a plant man."

"At least he's a man!"

A nurse burst into the room with Grace at her heels, just as Harry relinquished his grip and sank back into his pillow. "For God's sake!" the nurse hissed, knifing between the villainous son and the bed to check her patient's pulse "Are you trying to *kill* him?"

Alex backed away and stood frozen against the wall while his father kept talking, now with a faint quaver in his voice that Alex suspected was for the nurse's benefit. "Not since Sam's strike have things been so hopeless," were his last words before his body slackened and his eyes closed. The last thing Alex was aware of on his way out the door was the EKG going wild.

Back at the townhouse and with no clothes except those he came in, Alex changed into a pair of Harry's extra-large PJs. He was a baggy sight when he joined his mother in the kitchen for a midnight powwow. The disturbing sight of her slumped over the table, smoking a cigarette and drinking wine, prompted Alex to sit down and pour a glass out of commiseration.

"I just spoke to Gunther," she said, "and told him the news, that he's now in charge." While Alex winced at this, Grace snuffed out her cigarette and quickly lit another. "He's beside himself, utterly demoralized. You know how he worships your father...." She let out a beleaguered sigh. "I never realized things were *this* bad. Without a miracle, we're out of business by Christmas."

Alex sat up as though he'd been poked. "Define miracle."

"Oh, Alex," she snapped, as if he had no business asking, "I don't know all the details....What did Gunther say? Four million dozen in new sales, I think was the number."

Alex absorbed the full impact of this visceral blow. Did his mother realize that four million dozen represented an entire peak year worth of business for Halaby Hosiery? He was incredulous that things had degenerated this far and equally dis-

tressed that the business was now in the hands of Gunther Spear, the plant manager and chief operating officer stationed in Gastonia, North Carolina. An
undisputed engineering genius but devoid of people skills, Gunther was prone
under extreme pressure to manic-depressive mood swings. To those above him,
namely Harry and the customer, he was ingratiating; to those below a ranting
tyrant. A decade ago Harry had experimented with letting Gunther interface with
customers, but all it had taken was a raised eyebrow or a two-second hesitation on
the part of a buyer to scare the plant man into making sweeping price concessions. "Ve'll make it up vith efficiency!" Gunther would trumpet afterward.
Never one to make the same mistake twice, Harry had kept Gunther away from
buyers ever since, using him only as a prop on plant visits. Now the prop was in
change.

"Listen, Mom," Alex began haltingly, "I want to save this…turn it around.
Before Gunther does anything drastic, I'll meet with Larkin. Maybe call on some
other customers."

"People will never accept you," she snorted.

She wasn't entirely wrong. Why would Jack Larkin or anyone else on the
buyer's side of the desk give him the time of day? In eight years working for his
father, he had made no mark of his own. His track-record was blank, except for
quitting impulsively. "Just once give me some support, will you?" he persisted.
"Show some confidence in me."

"Why should I? You're much too young and inexperienced. Not to mention
unreliable."

"I'll turn my youth into an advantage," he said, not quite sure what he meant
by it. "What do we have to lose at this point?"

Grace closed her eyes, as if in pain, but then let out a sigh that indicated
grudging acceptance of the inevitable. Torn between her lack of faith in him and
wanting him back, she said, "Is this really what you want? A month ago you
hated the business."

"I did the right thing to quit, and I'm doing the right thing to come back."

"Then you'll live here, in the townhouse," said Grace, laying out her non-
negotiable terms.

He didn't know whether or not there was any hope for a relationship with
Emily, but he needed his own place, in any case. Now was not the time, however,
to disagree with his mother about anything.

"You should save your money," she continued, making the most of her sudden leverage. "The office is here. We're here. I would think you'd want to be
close to us, that you'd have other things on your mind besides getting another

swanky apartment at a time like this." She examined him with a faultfinding eye. "You can't go back to work with hair like that."

The wine and his mother were robbing him of oxygen. He couldn't believe that only a short month after he finally had begun to live his own life, he was back not only working for his parents, but living with them.

"You heard your father: He doesn't want you anywhere near the business," Grace said fretfully, "so for God's sake don't do anything stupid. The worst thing you can do is to pretend to be somebody you're not, to go off half-cocked and try to be a hero."

"You can't put me in a straitjacket and expect…"

"Don't you *dare* make any decisions without consulting Gunther or me," Grace cut him off, suddenly looking like a zombie as she rose from the table. "It's after midnight. I'm going to bed." She began shuffling away; halfway to the door, she stopped and turned. "Alex, this is no game. You can mess up your own life but don't you dare mess up ours. Just get a haircut and see if you can fix things with Larkin."

◆   ◆   ◆

"Our policy," said Jack Larkin, sitting behind his desk in his sterile cubicle, "isn't to hurt your company."

Alex nodded, trying to appear statesmanlike but feeling like an imposter, a banana republic dictator ruling without the consent of the junta. "Our companies have been partners for thirty years," he reminded the buyer. His Paul Stuart wool suit, pulled out of mothballs, felt scratchy and confining. A barber had shorn him of all but an inch or so of his hair, which placated his mother and completed the metamorphosis. He was now a company man. But based on the morning's cataclysmic report from North Carolina, the company needed more. It needed Superman.

Orders had dried up; the plant was operating just two days a week and still accumulating inventory. The gloom in Gunther's voice had been palpable as he described rows of idle knitting machines; dormant sewing, dyeing, and boarding departments; and footsteps echoing on the concrete floor of the normally deafening yarn-texturing room. Alex had never known the plant not to be humming, and the thought of all that expensive, state-of-the-art European equipment lying idle shook him, leaving him with a sense that the company's misfortunes had advanced beyond the point of no return.

Gunther, devastated by Harry's illness and abdication, was ready to step into the void. "Now is ze time to shut down ze entire plant. Ve keep ze shipping room, send out ze overstocks." Gunther's sigh made it through the phone line. "Harry said no, no, no, but ve have to. Layoffs. Twelve hundred, at least—even that might not be enough."

Alex listened respectfully, knowing that it would take a miracle to save the company, but also knowing that his father wouldn't throw in the towel so easily. Nevertheless, as Gunther had explained, each day they put off the inevitable meant sending tens of thousands of dollars out the door in payroll and unnecessary inventory accumulation. How could Alex defend that as a business decision? When he dared to question this extreme course of action, the Düsseldorf-born industrial engineer rattled off a barrage of statistics about soaring overhead and crumbling cost structure. In response to the best platitudes Alex could muster about finding additional business somewhere, Gunther went apoplectic. "You haf never solt anyfing in your life! You vaste my time!" he screamed, before hanging up in Teutonic disgust. Alex was aware that this was not a great way to begin a working relationship, but he wasn't about to let Halaby Hosiery be decimated without a fight. This was the Mother of all Battles: to save his family, define his life.

Earlier he had taken Larkin to lunch at trendy El Mariachi, the buyer's pet Midtown restaurant, where waiters fawned over him even though he himself never paid for a meal; it was enough that his power as buyer brought in clientele. Alex tried talking business; but Larkin, feasting on paella and martinis, kept the conversation infuriatingly superficial, babbling on at great length about the "store trip" he had taken last week to the San Francisco Bay area, a junket that seemed to consist mostly of golf with the "nice folks" at Wright-Fit Stockings. Whenever Alex brought up anything serious, his lunch companion, sporting a cinnamon tan, returned to a description of his escapades on the links, detailing to the writhing vendor the signature holes at Pebble Beach, Cypress Point, and Spyglass.

The walk back to the R. Havemeyer Building had been circuitous, a typical Larkin route. The buyer led him past the neighborhood's luxury stores—Gucci, Asprey, the Sharper Image—gazing acquisitively at the window displays and pointing at various exotic articles that caught his fancy: alligator valise, sealskin wallet, ostrich shoes, aardvark golf bag. Like his father, Alex had refused to take the hint, and now Halaby Hosiery itself was in the process of being skinned alive.

"It makes no sense for Havemeyer to buy all its pantyhose from a single supplier," Larkin pontificated, tipping back in his chair and resting his huge wing tips on the desk. Pink chewing gum was affixed to one sole. "There are plenty of fine manufacturers all over the world, none of whom have a monopoly on good ideas."

"Believe it or not, I agree," said Alex calmly. He was trying not to think about the last time he had been in Larkin's presence, when the man had called him "daddy's little ass-wipe." "It's unwise for either of us to put all our eggs in one basket. But why not have an orderly transition? No sense amputating a hand just to get rid of a hangnail. No sense imposing unnecessary hardships. Right now I desperately need orders. Our plant's running only two days a week, and still we're piling up inventory. Our shipping room's crammed to the gills." No matter how Alex modulated his voice, it sounded shrill and pleading and lacked authority. "Twelve hundred people are about to lose their jobs. And you're about to weaken a valuable resource."

With an air of supreme indifference, Larkin swung his enormous shoes back to the floor and removed a pouch of tobacco from his desk drawer. "You're people aren't my responsibility, and frankly the industry could benefit from a little retrenchment," he said to the pouch. "Since I became the pantyhose buyer, other companies have submitted prices well below yours."

"They're low-balling! Six months from now, their prices will be higher."

Larkin peered down at him as if he were an annoying, yapping puppy. "I was a buyer when you were in diapers. There isn't a trick I don't know. Besides," he said, addressing his pipe, "I *like* low prices." He tapped his pipe against the ash-tray to empty the charred residue and then dipped it into the fresh tobacco. All his attention was lavished on this unlovely apparatus. "When I took over the pantyhose division, Halaby accounted for 100 percent of our business! That's not only unheard of, it's stupid!" *Tamp-tamp.*

"It didn't happen by accident. We earned it."

"We?" Larkin chuckled, flicking his Bic. With a series of short breaths he drew in the flame until a foul, gray cloud permeated the office. The intricacies of loading and lighting his pipe seemed to interest him more than the discussion at hand. "Resting on Daddy's laurels, are we? No wonder you expect favoritism." *Puff-puff.* "It's all you've ever known."

"All I expect is fairness."

"And what do I tell my other suppliers?" Larkin posed. "You're not the only one with plants to run."

"They have other customers. We're totally devoted to you."

"Whether we like it or not."

"What exactly do you have against my father?"

So far Larkin's demeanor had been one of bored tolerance, but this remark seemed to galvanize him. "Shit, Halaby! Your way of doing business is prehistoric! Made in America—gimme a fuckin' break! No salesmen except your father, no designers except your father, no executives except your father! Now that your father's out of commission, what am I supposed to think? I mean, who's really running things over there? Bipolar Gunther? Your bridge club mother?"

"*I* am," Alex quavered.

Larkin shook his head with amused incredulity. "I see. And what has Alex Halaby done to merit our confidence? I heard you quit a month ago. How dedicated can you be? How do I know you won't quit again next month?" The buyer leaned back and cradled his pipe, like Bing Crosby about to croon "White Christmas." "Our objective is to scale you down even more. By the end of the year, you'll be down to a third of our business." Alex's stomach went into spasms, but Larkin wasn't through: "By next April you'll be leveled off at a quarter." He handed Alex a letter on R. Havemeyer stationery, signed by his boss, the director of merchandise, which made the carnage official.

Alex scanned the letter in stark panic as his heart pounded. He didn't need Gunther to tell him what this meant. "Jack, this kills us!" he gasped. How could he ever tell his mother?

"Any other vendor would give his left nut to do a quarter of our business."

"This decimates our cost structure!"

"I told your father to get new customers."

"It'll take years to replace what you're taking from us!" Alex exclaimed helplessly.

"Your father shouldn't have dragged his feet."

"He doesn't deserve this treatment, especially when he's in the hospital and can't defend himself!"

"It's not my job to make the Halabys rich."

"Nobody can match our quality," Alex retorted, realizing the futility of arguing but drawn into it anyway. "Nobody's been more loyal to the R. Havemeyer Company than my father. He gave you guys a competitive edge for years, and this is how you treat him when he's down? What you're doing is just plain vicious!"

"Telling me how to do my job, you little snip?" Larkin thundered, pointing his pipe at Alex's chest. "Your father had a reputation for that, but at least he earned the right to his opinions. You've been at the helm half a day and already you're..."

His tirade was interrupted by the ringing phone. Larkin grabbed the receiver and instantly morphed into another person: pleasant, gracious. Alex quickly deduced that he was talking to the Wright-Fit salesman. As the buyer prattled on about the new products Havemeyer and Wright-Fit were launching together, then casually switched to golf, Alex marveled at how efficiently this suntanned swindler was ruining his life, destroying Halaby Hosiery on his very first day as company savior. How he hated this business! Hated being responsible for twelve hundred employees he didn't even know. Hated being at the mercy of this corrupt, pipe-obsessed corporate tyrant.

When Larkin finally hung up, his tone was more conciliatory. "Look, Alex, I don't want any animosity between us. I'm sorry about your father, I really am. I have tremendous respect for him."

You caused his fucking heart attack.

"It's just that he's inflexible, stubborn—which is good in some ways, bad in others. He doesn't understand the human element."

"What human element?" Alex asked warily.

"That buyers are paid a relative pittance for making decisions that earn their suppliers millions. If I make your family millions with a stroke of my pen, shouldn't you guys, you know, show your appreciation? Or are you too sheltered to grasp that concept?"

As the buyer's eyes bored holes into his prospective pigeon, Alex remembered the Mercedes brochure that Larkin had flashed in Harry's office a month ago. He had never seen his father prostitute himself and instinct advised him not to set a sleazy precedent. He knew this wouldn't be the end of his problems but the beginning. Jumping into quicksand with the "nice folks" at Wright-Fit and a host of other industry whores was no way to build a business; you couldn't build anything on quicksand. Far from restoring Halaby to its prominence with R. Havemeyer, capitulation would only signal its karmic doom.

On the other hand, the price of a car was trivial compared to what was at stake. A tactical concession might very well buy him some much-needed time. Even a month—a week—could make all the difference, assuming he could get the junta's approval.

"Look, Jack," he leveled, "your decisions are putting us out of business. I can't bear to see my father's company go down the drain, especially on my watch. Please, just tell me, what will it take to keep that from happening?" Then, responding to the same hesitation that might have terrorized Gunther Spear into making widespread concessions, Alex ingloriously caved in: "You want that Mercedes, you got it!"

After some fumbling around in his pocket, Larkin produced a large black key with a gleaming metal Mercedes emblem, which he dangled in the air with a broad smile. "How about a Lear jet?" he said.

"Fuck you, Larkin."

With that little pleasantry Alex left, and minutes later he was tromping back to the townhouse, dejected and ashamed of himself for having sunk to bribery and profanity—to Larkin's miserable level. Much as he hated to concede it, his mother and Gunther were right: There was no conceivable way that even a seasoned veteran, let alone "daddy's little ass-wipe," could peddle four million dozen in the required heartbeat. It had taken his father a lifetime to accomplish that, and in this business environment, with the economy sputtering and everyone in corporate America fear-based and cautious, it was a task beyond Herculean. As his father's own life experience proved, it took years to generate meaningful volume with the chains. Typically they would start a new supplier out with a small item—a measly five or ten thousand dozen—to see how it performed. With the bomb lashed inside Halaby Hosiery's bowels down to its last few ticks, starting small wasn't going to cut it. As Alex marched up Fifth Avenue, he told himself that there had to be another way of dealing with the crisis, something he just wasn't seeing. For the moment, however, there was nothing to do but start knocking on doors.

◆   ◆   ◆

It was nine o'clock in the morning, and Joe Frank Russell slurped a cola, squinting at the pantyhose samples on his plain metal folding table, then at Alex's business card—curiously, back and forth. Prior to his sales trip and without telling a soul, Alex had taken the liberty of printing up cards identifying him as Halaby Hosiery's CEO to enhance his credibility. It never occurred to him that it would have the reverse effect of undermining Halaby Hosiery's credibility. What manufacturing company in its right mind would choose as its CEO a thirty-year-old with "lightweight" written all over him? Joe Frank Russell's squint stemmed more from deep-fried Southern bloat than from focus. His red neck sported an even redder birthmark, shaped like a hog nursing a trio of piglets—or so it seemed to Alex, who after three fruitless weeks on the road was bleary-eyed and punchy.

"Yer line's purdy fancy, son."

Alex couldn't tell whether the remark was meant as a compliment or a condemnation, but he suspected it was the latter. Three weeks of abysmal sales calls all around the country had all but shattered his confidence. He felt like an oft-beaten dog waiting for another painful wallop.

Joe Frank Russell bought pantyhose for BelMart, the largest and fastest-growing discount chain in America. With over five thousand outlets in malls throughout the heartland, and hundreds more in China, they had a decade ago shot past R. Havemeyer in annual sales, leaving them and every other retailer in the dust. No other prospect could have prompted Alex to fly through violent thunderstorms to Little Rock, Arkansas, rent a car and drive two hours in 105-degree heat to Tuckerman, BelMart's company town. The middle of Arkansas was certainly no place to be in June. The drive was dusty and sweltering, with nowhere to eat along the road but places like "Ray's Red Hot Ribs" and "Floyd 'n' Flo's Chicken BBQ." Starbucks had penetrated China but not this part of the world.

BelMart was the last stop on Alex's hastily arranged, whirlwind sales trip. In the rearview mirror were Sears (Chicago), Kmart (Detroit), Target (Minneapolis), Mervyn's (San Francisco), JCPenney (Dallas), as well as two large supermarket chains (Albertson's, Piggly Wiggly), two convenience store chains (7-Eleven, Cumberland Farms), and a shoe store chain (Edison Shoe). Now he was in Tuckerman, bracing for his umpteenth rejection in three weeks. It didn't seem to matter where he went or what he said; buyers supporting families on modest salaries seemed to derive sadistic pleasure from making the thirty-year-old "chairman" squirm in his fashionable worsted suit. Alex felt like a circus attraction. Quality, price, and service were of less interest to them than his pretentious title.

Last night—demoralized to the point of sickness, alone in his bleak cell at the Tuckerman Komfort Korner with nothing but a Gideon Bible to keep him company—a fierce longing for Emily assailed him. For hours he stared at the crumpled-up Post-it on which he had scrolled her Southampton number. Drenched in failure, he had been in no frame of mind to call her and explain the radical changes in his life. She would only see him as a colossal loser. She was married to Mr. Megabucks while he was chained to a sinking ship, helplessly watching three decades of his father's work slip down the drain. His father had saved his employees from NAFTA; Alex was about to preside over their demise in his very first month sans Daddy. Such comparisons, though unjust, were inevitable; like it or not, that was how he would forever be branded. He pictured himself walking into one of his East Side haunts years from now and generating catty whispers about his dubious lifetime achievement. He would have to move to Australia.

When he finally worked up the courage to dial Emily's number, he got the same grumpy housekeeper. Posing as a C-SAW functionary, he managed to extract from her that Mrs. Lukes was back in the city awaiting the return of Mr.

Lukes. When he pressed her for their New York number, she curtly informed him that she wasn't authorized to give it to anyone. Serenaded for the rest of the night by the rattling air-conditioner and the sporadic groans of the ice machine outside his window, Alex tossed and turned in spiraling depression, lamenting that he might never see Emily again. Now, after scarcely an hour of sleep, his nerves were raw.

"As a mattah uh fact," said Joe Frank, noisily sucking crushed ice through a straw, "I ain't evah seen a hosra line so s'phisticated." He cast a jaundiced eye at Alex's stylish New York suit and silk tie and added, "'Specially at these prices." The buyer's stomach slouched over his polyester pants; patches of sweat garnished the armpits of his short-sleeved shirt; a yellow fluorescent woodpecker adorned his bib-sized tie. "How much uh Hav'meyah's pantyhose d' y'all supply?"

"One hundred percent," Alex said, omitting Larkin's plans to cut them to twenty-five. At the start of the trip, the figure had been a boast, a selling-point to demonstrate Halaby's quality and legitimacy. But buyer after buyer had interpreted it as a sign that Alex and his company were entrenched in the enemy camp.

"Does Hav'meyah own a piece uh y'all?"

"Absolutely not," Alex declared, for the umpteenth time in three weeks.

"Hav'meyah's our archrival, yuh know."

"They seem to be everybody's archrival," Alex said edgily. "We must be doing something right."

Joe Frank examined a glittery sample with butterfly designs, flexing the waistband a few times before letting the garment drop to his desk. Alex imagined him fondling his wife in the same coarse manner and expecting multiple orgasms. "What yer showin' me heah ain't Hav'meyeh goods."

The hillbilly knew his pantyhose. "Our design team is constantly developing new items."

This, of course, was a bald-faced lie. Beside the fact that Halaby Hosiery didn't have a design team, the samples on Joe Frank's desk were the result of a last-ditch shopping spree at the Dallas Neiman Marcus. Gunther had made this little deception necessary, having ignored Alex's request for new sexy samples prior to his maiden sales trip. "Ve don't do sexy, ve do quality! Ve don't make styles, ve make products!" Alex's half-cocked sales trip—or "Gullible's Travels," as Gunther derisively labeled it—was a "colossal vaste of time and money." While Alex would be dashing around the country "like a decapitated chicken," Gunther ranted, the company was choking with goods it couldn't sell, losing money hand over fist. Meanwhile, Wright-Fit's factories in China were working around the clock. The situation was irreversible; to think that some mass market retailer would magically appear out of nowhere and bail them out with four million dozen was sheer folly. As if to make it a self-fulfilling prophesy, Gunther had sent Alex the same tired basics that Halaby had been churning out for R. Havemeyer year after year, styles that in Alex's opinion belonged in a geriatric health supply catalog. Worse, the garments bore R. Havemeyer labels and were sheathed in R. Havemeyer packaging, hardly the way to seduce a rival retailer. Hence his rush-rush visit to Neiman Marcus in Dallas. Halaby Hosiery needed a severe make-over, and so the "line" Alex was now presenting to BelMart consisted of sexy bikini cuts, silky yarns, and sophisticated patterns from Christian Dior, Calvin Klein, Evan Picone, and Donna Karan, without their identifying labels. With a pair of tiny nail scissors, he had cut out the designer size tags and discarded the packages, inserting the doctored hose into plain white sample envelopes—all of which he accomplished in the back seat of his Budget rent-a-car before turning it in and flying off to Little Rock. He had employed seat-of-the-pants pricing methods, calculating backward based on each retailer's probable retail and markup, lowballing just like Wright-Fit was doing with Larkin to get in the door. Designer styles at discount prices: How could any buyer refuse?

The buyer leaned back and interlaced his sausagy fingers behind his head, revealing more armpit sweat. "I'm curious how anybody kin make goods like these fuh these prices."

"I'm not in business to lose money," said Alex with a thin smile. "So, are you interested?"

The buyer picked up one of Alex's samples and stretched the foot. "Yew bet, I'm interested. I'm interested in what kinda backwoods yap yuh take me fuh. I'm interested in what this here 'CD' knit in the heel stand fuh. Civil Defense?" He hurled the Christian Dior garment into Alex's face, and then with one sweep of his pork-chop arm cleared the table of all the other samples. His birthmark now a blazing scarlet, he glared at Alex like a wild boar pawing the dirt.

Alex tiredly met his gaze. "The entire pantyhose industry steals ideas from France. I just didn't go to the trouble of making samples." With that, feeling like the lowliest form of vermin, he bent down to collect the strewn hose, stuffing them haphazardly into his briefcase.

Joe Frank eyed his visitor with a mixture of disgust and pity, before making a megaphone with his hands, one of which lacked a finger, and shouting, "Laverne! Git yer white ass in heah!" Into the cubicle lumbered Joe Frank's male assistant, a strapping, slack-jawed Neanderthal about Alex's age. Alex, on his hands and knees in "squeal like a pig" pose, was expecting to be forcibly ejected. Instead, Joe Frank handed Laverne some change and said, "See if yew kin bring us a coupla colas without spillin' 'em." Once Laverne left and Alex returned to his chair, the buyer's birthmark returned to its original dull hue, and he addressed Alex in Dutch-uncle fashion. "Why did yew pull that dumb-ass stunt? Designah crap don't fly down heah in Dogpatch."

"Nor does non-designer crap," Alex murmured. "I've been on the road for three weeks, showing what we actually make. The chains all have established relationships with other suppliers. Believe it or not, Halaby makes a great product. I'm in this mess because the new Havemeyer buyer is a shakedown artist. He gave my father his heart attack. What a crime that a man like that can ruin the life of a man like my father."

Joe Frank emitted a little *pffft* of disgust. "If it makes yuh feel any bettah, the hose y'all make fuh Hav'meyah 's the best value in the whole damn US of A, bar none. Jus' between yew an' me an' muh ugla fuckin' birthmark, even my wife buys 'em, and she kin git BelMart's fuh free."

Conditioned as he was to catastrophe, Alex was flabbergasted at this assessment. Hearing such encomiums from his father and Gunther was one thing, but hearing it from a rival buyer, especially on the heels of his designer fiasco, was quite another. He dropped the remaining fragments of his attempt to be a suave CEO. "Then why do buyers treat me like dirt?"

Joe Frank's belly shook with a country laugh. "Yer too fuckin' young tuh be runnin' a manufacturin' company. It's ridiculis."

"No more ridiculous than a lug like you buying pantyhose."

"Maybe so," the buyer conceded, "but at yer age I was an assistant buyah, fetchin' colas like dumb-ass Laverne. Don't git me wrong, son, I don't envy yuh one damned bit. I'd hate tuh be in yer shoes. Yer dripping with so many advantages that it's purd-near imposs'ble tuh succeed. Even if yuh do, it's stigmatized. Folks're jealous."

"But I'm the underdog! Wright-Fit's a billion-dollar company!"

"Y'ain't a typical undadog. Undadogs nawmally ain't got silvah spoons in they mouths." Laverne returned with two colas and set them on the metal table. "Shut the fuckin' door on the way out," Joe Frank told him, while his eyes remained squarely on Alex. "Yer different from the boot-lickin' hooers who nawmally set foot in heah. Uppidy, impatient—all the things a typical salesman ain't s'pposed tuh be. The way my screwed-up brain works, anyone who has the balls tuh pull the stunt yuh jus' pulled and then justify it without battin' an eye prob'ly has some redeemin' features."

The redneck downed his entire cola in one long gulp, his Adam's apple bobbing like a yo-yo. When finished, he let out a thunderous belch, seemingly proud of the decibels. Alex watched in wary wonder while he wheeled his chair over to a file cabinet and returned with a four-inch-thick folder, which he slapped on his table.

"These heah ah customah complaint lettahs, most of 'em angra sumbitches. All on Wright-Fit goods. Wright-*Shit's* mo' like it. They qual'ty's gone down the crappah. Our stores and customahs ah royally pee-owed. Wright-Fit used tuh be a good comp'ny befo' the Chinks started making everything for 'em. They been livin' on their laurels too fuckin' long. Like Shakespeah said, reputation don't mean shit."

"Since our product's so good and Wright-Fit's is shoddy," Alex ventured, feeling a glimmer of hope that maybe, just maybe, this disastrous meeting and his disastrous sales trip might be salvaged, "why not throw me a bone?"

"'Cause it ain't my decision."

"Aren't you the buyer?"

"That's muh title, but the boys upstairs tell me who tuh buy from. I'd luv t'buy from y'all, 'specially y'all's control-top and support. But co'prate politics bein' what they is, I cain't."

"Why not? Somebody greasing somebody's palm?"

"Not *my* palm. Wright-Fit's entrenched evrawhere—with my boss, my boss's boss, all the way up tuh the big cheese. Yuh don't get nowhere these days pitchin' tuh the hired help."

"I need a huge order, a grand slam!" Alex's desperate plea was directed more at the universe than at Joe Frank Russell.

"Hard tuh hit a grand slam with the bases empty, son. Be great if yew could give 'em somethin' they ain't never seen befo', but given that the hos'ra business ain't seen a majah innovation since spandex, my advice is tuh go out, git as drunk as yuh can, an' turn the page of yuh company ledger tuh chaptah 'leven."

With a long drive ahead of him before his Byzantine flight back to New York, which involved changing planes at Memphis and then at Cincinnati, Alex rose and shook the buyer's hand. "If anything changes—like if your management gets indicted—please keep me in mind. Sorry about my ruse and thank you for your time."

8

Blue Dots, Red Eyes, and Other Epiphanies

The Charles Lukeses, reunited after their three-week separation, had for the moment retired to their respective bathrooms in preparation for bedtime. Charles, dog tired from his twelve-hour flight but in the throes of a second wind, sang loudly in his white marble shower. He was obviously delighted to be ensconced back in the old castle. Twenty-five feet away, behind closed doors, Emily stood retching over her toilet, holding a home pregnancy test and gaping at the positive blue dot in disbelief.

"Spi-dex, Spi-dex, doncha love that Spi-dex," Charles crooned, to the tune of "Jeepers Creepers." "Spi-dex, Spi-dex, doncha love that string...Hey, Emmy?"

Emily was too stunned to respond. She was pregnant—and she didn't need to do the math to determine who the father was. She knew there was no way Charles could be.

"Emily!"

"One sec!" What had she done!

"Emily, my little geisha"—the cries were coming closer—"the whole time I was over there talking about gene splicing, about mating spiders and goats, I was thinking about our own gene blending project."

"Just a minute!" she said sharply, mind spinning. Since their night in Southampton three weeks ago, she had received no communication from Alex. This lack of gallantry—not to mention lack of interest—after what had been the emotional pinnacle of her life, had left her feeling scorned. Maybe she had been too off-putting at the end, but surely he had to understand her situation. It shouldn't have totally discouraged him—not after the way he pursued her, not after all his bold romantic talk and the incredible sex. At least *she* thought it was incredible; maybe for him it was just another night at the office. After a few anguished days of no contact, she had dialed information for his number; but his name wasn't listed, and she was reduced to the out-of-character gesture of driving over to his cabin. She had never chased men before; she had never had to. His Harley wasn't there and neither was he, so over the next several days she began the painful task of expunging him from her heart and mind. Hoping to reinvigorate her marriage, she had even planned to surprise Charles today by meeting him at JFK Airport—until this morning, when she vomited for no apparent reason and then remembered with a jolt of icy fear that she had been ovulating right around the time of that wild, rainy night with Alex. Scratching her airport plans, she went instead to the neighborhood pharmacy and purchased an EPT, only to procrastinate until she could no longer take the uncertainty.

As she eyed the blue dot, panic rising, she briefly considered the feasibility of abortion. The logistics of having one without Charles finding out were daunting, and while she knew several women, including Vanessa and Claire, who had gone through abortions as if having their eyebrows plucked, she knew it wouldn't be that easy for her. Already her maternal instincts were kicking in, and she realized that unplanned and inconvenient as this baby was, she wanted it—in part because it *was* unplanned and inconvenient. The lovechild she thought she would never have with her husband.

It wasn't as if she had any obligation to tell Alex it was his. Even if he miraculously reemerged with a reasonable explanation for his silence, she owed him nothing. It was Charles who desperately wanted a family and a child, who had promised to stop drinking once he became a father. A baby might force him to grow up, give them both something truly important on which to focus their energies, a common purpose. She and the baby needed someone who would be there for them—and she craved boundaries, before her life spiraled out of control. Yet when the bathroom door suddenly flew open, and Charles sauntered in wearing his striped Savile Row pajamas, she discreetly dropped the applicator into the wastebasket behind her and waltzed toward him in diversionary fashion.

"What's wrong, my darling?" he said, holding a large oblong gift and his usual glass of bubbly. "You look like you've just seen a ghost."

"I'm not feeling well," she muttered.

"Maybe this will make you feel better." He thrust the present at her.

She snatched it and ushered him out of the bathroom and over to the bedroom chaise, their traditional spot for dealing with his gifts. Gathering her poise and forcing a smile, she removed the scarlet ribbon and paper, squinting at the unfamiliar Japanese logo on the glossy beige box.

"Open it," he urged.

With some trepidation, she lifted the lid, expecting an overpriced designer peignoir. But she was pleasantly surprised. Beneath the tissue were a dozen sleek ten-inch-long tubes, made of what looked like teak. She picked up one and saw that it opened at one end. Inside was an elegant sable paintbrush, which she gingerly removed. She pressed the soft bristles against her palm.

"They're lovely, Charles. Thank you." This was the second gift he had given her recently that reflected a genuine effort to please her, that wasn't simply a crass monetary display.

"I went to visit this calligraphy shop," Charles explained, wrapping his arms around her from behind, "and the shop girl convinced me that it's the *pelfect* hobby for a *cleative* wife." He stepped back and gave a clownish Oriental bow.

The hope she had begun to feel was suddenly gone, like a rare breeze on a sweltering day. "Calligraphy?"

"*Carrigraphy*," he kept on with a toothy grin. "It's done with brushes, like painting, donchya see? You can use your paintbrush skills but without all the fumes."

"I like the way my paint smells."

"I thought you'd be thrilled to get something indigenous as well as artistic." He arched a droll eyebrow. "Once you master the skill, we'll never have to print party invitations again. You can do them all by hand."

He kissed her cheek and went over to the bed, where he began sorting through the stack of mail that had accumulated during his trip. Taking the teak tubes over to her side of the bed, just to avoid being pestered about them, Emily flopped down and switched on the TV, surfing to an African wildlife program on the Discovery Channel. Zebras and gazelles romped across the wide screen, bringing back the memory of her Noah's ark conversation with Alex. The tingle of fear in the pit of her stomach returned to butterfly mode. One stormy night and whammo—her life was in danger of being wrecked. The image of herself on the back of Alex's Harley in the rain, pregnant, on some dark highway in the middle of nowhere, looking for a place to stay for the night, ran through her mind. That was the reality of his situation; he had nothing.

But that thought was soon eclipsed by memories of Southampton: the cozy conversation, the lovemaking, feeling like a woman. Impractical as he was, Alex gave her everything her marriage lacked. Where was he now? Any number of things could have scared him off, from her off-putting good-bye to his tenuous existence. Yet try as she might to justify his desertion, she felt used, defiled. She couldn't conceive of a good excuse for his not contacting her. Was he a cad who had stereotyped her as just another unhappily married rich woman for the taking?

Did he think her a slut for sleeping with him so easily? That was it, she was just another notch in his bedpost! Suddenly her nausea returned. She took slow, deep breaths, feeling as doomed as the gazelle on TV that was trying to outrun a cheetah.

"We're going to make a whole bushel of money on this Spidex thing," Charles said. "With the military interested, we might even make it onto *60 Minutes*. How about a celebratory roll in the hay with the mad geneticist? With your looks and brains, and my money, our little munchkin will be perfectly engineered." He squeezed her knee and then moved his hand to her stomach, but she flinched. "Is that any way to greet the Spider-Goat King after his heroic journey to the Far East?" he asked. When she didn't answer, he snapped, "You know, I don't buy you all that lingerie just for you to fall asleep in."

They both fell silent. It was rare that Charles lost his sense of humor. For Emily it was almost refreshing. His unassailable irony was the material from which her prison was constructed.

Charles picked up a shiny gold-foil envelope—obviously an invitation—and pushed his new Kyoto reading glasses farther up onto the bridge of his nose. He tugged at the flap until the envelope ruptured, drenching him and the sheets in a shower of multicolored confetti. After eyeing the glittery mess with the fascination of a person who has never had to clean anything up in his entire life, he examined the invitation. "Ah, no wonder," he murmured. "It's an AIDS benefit. A confetti crowd if ever there was one. We'd better get our red ribbons dry-cleaned, my dear."

"Does everything have to be a joke with you?"

"What's gotten into you?"

"I told you, I'm feeling sick."

Charles's face suddenly lit up. "Maybe you're preggers," he said, sending chills up her back.

"Is that all you can think of when I'm sick?"

Charles was too fixated to listen. "Hey, why don't I send Riggs out to the pharmacy to buy one of those home pregnancy tests?"

"Don't bother Riggs at this hour."

"Don't be silly, that's what butlers are for." As Charles turned away and reached for the phone, Emily yanked at his pajama collar and the seam ripped slightly. Charles stared at her, as if trying to figure out who she was.

Despite the guilt raging inside her, Emily needed to lash out. "Making spider-goats and making babies—it's all the same to you, isn't it?"

"Excuse me?"

If she was going to raise this child with him and spend the rest of her life with him, then he was going to hear her out! "Having a baby is a serious matter! A lifelong commitment, not one of your stupid projects! It's not something you can just hide in a drawer, like your novel, when you get bored with it!"

"Where is all this coming from?"

"What will you teach a child?"

"I'll teach it not to go bonkers for no reason." Charles took a nervous gulp of champagne.

"You'll teach it where the wine cellar is, no doubt."

There was a profound and almost frightening silence. Countenance grim and tight-lipped, Charles swung his legs to the floor and stood up. He ambled over to the desk in the corner to retrieve one of his gold-filtered cigarettes, lighting it and taking a slow drag before casting his wife a cold look. "I think we need to have a little talk, my angel." The usual lilt was gone from his voice. "I don't know what exactly is the matter with you. Or what you think this is. But I think you need to be reminded that everything you have flows from me, that you are my *wife*, first and foremost." As Charles paced the room, he seemed to grow angrier. "Your primary duties are to be as beautiful as when I married you and to give me children."

"Funny, you never phrased it that way during our courtship," she said sarcastically.

"Claire used to get snippy for no reason, too—all the while she was *cheating* on me." His eyes were like police searchlights. "That piano man didn't tickle a few keys when I was away, did he?"

"Don't be absurd," she laughed, forcing herself to meet his gaze as her terror took a new turn. What if Alex had boasted of his conquest to Billy and Billy spitefully told Charles?

"I was abandoned as a child and abandoned as a husband," Charles sputtered. "That is never going to happen again! And if by any chance it does, I can promise you one thing: You will be very, very sorry!" He snuffed the cigarette out in the ashtray; his fingers were shaking. Emily had never seen this side of him, and it alarmed her. "This marriage is for keeps, and no one," he said, teeth gritted in an angry smile, "is going to take that away from me!"

"Jet lag's making you paranoid," Emily muttered from her pillow. "Our problems have nothing to do with piano players."

"What problems?" he scoffed. "Most women would love to have *your* problems." Emily could almost see a series of thoughts pass through his mind, changing his expressions until his eyes welled up and he issued a melancholy sigh. "Sometimes I feel like a fake, a dupe, like the gods are playing some sort of cosmic joke on me. I mean, if *I* can't manage to be happy, or keep my wives happy, after all I've been handed, aren't I the ultimate failure?"

"You're just over-tired," she said softly, feeling genuinely sorry for him all of a sudden. "You're babbling, not thinking clearly."

"Would you have married me if I was a hot-dog vendor in the park?"

"Would you want your daughter to marry a hot-dog vendor in the park?"

"Give me a daughter and I'll tell you," he snorted. "I need something organic in my life."

"The cook made some organic chicken; it's in the warmer."

Nothing like some silly word play to perk Charles's spirits, she thought, stroking his head, thinking that she was not a good liar and had no desire to become one. At least Charles needed her, and she had betrayed him horribly. As she held him, she considered the simplicity of choosing him as the father. She could force herself to forget about Alex, just as he had obviously forgotten her. How could Alex be expected to care for anyone when he hadn't even cared enough to use a condom? God knew how many casual partners he had had; she hoped a baby was the only thing he had given her.

"Let me get you a plate," she soothed Charles, "you'll feel better." She headed for the door. "But then you must get some sleep, or you'll be out of sorts for days."

"I'm too discombobulated to sleep."

"Close your eyes and breathe," she said on her way out, feeling herself decompress as soon as she left the room. She wondered where Alex was but forced the thought out of her mind. She hoped he was in Timbuktu.

◆   ◆   ◆

"Not one nibble?" asked Grace.

Alex had made it home from Gullible's Travels in time for dinner but was too dazed with failure and exhaustion to eat his spaghetti Bolognese—so dazed, in fact, that he wasn't sure whether the nibbles his mother was referring to concerned dinner or interest from potential customers.

"Gunther and I both told you it was a wild goose chase," she said. "But at least you tried."

"I feel like Willie Loman. Didn't he sell stockings too?" Alex sighed, slumping in his chair and listlessly sipping a Heineken from the bottle. "What time tomorrow are we picking Dad up from the hospital?"

"*I'm* picking him up at ten. *You're* flying to North Carolina. Gunther's closing the plant down, and he wants you there."

"He called *you?*" Alex croaked, feeling asphyxiated by his own powerlessness.

"Don't argue! He wants you there first thing in the morning. I had Flora make airline reservations. The tickets are on your father's desk."

"But I just got back from three weeks of traveling," Alex protested. "And I don't believe in giving up."

Grace spoke with an air of patience tried. "Someone should represent the Halaby family at a time like this, and your father obviously can't."

"Dad would never quit in this situation."

"Things are too far gone. We have no choice," she said.

"I can't believe you're letting that myopic mechanic do this! It's not his company!"

"The decision's been made, so don't fight it. Stop meddling and accept what we're doing." She pointed her trembling index finger an inch from his eyeball. "Now, listen! Don't tell your father—he's not supposed to talk about anything stressful—but I'm putting everything we own—the townhouse, the beach house—on the market. I'm auctioning off my jewelry. I suggest *you* start drastically paring your expenses as well, because your salary won't continue. We can't afford it."

"What expenses! I live at home! Mom, please, calm down. You're going bananas."

"I'm facing reality, Alex!"

"I just need time to figure something out, a big idea…"

"There are no big ideas in pantyhose. Now, up to bed," Grace ordered, belligerently lighting a cigarette. "You're making that plane tomorrow and not with bags under your eyes!"

"Don't tell me when to go to bed!" Alex argued.

"I'm your *mother!*" Grace exploded, slamming her hand on the table, tearfully releasing what seemed like a lifetime of repressed anger and martyrdom. "Do you ever think how *I* might feel? All those years of standing by your father! Bucking him up while he fought off unions, made payroll, built his business. Against hopeless odds! I *told* him to go off-shore and not to put all his eggs in one basket. Now we're losing everything. And all you can think of is your ego! Stop focusing on who's in charge."

"You're completely missing what I'm saying."

"Our lives will never be the same," she wailed. "We're too old to start over, especially with your father's ill health." She glared at him with bloodless cheeks and blistering eyes. "How could this happen! How could *you* let this happen?"

Alex bit his lip. There was no sense reacting. He didn't get angry when a crazy bag lady with Tourette's accosted him on the street, so why should he now? It was the same beast at the moment—and who could blame his poor mother? She had every reason to be upset; he could only imagine her trauma. He embraced her, but Grace remained as stiff as a snuffed candlewick. "Good night," he said.

As soon as he was sure his mother was asleep, Alex snuck out of the townhouse and headed for the parking garage that housed his Harley. He could barely breathe under her roof. Granted, there was nothing he could possibly do to help Halaby Hosiery or himself at this hour, motoring aimlessly around the city on this balmy night. Much as he needed sleep, he was too revved up. Restlessly aware that the imminent demise of Halaby Hosiery meant he would be on his own for real in a matter of hours, with nothing to fall back on, he felt the overwhelming urge to keep moving.

Cruising down Fifth Avenue, he saw Emily's apartment building coming up on his left. He pulled over, cut the motor, and peered upward. All the windows of the duplex penthouse were dark save one. He hoped the delay in contacting her hadn't completely soured her toward him; that when he finally emerged and explained the reason for his disappearance, she would forgive him. Emily had all the makings of an empathetic soul. The feelings they shared were too beautiful to discard. Emily and he would pick up right where they left off in his cabin, he was sure of it. Still, despite his artificial optimism, he would have given away his Harley right then just for her apartment phone number.

A glistening silver Bentley pulled up to the awning. As a homely but richly adorned young couple climbed out, fawned over by the doorman, all Alex could think of was that the cost of the emerald dangling from the woman's ear lobe exceeded his entire net worth. A wave of hopelessness swept over him. Fair or not, his place in history as the pampered, incompetent son who ran his father's business into the ground in less than a month while his father lay in a hospital bed was all but assured. He would spend the rest of his life with a scarlet "A"—for Ass-wipe—tattooed on his chest. The Hester Prynne of Pantyhose. And maybe an "H" on his back—for Hypocrite! After all his grand talk of living freely, what was he doing? Failing at the business he said he'd never go back to; living with his parents! No woman worth her salt could possibly respect him when he didn't respect himself.

With his self-esteem in free-fall, he succumbed to old habits and motored like a madman onto the FDR Drive and all the way to Williamsburg to pay Billy a visit, fully aware that this constituted a full-fledged regression. Clearly Billy had to be phased out; he had ceased to be amusing. Ever since Alex had given up drugs, their friendship had become increasingly forced. Despite their common predicament—the imminent demise of their respective businesses—their lives were heading in opposite directions. And anyway, all Alex wanted was Billy's Rolodex. With his life in shambles, he was in no position to pursue any woman, let alone Emily; yet, unworthy as he felt, he craved contact with her more than ever, if only as a friend. Nothing less could possibly console him. She was the only person who had ever made him feel euphoric. Just to be able to talk *about* her in passing was worth the trip across the river. Enough time had elapsed since his infamous toast, he figured, to cool Billy's rancor and patch their stretchable friendship for the time being. Once Billy learned that Alex was in even worse financial straits than himself, his *schadenfreude* was bound to kick in and snap him out of whatever funk he was in.

The club was practically empty—just a few stragglers at the bar, male and female, all vying to go home with Winnie the bartender.

"Hi, stranger," she greeted him, looking harassed. "Get stranded on an island somewhere?"

"Kind of."

"I'll be expecting my invitation anytime."

"Where's Billy?"

She gestured to the ceiling and Alex circled around back. As soon as he started up the steps, they began to shake from thundering footsteps. A second later he was almost trampled by two hulks stampeding down. As he backed against the wall to let them pass, he realized that he had seen them before. They were Billy's loan shark business partners—Warren Buffetini and Bill Gateseroni, as Billy had dubbed them. Only after they were safely out of the club did Alex peel himself off the wall and sprint up the steps. The door to Billy's dim, disorderly quarters was wide open, and Billy was sprawled on the floor with a swollen eye and a bloody lip.

"Jesus, you all right?" Alex cried, helping his friend sit up.

"*Owww*, you fucking towel-head! The ribs!"

"I'll call the police."

"Not with all the Bolivians marching in my bloodstream, you don't!"

Alex dashed to the refrigerator and pulled out an ice tray. He grabbed an End of the World T-shirt that was draped over a chair; but before he could assemble a makeshift ice pack, Billy was at his desk preparing a stronger remedy, dicing a chunk of cocaine with a razor blade.

"Those thugs own part of this club?" Alex asked.

"It's *me* they own," said Billy, his trembling hands chopping out several uneven lines. "Christ, I need to get some more people in here! I need some fucking customers!" He took a couple of desperate snorts and then thrust the straw at Alex, who wincingly refused it, to Billy's annoyance. Finding a hair in his coke, Billy yelled, "*Fuck!* The worst part of being broke is you can't afford the shit good enough to make you forget you can't afford the good shit!"

This incomprehensible rant caused Alex to scratch his head. "Charles didn't come through, I take it."

"Fuck no, thanks to your fucking toast. I even asked Saint Emily for money when Charles was away. Christ, what a tight ass."

Alex let the comment pass.

"I even hit up Emily's old man. And, you know, it ain't easy asking for money from a man who starts out by calling you a 'coke-head piece of shit.'" Billy sucked up another line of powder, then pleaded, "Don't make me beg, Sahib."

"My father had a heart attack. The business is about to fold."

"*Dammit!*" Billy exploded, kicking his loafer across the room. He punched the file cabinet, losing the skirmish. "*Owww! Fuck!* I can't even depend on my best friend! I need some customers, some fucking customers!"

"We'll figure something out," said Alex, taking his deranged pal's arm in an effort to calm him.

Billy, practically in tears now, violently ripped himself away. "*Nothing to figure out! Got no more alternatives, A-rab! End of the line!*" Before Alex could fathom what was happening, Billy threw open his drawer and reached inside. He put something long and black to his temple and closed his eyes.

Alex's body and vocal chords froze in horror. He tried to speak but nothing came out. "Billy *no!*" he finally croaked, lunging toward the desk to avert the unspeakable—only to see that the gun was a black corkscrew.

Billy, sniggering at his little prank, offered no resistance as Alex dragged him over to the bed, removed his shoes, and tucked him in. Alex applied the ice pack to Billy's wounds, assuming it would take hours for his coked-up friend to fall asleep; but seconds after Billy's head hit the pillow he was out, making Alex wonder what other drugs were in his system.

Cocaine was everywhere: mirror, desk, chair, and floor. The mother ship—an ample plastic bag—overflowed atop the dresser. Craving an escape from all his troubles, Alex found himself sorely tempted. He pulled out his wallet and rolled a dollar-bill tightly into a straw, recalling the good old days when he had used only C-notes. Fortunately, his body, recalling on a cellular level the miseries of cold turkey, shivered in rebellion just in time, and he caught himself. He then went to the opposite extreme, feverishly cleaning the premises of any traces of powder. While picking up the mother ship to flush it down the toilet, he discovered Billy's Palm Pilot underneath. Despite a sense that the Palm Pilot contained more danger than the entire bag of cocaine, he pulled out the stylus and punched his way to what he had come for in the first place.

Emily slipped down the hall to her art studio and softly closed the door behind her. She collapsed in her oversized armchair and expelled a titanic sigh. Now that Charles had finally fallen asleep, she was free to breathe, to ponder her dilemma and commune with her pregnant body without feeling she was being monitored.

Placing the unwanted calligraphy brushes at her feet, she rose and lit a couple of candles around the room, her custom whenever she painted. She resettled in her chair, cross-legged, palms up, closing her eyes in meditation while the candles sweetened the air. Try as she might to clear her mind of all thoughts, her meditation drifted inexorably into a medley of sexual fantasies involving Alex—making love among the dunes, in his cabin, in luxurious hotel suites, country inns. The more she tried to resist the images, the greater their onslaught, and the next thing she knew she was sketching erotica in her notebook as a means of feeling closer to him. Unlike her clowns, the style wasn't constrained by realism, but was energetic, improvisational. Entwining lovers flowed from her pencil as naturally as anything she had ever created, in all sorts of exotic poses, to the point where she herself became sexually aroused and had to stop to regain her composure. Not since college had she felt so inspired, at the height of her creative power, and it dawned on her with a good deal of excitement that she had stumbled upon a risqué new artistic direction, one that so perfectly dovetailed with her own issues. She couldn't wait to start experimenting on canvas.

In the throes of this artistic epiphany, the phone rang; her hand flew to answer it before Charles could be awakened. "Hello?"

"*Emily! Finally!*" It was Alex, and her heart jumped to her throat. Had her sketching telepathically triggered his call? "I've been all over the country! Thinking of you, dreaming of you!" he said breathlessly.

"I haven't given you much thought, actually." She said this partly out of pride, but also in the event her light-sleeping husband might be eavesdropping outside her door. Desire rekindled, anger melting, she could barely contain herself. Suddenly all bets were off. She was, after all, carrying his baby; the least she could do was hear him out.

"You have no idea what's happened to me," Alex rasped. "Please, Emily, you've got to let me explain—and not over the phone." The anguish in his voice was almost enough for her to forgive him on the spot. "I need to see you."

Emily was about to make a date against her better judgment when her studio door flew open. In a fearful reflex she hung up the phone, then calmly lifted her head and saw Charles standing in the doorway.

"Jesus, it's midnight," he grumbled. "Who was that?"

"Vanessa. Boyfriend problems." She rolled her eyes for effect, hoping that she had dodged a bullet and that Alex would have the sense not to call back tonight.

"Who are you, Ann Landers?"

"Why aren't you sleeping?" she parried.

"I started to doze off"—Charles ambled into the room, one hand in his pajama pocket—"but all of a sudden I was wide awake again." His penetrating stare made her squirm; she felt as though he was looking right through her, into the backrooms of her brain where all her secrets were kept. "Ran out of Ambien on my trip, so I wandered into your bathroom for that homeopathic sleep remedy you sometimes take. And look what I found in the wastebasket." In abracadabra fashion, his hand flew out of his pocket and produced Emily's EPT device.

"Oh…that," she said, too much in cover-up mode to rue the fact that her romantic ship had been torpedoed in the harbor.

"The dot's blue," he drawled. "According to the directions on the box, you're expecting, my darling." He peered at her. "So, were you ever planning to tell me?"

"I just found out a couple of hours ago, when you were in the shower. I guess I needed to live with the news for a night. I can't believe I'm pregnant." That much was true, which enabled her to state it convincingly.

"Well," he observed, "you don't seem all that overjoyed."

"Of course I am. Aren't you?"

"It's a rather unconventional way for a husband to find out, you must admit," Charles sulked. "Not that one should *always* be conventional, but when it comes to reproductive issues, it's probably a good idea, no?"

"Don't be upset," she said, casually closing her sketchbook as Charles approached. The last thing she needed was for him to see her erotic drawings. They would only fuel his suspicion; he would have to know he hadn't inspired them. Much to her relief, rather than come over to hug and kiss his pregnant wife, he stopped short and eyed her from ten feet, arms folded.

"Why the temper tantrum earlier?" he probed.

"I was sick, and all you could think of was whether I was pregnant," she frowned. "What's your excuse?"

Charles gave a shamefaced little smile. "I guess I *did* go a little Bela Lugosi on you. Sorry, my darling." All of a sudden he was giddy, as if the full impact of fatherhood just hit him. "I suppose this calls for a little champagne celebration."

"You promised you'd stop drinking if I got pregnant."

"When I became a *father*," he qualified, finally going over and kissing her brow. "I'll get the bubbly and see you in the bedroom. I guess you *were* ovulating that night after all," he gleamed, and then off he went.

Her creative spree over for now, and her fate sealed, Emily tiredly rose from her chair. She blew out the candles and the room went dark.

◆   ◆   ◆

Alex spent the wee hours of the morning tickling out "In the Wee Small Hours of the Morning" over and over on the End of the World's tinny upright. His mind brooded in circles trying to divine whether Emily's abrupt hang-up had been triggered out of necessity or anger. Winnie had gone home hours ago, and who knew when Billy would resurface? His loneliness and depression growing more abysmal with each rendition, he stopped playing and shut the piano cover over the keys. Rising from the bench, he glanced at his cell phone to see if his mother had called; thankfully there were no messages. Once she discovered he was AWOL, she would surely whip herself into frenzy, maybe call the police, knowing her. She would be even more irate when he informed her he wouldn't be flying to North Carolina. Not the answer…. Much as he craved a comfortable bed, there would be no peace at the townhouse. He couldn't endure another motherly harangue, not with both of them in hair-trigger mode. Wasted by failure, raw-nerved from lack of sleep, his future in darkness, he couldn't decide as he shuffled out of the club whether to check into the nearest cheap hotel or find a cup of strong coffee.

Apart from the usual litter swirling around, the street was empty—eerily so, like a ghost town. Neither soul nor vehicle was in sight. Hadn't he parked his motorcycle directly in front of the club? Panic rising as he got his bearings, he glanced down the windswept street in one direction, then in the other. Nothing! As the horror of his bike's theft began to register and spread throughout his body, to every extremity, filling his lungs with bile, re-shattering his heart, reducing him to the brink of tears, Alex glared up at the heavens and unleashed a primal scream. "*Fuuuuuuck!*" The obscenity echoed throughout the cavernous neighborhood, but not even God seemed to hear it. He went limp, too despondent to race around in frothing pursuit of the culprit. His cherished symbol of freedom and self-expression, the only inspired thing he had ever created from scratch, was gone forever. Probably in New Jersey by now with a new paint job. The identity theft was complete; he was at rock bottom.

Trudging around the corner, he bumped squarely into a burly sanitation worker. "Sorry," he mumbled, but the dusty man, who reeked of trash, hardly noticed. He was gazing raptly through the metal grates of an electronics store. Dozens of TV sets glowed and blared with the same image: an eye-popping commercial, featuring three masked supermodels in tight-fitting, fetish-oriented leather outfits and bull whips. The S&M flavor made Alex take notice. As the camera zoomed in on their faces, the girls threw off their masks one by one, to show how terrific their eyes looked.

"Feel the power!" purred the blonde.

"Feel the danger!" beckoned the brunette.

"Feel the Lash!" hissed the black model, making like a poisonous snake.

In menacing unison the leggy dominatrices declared: "Feel the Lash! The wicked new lash liner from Cresslon!"

The trio snapped their whips, and the Cresslon logo lit up in neon. An oiled, rippling male chest flashed supine on the screen, to be stepped on by a long, slender leg in a stiletto heel. Then another. Then another. *Boom, boom, boom.*

Alex glanced at the dumbstruck sanitation worker and wondered if his own face bore the same expression. "Who cares about eye makeup when ya got legs like that!" marveled the garbage man, as Alex kept gaping at the commercial.

"Don't be a slave to fashion!" exhorted the ebony beauty.

"Lash out at the world!" enjoined the brunette.

"It's time," said the breathy blonde, "to feel the Lash! Feel the Lash Eye Makeup, from Cresslon!"

Alex was about to turn away from the TV-set montage when a handsome, silver-haired, well-tailored man appeared on the screen, the Manhattan skyline as his backdrop.

"I'm Frank Shea," the apparition said, in a deep commanding voice. "I may be CEO of Cresslon Cosmetics"—to Alex, it seemed as if he was looking straight at him—"but *you're* in charge!"

The commercial ended with the models whipping the Cresslon logo for all they were worth, and suddenly Alex's stagnant universe exploded in a Big Bang, propelling every atom into the blue beyond. Out of his dense black hole he had fallen into a wormhole and was barreling through time and space, defying the immutable laws of pantyhose. Newton had his apple, Alex his TV commercial!

"Cosmetics!" he shouted, startling the garbage man out of his reverie, his stolen motorcycle completely forgotten. "For the legs! *Cosmetics for the legs*!"

"What are you on, kid?"

Whatever he was on, he began sprinting down the block chasing a taxi, punching his cell phone, dimly aware that it was possible he had lost all his marbles, that he had finally gone over the edge. But he was on fire and couldn't dial fast enough. "Gunther...Yeah, I know what time it is...Listen, keep the plant running one more week...No, I'm *not* coming down there...Don't argue with me...*Dammit*, Gunther! I will personally fly down there and cut your *nuts* off if you even *think* of closing that plant!"

9

Wild Pitch

Frank Shea propped his legs on the limousine jump seat and with a toothpick dislodged the last bits of sausage from his capped teeth. He had forsaken eggs because of their high cholesterol, but couldn't wean himself away from the smoky savor of cured meat, especially the way they seasoned it at the Regency Hotel.

Every morning he conducted power breakfasts there, plotting with his Cresslon lieutenants, conferring with his speech writers, swapping stories with fellow CEOs with whom he shared reciprocal directorships. But mainly he went to the Regency to be seen breaking croissant with the mayor, the cardinal, the NFL commissioner, a Hollywood mogul, a TV anchorman, an Ivy League university president, a leading feminist, a former secretary of state, and other prestigious citizens whose goodwill he cultivated. For most executives, heading the world's largest cosmetics company would be the pinnacle; for Frank Shea it was a base camp from which to scale heights beyond the reach of the corporate ladder. When he wasn't running Cresslon, he was chairing business round tables, presidential task forces, public philanthropies—collecting favors, celebrity friends, and useful humanitarian awards in the process.

A few years ago, consumed by political ambition, he had contemplated running for the U.S. Senate, with an eye on the presidency, figuring it was time for voters to stop electing political hacks and choose a businessman instead. Ad agency after ad agency was vetted until he found one that "insisted" he star in his own Cresslon TV commercials. At first he feigned camera phobia, only to succumb dutifully to the pressure and quietly quadruple Cresslon's advertising budget. Soon the whole country was exposed to dynamic Frank Shea speaking on behalf of the American woman—not only about their beauty and cosmetics, but about empowering them: from his company's impressive record of hiring female executives, to sponsoring breast cancer research, to setting up shelters for battered women.

As a business gambit the campaign was effective; as a political trial balloon it never got off the ground. Cosmetics and politics, those two fields of illusion, didn't mesh in the public mind. Shea took his disappointment in stride. Business, after all, was where the real power was. He continued to be invited to Camp David and Bohemian Grove; presidents still asked him for advice; he had a eight-figure salary, a shit-load of cheap stock options, and a small fleet of Gulfstreams at his disposal.

Not too shabby for a street kid from the Bronx, he reminisced in the plush quiet of his company limo, looking back for once instead of forward.

Fresh out of Fordham on a baseball scholarship, he had spurned a minor-league contract, knowing he couldn't hit a curve ball and would never make the majors. Making it in the corporate arena, on the other hand, was less a matter of pure talent than of cutthroat maneuvering and presenting a good image, and when Shea took an entry-level job in the mail room of a small ad agency, he knew he wouldn't be stuck there for long. Two years later, he became the agency's youngest account executive. When one of their clients, Venus Chocolate, needed a sales manager to drive it to the moon, it took a colossal gamble on the young marketing whiz. U.S. Foods, the country's largest purveyor of processed food-stuffs, subsequently acquired Venus and named Shea its executive VP in charge of all junk foods. When the multinational behemoth Galaxy Corporation gobbled up U.S. Foods in a hostile takeover and spat out its management like watermelon seeds, Shea, the sole survivor, was appointed the CEO of U.S. Foods. By his mid-forties, he had risen to the top of the artificial food chain—on such a fast track, detractors claimed, that he had never held a job long enough to be tested.

Boardroom intrigue could take an ambitious executive only so far. Back in those days, the real power people hung out at 21, where practically every night Shea schmoozed with the movers and shakers of New York—including Jacob Kress, the elderly patriarch of Cresslon. Kress quickly saw in Shea the driven, charismatic tiger Cresslon needed to claw past Revlon to the top of the cosmetics heap. A child prodigy concert pianist from a well-to-do banking family who had survived a Nazi concentration camp before immigrating to America to start a new life, Kress normally hired only Jews for top positions. However, call it moxie or chutzpah, Shea had it in ample doses, and the trusting old man recruited him to join the Cresslon family, despite widespread warnings from his inner circle that Shea, the closet anti-Semite, was out to hijack the company. Kress announced his desire to retire in three years and said his successor would be chosen from among three candidates, one of them Frank Shea. It took just a year and a half for Jacob

Kress to retire and place his life's work in Shea's custody. A year later, the old man died. The day after the funeral, Shea began cleaning house, replacing the old Semitic order with his hand-picked Irish mafia.

That was fourteen years ago. *Long enough to be tested. Fuck the critic! Teddy Roosevelt had it right: "It's not the critic who counts. The credit belongs to the man who is actually in the arena, whose face is marred by dust and sweat and blood...not those cold and timid souls who know neither victory nor defeat." Fuck the critic.*

As Shea's limo approached the curb on West Fifty-Seventh Street, he snapped his toothpick in half and deposited it in the ashtray, then sprayed his mouth numb with Binaca. Breakfast was officially over. For the first time in years, he had eaten alone, plotting his survival.

He resembled anything but a hunted man as he shot out of the limousine and strode briskly toward the Cresslon Building, a black-glass monolith he had erected seven years ago to cement his legacy. At sixty-three, he was still a vortex of vigor and vanity. His protruding blue eyes darted from side to side, his long arms swung with purpose. Though he received his inspiration from Teddy Roosevelt, his mop of sandy hair was Kennedyesque, tossing luxuriously in the breeze. By the stodgy corporate standards he adhered to and at the same time despised, he was a dapper dresser: double-vented Italian suit; silk shirt with monogrammed French cuffs; gold cufflinks; matching paisley tie and handkerchief; glistening alligator shoes; and the best facelift and capped teeth money could buy. He hadn't gotten to the top by being understated. Confidence had always been his ace in the hole; confidence, he hoped, would save his hide.

Revenues were flat, profits down. The racy "Feel the Lash" ad campaign, designed to catapult the company out of its doldrums, was bombing amid uncomplimentary fanfare. The Enron, Tyco, and WorldCom scandals had made his appearance in the commercials a distinct negative; heads of big corporations were now seen as greedy pirates. The price of Cresslon stock had hit a three-year low while Shea's compensation had hit an all-time high, which was why Lester "the Jackal" Ruby had over the past few weeks quietly purchased 7 percent of the company in the open market. Ruby had told the financial press that this was to be a passive investment, but nobody believed him. A bitter proxy fight was brewing. True to his moniker, the Jackal was always gunning for troubled companies and vulnerable CEOs, and the post-9/11 corporate carnage had him on a feeding frenzy. Only now, this raper of companies and elusive object of insider-trading probes was, incredibly, posing as a moralist, preaching about accountability, ethics, and the evils of self-dealing. Moreover, this latest foray of Ruby's had the tinge of personal animus. Ruby and Shea had once vied like warring stags—circumcised versus uncircumcised—for the affections of a former beauty queen. They heartily despised each other on personal, business, and even religious grounds. Shea seethed whenever Ruby appeared on "Page Six" with another glamorous woman—the latest, Vanessa Muss, had served a brief stint as his own secret midnight concubine. One of his scraps, but still it irked him. Whatever Frank Shea had, Lester "the Jackal" seemed to want it. Cresslon, with its high-fashion, socially conscious image, was the ideal crown jewel for a bottom-feeding gangster like Ruby, who had everything money could buy except respectability.

Looking like a dandy but feeling like a brawler, Shea shoved through the revolving door and headed for the elevator. He had become too complacent of late. Outside interests—especially of the female kind—had seduced him from the day-to-day conduct of the business and made him unpopular with certain puritanical stockholders, who were demanding that he forego the glitz and return to the fundamentals that had made Cresslon the largest cosmetics company on the planet. A hostile buyout would put tens of millions in his pocket, but it would also take him out of the loop. Power, perks, and action were his addictions—what he lived for. Without them he would be living a useless existence in somewhere like Palm Beach. *Time to get back in the arena. Once you're out of the game, nobody wants you.*

By the time the elevator reached the fiftieth floor, Shea's ruddy Celtic face was twisted in a pugilist's sneer. Marching through the executive reception area, a canyon of medieval tapestries and marble busts, he was appalled by the scruffy sight of young man in jeans and a motorcycle jacket, his blazing eyes scorching what looked like Internet printouts. When the creature glanced up at him, Shea, resisting the urge to bawl him out for his slovenly appearance, quickened his stride down the hallway and into the alcove of his secretarial bulldog, Mrs. Donovan.

"Who's the punk camped out in the reception area?" he barked on his way into his office.

She rose and followed him. "He insists on seeing you. Won't go away."

"Spray him for lice and call security," Shea ordered, lighting a cigarette.

"Says he's chairman of"—Mrs. Donovan consulted her notes—"Halaby Hosiery. I tried to get rid of him, sir, but he was so persistent that I wasn't sure what to do. Claims his father is a pantyhose pioneer and…"

"Pantyhose?" Shea snapped. "Haven't you heard, Donovan? We sell cosmetics. The Jackal wants to cut my balls off and stuff them down my throat, and some pubescent urchin off the street wants to sell me stockings! Jesus Christ! Throw his ass out!"

To kill time until the business day began, Alex had holed up in the twenty-four-hour Internet café across the street from the Cresslon Building, drinking espresso after espresso to keep awake and surfing the Net for whatever he could find on Cresslon and Frank Shea. Through the osmosis of living in New York, he was vaguely aware of Shea's existence as one of the city's hot-shot CEO celebrities, as well as an incurable publicity hound. The photos on the Net said it all: Shea posing proudly with the standard local icons, from the Yankee infield to The Donald to the mayor—but all that was old news. Alex had been so cocooned in his own problems of late that he was oblivious to what was happening in the world, including the fact that Frank Shea and his company had just recently become front-page news. Cresslon was in play. Lester "the Jackal" Ruby, the infamous corporate raider, was in the throes of a hostile takeover bid. As Alex dug further into the facts, reading the history backward from Cresslon's falling stock price, to Shea being accused of losing his golden touch, to Ruby's and Shea's ancient hatred for each other—scrolling so fast through cyberspace that he actually became winded—the seeds of a game plan began to germinate. It all seemed eerily perfect, too perfect. In his desperate, sleep-deprived condition, could he trust himself? Was his idea outlandishly brilliant, or was he being delusional? Feeling precarious as he printed the last article and paid the tab, he glanced up at the TV: CNBC's talking heads were debating which mogul would prevail. Outside, he passed a newsstand and saw the story plastered all over the tabloids. Suddenly the name Cresslon was everywhere, and the idea began to build just how serendipitous Ruby's hostile takeover bid might be for him. Was it possible that he, Alex Halaby, was about to become an integral player in this corporate brouhaha? When a "Feel the Lash" commercial being shot in the lobby of the Cresslon Building enabled him to use the confusion to slip past security and into the elevator, he wondered if Lady Luck was finally smiling on him.

Now, planted outside Frank Shea's office, he chided himself for his paralysis moments ago. The man had looked him straight in the eye, and what had Alex Halaby done? Sat there like a stump. With *l'esprit de l'escalier* tormenting him, reminding him of all he might have said, he churned for another bite at the apple. When Mrs. Donovan returned, he eagerly rose to his feet, only to be chilled by her bellicose expression.

"He can't see you without an appointment," she said. "How did you get up here?"

"Look, I know this isn't exactly the right protocol…"

"That's an understatement."

"If Newton had to make an appointment with the apple," Alex said, forcing a grin, "he never would have discovered gravity."

"You should put on a suit, if you own one," she said sternly, "and take whatever bright idea you have to our New Ventures Group."

"I don't have time to go through channels. And frankly," Alex said, brandishing his Internet reports, "neither does your boss."

"Well, that's how things get done around here. Now, are you leaving, or am I calling security?"

Could things get any worse if he got arrested? "Better call security," he said, and then sprinted past the horrified secretary and straight into the chairman's office. Enter David—with slingshot and red eyes.

Shea, seated behind his gargantuan kidney-shaped steel desk, recoiled in alarm. Undaunted, Alex extended his hand across the sleek, polished expanse, but Shea ignored it and roared at Mrs. Donovan, who was now quivering in the doorway.

"Call the guards! Get this crazy bastard out of here!"

"Since it looks like this will be a short meeting," Alex began, way too buzzed to be nervous, "let me cut to the chase. Your stock is at a three-year low. 'Feel the Lash' is underperforming, and you're about to lose your company to a guy you hate. Cresslon needs a miracle. Well, Mr. Shea, here it is: Cosmetics for the Legs."

Shea ominously flicked his cigarette into an ashtray.

"OK, OK," Alex said quickly, his mind whirling with all he had read about Shea on the Net, "let the Jackal have Cresslon. Who cares, right? That'll put what, twenty, thirty mill in your pocket? It's just that I can't picture you on the sidelines, watching Lester Ruby getting *your* fifth-row seats at the Oscars, *your* dinner invitations to the White House, *your* foursomes with Tiger Woods…"

While making this frantic pitch, Alex took visual snapshots of the posh but sterile office. Everything, from the steel desk to the abstract paintings to the ultramodern sofas and geometric area rug, was a slick silver-gray. For a fashion-conscious company offering a myriad of lipstick shades and eye shadows, the monochromatic scheme struck him as odd, but not nearly as odd as the antique grand piano off in the corner. That anomaly seemed to be the office's only touch of warmth and character. As Alex slid his business card across the desk—*we're equals, two CEOs having a meeting*—he noticed that the wall behind Shea was covered with photographs of Shea posing with celebrities, including Bill Clinton and both Bushes. There was a framed quotation of Teddy Roosevelt. No pictures of family to humanize the place, as far as Alex could tell.

"I've never seen a piano in an office," he said—a feeble stab at breaking the ice. "What's the significance? Do you play?"

The cosmetics baron tore up Alex's business card and dropped the pieces into a Lucite wastebasket. "Jacob Kress, the company's founder, was a concert pianist before he fled Nazi Germany," he said, "and you have thirty seconds."

"Oh, come on, Mr. Shea, it takes a big idea to stave off a hostile takeover and certainly more than thirty seconds to…"

"Security comes in thirty seconds. If I don't hear anything earth-shattering in that time, I'm throwing the book at you."

Alex's brain locked. Not even a super-savvy ad man like Shea could lay out a brand new marketing concept in thirty seconds, especially one so far-fetched and half-baked, with no facts to bolster his case…not under these kangaroo-court conditions, however self-imposed. Audacity had gotten him this far, and this was no time to change tactics. "You want to know what you can get in thirty seconds, Mr. Shea? Here's what you can get in thirty seconds." He stormed over to the piano, prepared to go up in flames of glory.

Flashing his best entertainer's smile, wryly telling himself that seventy-two virgins awaited him on the other side, Alex began to play the rapid preamble to Gilbert and Sullivan's "The Major General." The antique instrument was out of tune, a couple of notes were dead, but the action was easy and Alex felt remarkably relaxed under the circumstances. Shea's eyes practically popped out of his head as his weird visitor began rattling off Tom Lehrer's lyrics:

> There's antimony, arsenic, aluminum, selenium,
> And hydrogen and oxygen and nitrogen and rhenium,
> And nickel, neodynium, neptunium, germanium,
> And iron, americium, ruthenium, uranium.
> Europium, zirconium, lutetium, vanadium,
> And lanthanum and osmium and astatine and radium,
> And gold and protactinium and idium and gallium
> And iodine and thorium and thulium and thallium…

"I hope you're taking notes, Mr. Shea," Alex chirped, while playing the merry interlude, "'cause there's going to be a quiz afterward."

> There's holium and helium and hafnium and erbium,

And phosphorus and francium and fluorine and terbium,
And manganese and mercury, molybdenum, magnesium…

Somewhere between "dysprosium" and "sodium," Alex glanced at his grim audience and almost broke down in futility. It had seemed like a brilliant gambit at the outset, but now he wondered if he had gone completely mad. He was a buffoon, not a businessman—making a mockery of himself—and yet it would be infinitely worse if he quit in midstream. Imagining Emily watching him, spurring him on with her mellow smile and soothing green eyes, he persevered, knowing that his parents would be aghast at the way he was representing them and their company. His only hope was that underneath Shea's sneering upper lip lurked a sense of humor, a musical soul, or at least a manly appreciation of his *cojones*.

When Alex finished his flawless performance, Shea snuffed out his cigarette and looked like he was about to do the same to the piano player. Seeing no upside in sticking around, Alex gave a half-hearted bow and beat his escape through Mrs. Donovan's alcove. He marched through the reception area, past two onrushing security guards. At the elevator bank he hit the down button, feeling strangely elated, praying that the elevator would arrive before the guards doubled back and apprehended him. The doors opened, but just as he darted into the cabin a meat-hook of a hand grabbed his arm and yanked him back. In what seemed like one fluid motion, the guards roughly pressed him up against the wall, cuffed him, and dragged him off toward an ominous concealed door that looked as if it led to the bowels of the building, no doubt to a torture chamber.

The sound of scurrying footsteps caused the guards to stop and turn. It was Mrs. Donovan. "Mr. Shea wants another word with him," she told the guards.

◆   ◆   ◆

"Jesus, Mary, and Joseph!" exclaimed Flora, when Alex entered the townhouse later that morning. She took in his unkempt appearance with a mixture of relief and disgust. "Your mother thinks you're floating facedown in the East River!"

"Actually, I'm floating on Cloud Nine!" He leaned over the desk and gave Flora a loud kiss on the forehead. The fact that she angrily pushed him away didn't faze him in the least. "Is Dad back?"

"They got home an hour ago. He's resting up in his room. Your mother is livid."

Alex bounded up three flights of stairs to his parents' bedroom, but before entering he stopped to catch his breath and get his bearings. Ever so gently, he opened the bedroom door and peeked inside. The blinds were drawn and Harry was asleep, propped up on pillows, looking so peaceful that Alex couldn't resist edging into the shadowy room to be closer to him. He was relieved that his mother wasn't there, just the black private nurse off in the corner reading *Cosmo*. Alex gave the woman an affable smile and quietly approached the bed. On those rare occasions when Harry used to nap, it was with a pugnacious expression and balled fists at his sides—a repose which his son had always found comical. Today, Harry's visage was serene, his hands limp. As Alex watched his father's large stomach rise and fall, the accumulated exhaustion of the past weeks—especially the past few hours—hit him like he'd been smashed on the head with an iron weight. Suddenly he could barely keep his own eyes open. A mere three weeks of chasing business and he was wrecked. How had his father done it all these years, on top of building an organization and a plant and a product line from scratch, with no support system? Looking down at the sleeping warrior, Alex felt humbled, in the company of greatness.

The door creaked open. Grace, white and drawn and ready for battle, stepped in, and Alex immediately felt himself shrinking.

"I've been worried *sick!*" she hissed, her decibel level kept in check by the sight of her slumbering husband. "Gunther said you called him in the middle of the night ranting like a madman! Where have you *been* all night?"

"Ever hear of Cresslon?"

Grace heaved a sigh. "The cosmetics company?"

"And so are we about to be."

She studied her son's worn face. "Oh, Alex, I think the stress has been too much for you. Have you slept at all? What a harebrained idea!"

"Cresslon's CEO Frank Shea didn't think it was harebrained." He paused long enough for this information to register on his mother's enameled face, then began whispering in rapid fire some the ideas he had rattled off in Shea's office less than an hour ago. Strangely enough, he had been more articulate and less nervous then than he was now. "Imagine," he said, "pantyhose marketed like cosmetics, the colors tying in with foundations and eye shades. Tights to match lipsticks and nail polishes…fishnets with an eyelash design…colors listed as 'matte' and 'glossy.' High-end stockings sold in tubes shaped like lipstick or in old-fashioned compacts. Products to make old legs look young, to revitalize pantyhose, to bring back glamour…"

Grace stared at him like he was speaking gibberish. The nurse looked even more nonplussed.

"Don't you see, Mom? Cresslon desperately needs something new to boost its stock price and poison Lester Ruby's takeover bid. Their sense of urgency is almost as great as ours! With their name and distribution, the potential is mind-boggling. Huge!"

"For Chrissake, speak up!" It was Harry, and Alex whirled around.

"The doctor said no business," Grace warned them both.

"You met with Frank Shea?" Harry demanded.

Withholding good news, Alex figured, was as bad for his father's heart as burdening him with bad news; besides, he was aching to tell him—he was so excited. He had waited his whole life for such a moment, to earn his father's respect as an equal. "Yes, with *the* Frank Shea. This morning, in his office."

"How'd you manage that?" said Harry.

"If I told you, you wouldn't believe it."

"Goddammit, tell me what happened!"

"Let's just say that my presentation got his attention."

"You saw him looking like that?" Grace exclaimed.

"Quiet!" Harry barked, and kept grilling his son: "Shea actually likes this cockamamie idea?"

"He hasn't said no. We're having drinks tonight at the Four Seasons to discuss particulars."

"You'll be wearing a suit, I hope," said Mother.

"I'm gonna be there," croaked Harry, attempting to slide out of bed, but the nurse, surprisingly nimble for a person of her girth, was there to block him. "Out of my way! I'm not a cripple!" Harry roared.

"Sit still, Harry," said Grace. "You're not going anywhere."

"Shea'll make mincemeat of him!"

"It's *my* cockamamie idea," said Alex, slapping his CEO business card on the bed to complete the bloodless coup d'état. While his parents gaped at his card, he shuffled numbly down the hall to his bedroom. He closed the door behind him and yanked the curtains to block out the sunlight. He peeled off his clothes, showered, shaved, brushed, gargled, and slipped into fresh cotton PJs. For the first time in weeks he could bask in something positive, however nebulous at this stage, and experience the luxury of not having to rush to an airport or a meeting, of lying in a familiar sea of goose-down instead of a cheap hotel bed. Nothing pressing for seven hours. How glorious! His limbs melted, the inner noise quieted, he began to doze...

His eyes popped open with a jolt, chest churning, mind racing, in the same urgent mode he had been in Shea's office. No wonder Emily had hung up on him! A month of no communication after their glorious night—she had to think him the scum of the earth. How could he have let things slide this long without telling her what had happened? He couldn't wait another minute! He needed to explain himself, explain that he was doing something big with his life, fighting for his family, for her. She was only a few blocks away. He had to get things on track, tell her how he felt—before it was too late. He flew out of bed and began getting dressed in fresh business clothes, selecting his favorite red power tie. He had the rest of his life to sleep.

10

Million Dollar Baby

Recent events and brutal exhaustion had skewed Alex's perspective on what constituted normal behavior. Compared to storming Frank Shea's office looking like an al Qaeda bomber, staking out an apartment building in a blue suit seemed rather civilized. After two hours he continued to pace the cobblestone sidewalk, peering across Fifth Avenue at Emily's residence, waiting for her to appear. She had to at some point. Once she saw him and he explained everything, her old feelings would return. They *had* to; such mutual attraction was beyond either of their control.

Between all the early-morning espressos at the Internet café and the two cokes he had consumed on his current vigil, he was so hopped up on caffeine that it harked back to his old cocaine highs, complete with itching, paranoia, and chattering teeth. Vaguely aware that he might be borderline psychotic and could very well come unglued in front of Frank Shea tonight if he didn't go home and get some shut-eye, he kept trying to remind himself why he was here. After weeks of sensory deprivation, the memories of Emily had grown fainter; conjuring up a vivid sense of her in his mind's eye was more and more like trying to grab hold of a moonbeam. The images were fading fast, as if their wonderful night had scarcely happened, which only heightened his desperation to see her.

The cokes were pressing on his bladder. Somewhere at the bottom of the stairs behind him beckoned the Central Park Zoo's men's room, but after investing a good part of the morning waiting for Emily to show, and with the prime window of lunchtime approaching, he didn't dare leave his post.

Minutes later, however, the pressure was unbearable. He was about to rush down the stairs to relieve himself, when Emily, clad in a peach blazer and white jeans, emerged from the building and began strolling downtown. Was she a mirage? He beat a parallel path to hers down the opposite sidewalk while trying to clear a path in his brain. Defying the red light, he darted across the avenue. The clop of his onrushing footsteps caused Emily to turn. At first glance she didn't recognize him, but then she did a double-take and with a look of terror turned away and quickened her stride.

"My father had a heart attack," he panted, as he caught up to her.

"I'm sorry," she said politely, not slowing.

"Seriously! He almost died!"

"Is he okay?" Her tone was clipped.

"He's fine, recovering at home." Alex fished a business card out of his wallet, and when she shunned it, he began talking at breakneck speed. "I had to take over the company, which is about to go under. My father put all his faith in one customer, and the customer betrayed him. I've spent the past month flying around the country, doing absolutely everything and getting absolutely nowhere. But for the first time in my life I feel like I'm in my life, like this is what I was always meant to do. Sorry, Emily...I'm a little off-center. I've been up for two days trying to figure out how to save the company. And, knock wood, I think I found a way. Depending on how well this meeting goes tonight."

"You look different...very different." Whether she was frowning at his business suit and short haircut or at his strung-out aura, it was obvious that he had some serious repair work to do.

"Last time we were together, you said I was a dreamer," he rasped. "Well, now I'm doing something real. I'm taking control of things."

"Yes, and that's what I'm doing too," she said distantly.

At a loss as to how to get things on track, he gazed at her lovely face, breathed in her scent, and realized that her appeal, far from diminishing, was more potent to him than before. It had withstood the test of time. He had to get her alone, somehow, and kiss her again. "Have lunch with me."

"I'm booked."

"I'm free all afternoon." He placed his hand on her arm and gave her a tender, pleading squeeze. Emily shook him off.

"I'm not."

"Please, Emily, don't be this way. I didn't want to be out of touch, believe me, but..."

"That's not the issue. I'm married, Alex."

"I know, you keep saying that...but so much has happened," Alex flailed. "My life's been turned inside-out. My father needs me. Hundreds of people with families will be laid off unless I come through tonight. Our business is literally on the brink of ruin!"

"A lot has happened to me too," she said, directing her gaze straight ahead. Alex thought he saw her eyes glisten and her lips quiver.

"Tell me, Emily. What's happened? I want to know."

"Nothing!" she snapped. "My life doesn't concern you, and yours doesn't concern me." She came to a screeching halt and faced him squarely. "Look, it was a one-night thing. We lost ourselves."

"No, we found ourselves."

"It was a mistake. Don't compound it, get over it. Move on." Exasperated, she resumed her march downtown.

Alex followed her like a stray puppy. The pressure on his bladder was contributing mightily to his impatience and desperation. What kind of person was she, really, if she couldn't understand his predicament? "It was *more* than a one-night thing, Emily! It was the most incredible night of our lives. I love you!"

"You don't even *know* me. And I certainly don't know you. Suddenly you're a businessman? Supposedly running your father's company after telling me how much you hated it? Please, go away! Leave me alone!"

"Well, well," came a sultry female purr, "what a delicious surprise!" Merging from a side street, decked out in Coco Channel from head to toe and grinning from ear to ear, was the Baroness de Lapalisse.

"Hi, Claire!" Emily covered. "Look who I ran into. You remember…"

"I certainly do. Our Toastmaster General. How could I ever forget? Please, don't let me interrupt."

"You're not interrupting anything," Emily insisted.

"Emily," Alex said, "perhaps we can…"

"Gather 'round the piano and sing show tunes?" chirped Claire, as the two women came to a stop directly in front of Harry Cipriani's. "Are you joining us for lunch?" the baroness asked Alex, but then Emily provided the answer by disappearing through Cipriani's revolving door. "Well, I guess not. Pity. Ta-ta, Alex de Monk." She gave a little finger wave before following her friend inside, leaving Alex standing on the sidewalk, his heart and his bladder about to burst.

While Sergio the kissy maître d' ushered the girls to their center table, Emily glanced anxiously back at the door to make sure Alex wasn't going to follow them inside. She remembered the scene he had made at her birthday party. He was capable of anything. Composed as she tried to appear, his ambush had left her reeling. Perhaps she had reacted too coldly—but he had come on like a cyclone, looking crazed, jumpy, like he'd relapsed into his old drug habits. She hadn't heard a word from him in a month, and now he was calling her at home at midnight, accosting her on the street like a stalker a block from her building, with bloodshot eyes, looking like death. He *was* unstable! Even *Billy* had warned her about him. What a fool she'd been falling for Alex's phony idealism, his piano-playing charm, and that "You make my socks go up and down" nonsense! How many times had he used that line on other women? To think he was the father of her baby! Charles must never find out. No one must! It was a secret she would take to her grave.

Claire flagged down a waiter and cried out like a stevedore, "Two martinis."

"I don't want a martini," said Emily. "An Evian for me, please."

"Darling," Claire protested, "if you've ever needed a martini in your life, I think it's now, from the looks of you."

"But…"

"I insist. It's out of your hands."

"I can't."

"Why off the wagon all of a sudden?"

With the biggest smile she could muster, Emily went public: "I'm pregnant."

"My *God!*" shrieked Claire, turning heads. She gave Emily a theatrical hug. "I don't believe it! Charles must be out of his cotton-pickin' mind with joy, no?"

Emily nodded. "He's thrilled."

"It's just so wonderful! So amazing! Charles and I tried long and hard to get pregnant when we were married"—Claire cast Emily a sideways look—"and you know how fertile I am, four abortions and counting. I get pregnant when the wind blows up my skirt."

Catching her not so subtle drift, Emily slowly raised the menu over her eyes. "I can't believe we're actually starting a family. We're going out tonight to celebrate."

"By all means," said Claire, "you and Charles go cavort. And you and I will keep our dreamy Alex Monk *covert.*"

Down came the menu. "Please," Emily protested, with a laugh, "I just bumped into him on the street. Haven't seen him since he ruined my birthday party."

"What exactly did I witness out there? What were the two of you all lathered up about?"

"Lathered up? Honestly, Claire…"

"You both practically jumped out of your shoes when I showed up."

"I always jump out of my shoes when you show up. Alex was just telling me about his big career change."

"What big career change?"

"He's into pantyhose," Emily replied with a shrug.

"Whose pantyhose? Not yours, I hope," the baroness gleamed.

"Claire?"
"What?"
"Do you ever shut up?"

◆   ◆   ◆

Instead of sleeping, Alex spent the afternoon churning over how badly the long-awaited encounter with Emily had gone. He had practically attacked her. Seeing him as an obsessed businessman rather than as a motorcycle rebel no doubt had thrown her for a loop. But she had been different too, hadn't she? Closed off, fearful, in denial—not the breezy, affable Emily he had fallen in love with in Southampton. All he could think of as he approached the entrance to the Four Seasons was that he couldn't afford to screw up the meeting with Shea the way he had with Emily. He would try to fix things with her later. Right now, he needed to dig deep beyond his splitting migraine and muster every ounce of mental acuity left in his overtaxed vessel to save his company, his family, his future. In his mind, winning Emily and winning Cresslon were inexorably connected.

When he informed the slick-haired host in the Grill Room that he was meeting Mr. Shea for drinks, he was given VIP treatment and promptly escorted down a long hallway to the Pool Room, to an empty table abutting the square white-marble bubbling pool. He was relieved that Shea was late, which allowed him time to get his bearings, secure two Advils from the waiter and swallow them with a bracing aperitif, and soak up the tranquility around him. He looked around the legendary and uniquely spacious restaurant. The room was at least thirty feet high, with floor-to-ceiling windows. Elegant, airy window treatments with a geometrical motif complimented the modern design of the space. Six or seven towering palm trees marked the summer season and added to the feeling of a contemporary, secular cathedral—a place of worship for the powerful and mon-eyed. Alex noticed Jack Welch and Leslie Stahl sitting at one of the other poolside tables; NBA commissioner David Stern was off at the corner. The Four Seasons was a watering hole for tycoons, politicos, publishing bigwigs, and media celebrities. The rich and famous were pampered like members of an exclusive club; all others were treated with cold civility. Alex had a love-hate feeling toward the Four Seasons; he relished the cuisine and the luxury, but the pecking order always reminded him of his relative insignificance. Tonight, however, he was seated at one of the power tables, about to face off against one of America's most formidable businessmen. His own moxie and imagination had manifested this. The scent of power electrified him. This was where he belonged! Overmatched as he was, he was hell-bent on victory.

He saw Shea enter the dining room and glad-hand a local news anchor at a table by the entrance. The cosmetics king then briefly toured his realm, shaking hands with the various luminaries before joining his young guest. As Shea sat, Alex caught an asphyxiating whiff of his Bay Rhum cologne, as well as signs of his vanity that he hadn't noticed this morning in all the frenzy: facial tautness suggesting a lift; iron-gray roots in his sandy hair indicating a dye job; capped teeth.

"Sorry I'm late," Shea said, crushing Alex's hand as they clasped. He looked his young guest up and down, as if trying to reconcile his suit and tie with same person who had stormed his barricades that morning. "Punctuality is the courtesy of kings. Problem is, this king has a nasty little jackal nipping at his heels."

"How's it going?" Alex ventured.

"Ruby's an evil prick, but hell, that's what makes life interesting. One needs evil to showcase one's greatness. What would Churchill be without Hitler—a drunk! Gandhi without the British—a half-naked little wog! I know hundreds of leaders in business, the media, politics, religion, you name it. Many of them I met right here at the Four Seasons." Shea leaned close. "Let me give you some price-less advice: A year at the Four Seasons bar is worth an MBA from Harvard."

The two CEOs ordered drinks along generational lines: Shea a Glenfiddich on the rocks, Alex, buoyed by the affable beginning, a martini. Not that he planned to drink much of it; he'd had more than enough with the Advils, and sirens and red lights were already blaring and flashing in every corner of his body. His head was spinning and dangerously unfocused; he could barely think and was grateful when Shea dispensed with the small talk and got down to business.

"OK, you got your forum," he began, fondling an unlit cigarette. "But there's no piano to save you now. Tell me, how did this crazy idea come to you?"

"I was passing an electronics store and saw your 'Feel the Lash' commercial on three dozen TV sets. And, whammo, it hit me."

"Great ad. Problem is, only men watch the damned thing—not exactly our target market for eye makeup. Squandered a bloody fortune on that campaign."

"Don't be so sure, Mr. Shea. I saw it, and that alone could justify the expense," Alex said eagerly. "Like I said this morning, pantyhose and cosmetics are kissing cousins. Both are sold using subliminal promises of beauty, sexiness, romantic fulfillment. Both are sold side-by-side on the main floors of department stores. The connection is natural, the product tie-ins unlimited. Today, women either shun pantyhose altogether or buy it as a necessary evil. Remember when female legs used to be glamorous? Marketing pantyhose like cosmetics in a bold and sexy way can snap both industries out of their doldrums. Between Cresslon's name and distribution, and Halaby's manufacturing expertise, we can make some news."

"I get my best ideas when I shave," Shea mused. "Hard work followed by total relaxation: that's the formula for creativity, for tapping the subconscious."

Alex waited until he was sure nothing else was forthcoming. "I'm no expert on corporate takeovers—or on anything, really—but doesn't Cresslon need something new to crow about? If we do this right, the hype alone will drive up Cresslon's stock price and drive away the Jackal."

Shea seemed vaguely insulted by Alex's simplistic assessment. "Pantyhose is still a big market, even in this slovenly era," he grudgingly conceded, as the drinks arrived, "or I wouldn't be giving you the time of day. But novel ideas are a dime a dozen. There's the small matter of execution…." Shea stirred his swizzle stick for a long moment, during which time Alex remained attentively silent. "Tell me, how did a fellow your age become CEO?"

"Nepotism," Alex grinned.

"You comfortable with that?"

"Let's just say that a deal with Cresslon will go a long way to cure my self-worth hang-ups," he laughed. "My father, the company's founder, had a heart attack and retired on the spot."

"Must have a lot of faith in you. Where did you go to college?"

"Princeton."

Shea dismissed this with a wave of his hand. "Doesn't mean a thing."

"Never said it did. My father left high school at sixteen, and he's done better than most MBAs."

"I suppose he's calling the shots from bed?"

"Yeah," Alex sniggered, "he ordered me to barge into your office, unshaven, in blue jeans and a leather jacket, and rattle off the chemical elements on the piano. I was just following orders."

Shea issued a thin smile before turning serious. "I had my people run some down-and-dirty calculations on what Cresslon could do if we really got behind pantyhose. The numbers may scare you, may be too much for your little one-customer company to handle. Six, seven million dozen in the first year, in the U.S. alone, and growing from there."

Hiding his jubilant shock—this would not only save Halaby Hosiery from the gallows, but nearly double its size!—Alex struck a statesman's pose. "Precisely my point. Together we can become the biggest department store brand in the country."

Contemplatively, Shea sipped his scotch; he tapped his unlit cigarette several times on the table, obviously dying to smoke. "Why should the world's largest cosmetics company entrust a major program to a small outfit like yours? What's to prevent me from buying you drinks, picking your brain, and then cutting a deal with someone who knows what he's doing? Wright-Fit's CEO and I served on a couple of committees together. He belongs to my country club. We could make the deal on the putting green, and I could sleep nights knowing I'm in seasoned hands."

Alex felt like he had fallen from sunlight into dark, swirling water. The mere notion that Shea might hand his brainstorm to his father's nemesis on a silver platter assaulted his sense of justice, not to mention his sense of security.

"I have a cardinal rule," Shea expounded. "Never argue with success."

"Our company…"

"Is in deep shit. You think I didn't check you out? Though I really didn't have to. Your desperate performance this morning told me everything I need to know." Shea seemed almost irate now. "Your one and only customer is throwing you out."

"Only because my father's ethical and the buyer's a crook."

"Sounds like sour grapes to me."

"Look, Mr. Shea, while all the other hosiery companies went offshore after NAFTA, my father kept his manufacturing in the USA. Made in America—isn't that good PR? Wright-Fit makes everything in China!"

"Maybe *that's* why you aren't competing. Look, I applaud you for coming up with this interesting idea and bringing it to me. But it's basically a marketing gimmick—it's not as if you have a patent. Wright-Fit's eating you alive! Hell, your company might not even be around a year from now."

Alex felt pinned into a corner, not so much by Frank Shea as by life. Like a wounded bull with nothing to lose, he began to stir, ready to charge but not sure how or where. In an aggressive reflex he sipped his untouched martini, and as the cold liquid seared into his tongue, he realized that he was finished, that his brief forays into the romantic and business big leagues had met with resounding failure. Cresslon was gone. Emily was gone. And Alex Halaby, despite all the parental attempts over the years to prop him up with Choate and Princeton and a family business, had always been a nonentity. A loser from Aurora and destined to remain so.

"I'm not in the habit of backing losers," Shea underscored. "I'd be a goddamm fool to hitch my wagon to you."

The pressure in Alex's head was building like a blast furnace. Every synapse pulsed with hot contempt: for the odious corporate culture; for all the convention, tradition, and privilege that had dulled his senses for thirty years; for all that corrosive money and power that made kings out of hacks, queens out of barracudas, jacks out of jack-offs. So much depended on the luck of the draw. What had Frank Shea done to earn his position other than create his own hype? What had he built? The man couldn't carry Harry Halaby's jockstrap. For perhaps the first time in his life, Alex felt like a true have-not, and experienced the exhilaration of standing on moral high-ground; and when he finally blew, it was with the temerity of a world-class entrepreneur. "You're a goddamn fool if you *don't!* Wanna know why? *Me!* You need me, Mr. Shea."

"Don't you have things ass-backward? You're nothing but a cocky little punk who's been playing in Daddy's sandbox for, what is it, a month?"

"I'm the punk who's going to save your career. Who had the courage and imagination to blow past barriers. Risk arrest. Bring you the hottest idea ever to hit either of our industries! Sure, it's Daddy's sandbox, but I see past the sand. I see the possibilities. I'm a punk with vision!"

The irises of Shea's steely eyes dilated ever so slightly, as if recollecting some distant half-forgotten memory. But just as quickly he snapped out of it. "Nice speech, kid. You got testosterone, that's for sure."

"Well, I wish I could say the same of you! Going with those empty suits at Wright-Fit? How bland and mediocre is that!" Determination surged through every cell of Alex's body; his migraine had magically vanished. Win or lose, he had found his stride. "Nine-to-fivers sitting around the boardroom, wondering who ate the last Danish. They have no skin in the game. All they care about is holding onto their cherished little turfs and not making waves. I'm talking about starting a new fashion trend, Mr. Shea; changing the way women think about their legs! For this project to fly, it'll need energy, creativity, imagination! Already I've given you more ideas than they ever will."

Shea drew a breath as if about to speak, but Alex would not relinquish his hard-won momentum.

"Aren't you better off with a punk like me, who'll put himself and his company on the line twenty-four-seven? A hungry punk, just like the punk *you* used to be back when the mail room was your sandbox!"

At that critical moment, Shea's attention was diverted by someone approaching the table. His countenance turned morose. Resentful of the untimely interruption, Alex cast a dour glance at the intruder: a dapper semi-dwarf, bald as an egg, with a blazing gold tie and an unlit cigar as big as he was cocked out of his mouth. Alex almost leapt out of his chair. This was Lester Ruby, the man who inspired so much fear in corporate America. Alex had never imagined him to be such a pipsqueak.

"Hiya, Frank," said the Jackal, in an abrasively high-pitched, outer-borough accent. "Start packing up your office yet? I'll be redecorating, so you can take that flying saucer of a desk with you when you go."

"Look, Ruby…"

"Underestimating Frank Shea is what I call a really stupid career choice," Alex said, amiably jumping into the fray.

"Who's this?" Ruby chuckled. "Sorcerer's apprentice?"

"And for my first trick," said Alex, "I'm going to make your takeover disappear before your very eyes."

"Lester Ruby, shake hands with Alex Halaby," said Shea, with surprising zeal. "You're going to be sorry you ever met him."

Curling his upper lip like a toy rottweiler's at Alex's outstretched hand, Ruby said, "Keep my office warm for me, Frank. See you goys later."

Once the Jackal and his pair of upholstered henchmen had been escorted to their poolside table catty-corner from theirs, Shea grabbed Alex's forearm. His demeanor was calm but his grip vice-like. "I want every goddamn woman in the country wearing Cresslon pantyhose by Christmas." He smiled for public consumption, though his eyes burned with killer intensity. "I want our stock through the roof and Ruby choking on his vomit. Can you handle it?"

"You won't regret this!"

"Get a grip, kid, we're being watched." They shook hands, but Shea didn't let go. "I've gotten this far on my instincts," he said, as if trying to justify the impulsive decision he had just made, "and my instincts tell me this idea of yours is a winner. Normally, our people would spend a year doing market research, focus groups, and all that other cover-your-ass crap telling you what you already know, but I want to jump all over this baby now. I want to get it to the press!" With a flourish, he downed the rest of his Glenfiddich and slammed the jigger on the table. "'In any moment of decision…the worst thing you can do is nothing.' Teddy Roosevelt said that a hundred years ago, and it's even more valid today. Intelligence is knowing what to do when you don't know what to do—like playing Jacob Kress's old piano, or taking on the Jackal just now. It's time to shake things up, create a new tone around the company. I need warriors and scrappers around me, not ass-lickers with their fingers in the wind. Be at my office tomorrow morning, nine sharp, for a Cresslon pantyhose kick-off meeting. There's a ton of work to be done!"

It took all of Alex's self-control to keep from weeping on Shea's shoulder. "Perfect," he said, not knowing what else to say. He felt his rigid body begin ever-so-slowly to ease out of its ancient contraction. Now Halaby Hosiery had another problem, a delicious problem: how to handle Cresslon's six million dozen. Even if the plant ran full out—seven days a week, three shifts, like Seabiscuit down the home stretch—they would have to contract outside knitting and eventually acquire a second plant. It would be chaos, but nobody was better than rabid old Gunther at chasing production. Alex had done the impossible, with a most timely assist from an unlikely guardian angel: the Jackal!

Shea jabbed an index finger in Alex's chest and said sotto voce, "I take great pride in screwing people who screw me, and I'm sticking my neck way the hell out for you. Cross me and I'll cut your balls off!"

"I'll hand them to you myself, sir," said Alex, anxious now to beat his escape and proclaim the fabulous news to his parents before Shea changed his mind, and just as anxious to find Emily and show off his new plumage of success.

That opportunity came sooner than expected. As Shea peered toward the entrance, Alex followed his eyes and saw none other than Charles Lukes, smiling like a Cheshire cat. A step behind him and not smiling at all was Emily. Alex was so stunned to see them approach the table that he didn't notice Shea rising to his feet to greet them.

"Hey, Q-Tip!" Shea boomed. He embraced Emily and kissed her cheek.

"Hi, Dad." She saw Alex and blanched.

Dad? Alex's heart stopped beating altogether; for a millisecond he was technically dead.

"Frank!" Charles hailed. "We've got fabulous news!" Suddenly he noticed Alex politely standing, and his grin collapsed. "Why, if it isn't our own Gershwin."

"How do you two know each other?" Shea wanted to know.

"I was just about to ask you the same question," said Charles, casting Alex a withering look. "Halaby played at Emily's birthday party...and gave a truly memorable toast."

"You'd have known that if you'd come, Daddy," said Emily coldly, avoiding Alex's eyes.

"You miss a lot of things when you work for a living," said Shea. "You kids should emulate Alex here and try it sometime. He played his way right into a partnership with Cresslon. Anyway, so what's the big news?"

Emily's mouth did something odd, and she blinked furiously. "It can wait," she said, with a black look at Alex.

"Wait for what, Pumpkin?" said Charles.

"Better scram, kid," Shea told his new protégé, "this is family business. See you tomorrow."

"I assume this means you won't be playing at our Labor Day bash at the Ocean Club?" Charles drawled.

A crack had opened between two parallel universes; any minute there could be a nuclear explosion. "Nice to see you both again," Alex said cordially, but both Lukeses ignored his good-bye. As he slunk away, he overheard Charles proclaim his news:

"The thing of it is, Frank, I...I can't believe it. I'm going to be a father! Emily and I, well, we managed to ring the old bell after all."

Alex banged into a waiter. Entrees crashed to the floor. The only person who seemed to notice was Lester Ruby, who from across the pool was laughing with sadistic delight.

11

Fireworks

Feeling sucker-punched, unable to revel in his business triumph or plan one minute into the future of the company, Alex caught a cab outside the Four Seasons, barked out directions to the driver, and brooded all the way to Brooklyn. His need for sleep was suddenly eclipsed by his need to talk to Billy, who for all his warts at least knew all the players in this dicey drama. Say what you want about Billy, he had an eerie staying power.

Inside, the club had a real-life end-of-the-world feeling, with just a couple of barflies and a doom-like ambience that had nothing to do with the décor. Billy was upstairs sleeping off last night's beating and whatever else he needed to sleep off. Thirty minutes and three shots of tequila later, Alex's head was spinning along with everything else in his life as he improvised some slow blues on the piano. Winnie and a couple of cute waitresses were hanging at the bar, a finger snap away, but he was way beyond saloon camaraderie now as he tried to process all that had happened to him in one day.

Emily's hang-up and strong-arm behavior on Fifth Avenue now made perfect sense. It had to be the pregnancy. Either the poor thing was embarrassed and wanted to get on with her life or was bummed out at the thought of being irrevocably bound to Charles Lukes. Or maybe he, Alex, was the father! It was not beyond the realm of possibility. The way the passions had flowed that night, a baby would only be fitting. The prospect of a messy scandal might have put her into a state of terror. Maybe she was looking for some kind of reassurance from him. And how did he reassure her? By vanishing for a month and then ambushing her like a madman.

When he recalled her icy demeanor at the Four Seasons, he grew sick with remorse. One minute he's sleeping with her and proclaiming his commitment to a carefree lifestyle, the next he's doing a deal with her father like some kind of sneaking, corporate wolf. She had to think it was all premeditated. What a mercenary bastard she must think him to be, going to bed with her and then getting into bed with her father!

He stopped playing and eyed the four shot glasses on the piano—the Four Horseman Lineup—three of which were empty. He downed the last shot, concentrating on the slow burn all the way down to his stomach. Could he be blamed for being just a little crazed and preoccupied? Wasn't a guy with a sick father, who was on the brink of losing his family business, entitled to a little slack? And for that matter, how mentally stable could Emily be—the daughter of an egomaniacal womanizer and a mother who'd been ground into pulp. For all he knew, Emily might not be sure *who* fathered her child! Maybe he had misjudged her, idealized her to quench his emotional neediness. Maybe it was the best thing all around to let sleeping desires lie. She was married and pregnant! What other signs did he need to realize he was well out of it? Even the idea of his paternity withered in the face of deductive reasoning. Women of Emily's ilk didn't get knocked up by men other than their husbands, and he should count his lucky stars for that. If Shea took great pride in screwing people who screwed him, imagine what he'd do to an upstart vendor who screwed, and possibly impregnated, his married daughter…. So why, even through the thick haze of exhaustion and inebriation, did he have the distinct sense that he could never get her out of his system, that this wasn't over by a long shot and was somehow destined to end in tragedy?

Billy emerged from his upstairs lair holding an open bottle of Beck's in one hand and a handkerchief smeared with dried blood in the other, shuffling like an old man. "How was your day, darling?" he asked, through his bruised, puffy face. His voice was almost gone.

Alex's "day" had begun roughly thirty-eight hours ago. He hadn't slept since Dallas. "I cut a deal to save my business."

"What deal?"

"With none other than Frank Shea."

"Emily's father?" Billy's pallid face collapsed. "But he's in the cosmetics business."

"Now he's in the cosmetics-for-legs business."

Billy considered this before smirking, "Boy, you're good. How long have you been concocting this little scheme?"

"When Charles and Emily showed up at our table, I almost fell over."

"Yeah, riiiiight. Like a hungry little opportunist like you doesn't know who's who and what's what. Like it's some kind of cosmic coincidence you're toasting the fair Emily one minute and romancing her not-so-fair father the next."

"Trust me, Billy, I had no idea Frank Shea was Emily's father. You never told me."

"Anyway, man, who cares! You hit the big leagues. *Now* maybe you can lend me some money." Billy grabbed the tip glass off the piano and thrust it under Alex's nose. "*Baksheesh!*"

Alex had walked right into it, and he couldn't completely ignore Billy's face and the image of those thugs who had battered it. Halaby Hosiery's de facto CEO didn't have signature rights on company checks, but he figured that in return for a six-million dozen order he could cajole Gunther into authorizing a small no-questions-asked expenditure under the heading of "finder's fee" or "consultant." His resistance was sapped.

"How much do you need?" Alex groaned.

"Two hundred grand."

"What! Forget it, Billy!"

"Fifty, then. C'mon, you're a big fucking mogul now."

"All I have from Shea is a handshake."

"People want to kill me!"

"Twenty's my limit. That should be enough to hold off the dogs." As soon as he said it, he felt he was betraying his family, pouring their hard-earned money down a rat hole, though he tried to justify it in his mind: He had just saved the company, cut a deal worth tens of millions, maybe a hundred. Twenty grand was chickenfeed in that context. He needed Billy's goodwill; Billy was the only mole he had.

"I need it yesterday, Sahib!"

"No more drugs. I mean it, Billy. Get some help." His own shallow hypocrisy made him wince inside. If prison couldn't rehabilitate Billy, how could he expect his cajoling to?

"Promise, scout's honor!" said Billy, offering a three-fingered salute. He looked heavenward in gratitude, then gave his temporal benefactor a bear hug. "Thank you, thank you, thank you! You're the best friend I have in this fucked-up world! You know I'd do the same for you."

Unable to breathe, Alex pushed his mole away and asked, "What can you tell me about Shea?"

Billy's hand trembled as he took a swig of beer. He looked like he had aged a decade since last night's bender. "Beside the fact that he hates my guts?"

"Apart from his astute judgment, what sort of guy is he?"

"A great guy—other than the fact he's ruthless and soulless. He cut numerous throats to get control of Cresslon but poses as this enlightened humanitarian and family man. Meanwhile, he's all but destroyed his family. He turned his wife into the Queen of Re-Hab with all his philandering. He hardly ever sees her. His two sons moved to Montana and haven't spoken to him in years. Emily? Well, let's just say he tries to control her as much as possible. She's important for his image, so he can look like a normal American father."

"She's pregnant, by the way," Alex said. "Your brother, or whatever you call him, announced it at the Four Seasons."

"Uncle Billy's always the last to know," Billy mumbled, clearly miffed. But Alex also detected sadness in his eyes, as if something in him had died. "Surprised Charles had it in him. He shot nothing but blanks with Claire." Alex felt chills as Billy draped an arm around his shoulder. "Remember, a halo only has to fall a few inches to become a noose, so don't screw up. Frank Shea is the last person you want as an enemy."

◆   ◆   ◆

Over the next two weeks, Alex left several phone messages for Emily with Riggs the butler. He even had the factory ship her a case of clunky maternity pantyhose with stretch-lace front panels. A practical gift, he figured, was above reproach and wouldn't get her in any hot water. His overtures were ignored, however, and thereafter he tried to put her out of his mind and get on with his new life as a junior tycoon—which wasn't easy, considering who his new business partner was. Shea took Alex under his wing and dominated his every waking minute. The regular strategy sessions were the least of it. To Shea, there existed no distinction between business and personal; the two converged in an endless torrent of hyperactivity. With the Jackal breathing down his neck, demanding a board seat and criticizing his regime in the press, Shea's commitment to the new business venture was all-consuming, his energy both admirable and maniacal. Apparently he deemed the project too important to delegate to his minions, and Alex had no choice but to match him step for step.

There were golf outings with Shea and his corporate cronies; trips with Shea on the company Gulfstream to pre-sell Cresslon pantyhose to department store CEOs. Sponsored by Shea to take the lead in all creative aspects, Alex dreamed up the packaging concept for the campaign: to enclose pantyhose in classic makeup shapes—compact, jar, tube—produced in different colors of shiny plastic. Brainstorming sessions with Cresslon personnel yielded an endless array of spicy products to complement the silky nude and black basics: glitter pantyhose to go with glitter eye shadows; plasticine-based tights to match Cresslon's enamel nail polishes; novelty stockings with embroidered seams of puckered red lips or eyelashes up the back.

Gunther had initially balked at trying to produce these flashy samples—"Not zese silly things, not from my plant! It's flaky." It had taken a couple of head-banging phone sessions—"You want to keep the company alive, right? You want to make pantyhose, then make what sells!"—for Alex to convince his headstrong plant manager to get with the program. The beauty was, once Gunther saw that Cresslon was for real, he became a zealot.

Weekends, oddly enough, posed Alex's biggest challenge. With no motorcycle to take him to Southampton and no desire to face the bittersweet memories of his cabin, he holed up in the city with his parents in the air-conditioned opulence of their townhouse, practicing Alex-monkhood and charging his batteries for the next grueling week. He couldn't wait for Monday to come. While the dizzying heights of Shea's power-laden world and the headiness of success and parental approval kept him in a largely positive frame of mind, the possibility that Charles Lukes might end up raising his flesh-and-blood child gnawed insidiously.

His shaky equilibrium was tested one September evening, just before Labor Day Weekend, when Shea dragged him to a Republican fund-raiser at the Frick. Alex felt out of sorts and out of place and had nothing to say to the old money and corporate power that milled around the fabled indoor pond. As he wandered off in search of solitude, a beautiful arm reached out and grabbed him. It was Claire de Lapalisse, all black-and-white de la Renta.

"Last time I saw you at a party," she smiled from behind a provocative veil, "you were the hired help."

"Guess I'm coming up in the world."

"So I hear. Come, let's chat," she said, taking his arm.

As if the Frick were her own private castle, she lifted a silk rope and ushered him up an off-limits staircase. At the landing, she led him into a dusty, wood-paneled parlor, primly sat down on a leather sofa, and beckoned him join her. As he complied at a polite distance, she crossed her slender legs, thereby hiking her skirt halfway up her thigh and displaying the tiny C's for Cresslon woven into the pattern of her black stockings.

"Emily told me you thought up the whole Cresslon pantyhose idea," she purred. "As you can see, I'm wearing a sample pair tonight. I'm one of Frank's wear-test guinea pigs. And I must say, I'm thoroughly satisfied…which doesn't always happen." She stood and hoisted her leg onto the sofa's padded arm, her thigh inches from Alex's face. Slowly she ran her fingers up her shapely limb as she described the product in a sultry voice: "No gathering at the ankles, no clinging at the knees"—the dress was almost to her crotch—"no pulling at the thighs." Down came the leg. "I want you to do *me* next."

"Excuse me?"

She sat back down, her knees brushing his; her spicy perfume was hypnotic. "I was a successful fashion model in Paris," she said. "I know all the top designers, was a cover girl, have great connections, impeccable taste. I've always capitalized on my looks"—a coy head tilt—"and now I want to capitalize on my title, on the whole glamourpuss package, if you will."

"I'm not sure I understand."

"Imagine a Baroness Claire line of clothing, fragrances, lingerie, bath oils—anything having to do with style, fantasy, and sex. Help me become a franchise," she pleaded, touching his hand. "The American public is always fascinated with glamour and royalty, especially when one of their own attains it. It's itching for another Grace Kelly."

"But I make pantyhose." Just participating in this conversation made him feel idiotic.

"Don't be myopic, Alex de Monk. Be my partner. I know nothing about businessy things," she said, lifting her veil and gazing at him like an earnest kitten, "and you're just the marketing genius who could launch me. So, what do you say, why don't we run a few ideas up the old pole?" Her blue eyes dancing with devilment, she pushed him against the back of the sofa. Quick as a cat she straddled him and treated him to a mushy kiss, smearing him with lipstick, then placed his hands on her breasts. His lack of interest surprised him probably more than it did the baroness. A year ago he would most certainly have been swept into action. Now, he saw everything in terms of Emily. Could this be a set-up, a test of his character? Had Emily passed him on to Claire like a toy? While she struck him as Claire's antithesis, what did he know? Maybe she and Claire belonged to the same man-eating cabal. He dropped his hands and gently turned his head away, leaving the baroness bothered but far from crushed.

"I assumed you liked your women rich and unavailable," she said.

"If you're unavailable, then I'm the Sultan of Brunei."

"You know what I mean. Married. Don't you go for married women?"

"What are you talking about?" he protested, though he knew perfectly well.

"Emily is what I'm talking about. What I saw that day on Fifth Avenue, outside of Cipriani's. Remember? That was no casual meeting. Sure looked like a lovers' quarrel to me."

"Would you mind letting me up?"

"Now that I think of it," she said, "it's a real coincidence."

"What coincidence?"

Claire de-straddled Alex. "Emily's pregnancy. You know, all Charles ever wanted was an heir."

"So, I hear he got his wish," Alex murmured.

"Except that Charles has an urologist at Lenox Hill who once told me that he'd seen castrati with higher sperm counts."

He tried to keep a casual expression but felt himself flushing red.

"Oh, never mind, sweetie," said Claire, waving him off with her long French-tipped nails and whipping out her compact to fix herself. "I gather you're under exclusive contract. Run along, Alex de Monk."

◆   ◆   ◆

As Charles ushered his wife through the marble colonnade of the Southampton Ocean Club for its annual Labor Day party, the last thing Emily felt was festive. In spite of its majestic comfort, the Ocean Club had always struck her as a kind of minimum-security prison, the inmates shackled by their own snobbery and anachronistic traditions. It was a place where she couldn't quite relax, even though she was thoroughly accepted, a place where the slightest eccentricity was deemed subversive. The club's thirty-year-old dress code included guidelines for skirt lengths (nothing higher than an inch above the knee), bathing suits (thongs were no-nos), and fabrics (no leather or denim), as well as an archaic male tonsorial policy (no long hair, excessive sideburns, or facial hair beyond well-trimmed mustaches). Each member was issued a booklet delineating objectionable behavior, which ran the gamut from using cell phones, to conducting business on club premises, to engaging in inappropriate laughter—all grounds for expulsion after one official warning.

Then there were the unwritten rules, heinous acts the club frowned upon but couldn't formally condemn, such as saying anything negative about the Bushes or parking any car fancier than a Mercedes in the club lot. Gas-guzzling station wagons and SUV's were appropriate, while Bentleys, Porsches, and the like were deemed flashy nouveau riche vehicles that had no place in the family-oriented Ocean Club. Nor did blacks, Asians, Eurotrash, and Jews, though on that score the club was easing up a bit: Last year, a Jewess and her wealthy Wasp husband (the MacKenzies) were granted membership, refuting once and for all, at least among the members, the charges of anti-Semitism hounding the club. Emily had no problem conforming to the club's dress code. What disturbed her, even as much as the bigotry and xenophobia, was the very notion of clubbiness itself, which in her view fostered comatose intellects and social inbreeding. As if to prove her point, Mr. Fisk, the elderly club president, sauntered forward to greet them.

"Goodness gracious, Emily," said Mr. Fisk, sporting a huge red, white, and blue bow tie and leaning on his cane. "Your hair has gotten so long that for a second I thought you were Rapunzel."

The politely snide hint caused her husband to bristle. Unintimidated by this withered old hierophant, Charles reacted with what he no doubt considered an appropriate and proportional response. "Yes, Emily's hair is the envy of all our acquaintances." He studied the president's bald head for several seconds and smiled. "On the other hand, you, my dear Fisk, seem to be heading in more of a Rumpelstiltskin direction." He let the barb sink in. "Which is actually somewhat apropos, as my wife is now carrying our firstborn."

"Ah, that's wonderful news!" said Mr. Fisk, eyes still fixed disapprovingly on Emily's flowing mane. "People were starting to talk, Lukes. What took you so long?"

"Emily wasn't sure she was ready to set aside her illustrious art career and become a full-time mother." His black eyes were dancing.

"I see," said Mr. Fisk, clearly baffled by Charles's mocking tone.

Emily issued a thin smile. The truth was, she hadn't been this prolific with the brush since college. With her romantic hopes and dreams on ice, she was sublimating them. She painted late at night, elated, nearly giddy, even though she was careful to use the latest nontoxic acrylics so as not to expose her fetus to fumes. Her abstract erotica was so inspired that she was actually thinking of promoting it and herself after she gave birth and her life calmed down. Her new stuff was good, really good; and original, too—she knew it in her bones. If her one-night affair with Alex had contributed anything constructive to her life—besides the baby, of course—it was to reawaken her creative juices. Charles, who hardly ever set foot in her studio, was oblivious to all this, which was just as well. The subject matter would surely send him into a lather.

"Boy or girl?" Fisk quavered. "Do you know yet?"

"We're hoping for…" Charles stopped when he spotted a waiter approaching. "Actually we're hoping for a couple of bouncing baby gin and tonics." This elicited a snort of laughter from Fisk, who clapped Charles on the back and went off to mingle.

"Charles," Emily admonished, "you know I can't have alcohol." The waiter was standing at attention.

"I know, my pet. The two G and Ts are for Daddy-o." He turned to the waiter. "Bring two Tangueray and tonics and an Evian with lime to our table."

Emily shot her husband a look of betrayal.

"Yes, Mommy-o, after the stork delivers our bundle of joy, I am going to abstain from all relaxing liquids. But that's why I have to store up now, donchya know? Like a bear before winter."

Emily tried to smile, remembering how much she used to laugh at this kind of witticism from Charles. Now, with a child inside her, it felt pernicious. The marriage was just going through a down cycle, she rationalized. She would regain her affection for him; she had to. Everything would be better once the child was born. A real living baby will force Charles to stop being silly and become a complete person.

Charles guided her onto the spacious veranda, where they were enveloped in the anodyne buzz of dinner talk and orchestra music. Each table of ten was draped in a patriotic tablecloth. When the Lukeses found theirs, the Plums were already sitting, along with a half-asleep Baron de Lapalisse—abandoned as usual by Claire, who was off dancing the rhumba with a handsome young descendant of the Tsars—and two couples whom the Plums had invited, whose role, much like the skimpy seashell centerpiece, seemed to be essentially decorative. The Plums, a chronically social couple in their mid fifties, were longtime friends of Charles. Quintessential club people and champion gossips, they jetted from resort to resort, wintering in Palm Beach, summering in Southampton, never meeting a party they didn't like.

"We heard the fabulous news, Emily, darling! It's about time you two started a family. When are you due? Tell me everything!" crooned Lynne Plum.

"That is going to be one lucky baby," added Eugene. "Got it enrolled in Harvard yet?" Despite his slight lisp, bloated melon face, and a reputation for being light in his Gucci loafers, his position on the board of governors of the Ocean Club, as well as the Bath & Tennis and Everglades Clubs in Palm Beach, made him a man to be reckoned with in his sphere. "Better start making donations now if you want to get the kid into the right preschool."

"Don't be vulgar, Gene," his wife chided. She chided him often. Lynne's no-nonsense mannishness was the perfect complement to her husband's essential giddiness. She drove the car, balanced the checkbook, made the reservations, and organized their two houses along with their relentless social calendar, leaving Eugene to do what he did best: flit from party to party spreading gossip and offering unwanted advice. Years in the South Florida and Eastern Long Island sun had leathered Lynne's skin. Her sturdy legs were riddled with varicose veins, her frosted hair had the consistency of peanut brittle, and Emily suspected that she had to wax twice a week to conform to the club's no-facial-hair rule. Emily had always found Lynne frighteningly blank, but never so much so as tonight. "Anyway, what I simply must know," said Lynne, "is whom are you using to do the nursery."

Eugene sprang from his chair as if it were electrified. "Oh, please! Whatever you do, don't use Enrique! He absolutely ruined the Hayworths' nursery. He's stuck on that black-and-white visual stimulation theory, and the whole place looks like a frigging Holstein cow!"

"Gene!" his wife hissed. "You've got your elbow in your bread plate. Let Emily and Charles talk."

Charles had already polished off one of his gin and tonics. "The nursery is completely Emily's purview," he said, with an amused glance at his wife. "She's the artiste in the family."

Since getting pregnant, Emily had noticed that Charles's attitude toward her had grown increasingly vitriolic, had more and more edge, as if somewhere in the recesses of his subconscious he knew the baby couldn't be his. The nursery had been a sore subject between them ever since she had arrived home from a C-SAW board meeting two weeks ago and found Raoul, the society decorator who reminded her of a French used-car salesman, taking measurements in her studio. Luckily her erotic art was stored out of sight; still, the encroachment infuriated her. They had two other guest rooms the same size, so why, she confronted Charles later, had he decided to convert her studio into the nursery without bothering to consult her? How could he be so inconsiderate! "Because it has the best light and the best view, my darling," Charles replied, "and you don't want to deprive our little munchkin of the best when you can just as easily paint in one of the other rooms. Besides, Raoul says that it stands the best chance of getting into *Architectural Digest*." Ultimately it boiled down to the fact that it was his apartment and his money, and as furious as that ordinarily would have made her as his wife, her tortured conscience kept her from making too big an issue of anything these days.

Lynne reached over and gave Emily's hand a little squeeze. "I know how much you like to paint, Emily, but there's nothing more creative than raising children. Do as I do and think of them as little blank canvases."

"To the new Lukes masterpiece!" Charles toasted.

While the table clinked glasses, the Baron de Lapalisse awoke with a jerk and posed a question to the table: "Where is zee lovely Vanessa this evening? Playing around with zat meejit, Lestere Ruby? Surely zey would not let heem in here, yes? Iz he not a Jew?"

There were some coughs and embarrassed chuckles at this. The issue of race and club eligibility was not generally verbalized, though Charles, naturally, turned to Eugene with rosy cheeks and cocked eyebrow and added his own irreverent comment: "I hear it on good authority that when the Jackal dies he's going to be cremated and have his ashes sprinkled by helicopter all over the Ocean Club." As her husband said this, Emily noted, not for the first time, that his mannerisms seemed to be growing more effeminate with age. Whenever he and Eugene were together they drank excessively and seemed to forget themselves, bantering like a couple of poufs. "What's the board of governors going to do about that, hmm?" Charles posed.

"The Jackal will get into the club one way or another, even if he's blown in by a couple of giant fans," howled Eugene. "I wonder how Miss Muss and her gargantuan implants became members in the first place. Perhaps we should incorporate some rules about plastic surgery into the dress code."

Emily had thought she was by now anesthetized to such talk, categorizing it as harmlessly inane; but with a new soul growing inside her, completely dependent on her, she wanted no part of it. "The way the club discriminates is petty and disgusting. Shutting out the world is no way to go through life,' she said, silencing the table for a long moment, but also feeling hypocritical. Either no one wanted to argue with a pregnant woman, or no one had a reasonable answer.

"I don't know how *you*, of all people, can say that, Emily," Lynne finally said. "Lester Ruby's trying to steal away your father's company, and you'd still let him in?"

"It's not my father's company; it belongs to the stockholders."

Charles's look of shock quickly gave way to one of amusement; he seemed to enjoy a private laugh, as if her brashness were attributable to hormones rather than to any threatening conviction. But Emily's refusal to participate in Jackal-bashing clearly galled Lynne Plum. The Ocean Club was absolutely the last bastion in the New York area where she could vent against God's Chosens without suffering permanent social mortification, and she was bent on keeping it that way. "The Jews have poisoned every profession and resort area they've ever touched, and they'll poison our club if we relax our standards." Even the anti-Semites at the table stared at her in astonishment; the discussion had become far too uncouth for their appetite. "What's wrong?" Lynne said at all the gaping faces. "You think they don't say worse things about us? Don't tell me you've all become self-hating Christians, like Emily."

Rather than rush to the defense of his wife, and create an unwanted enemy, Charles tried to smooth things over with Biblical humor: "'Tis easier," he said, raising his glass, "for a camel to pass through the eye of a needle than for a Jew to have lunch at the Ocean Club."

"Excuse me," said Emily, pushing herself away from the table and rising to her feet, "I need some fresh air."

"But we're outside," said Eugene, as Emily fled.

The orchestra was playing an Ocean Club version of "Bad, Bad Leroy Brown." A few oldsters fox-trotted gamely on the sidelines, while the younger couples—those in their forties and fifties—jerked and ducked and flailed their arms feverishly in a comical simulation of hip, youthful abandon. The genuinely youthful, who would rather have died than acknowledge this Jurassic music in any way whatsoever, clustered in a bored, sophisticated knot by the bar on the far wall, hard by an enormous buffet, which was as yet untouched and laden with lobsters, stone crabs, giant salads, and whipped cream-laden desserts. The elderly were all striving desperately to be young; the young were striving desperately to be old. Still, it was a pleasant enough scene, Emily thought, had she not felt so trapped in it. Trapped in her own web of immaturity, gutlessness, and deceit, with no one to blame but herself. Clusters of pink and green balloons attached to the Doric columns bobbed back and forth in the ocean breeze. Torches flickered. The women were attractive, Puccied, impeccably turned out, except for the usual smattering of mutton dressed as lamb. The men were universally uninteresting to her, a gaggle of parasites: legacies with hidden mean streaks, feeding from the trough created by their forefathers; maggot investment bankers feeding off the sweat and vision of risk-taking entrepreneurs. Everything about them, from their choice of careers to their choice of wives, was calculated; passion was anathema to them.

But then conventional wisdom, like a rubber band, snapped her out of her heady rebellion and back to "reality." All the empirical evidence she had seen in her thirty years suggested that you can't build a relationship on passion; passion doesn't last; it exists during courtship and was never meant to be integrated into marriage. This aperçu was fortified everywhere she looked. Phony laughs, furtive leers, invisible knives; people more interested in their neighbors' mates than in their own. To think that Alex and she would be different was the height of delusion. Every couple had problems, and Charles was right: most women would gladly exchange theirs for hers.

Tired of this circular argument, she couldn't wait to go home to bed. Bed was the only place where she was exempt from playing the role of wife, especially now that she was pregnant. Turning away from the party, she took in the immensity of the starry skies and the roar of the ocean and began to feel a modicum of peace.

"Makes you feel small, doesn't it?"

Recognizing the voice, she spun around and came face to face with Alex. Apart from the pink handkerchief flowing a bit too brazenly from the breast pocket of his blue blazer, he was appropriately dressed—blue oxford shirt, khaki slacks, Hermès tie dotted with cute little bunny rabbits—but all she saw was a dangerous desperado.

"How did you get in here?" she croaked.

"I told the gal at the front desk I was meeting the baroness. Then I just winked."

"So, why don't you go find her?"

"Not without a chair and a whip." He took her arm and led her toward the crowded dance floor, and the next thing she knew they were pressed together, moving slowly to Cole Porter's "Easy to Love." Emily was trembling, fighting off feelings of desire, unable to savor the delicious comfort of his embrace.

"You shouldn't be here," she warned.

"Why didn't you tell me you were pregnant?"

"Why should I?"

"The baby's mine, isn't it?" He stopped dancing and stood there awaiting her reply, but Emily pulled him back into the dance.

"You really impressed my father, by the way. He must have told that piano-playing story a thousand times."

"I didn't know he was your father, Emily."

She forced a smile as Claire and her good-looking young Romanov glided alongside them. The baroness flashed a little gleam of complicity before whirling away to the music and vanishing into the crowd, whereupon Emily's scowl returned. "Everybody knows Frank Shea is my father!"

"I'm not everybody. I don't go through life with a who's-who mentality, Googling everyone I meet. Look in my eyes and tell me this is not my child."

"This is *my* child."

"That much I know," he smirked.

"Why can't you believe Charles is the father?"

"Because that would make the universe all wrong, like a puzzle that doesn't fit together. It can't be his child! It just can't!"

"Talk about puzzles that don't fit!" she shot back. "One day you're Henry David Thoreau, the next day you're Donald Trump!"

"All I know is," he whispered, "I love you so much I can hardly breathe."

Emily squelched her shivers of longing. "Tell that to my father and kiss your business good-bye."

"He likes me—says I remind him of himself when he was my age."

"God, I hope not," she muttered.

As the music stopped, Emily suddenly felt a sticky Post-it being thrust into her palm. "Here are my phone numbers," Alex said, "cell and business. Call me when you can."

"Obviously your big Cresslon deal means nothing to you."

"It's life or death for my company, and all I can think about, every minute of the day, is you and the ba…"

Abruptly he stopped, as both of them noticed Charles weaving through the crowd in their direction, his black eyes like gun barrels. When he caught up to them, he threw a possessive arm around Emily's shoulder and glared superciliously at her dance partner.

"Well, well," he said, "you turn up everywhere these days, like a bad penny. By the way, who are Grace and Harry Halaby?"

"My parents," Alex replied guardedly. "Why?"

"Saw their names posted on the club bulletin board as prospective members and wondered if they might be related to you. At least you come by your social climbing honestly. Who invited you tonight?"

"Uh, the…the Phippses."

Emily breathlessly watched Charles survey the party and count three tables hosted by three generations of Phippses. "Which Phippses?" he asked. "Not the Greenwich Phippses, surely."

"Actually, the Syrian Phippses," Alex smiled.

"Come, Charles," Emily intervened, taking her husband's arm, "the fireworks are about to start, and we haven't eaten. I'm eating for two now."

Like a mother hen, she herded Charles off to the buffet and didn't look back. When they returned to their table, Alex was nowhere to be seen. Her initial relief became an aching void when the fireworks began. They were launched from the beach and extraordinary, the best pyrotechnics money could buy. Preoccupied with her own explosive situation, Emily watched the brilliant display, picking at her food with a fork in one hand, fondling Alex's Post-it under the table with the other. People always say you should follow your heart, she ruminated, but how do you know it's your heart—and not your hormones—that's doing the talking? One thing her heart told her: a stress-free pregnancy was paramount. She needed to feel secure, which meant treading very carefully. There was no room for a wild-card like Alex in her life, no matter how he made her flutter. With everyone riveted to the crackling, eye-popping grand finale, she crumpled up his Post-it—but somehow she couldn't bring herself to part with it. It seemed too drastic, not to mention childish. Alex wasn't going away—he was doing business with her father—so what was the point? She might as well get used to the fact that their paths were destined to cross on occasion and learn to deal with it. With that rationalization, she quietly slipped the Post-it into her purse. The weight of the world left her body, and she was actually able to enjoy herself for the rest of the evening, for the first time since Memorial Day weekend.

12

Dryouts and Buyouts

A small gift-wrapped painting under one arm, a holiday basket dangling from the other, and a bundle in her belly, Emily trudged through the revolving door and into the Sunnyvale Rehab Center. Incense and Christmas music filled the bright, glassed-in atrium. The receptionist greeted her with a sympathetic smile, like an old friend, and told her before she had to ask the way to her mother's room. Emily's day had begun at 5:00 AM, when she received a call from her mother's friend Janet that her mother had suffered another one of her pill overdoses. She had prevailed on Charles to postpone their mid-morning flight to Palm Beach—an easy enough task considering that he owned the jet—but not before Charles, cranky from being awakened early, had gotten in his digs.

"It's her regular holiday routine. Some people fast, she overdoses."

"Do you think that's witty, Charles? It's my mother!"

After enduring several of Charles's inevitable *Valley of the Dolls* jokes while she dressed, Emily had driven out to Greenwich to lend comfort to her mother and get her affairs in order. Or rather, the chauffeur drove her; her husband has insisted on this, though Charles would never think of coming with her. When it came to extending himself to help others, Charles was detached and useless, and her family wasn't much better. With her father in a perpetual business meeting and her brothers living a Rocky Mountain fly-fishing existence, it invariably fell on her to tend to her mother during these episodes. On this brisk morning before Christmas, however, she was tired and had little to give, a fatigue stemming less from being seven months pregnant than from living a lie.

Leigh Shea didn't bother to turn her head to see who had entered her spacious corner room, which more resembled a Four Seasons Hotel than a clinic. She sat motionless in bed, propped up on pillows, gazing through the picture window at a frozen lake fringed by woods. Although an IV dripped fluids into her arm, she looked her usual elegant self from a shadowy distance. Her chestnut hair still had fluff and bounce; a peach cashmere shawl was draped around her shoulders. But as Emily edged closer and saw past the silhouette, her eyes received a Dorian Gray shock. Just two nights ago at dinner her mother had looked reasonably good; now, years of pain and narcotic escapes showed their sudden cumulative effect, leaving her delicately chiseled face ravaged.

Emily had hoped her mother might have been out of the woods. For the past eight months Leigh had been substance-free, having rallied back from a severe downward spiral following the fall of the Twin Towers. Like many people she had been thrown into a state of free-floating anxiety and depression; unlike most people, she had used it as an excuse to fall off the wagon. Off the whole wagon train, in fact. Adivan, Halcion, Percocet, Vicodin, Xanax—she managed to find doctors who would still give them to her, until Emily had staged her own one-woman intervention and checked her into Sunnyvale last spring, a month or so before meeting Alex. The program had worked wonders, until this most recent regression. Emily fought back tears and found herself thinking like a parent. Could she have prevented this by being closer? Stronger? More grounded in reality and honest with herself? Her mother had toiled selflessly, like a saint, to raise and nurture her three children, while her husband was off in the limelight seizing corporate glory and its accompanying luxuries, too busy extolling family values in his speeches to have time for his own brood. His career advancement, he believed, was all he owed his family, all they ever should need. On top of her domestic chores, Frank had demanded that Leigh treat certain business dinners as command performances, and despite her emotional shakiness and lack of spousal appreciation, she always managed to hold things together when it counted, with the help of bubbly white wine and little white pills.

"I tried to get here sooner, Momma."

"You beat everybody else," Leigh quavered.

Emily set the cumbersome Christmas basket on the bed. Decked in shimmering gold cellophane and red ribbon, it was so tall and blindingly festive that Leigh didn't seem to notice the gift that Emily placed down beside it. "I stopped by the house and canceled the *Times* delivery for two weeks," said the dutiful daughter. "I couldn't find the number for the man who's doing the bathroom; half the new tiles arrived cracked. Um, the cats are with Janet. And I figured this was a good time to get the car a tune-up." She didn't bother to mention the fact that she had emptied her mother's medicine chest of all narcotics and tossed them in the garbage.

"You're living my life better than I ever did," Leigh mumbled.

If she only knew the half of it, Emily thought bitterly, as her mother peered curiously through the basket's cellophane at the cornucopia of gourmet sweets and delicacies.

How Emily wished she had chucked the basket in the garbage before coming! Her father had dropped it off at her building early this morning on his way to Teterboro Airport, asking Emily in an accompanying note to take it to her mother as a favor since he had been called away on urgent business related to his takeover battle. Frank Shea hadn't expected to run into his relatively late-rising daughter in the downstairs lobby. Nor had he counted on his traveling companion—Oxana, the twenty-two-year-old Russian supermodel and Cresslon pantyhose girl—to open the limousine's tinted window for air just as Emily emerged on the sidewalk. Oxana's smug expression told Emily all she needed to know. She stormed off without wishing her father a Merry Christmas and without bothering to inform him of her mother's condition. He didn't merit either courtesy.

But that wasn't even the worst part. Two evenings earlier, at a small holiday dinner party thrown by her father in the 21 Club wine cellar, the same Oxana had posed as Alex's date. Attended by the Charles Lukeses, the Frank Sheas, and a handful of Cresslon executives, it was the first time Emily had laid eyes on Alex since the Ocean Club's Labor Day gala three and a half months ago. Seeing a diamond-studded sex-bomb on his arm, while Emily herself was beginning her third trimester, had nearly compelled her to feign an illness and go home. Rather than give Alex that satisfaction, though, she feigned contentment throughout the excruciating evening, ignoring his furtive glances across the table—so caught up in her own drama, she realized now, that she must have been blind to all the other intrigue swirling around her, and to the wheels coming off her mother. Only in retrospect, after seeing Oxana in her father's limo, did she realize that the rapport between Alex and Oxana had been nonexistent, which irked her almost as much as if they had been in love. All she could think during this morning's half-hour ride out to Greenwich was what a swine Alex was for consenting to be her father's beard. He had helped push her mother over the edge; she could never forgive him. Admittedly, there was plenty of blame to go around, but it didn't lessen the fact that Alex was no different from the other heathens she had met over the years who had fallen into her father's clutches.

Leigh undid the ribbon. "What a lovely basket. Thank you, dear."
"It's from Dad."

Leigh recoiled from the basket as if it were diseased. "Your father and I haven't exchanged Christmas gifts in fifteen years."

"He wanted to come," Emily said, loathing the twisted position she was in of having to lie for her father for her mother's sake, "but he had to fly to Aspen on some emergency business. He sends his love and will call you when he gets there."

Leigh shoved the basket and sent it sprawling to the floor. Emily went erect with surprise as jars went tumbling every which way. "Don't tell me he has *you* on the payroll now," Leigh snarled.

"Payroll?"

"I may be a pill-popping old drunk, Emmy, but I haven't lost *all* my faculties. Business in Aspen, over Christmas! Your father's off cavorting with that Russian model, isn't he—the one who's on all the billboards, who came to dinner the other night pretending to be with that handsome young Faust." Leigh let out a grudging chuckle. "Was that guy ever squirmy! It was almost endearing."

"Endearing? You must be kidding," Emily muttered, sitting on the bed and giving her mother a long embrace. Contritely, she whispered, "I'm sorry, Momma. I didn't mean to lie or to hurt you. I was put in the middle. I didn't know what to do."

"I'm sure young Faust felt the same way. He seemed more interested in you than in his date. Didn't you notice? He kept looking over at you."

Emily sat back up. "What sort of man ogles a pregnant woman?"

"Charles certainly seemed threatened by him. All those digs. You'd think having a gazillion dollars and a pregnant wife would be enough for him to feel secure."

Emily was sorely tempted to confide all that had been preying on her these past seven months. If anyone could understand a woman's unsung marital misery, it was her mother, who even in her sedation remained uncannily intuitive.

"So," Leigh asked, patting her daughter's protruding belly, "do you know what you're having?"

Flabbergasted that her own mother could have forgotten, Emily summoned all the patience she could muster. "I told you," she said, "a boy."

"I hope Charles will play with him once in awhile. He's awfully self-absorbed, isn't he? Not unlike your father in that respect. I don't mean to pry," Leigh added, "but the other night you looked so tense. Being pregnant was the happiest time of my life. It should be a joyous time for you as well."

"Just like you to worry about *me* at a time like this," Emily said, sucking back tears, her desire to unburden herself kept in check by fears that it would be too much for her mother's fragile constitution. Despite some astute flashes, Leigh was without moorings; taxing her any further would be unkind. "I should cancel my trip and take care of you."

"Nonsense, you have your own life to live. And stop treating me with kid gloves, like I'm a pitiful victim. I screwed up my life all by myself!" Leigh snorted almost proudly. "For heaven's sake, don't take *that* accomplishment away from me. Your father met his match this time; those Russians will slit your throat for a buck. Would serve him right. Would serve him right as well if the Jackal took away his company. Maybe it would humble him." Her eyes grew glassy, faraway. "Maybe he'd have time for me again."

"Just divorce him! He's unworthy of you. Unworthy of your good nature."

"You don't think I knew that when I married him?" Leigh warbled. "I weighed the good with the bad and thought I could change him, just like every other stupid young thing does when she decides to marry. Just as I'm sure you did with Charles. Every good trait has its flip side, doesn't it? What makes your father driven also makes him a prick. Glad you didn't go for a business killer. You were wise to pick someone who needs you, who's gentler and more refined. Though I imagine Charles can be a handful, too. Ruthless, in his own needy way," Leigh added, with a world-weary *pfff*.

"At least he's faithful and loves me." Even to Emily it sounded like a lame attempt to convince herself. Leigh must have perceived it the same way, given the patronizing way she reached out and stroked her hand.

"Just don't make the same mistake I did and let yourself be defined by a relationship. And don't blame the man when the relationship cracks—it takes two to tango. We can't belong to others until we belong to ourselves. Now, please, Emmy," Leigh said, pointing at the basket on the floor before closing her eyes, "get that despicable guilt offering out of here!"

Emily watched her mother drift off to sleep before bending down to gather up the spilled jars and tins back into the basket. Horrified to find a champagne bottle among the contents, she hauled everything outside to a trash bin down the hall. Among the basket's tinsel she spotted an envelope, which she ripped open. "I'm off slaying dragons," it said, in Mrs. Donovan's distinctive handwriting. Emily could only guess what nasty little secrets Mrs. Donovan knew after twenty years of covering for him.

Tearing up the note and dumping the basket in the garbage proved mildly therapeutic, though as soon as Emily returned to her mother's room, claustrophobia assailed her. She gazed at her slumbering mother with the disturbing sensation of looking into the mirror of her own future. Narcotics and booze didn't pose any danger for her, but wasn't she already in the throes of destroying herself from within? Trapped in a loveless existence, carrying the wrong man's child, wasn't some kind of physical sickness inevitable? She wished she could start life anew incorporating all that she had learned. But that, she knew, was a nonstarter. Upheaval and confrontation weren't in her makeup, and the forces against change in her life were unshakable.

She had brought no reading material, and with nothing for her to do but sit there while her mother slept, her attention gravitated to the gift-wrapped painting on the bed. The urge to look at it, to reassure herself just one more time, gripped her. Was it appropriate to show to her sick mother? Was it really as good as she thought? Gingerly she lifted the painting off the bed; doing her best not to make a sound, she peeled away the paper. She placed the untitled canvas on the chair and stepped back to behold the sex goddess she had created with a series of strokes, swirls, splashes, and pin-dots. A voluptuous mix of Caucasian and African features, she was straddling an amorphous man, completely in charge. Doing her best not to analyze the painstaking detail of her work, but just to take in the feelings it stirred in her, Emily savored its primitive energy. It pulsed off the earthy brown background, warmed her blood like music, with the steady drumbeat of life and lust. At least she was able to paint these feelings, she mused ruefully. The one-dimensional splash of yellow emanating from the side of the goddess's head still gave her doubts. She had added that whimsical touch at the very end, not quite sure why, fearful that it was overly mental and incongruous with the piece. Still, squinting at the portrait, she couldn't imagine it without that instinctive cerebral touch. It balanced out the raw life force. In a strange way, it gave Emily hope.

"What're you looking at?"

Startled by her mother's voice, Emily picked up the painting and presented it, feeling like a little girl at her first piano recital. "I did this for you, Momma," she said, steadying her work in Leigh's shaky hands. "Merry Christmas."

Leigh eyed it for several moments with changing expressions. "Oh, Emmy! It's wonderful!"

Emily eyes welled up. She still craved mother's approval, still yearned to reach her, to show her the way out of hell. "You like it?"

"No, honey…I *love* it! So…inspiring…liberating. I actually love the risqué overtones."

"Really?" Emily blushed. "I wasn't sure how you'd react."

"Course, what do I know?" Leigh grumbled, sinking back into her pillow. "Charles is the art expert. You should ask his opinion. I'm sure it's more worthwhile than mine." As Emily's spirits plummeted back down to the pits, Leigh murmured, "You know my black Chanel? When Janet found me—apparently this all happened in the bathroom—maybe I took, I don't know, a few extra something...Xanax or Paxil, something with an X. Anyway it doesn't matter what it was...the point is, I must have dropped my glass. *Spoosh!* Champagne everywhere. The good stuff, too—Louis Roderer Cristal. And Janet says I must have slipped and fallen on the glass, because there's a rip the size of..."

"What can I do, Momma?" said Emily, unable to listen to any more.

"Just take it to that Chinese dry cleaner in Old Greenwich. He always does such a good job."

A sober chill fell over Emily. "All right. Yes. Okay, I will."

"Now, you run off and have a good time in Palm Beach. I'll be just fine here. The staff and I are old friends." Leigh's eyes fixed blankly on the frozen lake. "You'll be so proud of me, Emmy. I was very firm this time. I told them, 'No view, no rehab.'"

Once she left the room, Emily almost swooned from the crushing weight of her existence. She felt drained and weak. Suddenly worried about her own health, she collected herself with a series of deep breaths before shuffling outside to the limo. The visit had ended sooner than she had expected, and despite her frailty, she had no desire to go straight home. Her bags were all packed and Charles wasn't expecting to leave the house until mid-afternoon. She had time on her hands and yearned to do something contrary to her blasted routine, yet her options seemed almost as barren as her mother's. As the limo pulled out of Sunnyvale's parking lot, she understood why her mother always fell apart over the Christmas holidays. And why the suicide rate skyrocketed. Without companionship, no time was more dismal.

Suddenly her baby kicked—hard—as if trying to remind her of something important she needed to do.

◆   ◆   ◆

Tentatively, Alex opened the walnut humidor on the office credenza and was bowled over by the asphyxiating waft of tobacco. He eyed his father's stash for a long moment before removing an eight-inch Cohiba Esplendido. He had never smoked a cigar before but had learned through osmosis that the Esplendido was the choice of dictators—not only Fidel's favorite but Harry's, who prior to his heart attack had reserved it for special occasions. With Christmas tomorrow and Cresslon blitzing the media with a sizzling pantyhose ad campaign that made

"Feel the Lash" seem like Girl Scout spots, this was an Esplendido moment if there ever was one. Halaby Hosiery was awash with orders; the plant was humming seven days a week, three shifts, and Gunther was putting out feelers to Honduras for a second plant despite Cresslon's "Made in America" PR campaign. There was no available production anywhere in the States, and both Gunther and Shea were adamant that since Honduras was in *South* America they were within the parameters. Alex was too busy to argue with his elders. News of his coup had spread to the industry heartland, and the same buyers who had once treated him like dog meat were now curious to do business with him and his innovative young company.

"Hark the herald angels sing, Glory to the pantyhose king!" Alex sang, loudly enough for Flora to hear from her desk outside. Despite his false bravado, he dreaded the upcoming holiday, not sure how he could handle a week of leisure. Work had become his crutch, his means to keep his mind from dwelling on Emily, as well as, ironically, the center of his master plan to win her back. In his mind, he had been wooing her from afar, operating under the assumption that she was cognizant of his business deeds, not the least of which was the fact that he had won her father's respect in a way Charles never could. With patience and discipline he had never before displayed in his life, he was biding his time in the faith that her heart would ultimately prevail. Given the most recent development two days ago, however, that prospect was looking exceedingly grim.

When Frank Shea had personally called to invite him to a holiday dinner party at the 21 wine cellar—rattling off the guest list, which included Emily—Alex had gleefully accepted. Only then did Shea impose his caveat: that he bring Oxana as his date. There was no wriggle-room; Shea would have it no other way, and Alex's eagerness to see Emily after three and a half months eclipsed this squeamish little detail. He hoped that showing up with the Cresslon pantyhose girl would make Emily jealous and shake her out of her siege. He could barely wait for the big night, certain that Emily and he would experience an overpowering connection, which would lead to a tryst and some honest reckoning in days hence.

How wrong that prediction proved to be! Emily froze him out, as if he didn't exist. The entire night was strained and filled with undertones:

"Sometimes you need to soar with the eagles, sometimes you need to crawl with the snakes," Shea had pontificated, seemingly for the benefit of his do-nothing son-in-law. "Alex, here, knows exactly what I mean. You gotta be resourceful, right Alex?"

Alex shrugged uncomfortably, not knowing what to say.

"I hear both eagles and rattlesnakes taste like chicken," said Charles, as Emily clung to his arm. "Hey, why don't we have the chef whip up a little tasting platter and see if anyone can tell the difference?"

Unamused, Shea stressed, "I want my grandson to be raised with the work ethic, to be fit for this world,"

"I'll settle for a decent person," Leigh slurringly threw in. She had gone through several glasses of wine by then, struggling to hold herself together while her husband strutted like a giddy peacock for Oxana.

"As long as 'decent' isn't a euphemism for 'dilettante,'" Shea retorted, with a quick glance at Charles, whereupon he segued into his favorite Teddy Roosevelt "man in the arena" quote. The ravishing Russian nodded in accord, though it was fifty-fifty she knew who Teddy Roosevelt was.

It was only during dessert, when Alex bent down to retrieve his fallen napkin and saw Shea squeeze Oxana's thigh, that it dawned on him what his real role was; but by then the damage was done, and all he could do was bob in the water like the wooden decoy he was. If the night belonged to anyone, it was Charles. Preening in all his paternal glory, touting his procreative success both at home and in Japan, he unleashed the evening's most memorable zinger, at Alex's expense. "Immersing ourselves in all aspects of the pantyhose business," he said to Alex, glancing suggestively at Oxana. "Vertically integrated, are we? Enjoy it while you can, Halaby, because Spidex is going to put your old-fashioned nylons out of business."

And a blood test will put you out of business, Alex was aching to say, though he knew such a move would only make Emily despise him—not to mention be bad for business, to say the least. He shuddered to think of the casualties that would occur if he got a court to order a blood test and it proved he *wasn't* the father. One family would be permanently scarred, another financially wiped out, all for nothing. With the birth just two months away, anxiety was a constant. He wondered if he would ever learn the truth.

Clinging to the fading hope that he and not Charles would be handing out cigars in two months, he ran the pungent Havana under his nose. He was about to bite off the tip when he spotted the brass cigar cutter inside the humidor, which enabled him to conduct the proper surgery. Sticking the cigar in his mouth and flicking Harry's gold lighter, he drew the fire upward with his breath, slowly turning the cigar until the tip glowed evenly, a ritual he had watched his father perform countless times in more elegant fashion. Seconds later the junior industrialist was overcome by a violent coughing fit. He was hacking and swooning when Harry entered in his dressing gown and slippers.

"Better finish what you started," chortled Harry. "That's a fifty-dollar Havana."

Alex dizzily relinquished the Esplendido to his father, who sniffed it nostalgically before placing it on the desktop ashtray.

"Saw Sprinkle yesterday," Harry said. "I've lost fifty-five pounds! Haven't weighed under the Mendoza line since Carter was president."

"You look great, Dad! I never thought you'd…"

"How's my business?" Harry cut him off.

After six months of operational freedom and stunning success, Alex had thought he'd be immune by now to fatherly intimidation; yet the question triggered the classic Pavlovian response in him: shriveling gonads, dry mouth. Luckily, before the symptoms could fester, Flora's voice shrilled over the intercom: "Jack Larkin, line one."

"Use the speakerphone," Harry barked like a drill sergeant. "I want to hear what that dirtbag has to say."

Alex was firm: "Only if you promise to be quiet."

After a grudging hesitation, Harry muttered, "Fine."

Alex assumed the throne behind the desk, hit the speaker button, and bellowed, "Jaaack!"

"Happy holidays, buddy!" Larkin boomed. "Just calling to see if you've thought any further about my proposal."

"Letting it percolate," Alex grinned, grabbing the cigar as a prop and hoisting his feet onto the desk in a classic tycoon pose. "Been too swamped to focus all that much on it, frankly. Not just Cresslon, either. We're making strides with BelMart, Target, JCPenney, Mervyns—all your competitors."

"Which is why you need a sales manager. You can't continue being a one-man show—unless you want to end up a cardiac case like your old man."

With a frantic wave, Alex kept his father from detonating, while Harry's scowl told Alex to take his goddamn feet off Harry's desk. "I'm hardly a one-man show," Alex laughed, swinging his feet to the floor and giving the Cohiba a tentative puff.

"No time for false modesty," Larkin said. "You've got a tiger by the tail, and you need a strong right-hand man like me to handle the day-to-day stuff, to free you up for bigger things, like acquisitions, building your empire. Look, I know we've had our differences. I was rough on you in the beginning, but only to toughen your character. You did what I suggested—got new customers, created new styles. Aren't you glad you listened?"

"Sure am!" Alex played along, trying not to laugh at his father's bilious expression. "Problem is, the townhouse doesn't have the office space for an executive of your caliber."

"Isn't it time you moved and got a real Midtown office? Face it, your father's way of doing things is over."

Alex puffed a bit more confidently on his cigar, while his pacing father writhed and reddened like a madman in a straitjacket, ready to jump right through the phone and head-butt the insolent bastard.

"With your momentum," the bastard continued, "there's no reason you can't surpass Wright-Fit and become number one in private label. But you need help—someone who knows the industry, who has a little gray hair. I know the customer side of the desk, which can be a real asset to you. All I ask is the same salary and benefits I have now with Havemeyer, plus an equity kicker, and I'm yours." There followed an unflattering silence, prompting Larkin to add, "Don't decide now—think about it over the holidays."

"Thanks, Jack, I'll do that." Fearing that Mount Harry would blow at any second, Alex graciously wished the buyer a Merry Christmas and hung up. He grinned over the glowing Esplendido at his father. "Eight months ago, Larkin called me your 'little ass-wipe.' Now he wants a job."

"Are you crazy?" Harry blustered. "That whore caused my heart attack! He's everything I despise! I'll kick his equity kicker right up his..."

"Calm down, will you!" Alex raised his hands to fend off his father's domineering energy. "I'm just stringing him along until Gunther gets more production. Thanks to Cresslon, we're behind on delivery to Havemeyer. Larkin could be sending our orders to Wright-Fit, but he's looking the other way, throwing us all the business he can in hopes I'll make him my right-hand man."

"Nobody makes hiring decisions but me!"

"Well," Alex winced, "he's right about one thing: We need to hire a couple of first-rate account executives to service the new customers we're about to bring on. Which means a bigger headquarters."

"Forget it! I won't give up my write-offs!"

"How do you expect us to grow?"

"You said we need more people. Who better than me?" Harry preened.

This proclamation chilled Alex; his jaw set, his spine stiffened. "Your heart..."

"Is fine." Harry slapped his flattened belly, like a gung-ho marine fresh out of basic training. "I'm getting re-involved."

Alex knew that his father was no more capable of sharing power than Genghis Kahn. "Exactly what role do you intend to play?"

"How about grooming my ingrate of a son to take over?"

"I *have* taken over," Alex shrilled, "even though *you* told me to get lost! This company was on the brink of extinction six months ago!"

"Success is proven over years, not in six months! You know next to nothing about manufacturing. You have no financial experience. You couldn't read a balance sheet if your life depended on it."

"That's why you pay accountants! Who's the ingrate?"

"I *built* this company!"

"I *saved* it!"

"Frank Shea, line one," burst Flora over the intercom, silencing them.

"Not a word," Alex growled at his father. Not even Harry could argue in whose trophy-case Frank Shea belonged. Only after staring his father back down into his chair and establishing momentary alpha-male dominance, did Alex hit the speaker phone. "Hey, Frank," he said, trying to project confidence despite feeling like a de-clawed house cat, "Merry Christmas!"

"By God," bellowed Shea, "that's the first 'Merry Christmas' I've heard all season! All that 'Happy Holidays' crap irritates the shit out of me. Since when is it a crime to be Christian? Anyway, the goys are winning. The pantyhose are blowing out of the stores! Women, it seems, want to show off their legs again!"

A faint roar in the background prompted Alex to ask, "Where are you?"

"On top of the world," Shea said, brimming with optimism. "Looking down at the snow-capped Rockies from my jet and barreling toward Aspen. See how our stock's shot up? Wall Street loves our new direction, though I doubt the Jackal shares its enthusiasm."

"What's his next move?"

"Who cares—he's a rotting piñata. You'd think he'd throw me a testimonial dinner for making him a fortune on his Cresslon stock." Shea cleared the gravel out of his throat. "I just hope Avon and Mary Kay don't copy us. The last thing we need is their door-to-door reps peddling pantyhose, one-on-one. They could undercut us. That's my only fear."

Alex jotted "Avon" and "Mary Kay" on a note card and stuck the reminder in his top drawer for a rainy day; but before he could think any more about it, Shea dropped a bombshell:

"I want us to meet right after the holidays to discuss a buyout of Halaby Hosiery. And I want a young punk with vision to run my new apparel division."

The cigar dropped from Alex's mouth. Quickly he snatched it before it could burn a hole in his slacks and brushed away the ashes, whereupon he and his father shared an astonished look, animosities forgotten. His very first thought was that a buyout would turn him into a worthy provider and enhance Emily's esteem for him. He couldn't hope to have even a fraction of Charles's money—and Emily, despite appearances to the contrary, wasn't money-driven, he was sure of it—but she and the baby would still require a stable financial situation. If this worked out, she would admire him, and come to him—not for his money, but for his mastery. She had originally fallen for him because he was a quixotic dreamer, yet who but a quixotic dreamer could have pulled this off? All this by age thirty! A few years of corporate slavery were nothing in the larger scheme of things.

Snapped back to the present by Harry's frantic hand signals, which seemed to say that Alex's authority as CEO didn't extend to making financial commitments, Alex stammered, "I…I'm just a minority stockholder. My…my father owns 90 percent, so it's really up to him. The company's been his life; any offer would have to reflect future growth."

"Down boy!" Shea chuckled. "It's Christmas Eve. Circle January fourth on your calendar. Ten AM, my office."

Coaxed by Harry's glare, Alex asked, "Mind if I bring my father along?"

"Delighted! See you guys on the fourth."

After hanging up, Alex looked at his father. Fear and loathing were gone from the old man's eyes. He and his son had achieved, or were about to achieve, what neither had believed was possible.

"Christ," Harry exhaled, "I might be able to retire from this goddamn business after all."

Alex sulkily turned away to his computer screen.

"For a budding mogul," Harry observed, "you don't look so happy. I hate to say it, but maybe you're working too hard. Where's the playboy son I used to frown upon?"

"He lost his groove."

"Then go for a walk."

"Why?"

"Because I feel like smoking a cigar," smiled Harry, "and if you're not here to see it, you won't have to turn me in to your mother."

Alex listlessly stood and headed out, but before he got very far Harry sprang up and smothered him in a bear hug.

"I'm so proud of you," he said.

"It took a buyout for you to feel that?"

"Stop it. Last night," Harry soothed into his ear, "your mother and I were talking about you, and she reminded me of something."

"What?" said Alex glumly.

"That you saved my life."

An earthquake of buried emotions rumbled from Alex's depths and shot straight into his unsuspecting heart. "She actually said that?"

"Yeah...and I agree. I just wanted to say thanks—for everything."

Alex wasn't sure whether he was touched more by his mother's observation or his father's admission, but it took all his effort not to erupt in tears.

A brisk stroll down Madison Avenue, Alex decided, was the best way to assimilate this new buyout development. It was also, in theory, his best chance of running into Emily, though the past four months of patrolling up and down Madison between Sixtieth and Ninetieth Streets hadn't produced a single chance encounter with her, making him wonder whether their orbits were intrinsically out of sync. The air contained a bitter chill, and against the ice-blue sky Alex's breaths rose like cumulus clouds. Parents with prams and small children were everywhere, converging on him from all directions. Freshly seeded hopes of a buyout caused his brain to dance with hypothetical millions. Soon, if the transaction went as smoothly as everything else was going with Shea, Alex, with his 10 percent stake, would be able to afford a Fifth or Park Avenue apartment, or better yet, a Soho loft large enough to accommodate a couple of kids and maybe an art studio—nothing nearly as grand as Chateau Lukes, but a much happier place to be sure.

Yet the caprice rang hollow. She had closed the book on him months ago. It would take far more than a buyout for her to trust him and chuck her marriage, to make a blind and gargantuan leap of faith based on one night eons ago. It hardly made sense to him. On the other hand, neither did Cosmetics for the Legs, and look how that had turned out. Life's secrets are seldom revealed through logic.

A deafening bus rumbled by. Plastered along its side was that sultry, bosomy symbol of corporate sleaze, Oxana—seductively horizontal; her exquisitely tapered legs clad in sheer black pantyhose—under the caption, *"CressLegs—Made in America! Flaunt 'em!"* The bus roared away, revealing a bus shelter across the avenue featuring the same ad, causing Alex to reflect on all that his feverish mind and will had manifested. Feeling invincible had its place, he mused, with a gaping pang in the pit of his stomach.

The traffic noise almost caused him to miss the chirp of his cell in his breast pocket. Quickly he fumbled for it and answered, "Hello?"

13

Pop Goes the Easel

"Just how low can you stoop!"

"Emily?"

"Isn't it enough that you almost ruined *my* life? Must you also ruin my mother's?" she shouted through the phone. "I thought you should know that she collapsed in her bathroom and is spending the holidays in rehab, thanks to your shameless performance the other night as my father's beard!"

Full of holes as her blame logic was, he was too overwrought to refute it then and there. "Where are you? We need to talk."

"We *are* talking."

"I mean in person."

"What for?" she said icily, just as an equally icy gust of wind smacked Alex's face.

"Please, Emily—we've got to clear the air. It's important for both of us. Have lunch with me."

"You actually think I want to be seen in *public* with you?"

Shivering in the cold, he offered, "How about somewhere downtown? Where nobody will know us."

"I don't have time to go downtown."

Alex looked up and saw the Hotel Carlyle looming ahead of him. "Meet me at the Carlyle. I'll get a room—just for privacy's sake, so we can talk. Give me ten minutes? *Please!*"

"A *room*?" she said incredulously.

"You're seven months pregnant. What am I going to do?"

After what seemed like an interminable silence, Emily said, "Fine!" Then the line went dead.

At the august, marble-floored Hotel Carlyle, Alex made a beeline for the reservation desk and secured a room, a process made somewhat awkward by the fact that he was huffing and puffing and had no luggage for the bellman. Moments later he was pacing upstairs in his junior suite, heart racing at the prospect of being alone with Emily after all these months, convinced from the fury in her voice that she still had feelings for him—feelings of hostility, for sure, but still feelings. Indifference, not hatred, was the ultimate rejection. At least she cared on some level. At least he'd get his long-awaited day in court, assuming she showed up.

Sooner than expected the door knocker rattled. He peered through the peephole to behold Emily's distorted image, then threw open the door. His heart skipped a beat as she strode in right past him without any acknowledgment, a bulging stomach but no pregnant glow, her countenance drawn and warlike. Alex quietly closed the door, and as he turned back into the room, his face received a stunning slap. The sting reverberated in his cheek, his eardrum rang.

"I hate you!" she declared, and slapped him again.

"Please, calm down…you're pregnant," he said, rubbing his face. "Sit down." He took her elbow, but she violently shook him off.

"You're my father's little pet! His clone!"

"No, no, *no!*" said Alex vehemently. "Men escort women all the time, so I didn't give it a thought when your father asked me to bring Oxana. She's the model. She works with us. I had no idea she was your father's *mistress!* Look, my father pats the models' behinds, but he doesn't *sleep* with them. It never occurred to me I'd be hurting your mother. All I could think of was that I was going to get to see you. I love you, Emily!"

"Stop saying that! You don't even know me!"

"I knew you better after one hour than Charles knows you after four years of marriage! And I want nothing more than to spend the rest of my life with you, even if it means pissing off your father and putting my business at risk! You're the only thing that really matters to me."

"What if I told you it was Charles's baby?" she taunted. "Would you still want me?"

"I wouldn't believe you," he said bravely, hoping she was merely testing him.

"Just as I thought—you can't answer my question. For you, it's all about conquest, isn't it? All about the chase."

"It's all about the fact that I've never loved a woman before you. I mean, Jesus, Emily, look at all the crazy things I've done because of you. I never made a toast, never crashed a party in my life until you came along."

"You may call that love. I call it pathological."

"I don't care whose baby it is!" he cried.

"You don't know what you're saying. You just want to win. After that, you're clueless."

Staggered that she held him in such low regard, Alex closed his eyes in pain and gathered himself with a deep breath. Defeat blanketed him like molasses; all that was left to save, he realized, was his dignity. "Just tell me that you love Charles and want to stay with him," he said, with resignation, "and I'll never bother you again. I promise. I'll support whatever makes you happy." Like a man before his own firing squad, with no realistic hope for a gubernatorial reprieve, he braced for the lethal fusillade. He stared at the floor; he couldn't look at her.

"The baby's yours," she finally exhaled.

Slowly he lifted his head and gazed into her anxious eyes, the eyes of someone who could not bring herself to lie. Despite all his previous speculation, nothing could prepare him for the spine-tingling certainty that he had actually sired a child, or the fact that Emily was admitting it. Not even taking on the crumbling mantel of the family business after his father's heart attack could match the lofty sense of responsibility he felt now, or the outpouring of love he felt for her. Their eyes deepened in a moment of silent reckoning before the force of nature swept them into a kiss. He tore off her overcoat and they collapsed onto the bed, unable to get enough of each other.

"I'm glad it's yours," she said defiantly, "though when I saw you the other night with Oxana I felt so sick with jealousy I thought I might miscarry!"

"She can't hold a candle to you." Holding her in his arms, Alex felt as though his Christmas dreams were coming true. "You've got to stop living under all this pressure. You need a safe harbor."

She shushed him with a kiss. "Please, Alex…make love to me."

"Can we? I mean…"

"Don't you want me like this?"

"Is it, you know…safe?"

"I'm already pregnant," she said with half a laugh.

He gazed into her eyes. "And you've never been so sexy."

Soon they were naked and under the covers, and Alex experienced for the first time the all-consuming bliss of making love to a pregnant woman. What a sensuous bundle she proved to be: so innocently erotic, completely vulnerable. There was far less motion, of course, but the emotion of it all enveloped and devoured him. Never before had he experienced such a supernatural level of pleasure or a deeper wellspring of feeling, though he was no match for the force of seven months of pent-up desire. Like an overly excited schoolboy losing his virginity, he couldn't hold back.

No apology nor explanation seemed necessary; Emily's coos of contentment and soft caresses were all the reassurance he needed. They lay silently in each other's arms, hearing only their own breathing and the muffled city traffic.

"I've really made a mess of things, haven't I, Alex?"

"We can be in this together if you want," he whispered.

Emily burrowed her head into his chest and fell silent.

Twenty minutes later, Emily, with a quirky southpaw tilt, was sketching her naked subject, who lay on the bed, a pillow as his fig-leaf. The intensity with which she studied each bodily detail and her deftly whimsical strokes had an erotic charge on him, but he was more concerned with her pensive demeanor. Was she capable of standing up to the pressure that would surely be heaped on her by the same people who had kept her down for most of her life? Was it fair to expect that of her? Just thinking of all the stress this had to be putting on her symbiotic eco-system made him feel guilty. At this delicate crossroads, he knew better than to pressure her. An hour ago he had been nowhere; this tryst had been a gift from God. She wouldn't have admitted his paternity, he reasoned, if she weren't planning to make changes.

Emily stopped drawing and expelled a tortured sigh. "My baby needs me to be a cocoon, not a bundle of nerves."

"Let *me* be the cocoon," Alex offered. "Leave Charles and let me bear the brunt."

"How? By carrying my baby? By having a civilized chat with Charles and my father over cognac and cigars?" She spoke softly, pleadingly, and even before she expressed her final verdict Alex's heart slowly began to break: "Don't think I haven't fantasized about running off with you. I do all the time, Alex, but it's wrong...on so many levels."

"Then why did you call me? Why did you come?"

"I don't know," she said weakly. "To see if I could go through with it? To get you out of my system once and for all? I don't know. If you knew what a mess I was inside, you couldn't possibly want me."

"Then why tell me I'm the father?"

"I wasn't planning to, believe me. I guess I needed to be honest with *someone*. I shouldn't have come, shouldn't have told you. No matter what I do, it turns out to be cruel." Her eyes grew dark for a long instant, then she looked at him with steely resolve. "I need your blessing, Alex. Please, if you care for me at all, let me go."

His gut turned rancid. He couldn't speak.

"I'm in my third trimester. The stress is eating me alive," she said, in such a way that there could be no rebuttal. "Running off with you won't alleviate a thing; it'll only make things worse. You have no idea what a backlash we'd face. When I think of all the tragedies that could occur—to the baby, to Charles, to me, to your business—I can't go through with it. I can't! I know I'm supposed to be sophisticated, but the guilt is unbearable. Please let me go. Give me your blessing so I can move on with a clear conscience."

"And abandon my own child?" he croaked.

The notion prickled her. "You seduce me seven months ago, and you think that entitles you to wreak havoc with everyone else's life? Look at the big picture, like you always tell me to do. Think of my health. The baby's. Think of all the people we'd be hurting."

"But it's okay to hurt me?"

"You're strong, fit for the world. And you're not my husband."

"You don't love your husband."

"Sometimes you can be so naïve," she snapped. "Marriage is complicated; it's not just about sex and passion. Poor Charles is buying rattles and baby clothes, boasting to all his friends. I'm his last chance at happiness, he says. If he's humiliated like this, he might kill himself! Or hire a hit-man to kill you—unless my father beats him to it. I know you think Dad likes you, but wait till this turns into a full-blown scandal. The adverse publicity in the middle of the proxy fight will infuriate him. He's vindictive, capable of almost anything—even murder, I suspect. Those he can't control, he destroys."

Alex deemed this overdramatic. "What about *your* life?"

"What makes you so sure we'd be happy?" she said, growing more distant. "The only thing we've done together is have sex. Marriage is hard enough without all the pressures we'd face, especially once you lost your business and we became social outcasts. Chances are we'd end up hating each other—just like every other married couple I know. It's hubris to think we'd be any different." She gave him one last hard look. "God, I hardly know you," she said, and then glanced at her watch. "I have to go. Charles and I are flying to Palm Beach for the holidays."

She snatched her clothes and disappeared to the bathroom, leaving Alex sitting there on the bed in a lump of dismay. Noticing her sketchbook, he crawled over and examined her drawing of him. His face had been expertly rendered—it was unmistakably him. His body, seen through her eyes, was more buffed than in reality. Small consolation. Desperate to put his own imprint on the picture, to give her something to ponder later on when she looked it, he seized her pencil and quickly wrote, "Dear Emily, I want to spend the rest of my life with you and our baby. I love you. Yours forever, Alex." Lamenting that Emily might be essentially spineless, he closed the sketchbook and stuck it back into her bag just before she returned fully dressed.

"We need to do what's right and elegant, Alex," she said, giving him a limp embrace before sliding away. "Love can never flourish at the expense of others."

"Love is always at the expense of others," he blurted, not sure what he was saying. Having learned from his business adventures that fortunes can swing on a dime, he tried to remain unruffled in his disappointment and cling to the long view. What other option did he have? Yet he felt sick inside, utterly helpless. "You can't be in love without causing resentment somewhere, without threatening someone who's grown comfortable with the old you, who has an emotional stake in your limitations."

"It's way too complicated. Nothing but bad karma can come from it."

"Please don't leave, Emily," he begged. "I've never loved anyone but you."

"You'll get over it. People always do. A year from now you'll be thanking me." She hoisted her bag's leather strap over her shoulder and headed for the door. Alex followed, wrenching in pain.

"Maybe instead of blaming one honest, passionate night for your predicament," he said, "you should direct your anger at the head games played on you over the years, tying you in knots. Maybe *that's* the real scandal."

"Good bye, Alex." With an icy countenance, she left.

◆   ◆   ◆

Emily arrived at her building forty-five minutes late, just as Riggs was slamming the limousine trunk over a pile of Louis Vuittons.

"Where's my husband?"

"Up in the future nursery," said the butler, with a hint of disapproval at her tardiness, as if he himself couldn't wait to start his vacation, "with brother Billy."

Alterations for the nursery wouldn't begin until after the first of the year and wouldn't be complete until mid-February, and until she moved her art supplies she still deemed the room her studio and sacred space. The thought of Charles and Billy poking around in there felt like a foreign occupation. Charles hardly ever set foot in her studio; the place almost seemed to threaten him, and in the state she was in, the last thing she needed was to have to explain her recent erotic canvasses. They were stacked against the wall under a thin white sheet. In a mild panic, she scurried into the lobby and caught the elevator, racking her brain for explanations for her paintings in the event Charles discovered them, but nothing compelling came to mind. Once inside the apartment, she headed up the staircase to the second floor. Trudging up stairs took all her energy these days. When she arrived at her studio, Billy, standing with Charles over near the window, was making yet another pitch for money.

"Forget the End of the World, bro. I'm calling it 'Wired.' Computers built right into the tables. Want a drink? Click. Menu? Click. Music? Click. Pick up a chick? Click."

"Please stop saying 'click,'" Charles scowled, "I get it."

"What's going on?" said Emily. She was relieved to see that the sheet was intact. Billy's Chesterfield overcoat was draped over it, providing an additional layer of protection.

"Nice of you to join us, my dear," came Charles's frosty greeting. "The driver said you got back hours ago. Where the devil have you been?"

"I did some Christmas shopping," she said, avoiding his stare.

"If I didn't own the plane, we'd have missed our flight," Charles said, with a frightening skull-and-crossbones smile. "Anyway, I was showing 'Uncle' Billy here the plans for the nursery." He gestured at Raoul's drawings on the table beside her copier.

"The renderings look great, Emily," said Billy unctuously. "A baby brings everyone together, doesn't it?"

"Charles," she said, "I don't want to go to Florida."

"What do you mean?"

"I just don't want to go with my mother in her condition."

Charles crossed the room and put his arms around her, looking intently into her eyes. "The Plums are expecting us tonight for dinner—and, my love, as boring as Lynne is, you've got to admit Gene is as amusing as a wind-up toy."

"I can't think of a worse way to spend Christmas Eve," she muttered.

"To cancel at this late hour would be rude," said Charles, with a droll smile. "You know that's my only virtue, that I am never rude. Besides, the doctor said this is the last time you can fly before you give birth."

"I personally think Palm Beach is overrated," said Billy.

"Oh, do shut up, Billy!" Charles exploded.

"Just trying to be helpful."

"You can be helpful by leaving!"

"Fine," Billy huffed, throwing up his hands. As he began to storm off, Emily had a sudden premonition of what was about to occur, but stood strangely paralyzed. In grabbing his overcoat, Billy also took the sheet, dragging it across the floor along with several paintings. By the time Emily could react, her work was strewn all over the floor, much of it face up.

"Hey, now," said Billy, picking up her most recent canvas, an abstract depiction of a man mounting a pregnant woman from behind, "these will sell!" He was practically salivating.

"Billy, put that down," Emily cried, dropping her shoulder bag to the floor and dashing over, but by then Charles was staring at another painting. He studied her new portfolio in pallid shock and then examined her with a cocked eyebrow, as if wondering who she was.

"I preferred the clowns," he said.

"I wanted to try something new."

"I gather who the woman is," Billy teased, completely regaled, "but who's the man? Is that you, Charles?"

"I told you, Billy," Charles bristled. "Shut up!"

Billy was too spellbound by the erotica to pay heed. "They're fantastic, Emily. Please let me hang them in my club, and I guarantee you…"

Ignoring his pregnant wife bending down to gather her canvases to their former upright position, Charles whirled on his brother. The muscles of his jaw were convulsing, but when he spoke it was quietly, his brow arched to its highest altitude. "Billy, get this through your cocaine-addled, pedestrian little pea brain: Emily is not hanging her paintings in your club. She's not hanging her laundry in your club. And I am not investing in your barroom version of the Titanic, whether you decorate it with computers, crap tables, or compost. Do you understand what I am saying, or do you need someone to translate?" Billy stood motionless. "So Merry Christmas and good-bye." Charles seized his wife's arm and propelled her out of the room and down the hall.

"That was unnecessary," she scolded.

"I'm fed up with that money-grubbing hyena."

"And I," she said, balking at the top of the stairs, "don't want to go to Florida and leave my mother alone on Christmas." She was thinking solely of Alex; the Lukes family dysfunction was already making her yearn for the warmth and tranquility of his bed.

"We're going, and that's that." Charles ushered her down the stairs. She felt too weak and guilt-ridden to resist as he herded her into the elevator. The cabin descended. Moments later, she looked into his face and got a shock: The famous Charles Lukes mask was gone; in its place was the visage of a scared little boy. "Listen, something horrible has happened," he said, lower lip trembling. "The goats got out."

"The *what?*" she exhaled, relieved that his consternation had nothing to do with her infidelity.

"I just got a call from Japan. The Spidex goats escaped from the complex! Nobody can find them! We suspect foul play; some radical faction may have freed them."

Emily stifled a laugh. "So what?"

"So what? So *what?*" Charles ran nervous fingers through his hair. "It's a nightmare, that's what! An international incident. They're saying that the whole Japanese ecosystem could be affected. People drink goat's milk. And these goats are part spider! Nobody really knows how the spider gene can change the bio-chemical makeup of milk! Nobody knows how it will affect children. I may get sued."

"I didn't realize the Japanese drank milk; I thought they were lactose intoler-ant."

"The Japanese press broke the story yesterday. Once the American press gets wind of this, we'll never hear the end of it. No one will find me down in Florida."

She struggled to keep a straight face. "How far can a few runaway goats get? How much damage can they do?"

"I don't know, but I need you. More than ever. You and the baby are the only things in my life that mean anything. I know you haven't been that happy recently, that I haven't been, perhaps, the husband you bargained for." His eyes had the forlorn look of a hungry beagle. "Can't seem to get hold of anything real, that's the problem. Nothing ever works, no matter what I do. I feel like I'm drowning, Emmy." He forced a laugh and took a swig from his silver pocket flask in an effort to return to his sardonic self. "Good god, I sound like Billy."

"Maybe you wouldn't be drowning if you didn't drink so much."

Instantly the mask was back in place. "Your middle-class morals are showing, my dear," he said, "though you'd hardly know it from your Kama Sutra art." The elevator opened and deposited them in the lobby. "I'm through with venture cap-ital. It's for scoundrels. People are basically an untrustworthy species. Scratch almost anyone and he'll disappoint you. I don't know what I'd do without you as my anchor."

Charles practically dragged his disconcerted anchor outside and toward the idling limo. She felt rushed, scatterbrained, and just before climbing inside the vehicle, she realized why: "I forgot my bag," she said with a gasp.

"Your bag! Jesus! Who cares?"

"*I* care. It has my wallet and cell phone." In a panic, she started back toward the building.

"Wait, you're pregnant, let me get it," said Charles half-heartedly.

She pretended not to hear him and quickened her stride inside. Her wallet and cell phone were the least of her worries; it was her sketchbook that she was desperate to secure. Just as she got to the elevator, the doors opened and there stood Billy, holding the bag with the sketchbook sticking conspicuously out of it. A tremor of fear shot through her lungs.

"I thought you might have forgotten this," he said, stepping out of the elevator cabin.

"Oh, thanks," she said, snatching the bag. "Sorry about Charles's rudeness."

"Don't worry. After thirty years, I'm immune. Merry Christmas." Billy pecked her cheek and then started to leave. At the doorway, he turned back and said teasingly, "Love you, love your work."

"Ha-ha, very funny," she smirked. Once he was gone, she took a cursory inventory of the bag's contents—sketch of Alex, money, cell phone. Finding everything intact, she shoved the sketchbook deep into the bag out of sight and returned to the limo and her impatient husband.

As the vehicle pulled away from the curb, Charles began crooning "White Christmas." She put on her iPod earphones and switched on some Vivaldi. Cradling her baby bundle in her arms, she sank into the cushy leather, closed her eyes, and conked out.

◆   ◆   ◆

Caressed by a South Florida breeze, grateful at long last for solitude, Emily strolled down the shaded path that ran along the Intracoastal Waterway separating Palm Beach Island from the real world. She hadn't heard another word about the missing goats and couldn't decide whether Charles was sadistic or simply clueless for hauling her pregnant body down to this heat, parading her from one social function to another and hovering around her all week. What a relief it was today not to have to put on a happy face for people in whom she had no interest. She squinted out from under her floppy sun hat at the white yachts. After some pasty, flabby bikers glided by and she was alone, she lowered her shoulder bag and took out her sketchbook for the first time since coming down here. She flipped to her drawing of Alex and was somewhat irked to see his inscription. It was selfish, manipulative; she did not appreciate the pangs of longing and regret it evoked. As she studied her rendering of his face, she once again decided that she didn't have enough history with him to feel trust; she barely knew where he came from. Their bond was untested, based solely on the allure of forbidden fruit. The upheaval would be too bloody and acrimonious to endure. She wondered how he might be spending the holidays. Hopefully not in another woman's arms, though could she blame him at this point?

It was New Year's Eve morning, a week since their tryst at the Carlyle. Two hours ago Charles had motored off to Wellington to attend a luncheon honoring the Prince of Wales and to watch His Royal Highness play polo. Charles—Lukes, not Windsor—had complained that it would look bad for him to attend the party of the season without his pregnant wife. But Emily, drained by all the social activity, was firm.

"You'll miss out!" was Charles's parting shot just before speeding off in his vintage Aston Martin, which had once been his mother's toy.

No one ever missed out here. You could disappear for years, then return, throw a party, and be in the social loop as if you had never left. What distinguished Palm Beach even above all other hallowed resort communities of America's rich was its air of timeless permanence—as if its sprawling sun-drenched Italianate villas and Mizner mansions had been dreaming on their vast well-watered lawns forever and would dream on into infinity. During the winter season there was always the same cavalcade of luncheons, teas, cocktail parties, and charity balls in the villas and mansions, which belonged to Palm Beach's supernal wealthy families—people who had always been wealthy and who would always be wealthy, until the last tick of time. At first, your expectations of unalloyed pleasure ran high, but by the second or third of these galas the luster wore off and the tedium took over, and before you knew it you were spending another jaded day in paradise. During this visit, Emily, feeling more like an observer than a participant and relishing it, could barely converse with the women in their circle, most of whom were in Lynne Plum's age group and had bitter marriages, vicious tongues, conventional answers for everything, and no real intellectual interests. Not that she cared, but since they gossiped about everyone else she had no reason to assume that they didn't gossip about her—probably along the lines that she was going through a juvenile artistic "phase" and was too young and quirky to take part in their insightful discussions of caterers, clothes, and interior decorating. What a field day they'd have if they got wind of her little secret.

Charles, of course, flourished in this venue and was always at his bantering best with glass and cocktail napkin in hand. His never-flagging wit on constant display, he discussed politics and current affairs with the same aplomb he did the finer points of croquet. Even more than New York, Palm Beach was his turf. Here, it didn't matter whether or not you worked; Charles's core group actually considered having a vocation a sign of mediocrity. What mattered was that Abigail Lukes's grandfather had spread enough money around the island to have a street, a museum, and a bridge named after him, which was why the adopted grandson belonged to the Bath & Tennis and Everglades Clubs and had the power to blackball anyone from entering the gilded gates of Palm Beach society.

Palm Beach might have been a utopian hell for Emily, but she loved their house. It was a pink-stucco Spanish Colonial, designed by Addison Mizner and built by Abigail's father in 1912. Though not overly large, it had the easy grandeur of that era, with ranks of high arched windows and broad yellow awnings. Brilliant flowers and flaming red bougainvillea thrived everywhere, tropical birds lilted in the trees, and, pregnant or not, it was still a treat early each morning to pull on a bathing suit, take a solitary dip in the mosaic-tiled pool, and then enjoy a freshly picked breakfast of oranges and mangoes—before Charles arose at ten and poured his unique brand of bitters over her airy mood. Palm Beach seemed the perfect environment in which to paint, until she actually tried it. Was it only the heat that sapped her energy and dulled her brain? Or was it the everlasting sameness of each long sunny day, the incessant serenity, the implacable orderliness, the utter absence of growth, of change, of nature? Every square inch of this island was manicured, down to its collective unconscious.

Arriving at Worth Avenue, Emily strolled on aching feet past the expensive boutiques—Armani, Hermès, Chanel, and those porcelain shops catering to the blue hairs. Feeling assaulted by sterility and banality in all directions, by the imagined stench of old people, by fatigue and dehydration, she ducked into a shaded travertine promenade. She bought an Arnold Palmer from a deli and parked herself on a wooden bench, feeling lonely, doomed. After a few sips, she remembered the pain in Alex's eyes back at the Carlyle. How callous she had been: making love to him, declaring his paternity, and then walking out of his life. It was unconscionable, and he had handled it with surprising dignity. Desperate to make amends, she rummaged through her bag for her cell phone and Alex's crumpled-up Post-it. Glancing about for eavesdroppers, she punched in his cell phone number, only to get voice mail. At a loss as to what to say and how to say it and afraid that leaving a message might be somehow unwise, she promptly hung up. Seconds later she mustered the courage to dial again, this time Alex's business number. After just one ring, an older man barked "Hello!" so brusquely that she nearly hung up in terror.

"May I please speak to Alex?" she managed to ask.

"He's out," the man said, and her heart sank. "Who's calling?" he wanted to know.

"Emily," she said a bit timidly. "Are you, um, Alex's father?"

"Not long ago I was known as Harry Halaby. Now I'm known as Alex Halaby's father," he said. "He's down in Soho looking at lofts."

"Soho?" she smiled. "Really?"

"He's sick of living with his parents, and who can blame him?" Harry Halaby gave a little bark of a laugh that made him sound more human. "What CEO lives with his parents?"

"You sound proud of him," she ventured.

"I'm in awe of him—but don't you dare tell him I said so. May I give him a message, Emily?"

Something about this charming gentleman, and especially the esteem in which he held his son, altered her chemical balance and worldview. Even over the phone the man felt like a blanket of protection. Beneath the crust she sensed an enormous, generous heart; the antithesis of her own father; the father she had always wanted. That Alex came from such earthy stock reassured her in stunning fashion, humanized him in a way that took root and made him viable. Suddenly her reservations about him seemed silly and unduly fear-based, and she found herself in sync with what truly mattered to her. Her child deserved its real father; their love deserved a chance. She couldn't go through life being a martyr like her mother or living under the thumb of a big lie. There would be consequences to going off with Alex, she realized soberly, but what about the consequences of *not* going through with it? Poor Charles…this was going to hurt him. He couldn't help who he was. He needed a woman who loved him, but Emily Shea simply couldn't be that woman. Not without destroying herself. Dozens of appreciative ladies would be lining up to take her place; and Charles would always have Palm Beach and his cadre of like-minded friends and sycophants, who equated money with virtue, who could be counted on to prop him up and blame her for everything. That was only fair, how it should be.

"Please tell him I called," she said, tingling with courage, "and that I miss him. And that I'll call as soon as I get back."

"I have no idea who you are, Emily," said Harry Halaby, "but you sound like another difference in Alex's ways. Any woman who misses my son is automatically a friend of mine."

"Thank you."

"Perhaps we'll meet early in the new year," he said.

"I'd like that very much," she beamed.

14

Smoke and Mirrors

Harry was incredulous as father and son strode briskly down Fifth Avenue, under umbrellas, to their highly anticipated rendezvous with destiny at Frank Shea's office. Despite the icy January drizzle, Harry had insisted on sticking to his health regimen of a morning walk. The prospect of a generous buyout accounted for the extra spring in his step, giving Alex the courage to relate, only now, the unabridged story of how he had originally stormed Shea's office. The anecdote was too priceless, he figured, for Shea not to bring it up today as he met Harry for the first time, and it would look bad if Harry was out of the loop.

"What's a piano doing in Shea's office?" Harry asked.

"It's a historic relic; Jacob Kress was a concert pianist," Alex explained, just as they passed beneath the gray awning of Emily's building. The numb depression with which he had spent the holidays suddenly seared like a knife. Despite Emily's resolve to enforce the status quo and stay with Charles, most of Alex's holiday energies had been spent waiting in anticipation of her phone call, figuring that the sentiments of the season would intensify her loneliness and cause her to miss him as much as he missed her. Even as each aching day had passed without a word, he refused to accept the fact that things were over. Only now was it beginning to sink in that she might be a lost cause. Maybe she *was* doing the right thing for all concerned, he thought; maybe she was the wise one between them and was protecting him from himself.

"And you really played that idiotic Gilbert & Sullivan song that's driven your mother and me bonkers for years?"

"Tom Lehrer," Alex corrected, a tad glumly, musing how he had relied on another man's creative talent to woo both Emily and Cresslon. At least he knew how to delegate.

"Well, it sure took balls," Harry laughed, the highest compliment he could bestow.

Alex fought through his pain and slapped his father's back. "Are you ready to retire to a life of luxury?"

"Are you ready to spend the next five years working for Shea?"

"I spent eight working for you," he teased. Concerned that he and his father might have vastly different ideas concerning the value of Halaby Hosiery, he threw in, "Shea has to pay us a premium, or it's no deal."

"Nobody's paying up these days. Everyone wants a bargain."

"Dad, Dad, Dad...we're growing like a nineties high-tech company!"

"And we know what happened to most of them. Just listen," Harry ordered, "and don't say a word until I get a feel for where Shea's coming from. You talk as if we're just going to waltz in there and pick up a fat check."

Alex gave his superior a mock salute. "Soon you'll have only your golf clubs to boss around."

"Speaking of clubs, your mother and I have our final interview at the Ocean Club. Just a formality, they tell me."

"Whatever floats your boat."

"By the way," Harry asked, "who's Emily?"

Alex's heart skipped a beat. "A woman I know," he said warily. "Why?"

"I forgot to tell you, she called on New Year's Eve."

Blood rushed into his cranium. "She *called*? You forgot to *tell* me?"

"She misses you," Harry teased.

A mammoth burden lifted from Alex's shoulders. Relief surged in one giant exhalation. Suddenly the bare Central Park trees were leafy green, the bleak gray skies cobalt blue. The sun shone, bluebirds sang, and a full-piece orchestra played Gershwin's "'S Wonderful." "What else did she say?" he asked, trying not to betray his glee as he walked a foot off the ground.

"Just that she'll call when she gets back. She seems nice.... Jesus, finally!"

"You make a lousy secretary," said Alex sourly, stifling a grin.

On that sparkling up-note they entered Cresslon's tower of black glass. In silence, they rode the elevator to the executive office floor. They removed their damp overcoats in the reception area, where Harry's eyes popped at the opulent trappings: Flemish tapestries depicting medieval knights on horseback, elegant marble busts in the wall recesses, carved mahogany sofas and reception desk. Mrs. Donovan was waiting there for them, and as she escorted them down the plushly carpeted hallway, Alex saw his father's skepticism dissolve. Animated by the ambience of power, Harry began to stride like a king—maybe only the King of Pantyhose, but as regal as any monarch. His chin lifted, his chest billowed. All those years of adversity and hard work, of being a standard-bearer for quality and integrity, had finally led to this Olympus, his just reward. There could be no better heart medicine, thought Alex with deep satisfaction, thrilled beyond financial considerations that he had brought his father to this pinnacle. He was even more elated that Emily had called. Talk about heart medicine!

The slick gray office with the panoramic view was empty when Mrs. Donovan ushered them in. With her usual professional reserve, she asked them to be seated and then withdrew. While Alex settled into a chair by the massive kidney-shaped desk, opposite Shea's throne, Harry was drawn to the floor-to-ceiling window. He gazed out at the expanse of Central Park for a long moment. Turning back to the room, he noticed the piano off in the corner. He smiled to himself, then went over and joined his son. They waited in anticipatory silence, Harry drumming his fingers. A minute passed before the door opened and Shea strode in.

"Don't get up, gentlemen," Shea said, in a clipped, business-like tone. "Congrats, Alex—the takeover's dead. The stock shot so high that the Jackal sold his shares, took his hundred mill in profit, and crawled away."

"That's terrific!" Alex beamed.

"Not necessarily," came another voice. It was Charles Lukes, his crooked smile both coolly pleasant and strangely menacing, who entered the room and crossed behind Shea.

Alex broke into a cold sweat; his mouth parched. Despite an effort to appear calm, he felt his face burning red. He prayed that this wasn't what it appeared to be, but the grim countenance of their host told him it was all over. His life, as he knew it, was finished. Forgoing handshakes, Shea sat; his ice-blue eyes burned a hole in Alex, stripping him of all pretense. Charles remained standing behind his father-in-law. With his navy blue suit and amused demeanor, all he needed was a top hat to complete the image of the ultimate master of ceremonies.

Without bothering to introduce himself, Shea addressed Harry. "We were supposed to discuss a buyout today, but something very disturbing was brought to my attention."

"What's going on?" Harry inquired.

"Why don't you ask your son?" said Charles, jutting his cleft chin.

All eyes focused on Alex, who feigned puzzlement. He was not about to utter a word until Shea and Charles revealed what they knew.

"Since Alex isn't man enough to tell you," said Shea, "allow me. Throughout our business relationship, your son has been having an affair with my daughter, who is married to—and pregnant by—my son-in-law here, Charles Lukes."

"My wife came to me last night and confessed everything," Charles added, gazing at the two Halabys with his patented arched eyebrow. "She couldn't take the pressure anymore. I came to inform you, Halaby, that she doesn't want to see you or talk to you. She realizes her terrible mistake. She hasn't had a lot of experience with predators and was fooled by you during a rather severe bout of depression. She's getting therapy now, thank heavens. As for me, I know these insignificant dalliances occasionally happen, and luckily I have the capacity—as well as the good breeding—to forgive her." He strolled to the window and looked out. "We're putting this little episode behind us for the sake of our child. We love each other, you know."

Harry was aghast. "Is this true, Alex?"

Alex couldn't bring himself to face his father. This supposed confession of Emily's didn't ring true, and yet who else could have told Charles? With no other plausible explanation, he began to suspect the worst: that she had cracked under the pressure and decided for whatever reason to make a clean breast of the affair. Obviously she had not told Charles the truth about the child—either that, or she had lied to her lover. But then, why had she called him on Christmas Eve and conveyed the message to his father that she missed him? Angry, desperate, confused, he abandoned all caution: "She told me the baby was mine."

"That is an outrageous lie!" Charles bellowed, his mien suddenly black and dangerous. "If you don't stop harassing my wife…"

"Harassing her! You must be kidding!"

"Oh, dear God," muttered Harry, head in hands.

"Let me talk to her," said Alex, only to have Shea slam a document on the desk.

"This," he said, "is a court-issued restraining order. If I find out you're even looking at a picture of my daughter, I will do everything in my very considerable power to destroy you. Both of you."

"My father has nothing to do with this."

"As of today our business relationship is dead. And you'll be dead too," Shea said, looking squarely at Alex, "if any of this ever leaves this room."

Alex refused to flinch as his eyes locked with Shea's. Raw instinct told him not to be railroaded, to insist on confirming the facts with Emily. Despite the restraining order, despite feeling sick and intensely guilty for dragging his father through such ugliness, he defiantly clung to his last thread, "What if she calls me?"

"Don't hold your breath," Charles snickered confidently from behind the cosmetics juggernaut, who added:

"Make one phone call to my daughter, get within a mile of her, breathe one word about any of this to anyone, and I'll sic so many lawyers on you you'll be paying legal fees for the rest of your life. I can take more drastic measures, too," he threw in mysteriously. He lit a cigarette, allowing time for his words to settle. Through the rising smoke, the photos of celebrities and money men on the wall behind him loomed menacingly, testimony to his vast network of influence. He glared at Alex. "What sort of lowlife prick would behave like this, after all I've done for you! You piece of shit! I saved your fucking company!"

"Now, just hold on!" Harry said. "My son saved your corporate ass! This is the first I've heard of this, but it seems to me your daughter has to bear some responsibility for this mess."

"My daughter was victimized by your scumbag son!"

"*Watch* it!" cried Harry, shooting to his feet and thrusting his index finger an inch from Shea's throat. The look of surprise on Shea's face suggested that it was unlikely he'd ever been spoken to in such a manner. "You don't address me or my son that way! And you don't threaten us—I don't care who you think you are! The only thing you've built is your own carrer."

"Get out!" Shea warned. "And tread carefully."

Harry snatched the restraining order off the desk and dumped it in Shea's wastebasket. "Let's go, Alex."

As the Halabys headed for the door, Charles, slipping his hand in his pocket and donning his ironic smile, got in the final word: "Oh, and by the way, Harry, old boy. I think you and the Mrs. may want to forget about the Ocean Club."

Only when they were out on the sidewalk did Harry square off with his son: "So *this* is your Emily—Shea's *daughter!*"

"I didn't know she was his daughter at the time."

"You knew she was married! Goddammit, Alex! Your dick's destroyed my whole life's work, as well as your future!"

"We only made love twice. Once Memorial Day weekend, once on Christmas Eve."

"Well, I hope it was worth it."

Alex whipped out his cell phone. "Dad, I'll make this up to you."

"Oh, no you don't!" Harry grabbed his arm to restrain him.

"I don't know what's just happened, but…"

"You don't know anything! You don't know who she really is or what she really wants."

"I know she's pregnant with my baby."

"Yeah, yeah," Harry said, all sarcasm, "she's having your kid. That's why she confessed to her husband and left you for roadkill. And why her husband wants the child. Jesus Christ, think!" Harry coaxed the cell phone out of his son's suddenly listless hand.

"None of this makes sense," Alex said.

"Well, it sure does to me! Just another in a long line of disasters you call relationships, though I must say this whack job takes the cake. She and her pantywaist husband deserve each other. If he were any kind of man, he'd have beat the crap out of you, not run to her father and blackballed us from his stupid club. No wonder she screwed around on him."

Only lamely could Alex defend her honor. "She's not that way, Dad."

"She probably has no idea who the father is. Her tennis pro, her personal trainer, her masseur."

Alex was fighting to keep intact his memory of the Emily he knew. Had he imagined it all?

"It's over," Harry decreed, flagging a taxi. "I don't want this to get any worse than it already is. My business is in deep shit again. I don't want my son's kneecaps broken as well." Pocketing Alex's cell phone, the old warrior looked into space with a tired, faraway gleam, like Sisyphus mentally readying for another strenuous upward roll of the rock. To Alex, seeing that look was as unbearable as Emily's confession; it spoke volumes about his own failure and uselessness. "Let's go home," Harry said, herding his shell-shocked son into the cab and climbing in behind him. "I'll do my best to pick up the pieces and calm Gunther…not to mention your mother." He slammed the door with extra oomph.

"I'll help…however I can," Alex offered, fighting back tears.

"No! Take another sabbatical and take serious stock of your life." After barking out the address to the cabbie, Harry turned his back on Alex and peered bitterly out the window. Much as Alex longed to talk, not another word was uttered by either of them on the ride home.

◆   ◆   ◆

Huddled under the awning of her apartment building, shielded from the bleak January downpour, Emily tried to remember the last time her father had invited her to lunch. All her life she had longed for a closer, warmer relationship with him, and despite her antipathy toward him and her suspicion he had an agenda, she had accepted his last-minute invitation. Most likely, he wanted to explain away the presence of Oxana in his limousine on Christmas Eve, say he was sorry about her mother's recent episode, mend fences with Emily—something along those lines. Still, his spur-of-the-moment request—"I want to take my grandkid to the Four Seasons," was how he had tenderly put it—filled her with guarded hope. Even now, she clung to the little-girl fantasy of sitting at Daddy's table and having a loving heart-to-heart, the plutocratic Frank Shea miraculously trans-formed into an apologetic, caring human being. An improbable notion to be sure, but as she stood under the awning she pondered an even crazier possibility: that she confide in him about Alex and the baby. With her father on the moral defensive, the timing might be propitious, assuming she found him to be in a conciliatory frame of mind. A naïve, risky idea perhaps, but what an unexpected boon it would be if she could somehow secure his assistance in dealing with Charles. If it had to be Alex and her against the world, she was prepared—if Alex still was. Whatever happened at lunch, she was planning to call him immediately afterward and arrange a rendezvous. She couldn't wait to see his face when she told him of her decision.

As the silver limo pulled up to the awning, the doorman opened an umbrella, enabling Emily to climb into the vehicle without encountering a single raindrop. Inside, her father was pressing the button to raise the glass privacy screen separat-ing them from the driver. His icy expression dashed any hopes of a pleasant lunch. As soon as the door closed, he said, "It's over—you and Halaby."

His words knocked the breath out of her. From his steely air, she knew it was no use bluffing. "Who told you?"

Mysteriously, he gazed out the fogged window at dreary, leafless Central Park. "Why don't you tell me your side of the story?"

She took a deep breath, determined not to cower. "Charles isn't right for me. I don't love him," she said, eyes welling.

"And so you get knocked-up by some stray cat?"

"Only you could imagine something like that."

"You betrayed your husband! And me!"

"You're a fine one to talk about betrayal," she shot back. "You, who screw Russian gold diggers younger than your daughter while Mom rots in rehab over the holidays!"

"I was just giving the girl a lift to the airport."

"To Teterboro? Awfully young to be flying private, isn't she?"

"Watch your mouth, young lady. You're hardly in a position to give anyone grief." His face was beet red; a V-shaped vein pulsed in his forehead. "I had no idea about your mother's episode, because *you* didn't bother to tell me."

"Why should I? *You're* her husband!" As her father grabbed her arm to restrain her, she ripped it away and cried, "Get your hands off me!"

"It's over, I tell you. The scumbag is out."

"Alex is ten times the man you are!"

"He's a conniving parasite who was playing us both for fools! Just to let you know, he's incapable of supporting you. I just ruined his company. It'll never recover from losing its biggest customer. And that's just child's play compared to what I'll do if he shows his face again. I'll hound him for the rest of his no-good life if I have to."

"This has nothing to do with you. You had no right to interfere."

"I had *every* right! Everything you do is a reflection on me. I'm a public figure. Stockholders deplore scandals—especially these days, when everyone's looking for reasons to crucify CEOs."

"So, as usual, it's all about you."

"For your bubble-headed information, Alex threatened to go straight to Ruby, straight to the press, and straight to a judge to order a blood test, until I blew his blackmailing ass out of the water."

Skeptical of anything her father said, Emily immediately began to poke holes in his story. "He was doing well with you. What would he stand to gain by black-mailing you?"

Shea expelled a long, put-upon sigh and slowly shook his head. "A couple months ago," he said indulgently, "Alex came to me claiming his company was losing money on the pantyhose deal and needed to raise prices. We'd already pre-sold the program to several department stores, and we'd issued price lists; we couldn't suddenly hike prices before having shipped a single pair. We'd look like jackasses. I explained this to him, told him a deal is a deal and that if he didn't like it, Cresslon could always switch suppliers. Didn't hear another word—until two days ago. He paid me a visit, thinking he could bring me to my knees with his shocking tale about you and him and the baby—only this time he wasn't seeking to raise prices but to extort millions for himself—not only betraying me, but his own father." Shea gnashed his capped teeth in anger. "He played hardball with the wrong guy. I cut him off at the knees. Set his shitty little company adrift and told him what else would happen if he tried anything. I doubt you'll be hear-ing from that garbage again."

Emily was reeling, too nonplussed to think. "I don't believe you."

"Then tell me: How else could I have found out?" When no answer was forth-coming, her father went on: "You should thank me. This scandal would have been all over the tabloids; you and your baby would have been tarnished for life." Notwithstanding his daughter's pregnant condition, he cracked the window and lit a cigarette. After a couple of drags, his tone mellowed slightly. "Everyone makes mistakes. He fooled me, too, so there's no sense for either of us to engage in self-flagellation."

Emily's spirits were in shambles. Maybe her father was right; maybe she was a fool.

"You should thank God Charles Lukes is your husband. He could've sued you for emotional cruelty—for a host of things—could've made your life a living hell. But instead he's rising above everything and is willing to take you back. I don't know any man big enough to do that in this situation—to forgive you and care for a baby that isn't even his. Jesus, I sure as hell couldn't."

"You've never had any respect for Charles before."

"I obviously failed to grasp his depth. He showed me incredible strength of character."

"He cares about appearances. That's the only reason he wants me back."

"He's a saint."

"If he were a saint," she sniffled, "he'd let me go."

"To where, your two-bit blackmailer? Better patch things up," her father warned, "because a divorce court won't give you a dime. And neither will I. I'll cut you out of my life and make sure your mother does as well. You won't exist."

"You cut your family out years ago!" With disgust, Emily seized her umbrella and threw open the door of the moving limo. The vehicle screeched to a halt in the middle of the avenue.

"Go on," taunted her father. "Run to your lover—if he'll speak to you. See what happens once the world knows what kind of slut you are. See how far you get in this city with no husband, no money, no talent, and no me to keep your pretty little head above water. See how many of your Park Avenue friends flock to your aid, or what kind of lousy pre-school your bastard kid gets into. See what kind of great life you can give your kid with those odds."

Despite her broken heart, Emily bravely met his eyes. "You always win, don't you? Well, guess what, Daddy? I have a lot of you in me! And I guarantee you, when you see it, you are not going to like it!" She pushed open the door and hauled herself out into the rain. She opened her flimsy umbrella, but a gust of wind inverted it. "All my bad dreams have you in them," she shouted above the downpour, and then stormed off, leaving the limo door wide open.

No matter how she looked at things, she couldn't picture Alex stooping to blackmail, or being so vengeful. It didn't jibe with any of her impressions of him—and yet how well did she know him? Whatever desire she had to call Alex right then and get his version was buried in fear, in the emerging sense that her father was probably right about him being a dangerous con. With her baby's well-being and her own future in dire jeopardy, this was no time to indulge in idle hopes. Survival was paramount. Her father meant business, and she shuddered to think what reception Charles had in store for her. If Alex was innocent, he would find a way to prove it, though she wouldn't hold her breath.

Not ready to face Charles and suddenly quite famished, she slogged over to Madison Avenue and ducked into a diner. She slipped into a pink plastic booth in the back, turned off her cell phone, and ordered a cheeseburger and a chocolate milkshake. For the next two hours she numbly indulged in comfort food, sketching the faces of the other diners on paper napkins, retreating into her body and her surroundings, trying to self-induce serenity. Her only concern right now was her baby—which meant sheltering herself, blocking out the world, and gratefully accepting whatever crumbs Charles threw her way.

By mid afternoon, as ready as she would ever be, she returned home. The gloomy weather made the apartment darker than usual, and as her wet shoes squeaked on the gallery's marble floor she heard a single piano note striking over and over—a high note. *Bing…bing…bing…*

"Charles?" she called out timidly. The note grew louder.

She entered the living room and saw Charles slouched over the Steinway keyboard. His left hand clutched a bottle of scotch on top of the piano, while his right hand ceaselessly plunked out the one note. Suddenly he stopped and sat up; as he did, something slid off his lap and clattered on the hardwood floor. It was a pistol. As he bent to pick it up, Emily jumped and took a step backward.

"How very clumsy of me," Charles slurred, once he was more or less upright again. "But we are all clumsy at times, aren't we, my dear?" Waving the gun, he gestured in her general direction, causing her to flinch. "You. You've been very clumsy too, haven't you?" Emily stood frozen, eyes riveted on the gun. "My perfect, proper little wife. You should have been more discreet in your choice of lovers, my dear. Didn't Claire teach you anything? Hmm?" He gave her an exaggerated puzzled look. "What's wrong? Oh, this?" He looked at the gun as if he'd forgotten he had it, then placed it gingerly on the piano keys, somewhere around middle C. "I thought as the wronged husband I should have a gun. It's in all the best plays."

"Charles, please…"

"I could actually kill him, you know." He said it as if he were mulling over what kind of tea to have. Icy terror shot through her, followed by a deeper distress: Her baby was feeling this! "A man with my kind of connections could get away with it, quite easily. Or I could always just blow my own brains out, right here, right now. Would that be your dream-come-true, sweetie pie?"

"Stop it, Charles. You're upset, and you have every right to be. Let me explain…"

"*Explain?* Would you like to *explain* the fact that you're having Halaby's baby?" He produced a piece of paper from his breast pocket, which he wadded up and threw at her feet.

Emily stooped to pick it up and smoothed out the paper: a photocopy of the sketch she had made of Alex, and his incriminating inscription. She dropped onto a sofa. "How did you get hold of this?"

"Ah. That is a great story, actually. Remember Christmas Eve, when we were about to take off for Florida and left Billy alone in your studio for three minutes? He was so enthralled with your pornographic art that when he saw your sketch pad sticking out of your bag, curiosity got the better of him. And guess what the little bugger found and copied on your Xerox machine?"

"Billy?"

"Instead of keeping it in the family and informing his brother, the weasel took his discovery straight to Alex. You know what they say about loyalty among thieves. Billy must've figured that Cresslon has deeper pockets than I, and that Alex, being the more ruthless of the two, could cut the best deal for both of them. Or maybe Billy did it out of hatred. Was hatred *your* motive as well, my dear?" Charles placed the gun on the bench next to him and made it spin like a top. "Your lover threatened to give his little prop to the tabloids—which really might have made an entertaining addition to the society pages—*and* get a court to order a blood test *and* tell the Jackal everything, if old Frank or I didn't pay him off. Fortunately, we don't scare easily. We have other ways of dealing with low-lifes. Here I was thinking Alex a second-rate garmento, and it turns out he's a third-rate extortionist! Just goes to show how you can misjudge some people, don't you agree, my dear?"

The room suddenly went off-kilter for Emily. She stared at the drawing, trying to comprehend how she could have been so careless on all fronts and so open to being trifled with. "Charles, may I please have that gun?"

"What for, my pet? You've already mortally wounded me." He chuckled bitterly.

Emily began to surrender to her grim fate. Weakly she asked, "What do you want from me?"

"You're not going to leave me. I'm tired of starting over. I want this baby. Everyone thinks it's mine. It *is* mine—as much as I belonged to Abigail. And here's the kicker: We're going to call him Charles Lukes Jr. How does that sound, my pet?" Charles stood up, gun in hand, and joined her on the sofa. Emily felt pinned down by his fierce eyes, like a dead moth behind glass. "All marriages have their little ups and downs, eh?" He was actually smiling! He slid closer to her and wrapped an arm around her quivering shoulders. "Now tell me you love me."

Emily shut her eyes, thinking about the years she had spent with this man—the trips, the parties, the bedroom conversations. It had not been all bad; in a strange way she still cared for him. Was it really possible that her passions had led her straight into the clutches of pure evil? She would never be able to trust anyone again, least of all herself. For the rest of her life she would be atoning for her stupendous mistake, for having driven her husband to a near-suicidal state when the poor man had done nothing to deserve it. "I'm so sorry, Charles," she said, lowering her head in shame. "I don't deserve your forgiveness."

"Tell me you love me," Charles persisted.

She couldn't bring herself to accommodate him. She had lied enough already.

"No matter," said Charles, with eerie poise. "I can wait. You have the rest of your life to tell me."

15

Silk Stalkings

A brutal February gust seared through Alex's overcoat as he peered across Fifth Avenue at Emily's building. He wasn't sure what he would do if she actually showed her face. All her phone numbers had been changed. Futile as this stakeout was, it was the last remaining thread to his life as he knew it.

Emily's betrayal had plunged him into a monthlong aimlessness and depression, from which the pills in his mother's medicine chest were his only means of coping. He needed white ones to sleep and peach ones to get through the day, though the numbness they afforded only served to deepen his apathy and disconnect him further from the world. When it came to Freud's maxim for self-realization—"to love and to work"—he couldn't have been a bigger washout. Thankfully, his parents, despite their own worries, had the decency not to rub his nose in it. His mother especially saw that he was suffering enough and kept a respectful distance, a veritable first for her. "At least you fell in love," she said, managing to pick something good out of the wreckage, acting more like the empathetic mother he had known as a boy. "Maybe next time you'll show more judgment, though this really wasn't your fault. It was the girl's for dragging your through this mess." Still, living with them under the same roof, sitting across the dinner table from their vanquished faces night after night, dealing with the palpable gloom, was hellish. His shame was too much to bear, yet he couldn't afford to move out. Nor did he have the energy; he was too despondent to muster any sort of action plan for his shattered life. He could barely rouse his groggy self in the morning; his heart wasn't in anything, and he actually was grateful that his father was back in charge of the family business. Once again, the junior Halaby was desk-less, relegated to sporadic paper shuffling in the back conference room. Unable to tend to anything but his misery, he paid little attention to what his father was doing in the outer office—until a week ago.

He was snapped out of his self-absorbed daze when Jack Larkin showed up for a one-on-one meeting with Harry. Made aware of the Cresslon debacle by the

Wright-Fit salesman, Larkin machine-gunned Harry with questions, while Alex eavesdropped from the conference room.

"Why did Cresslon dump you, Harry? What the hell happened? Quality problems? Delivery? Price?"

"We had philosophical differences," Harry said defensively.

"C'mon, Harry, level with me. Why are you back running the show? Where's Alex? Don't tell me he quit again!"

"Leave my son out of this."

"Well, fine, but this only underscores the point I've been making all along. If you guys can't keep other customers happy, why the hell should R. Havemeyer…"

Listening to his tired father stammer at the hands of this louse electrified Alex's conscience, shook him into facing his obligations. After having expanded production, the company was in even worse straits than it had been at the moment of Alex's motorcycle theft; and with Larkin up to his old whoring tricks, there was simply no way the company could compete. The business had passed Harry by and was at death's door, and Alex had serious doubts whether his father could personally survive its demise. Harry and his company were inseparable. Saddled with the burden of trying to resuscitate his fading Siamese twin, Harry was looking frailer by the day, and it sickened Alex to think that all he had done during these weeks was wallow in self-pity and humiliation. Unless he rose above his pain and did everything humanly possible to fulfill his duty and rectify the situation, he would be forever mired in hell.

He became proactive. Without telling either parent, he called the national retail chains he had been cultivating—JCPenney, Target, Mervyn's, Kmart, Sears, BelMart, and the rest—most of whom had expressed interest in buying product back when Alex was riding the Cresslon crest. However, he soon discovered that bad news spreads even more rapidly than good news, and that herd mentality was the prevailing ethos. Of the dozens of buyers he called, only Joe Frank Russell had the courtesy to get back to him, though his lethal message said it all: "Yer radioactive."

A bitter pill, yet Alex had been down before. He had learned that when one door closes another one opens. He had proven himself resilient, capable of miracles, and the more he pondered the first miracle the more he believed it to be the tip of a larger phenomenon. Cresslon wasn't the only cosmetics company out there. Hadn't Shea himself expressed fears of Avon and/or Mary Kay knocking off Cresslon once the concept was proven? There was no reason why one or both of these door-to-door giants couldn't work with him to develop lower-cost products, and then unleash literally hundreds of thousands of reps into American homes—women who could be walking testimonials to Halaby's quality. Halaby Hosiery's own private army of missionaries spreading the gospel—whether it be Harry's Old Testament of fit and wear-life or Alex's New Testament of fashion and flash. What could be sweeter, Alex mused, regaining his mojo by the minute, than hoisting that old son of a bitch Shea by his own petard!

A great plan in theory, but like an abortive Roman candle it fizzled at liftoff. Since neither Avon nor Mary Kay was in the pantyhose business, there existed no designated person in either company with whom he could speak about it. Alex's experience with both switchboards was the same: sent down one blind alley after another, bounced from bureaucratic pillar to post, before he finally left voice messages with various new-product and procurement people at middle-management levels. He knew he was dead. Pantyhose wasn't on either company's radar screen. Storming the CEO's office wasn't an option; he had shot his wad on that sort of antic. The more he wracked his brain for novel marketing ideas and creative means of distribution, the more he realized he was sunk. There was no one left to turn to, no more time. Every door imaginable had been slammed in his face.

Maybe he was just a one-trick pony, but at least he was young and well-educated enough to survive and carve out some kind of life for himself. Far more distressing to him was the fate of his parents: forced to put the townhouse and beach house on the market and facing the prospect of entering their golden years in mortifying, if not fatal, retreat.

His efforts, however for naught, had propelled him back into a fighting mode. He felt unjustly treated by the universe. The drastic punishment, the financial wipeout of his entire family, didn't fit the crime of falling head-over-heels in love with a married woman, especially since he had fallen before re-joining the family business and had no inkling whose daughter she was. Sure, he should have known better and expected some snarls, but who on earth could have predicted this? His soul ached for its fair share of vindication. Huddled across from Chateau Lukes as an icy wind whipped around the concrete buildings, nearly knocking him off his feet, he was growing feisty even as he took responsibility for his predicament. Maybe this total crack-up was his karmic payback: for taking for granted all the blessings God had given him, sport-fucking all those women, being cavalier about intimacy, and meddling in a marriage. And maybe the ties between the Lukeses ran deeper than he could possibly fathom. Who was Alex Halaby to judge a committed relationship? Still, despite all the introspection swirling around in his brain and his imminent destitution, his heart refused to accept that Emily's baby wasn't his, or that she had double-crossed him out of weakness or malice, or that fate was against them. There *had* to be another explanation! Maybe Charles, sensing something strange in her behavior, had hired a private detective, who had tapped her phone or tailed her to the Carlyle on Christmas Eve. Maybe Emily had confided in Claire or some other treacherous girlfriend she thought she could trust. Maybe she'd been told lies about him; been brainwashed by scare tactics. Before Alex disappeared from the scene, he was determined to find out what really happened and who she really was. Somehow, before the baby was born, he would find a way to look her in the eye and get the truth. Fuck the restraining order! What could Shea take from him that he hadn't taken already?

He couldn't believe his eyes when Emily and Charles emerged from their building, a yard apart and looking less than enthralled with each other. Alex actually felt compassion for both of them, until the sight of her stomach protruding under her open sable coat incited a possessive frenzy. He started across Fifth Avenue, only to freeze in his tracks as a burly man in a buzz cut shepherded the Lukeses into the back cabin of their limo. Alex thought he saw a pistol flash under his trench coat. He stood transfixed, until screeching tires and a blaring horn made him jump out of his skin. A Lexus had nearly slammed into him. Quickly he retreated to the curb, amazed as the Lukeses' bodyguard circled around to ride shotgun with the chauffeur and the long black limo pulled away that Charles felt the necessity to hire a goon. In a strange way it emboldened him, made him question the prevailing reality. If Emily had confessed of her own volition, why was Charles acting so paranoid?

He hailed a cab and headed to Brooklyn, determined to cash in on a favor. Billy owed him twenty grand and was morally obligated to give his benefactor the Lukeses' new phone number, especially if Alex asked for it casually. It was almost certain that Charles and Emily had kept the whole episode hush-hush and Billy in the dark.

Alex hadn't set foot in the End of the World since August. He didn't miss it; it was firmly in his past. He could barely fathom that he had frittered away so much of his life force there. With Halaby Hosiery all but engulfing him these past several months, giving his life more meaning than he had bargained for, his contact with Billy had tapered off considerably. The two hadn't even spoken to one another since before Christmas, and so Alex was surprised to find the club under massive renovation—a chaos of Sheetrock, wires, workmen, and dust. The wall dividing the former health food emporium next door was being razed, doubling the club's space. Billy, observing the demolition, was conferring with a construction foreman.

"I don't care about cost overruns," he shouted above the drilling noise, smoking a cigar and holding a glass of vodka in all his toxic splendor. "I want everything completed by April Fool's Day! Understand?" As the bedraggled foreman returned to work, Billy spotted Alex. "Christ," he barked, with a frat-boy chuckle, "my sister-in-law! What the hell were you thinking?"

"You *know?*"

"Of course I know. I was the one who introduced you into their lives, remember? I'm in the dog house, too—though not nearly as much as you."

"What's all this?" Alex asked, gesturing at the construction.

"Found an investor to buy into my vision."

"Who?"

"Some rich Kraut from Frankfort who wants to dabble in nightclubs," Billy said with a shrug. "We're calling the new club 'Wired.' Computers built right into the tables. What a drink? Click. Pick up a chick? Click. What do you think?"

Alex was too disconsolate to render an opinion on anything.

"Geez, you look like shit," Billy observed.

"I need to talk to Emily. All her numbers have been changed."

"You must be joking," Billy frowned, turning away.

Alex followed at Billy's heels while he made the rounds. "Please, Billy, I'm begging. I'll retire the debt."

"I'll pay you back the ten grand. *No problemo.*"

"It's *twenty*—but I don't want the money. I want to talk to her."

"You're asking me to betray my family."

Alex found this excuse infuriating. "You *hate* your family, Billy! Since when are you such a loyal Lukes?"

"Forget it," Billy said, putting up his hands. "I was over at their apartment last week, and they were ripping you to shreds. Shea was there too. Trust me, you don't want to get anywhere near her. Since her big confession—which took a lot of guts, by the way—she and Charles are tighter than ever."

Hearing this all but crushed him. "I don't believe it."

"What's not to believe? She has no desire to see you. I mean, Jesus Christ, man, she's having a *baby*!

"*My* baby!"

"Another Lukes heir without Lukes blood—the noble tradition lives on," Billy sniggered. "Anyway, what makes you so sure it's yours? Saint Emily lead you to believe that? Or did you just assume…"

"She told me flat-out."

"Look, Sahib, I don't know. Maybe she doesn't know who the real father is and strung you along for kicks. Maybe underneath the sweet facade she's just another head case. Who knows about anyone anymore? Or maybe you frightened her off with that loveably intense psychopathic stare of yours. You should be grateful she slept with you—I'd sure be. That's quite a notch in your belt. But I wouldn't mess with Shea. The man will kill you."

"He'd only be doing me a favor," Alex muttered. "Why can't I hear all this from *her*?"

"Good luck. She hardly leaves the house these days, and when she does she's accompanied by a trained killer named Vincent." Billy draped his arm around Alex's shoulder, though it felt more of a buzz-off gesture than a comforting one. "Look, pal, I got enough on my plate getting the new club ready in time without getting involved in your seedy business. You had your fun, now back off."

Alex's heart went into spasms. "Jesus, Billy, I've always been there for you."

Whipping out his checkbook, Billy hastily made out a check for $20,000 to "Alex Halaby," forgetting it was the company that technically had loaned him the money. He thrust the check at his forlorn friend. When Alex balked at accepting it and refused to go away, Billy, with a look of pity, scribbled a phone number on the back—but it was not the number Alex was seeking. "If you want Emily's number so badly," Billy said, "call Claire. A few carnal courtesies with her might do wonders."

◆   ◆   ◆

Entubed in a strapless seafoam-green evening gown, the Baroness de Lapalisse struck a pose in front of the three-way mirror. At her knees, the dress fishtailed in ruffles to the carpet. "Honestly," she asked, "how do I look?"

"Positively glam!" gushed Victor, the swishy Bergdorf-Goodman sales clerk who had attended to the baroness for the better part of the morning. "Just like a mermaid!"

Claire pouted at the mirror as if it were paparazzi, parading back and forth, swaying her bound hips with a look of concern. "How do I look, Emily? Luscious? Ludicrous? I can't decide."

From her perch on the window-seat, Emily pretended not to hear and continued to stare out at the plaza. Despite the fact that Charles had changed their phone numbers and hired a bodyguard, she did not consider them impenetrable barriers for a man of Alex's resourcefulness and determination. From getting her into bed to miraculously saving his business, he had always found a way to get what he wanted, and his total silence over the past month pretty much confirmed him to be the reprehensible rogue her father had portrayed. Still, she didn't feel any peace or closure. Ransacked of hope, paralyzed with remorse, she had spent much of the past month holing up in her bedroom—reading magazines, watching TV, catching up on sleep, letting Riggs bring her meals. In her quasi-catatonic state she had no desire to be social, leaving Chateau Lukes only for doctor and sonogram appointments, which at least verified that her baby's vital signs were in perfect order despite everything. She told herself that she was glad to be done with the lying that had marked her pregnancy, relieved in a strange way that the truth was out. All her love was now being channeled into her baby. Withdrawing into herself, she had become a human cocoon.

As her belly grew, the mere act of walking became a chore; her feet ached and she waddled like a duck. Water weight, heartburn, and lack of sleep added to her discomfort, but they weren't nearly as unpleasant as interviewing baby nurses and putting the finishing touches on the nursery with Charles and the insufferable Raoul—entrenching herself as Mrs. Charles Lukes. Such shared activities were so draining that she invariably had to lie down in solitude afterward. Oddly enough, Charles was behaving with eerie civility, showing no sign of instability since the gun incident, drinking less, and even attempting to cater to her needs. Though noble on the face of it, it struck her as manipulative and made her feel even lowlier. Still, as she headed into the final month of her pregnancy, she began to entertain the notion that she might be able to pick up the pieces of her marriage and learn to love and respect him again. It was the least she could do, she figured, considering the unspeakable atrocity she had put him through and the effort he was making. Yet whenever she made the attempt, something in her heart died.

Yesterday, beset with cabin fever and weary of Charles's attentions, she had attended a baby shower in her honor, hosted ever so graciously by Claire. Of course, she never went anywhere without her constant companion, Vincent, who escorted her all the way to the lobby elevator and waited for her until she came down. Much as Emily resented this, Charles and her father were both adamant, convinced that Alex, having lost his business, was psychotic and liable to resort to almost anything, even kidnapping. She was in no moral or physical position to argue.

The Baron and Baroness de Lapalisse had just moved into their much-heralded new flat on the corner of Seventieth and Park, which Claire had turned into a garish slice of Gay Paree. Emily, in her droopy state, had left the baby shower guest list entirely to her hostess, never dreaming the baroness would delegate that task to her newly retained publicist. In the process of upgrading her address, Claire was also striving to upgrade her social status: from Eurotrash to socialite. Far from an intimate gathering of Emily's friends, the event was populated entirely by the future *grande dames* of Manhattan, a set to which Emily belonged to by default even though she largely eschewed it. They came all dolled up, face-lifted, and bearing absurd baby gifts—from a teeny-weeny tuxedo, to a wee U.S. Marine uniform dripping with medals, to a miniature Harley jacket that reminded Emily of Alex. Predictably, it was all about them and their shopping prowess, not her baby, and pretending to be thankful for their useless gifts felt almost degrading. Later, as the mothers in the group droned on about epidurals, breast feeding, and English nannies, Emily went into a trance, until a furious scream began to build inside her. She slipped away to hide out in Claire's idiotically enormous powder room, where for ten minutes she sobbed uncontrollably. It was then that she realized just how badly she needed to talk to someone.

Her first thought was a shrink, though Charles had been seeing numerous shrinks for years, only to become more entrenched in his personality. Lately he had ceased therapy altogether, not wanting his shrink to know he'd been cuckolded. He was loath to lose face, which struck his wife as defeating the purpose of therapy. Emily craved an immediate ear, not a string of professional appointments, and so when Claire suggested a shopping date for the next day, Emily, desperate to unburden herself, decided that for all her bitchiness, the baroness was actually not a bad choice. She already suspected something and had enough skeletons in her own closet not to judge anyone too harshly when it came to sex-capades. Emily certainly hadn't lugged herself to Bergdorf's, looking like a whale, to shop for clothes.

Claire devoured her various images in the angled mirrors, albeit with a certain grimness. "Shit," she hissed, "my neck's a tea sandwich away from liposuction. Oh, well, I'll take the mermaid costume and starve for a week." While Victor picked up the phone and summoned a seamstress before his rapacious client could change her mind, Claire aimed a lacquered nail at the mountain of designer plunder piled atop the apricot-colored chaise—suits, skirts, blouses, bathing suits, accessories. "And all that stuff, too." She began riffling through a row of formal gowns. "And this one...and this one." She slapped her charge card into Victor's eager palm. "Be a lamb and bill me over three months. If my hubby sees this all on one invoice, he'll croak." Her eyes gleamed impishly. "On second thought, bill me all at once."

The seamstress arrived. Claire got her dresses pinned and changed back into her Valentino street clothes, whereupon the two women rode the escalator down.

Once on the main floor, they were shadowed ever-so-discretely by the trench-coated Vincent, whose marching orders besides guarding Emily were to remain anonymous and invisible. Once outside, Claire suggested they grab lunch up the street at Cipriani's. During the short walk, Emily wondered if the eagle-eyed Claire had any idea they were being tailed.

As soon as she and Claire stepped into the raucous restaurant, Emily had regrets; she wished she had spoken up and suggested another spot. None of the tables afforded the space and comfort her bloated body deserved, nor, more importantly, the privacy she desired. When she asked Sergio for a table away from the action in back, past the bar, Claire was mildly livid.

"Siberia. What a bore," she pouted.

"Indulge a pregnant woman, will you?"

Not even Claire had a retort for that, though once they were unfurling their napkins, she quickly demonstrated her keen powers of observation. "So," she asked, pointing at the distant window just as Vincent was peering in at them, "who's the muscleman following you all around?"

Looking down at the tablecloth, Emily falteringly replied, "My bodyguard."

"You mean, in case your water breaks he can rush you to the hospital?"

"No, *bodyguard* bodyguard." Her stomach leapt as she said it; there was no turning back.

Claire made a little moue, as if the Lukeses were getting above themselves. "I don't quite see why you need a bodyguard. Are you being stalked? Have you been threatened by kidnappers?"

A smiling waiter materialized with menus, and Emily went silent. She waited until he left before leaning toward Claire and saying in an urgent whisper, "Claire, I need to talk. I need to be able to trust you. I mean *really* trust you."

Up shot Claire's penciled eyebrows. "Of course you can trust me, darling. If you can't trust *me*, who can you trust? Bad girls are always more trustworthy than good girls."

Accepting this ironical logic at face value, and relieved to shake off at long last her heavy secret, Emily took a deep breath before launching into the saga of her romantic holocaust. The raw emotion of reliving it was aggravated by constant interruptions from busboys bringing bread and water, waiters taking orders and serving food, and Sergio stopping by to schmooze. Clearly, Cipriani's was the wrong venue for any heartfelt discussion, though Emily patiently took the disruptions in stride and persevered, making sure to include every vital nuance and detail so that the ensuing discussion could be productive. The baroness, for her part, proved to be a model listener, nodding her head in understanding, eyes glistening with compassion at the right moments. Though hardly an empathetic soul, this was a pickle to which she could thoroughly relate. Not until Emily was finished did Claire render her first comment:

"You're not getting divorced over this, I hope," she said, as if the child's paternity were incidental.

"Charles doesn't want a divorce under any circumstances. He'd rather raise the child as his own than be publicly humiliated."

"Jesus, do you ever live a charmed life!" Claire chortled, glancing around the room to make sure no one was straining to listen. "I can't believe Charles wants you back. I mean, compared to what you did to him, I was a great wife! A fucking saint! He must really love you."

"He's terrified to be left alone. He'd have no one left to play to."

"Left alone? Please! Thousands of women would be crawling over themselves like soldier ants to take your place."

Emily didn't know whether to feel relieved or threatened. "He's doing his best to put everything behind us," she said, "but he'll never really forgive me. He'll resent me and the baby forever."

"Every marriage seethes with resentment," Claire tossed off.

After a contemplative silence, Emily came to her main point: "Something tells me my father lied to me about Alex."

Claire slowly rolled her eyes. "Has Alex called or tried to get in touch with you?"

"Not to my knowledge," said Emily sheepishly, "but Charles changed our numbers and hired the bodyguard. And it would be just like my father—being the devout Catholic he is—to threaten the bejesus out of Alex and enforce the Frank Shea Inquisition on him."

"Alex isn't exactly a timid soul, my dear," said Claire, with a world-weary air. "Remember your birthday toast? How he stormed your father's office? Crashed the Ocean Club party? If he wanted to see you, if he was the least bit interested in clearing his name, claiming his baby, asserting his love, believe me, he'd find a way. Take it from a street-smart hussy: He's guilty as sin; a sleazebag. I mean, look at the circumstantial evidence you *do* know: hanging out with Billy, riding a Harley as his only means of transportation, using an alias! Besides which, how else could your father have found out?"

"Billy could have been the blackmailer."

"How utterly sloppy of you, by the way," Claire digressed. "Were you subconsciously trying to get caught?"

"Billy wouldn't need a co-conspirator for that," Emily reasoned, "and we all know about his money problems, the family history. Call me a fool, but I don't believe Alex is capable of stooping to blackmail, or that my own judgment of him could be so far off."

"Hormones and judgment don't mix," advised Claire, smiling over her martini, sticking the plastic saber into her glossy mouth and devouring the olive. "And good con men are impossible to detect until it's too late, which is why they're good. Remember, everyone thought Ted Bundy was charming. Say what you want about your father: he's still Frank Shea. He's been around, seen it all, and in my opinion did you a huge favor by cutting Alex's nuts off before they could inflict more damage."

"Fine, Claire, you're probably right," Emily conceded. "But just suppose for a moment that things aren't what they appear."

Claire leaned forward, placing an earnest claw on Emily's knee in a simulation of sisterhood. "I have this once-stunning girlfriend named Oona, an American, who was married for five years to an older but *très sympathique* English lord. They lived a very respectable life in London and had a baby daughter. While Oona was back in New York visiting her mom, she met this devastating young partner at Goldman Sachs named Chandler. Tall, Yale, old money *and* new money rolled into one—the total package. He followed Oona back to London and pursued her relentlessly. He told her he loved her, begged her to leave her husband, showered her with gifts. The sex was dynamite. He wore her down, until Oona left her husband and brought her daughter back to live with him. A month later he informed her, and I quote, 'You're robbing me of my air space,' whereupon he quit the bank and moved to Santa Fe on some fucking New Age metaphysical pilgrimage. Poor Oona had a life everyone envied and threw it away. Last I saw her she was all haggard, working twelve-hour days in some grunt PR job to make ends meet, shuttling her kid to and from a third-rate school, with no man in her life. If you saw her today, you'd never believe she was once beautiful."

"That's a horrible story, of course, Claire. I know how much you enjoy stories like that."

"My point is, whenever a woman lowers her guard, the man does something hideous. It's a law of nature." Claire twirled linguini around her fork. "I'm no moralist, as you know, but any woman who leaves a rich husband for a lover is a fool and deserves what she gets. Life's been too easy for you, which is probably why you let things get out of hand with Alex de Monk."

"What if he's innocent?" Emily persisted. "What if we're both being deceived?"

"Okay," Claire smiled, "suppose, just for the sake of argument, he *is* innocent. Better to idealize him from afar, because once the novelty and drama wear off, and you come face to face with the humdrum of daily life, and with the fact that you no longer have the lavish homes, the car and driver, the social status, the private jet, he'll repulse you. You'll kick yourself for giving it all up and depriving your child. All marriages eventually sink to the lowest common denominator, so you might as well be practical. Marriage is a business arrangement, a contract. It's about finding security in a tough world and learning to live with disappointment. And, believe me, even a well-meaning Alex would disappoint you. And so would you him. Think about it from his angle: inheriting an instant family under duress when he's been a freewheeling bachelor all his life, failing to give you the life to which you've grown accustomed, forever knowing he isn't measuring up. Eventually he'll blame you; he'll associate you with the death of his family business." Claire downed the last of her martini while Emily sat pensively. "If you're going to be miserable, you might as well be rich. Nobody's making money these days except those who have it already."

As she paused to let her wisdom sink in, Emily's head was spinning from the cynical barrage.

"Anyway," said Claire, "now that Alex is out of your life, I'm sure you won't mind giving his phone number to someone who's in a better position to take advantage of his attributes, who knows how to lay down with scoundrels and end up smelling like a rose." She smiled broadly.

Emily was appalled, speechless.

"Oh, don't look so shocked," Claire frowned. "What better method to test which one of us is right about him, no? Besides," she threw in, with a sadistic gleam, "we already had a little make-out session a few months ago, upstairs at the Frick."

Disgust rippled through Emily; it had all become too much for her. *This* was her reward for spilling her guts? The forces of evil were too ubiquitous for any sort of wholesome aspiration on her part. Maybe Alex and Claire were members of the same reptilian subspecies; maybe they deserved each other. Trembling, unable to do it fast enough, she riffled through her purse for the Post-it with Alex's phone number. Trying to dispose of the whole sordid episode once and for all, she stuffed the crumpled yellow paper into Claire's hand, sorry she had ever confided. "Here, he's all yours."

"I'll report back," Claire said dutifully.

"No! I don't want to hear about it! I'm done!" She tossed her napkin on the table, hauled herself to her feet, and toddled out of the crowded restaurant.

Moments later, as her pockmarked jailer accompanied her home, she felt the walls of her life closing in on her. She had no real friends, no real family. An image came to her mind's eye: she and her tiny son holding hands on a deserted isle.

◆   ◆   ◆

The doorman sent Alex right up without bothering to buzz the apartment. A French-speaking maid in a black dress and a frilly white apron answered the doorbell. She helped Alex off with his wet raincoat and escorted him into the salon, where a fire crackled in a marble hearth and lilac candles sweetened the air. The maid promptly left, closing the painted double doors behind her. As if on cue, the baroness entered from an adjoining room with two tuxedoed toy poodles at her heels. Her smile oozed Euro-poise; she had prepared for his arrival by pinning up her platinum hair in a prim French twist and donning a conservative Chanel suit, as if she were planning to broker a deal. Her vampish rouge and perfume reminded Alex that if all else failed there were always "carnal courtesies" to explore as a last resort.

"Alex de Monk," she gushed, "I'm *so* glad you called! Believe it or not, I was just about to pick up the phone and dial you when the phone rang and, low and behold, *you* were on the other end. Imagine my surprise! Must be a sign." As she kissed the air around each of his ears, her yipping dogs dug into his pant cuffs. "*Silence!*" she snapped at the dogs in French. "*Taisez-vous!*" Either the dogs were disobedient or didn't understand the language, so she leaned over, swept them into her arms, and made for the foyer. "You must excuse my babies," she explained. "They haven't been the same since I took them off the Prozac."

As she disappeared with her little nuisances, Alex looked around the de Lapalisse digs, unable to decide whether the myriad of silks, velvets, and taffetas in peach, scarlet, and saffron harmonized in a way he didn't understand, or simply reflected Claire's penchant for havoc. All those patterns and colors were making his head spin. The décor was pure *Gaiété Parisienne*, with an overabundance of Louis-something antiques and painted wood paneling. For some strange reason, it made him think back fondly on the old beanbag chair in his former bachelor pad. He paused to admire the exotic oil painting of a Moroccan souk over the mantel, when Claire returned with a bottle of champagne and two pinkish Venetian flutes.

"This occasion calls for it!" she declared.

He was in no mood for bubbly, but if humoring Claire meant getting to Emily, then he was willing to get plastered.

She handed him the dewy bottle and set the glasses on an ormolu-encrusted side table. "I need a big, strong man to get the cork out."

The cork popped effortlessly; an arthritic octogenarian could have done the trick. Bubbles spewed onto the Aubusson rug before he could get a glass under them, but the baroness didn't seem the least bit perturbed as she slipped out of her suit jacket and tossed it casually over a pleated pouf. Her azure-blue silk blouse amplified the hue of her eyes; its feathery fabric slid over her pert, lace-clad breasts like a shadow.

"Remember the first time we bumped into each other—at the bottom of Emily's stairs?" she smiled, raising her glass. "Here's to storming the castle, not to mention its sad little queen."

"So," he said, as they clinked crystal, "I guess you know why I'm here."

"I was afraid you'd say that," she said, with a mock pout.

"How is she?" he asked, fearful her answer would crush him.

"Vanessa bet me a hundred bucks she won't drop the baby until after next Wednesday," said Claire, arranging herself artistically on a large settee replete with embroidered pillows. "I say before."

"What's the significance of next Wednesday?"

"It's the day of my lapdog fund-raiser." Seeing his mystified expression, she explained, "It's my 'cause.' Emily has her kiddie project; I have my doggie project. I'm dedicated to restoring the rights of lapdogs to eat with their masters in restaurants, just like they do in Europe."

Was she kidding? "Is my invitation in the mail?"

"Sorry, but Charles is one of my biggest benefactors. He'd never forgive me." She hugged a small, tasseled pillow with a sultry look of yearning and with wagging index finger beckoned him to join her on the settee.

He settled stiffly on the edge, a yard away from her. "Need a piano player for your party?"

"Got it covered."

"If you just happen to call now and invite Emily over, and I just happen to be here..."

"Sorry, darling, it doesn't work that way."

"I thought you had a proclivity for mischief," Alex teased.

"Oh, but I *do*, Alex de Monk. Mischief is my middle name."

Breasts bobbing under her blouse, she rose and sauntered over to an eighteenth-century armoire housing a home entertainment center. She twirled a few buttons and seconds later Edith Piaf was belting out *"Non, Je Ne Regrette Rien"* and transporting them to a Parisian boîte. On her return, she reached up and unpinned her hair, which tumbled in luxuriant waves to her shoulders. "Now that Emily's father has tossed you out on your ear and you've hit bottom," she cooed, gliding onto his startled lap with nymph-like grace, "don't you just ache to be on top again? It's so cold and wet outside. Why don't we order up a nice hot dinner? My husband's off in Scotland, shooting small birds with big guns, so it's just the two of us, I'm afraid. What do you feel like eating? Cajun? Thai? *Moi?*"

"Look, Claire…"

She shushed him with a kiss and draped her arms loosely around his neck. "Don't be a fool. Emily and Charles are ideally suited, both bravely peeking over their piles of money to see what life really looks like. Why don't you concentrate on *me* for a change? Ironically enough, I'm much less trouble. Besides, haven't you wreaked enough havoc in her life?"

"What exactly do you know?" Alex asked.

"Emily told me the whole story," she said, eyes dancing as she caressed his neck. "And the only part where you come out a hero is in bed."

"Did she tell you why she confessed to Charles?"

"Confessed?" Claire laughed.

"Her father and Charles confronted me and told me she confessed."

"Oh, please! Our little mouse would never have done that."

Blood surged; Alex began to shake. "Then who spilled the beans? Not you!"

"I may be many things, but I'm *not* a rat," Claire scowled, her porcelain visage suddenly dark and cloudy. "Besides, I just learned everything yesterday. Anyway, what difference does it make? What's done is done. Face facts, Alex de Monk: rich or poor, you're affair material, not marriage material. Everything turned out for the best. You're better off as my playmate, and Emily is better off with Charles."

"Even if he isn't the father?"

"One lousy sperm should hardly dictate human behavior. That's like the tail wagging the dog."

"Being rich is all that matters, huh?"

"Puh-leeze," Claire drawled. "As if money isn't all you're about. Some gallant knight you proved to be, impregnating Emily and then blackmailing her father when you were about to lose the Cresslon account."

"*What!*" He shook her off his lap. "That's a *lie!*"

"Come now, de Monk, the required denial needn't be so vehement."

"I did nothing of the sort!" he declared. "You don't understand: I *love* Emily!"

Startled by his fury, Claire peered at him in wonder. "Honestly? You *didn't* blackmail her father?"

"Of course not! And according to you, Emily didn't confess. So, how the hell did Shea and Charles find out?"

Claire's eyes shifted back and forth, before regaining their coy composure. "I don't know for sure. I can only make an educated guess."

"Please, Claire, I need to know."

After appearing to give his appeal serious consideration, the baroness broke into a beguiling smile and slid toward him. "That," she whispered, planting the softest of kisses on his lips, "is going to cost you, Alex de Monk."

He took her by the shoulders and treated her to the most succulent French kiss in his arsenal—a tawdry though not altogether unpleasant experience, something he might have relished a year ago.

"Ummmm," she purred. "No wonder Emily got into so much trouble."

He wrapped her in his arms and kissed her again. "How did they find out?" he whispered, grinding his body into hers, moving his lips to her neck, while her legs slowly parted.

"Who had the most to gain, and nothing to lose?" she said breathlessly, reclining back and unbuttoning her blouse. "Follow the money. Isn't that what they always say in murder mysteries?"

Alex's mind went momentarily blank. Then, like a laser, the realization smacked him right between the eyes. "Billy?"

"Elementary, dear Sherlock," Claire said, sliding out of her blouse and bra and reaching for him.

Alex dodged her and shot to his feet. "How did Billy find out?"

"Apparently he got a sneak peak at some kinky love drawing of you. Which is more than I'm getting," she bristled. "I advised Emily that she was well rid of you, though she did say you were wonderful in the fucking department."

"I doubt she was that crass," said Alex, sick to think of Emily being under the influence of this harpy.

Beckoning with both arms and both breasts, the inexorable baroness launched a final forward pass: "I may be crass, darling, but if you're unemployed I've got one hell of an opening for you."

Alex blew into the foyer, where he was viciously attacked by the two toy poodles. "Sic 'im, Basil! Sic 'im, Babette!" he heard Claire call out from the living room. He had to practically kick the canines off his ankles just to get into the elevator without them.

Moments later he was standing out in the sleet on Park Avenue, too frenzied to go back and retrieve his forgotten overcoat. After five wet, frantic minutes of trying to find a free taxi, he dashed over to Lexington and descended into the bowels of the subway. He took the Number 6 going downtown and changed to the L at Union Square. After a slippery three-block sprint to Billy's club, he rocketed past a sign that read "Hard Hat Party Tomorrow." Wired, or whatever the End of the World was to be renamed, was more than half-renovated, with black marble, smoked glass, and scaffolding. Some workmen were just leaving, and with Billy nowhere to be seen, Alex dashed up the stairs to his private quarters. The clomping on the stairs brought Billy out of his newly furnished ultra-modern digs.

"Hey, buddy!" Billy cried, opening his arms for a hug, only to get a hard fist to the jaw. The punch staggered him back into the room.

Alex, completely rain-soaked, kept advancing until Billy tripped over a fancy ottoman and went sprawling. "German investor, huh! Who, you slimy little worm? The Baron von Shea?"

Scrambling on all fours to his desk, Billy rose and seized a letter opener, waving it in menacing desperation. "Christ, Alex! You were humping the billionaire's wife, the boss man's daughter! Did you really think you could get away with it?"

Figuring that if Warren Buffetino and Bill Gateseroni couldn't beat any sense into him, then there was no use in him trying, Alex shouted, "*When you were going fucking crazy in prison, who was there? Who came to see you? Who gave a fuck? Charles? Shea? Who gave you money when you were down and out? Who was there for you, Billy?*"

"Alex, c'mon, you…you've always been my *real* brother, right? *Right?*" Billy flashed Alex his most winning smile. "I never meant to…you know I've been in a hard place, right? People wanted to kill me, man, they really wanted to *kill* me!"

"I don't blame them."

"Alex! Sahib!" Billy put his arms out wide, an appeal for letting bygones be bygones. "I'll cut you in on the profits. We'll be partners. Aren't you broke? Don't you need the money?"

But Alex was out the door, leaving Billy ranting.

"You didn't really think she was going to leave the richest man in the fucking world for *you*! Did you? Well, *did you?*"

16

Curtains

"She gets too hungry for dinner at eight," warbled Charles merrily, as if the previous year had been a mere bad dream. "She likes the theatre but never comes late...." His labored impersonation of Ol' Blue Eyes, as they dressed for Claire's lapdog party, made Emily want to hurl a vase at him. His crooning had charmed her during their courtship, but over the course of their marriage it had come to epitomize his shallowness. What irked her most was his behavior of late: carrying on like a stereotypical expectant father, putting the last finicky touches on the nursery, ordering boxes of Havana cigars from his tobacconist in Geneva for the big event, showering her with affection as if nothing awful had ever transpired. It was psychotic; she preferred his former sarcasm, which at least she could trust. One thing hadn't changed: After a brief tapering off, Charles was back to his magnum-a-day alcohol regime, though he cheerfully ascribed his puffy face and weight gain to a sympathetic pregnancy.

Her camel-colored cashmere dress was the most elegant thing in her closet that still fit her, but it felt like a potato sack as she slipped it over her head and braced for a formal gala that she knew would be populated by slender glamour cats in filmy gowns. Tired of lugging herself around, she couldn't wait to give birth, sure that even the worst postpartum depression would be an improvement over her current marital numbness or the grief she felt whenever she thought about Alex's callow betrayal.

"That's why the lady...that's why the lady...that is why the lady is a traaaaamp." Charles looked at her expectantly.

"What a ridiculous premise for a party," she said. "Lapdog rights, when there's a war going on?"

Charles put his champagne glass down on the table to pour himself into his tuxedo jacket. "We're benefactors, my sweet."

"We don't even own a lapdog."

"Vincent sort of looks like a pug—on steroids."

"You're not actually bringing him! People will think…"

"That my wife's about to give birth, and that I spare no expense for her well-being," Charles explained. "Besides, I actually sort of enjoy having a bodyguard. It gives me a certain Mafioso mystique, no?"

It never ceased to amaze her how Charles could live day after day in such flagrant denial, so adeptly compartmentalizing reality. She feared that the longer he kept it up, the worse the inevitable blow-up would be when it came. She eyed her bloated body in the mirror with dismay. "I look like a cow."

"Those topaz earrings I bought you last year will go perfectly with what you're wearing," Charles said, and as usual about such matters he was on the money. "They'll spruce you up."

"What about a bell around my neck?"

"It's good for us to go out. I've been feeling cooped up like a bird, and you may not get another chance for a while." He gave her belly a pat. "I'll be downstairs."

Charles disappeared and Emily resumed applying makeup. Moments later, on her way to the safe to retrieve the topaz earrings, she heard a knock on the door.

"Come in," she called out.

It was Riggs, who edged into the room and announced, "Mr. Lukes requested that I bring him his pearl studs."

"Come," she said, "I was just about to open the safe."

She led Riggs into Charles's private closet and unlocked the safe, only to discover Charles's pistol. The sight of the weapon made her blood run cold. Quickly she retrieved her earrings and Charles's studs. Ever so gingerly, she pulled the pistol out and handed it to Riggs.

"Please get rid of this," she said. "I don't want it in the house."

Riggs gave the pistol a cursory examination. "It's capped, ma'am."

"Capped? What does that mean?"

"It's a prop gun. Perfectly harmless." Riggs put the barrel to his head and pulled the trigger a couple of times. *Click…click…*

Suddenly she felt like laughing. Charles had put her through all that trauma with a prop gun! How fitting it was.

Sensing Emily's displeasure on the elevator ride to the lobby, Charles asked her what was wrong, but she simply muttered, "Nothing," and turned away. What was the use of getting all lathered up about the prop gun with a public appearance looming in a few minutes? She had no energy for an argument. It could wait until tomorrow, or next week, or never, for that matter. Nothing about her situation had really changed. She would still be his wife for the foresee-able future. It wasn't as if her respect for him had plummeted all that much.

Vincent was waiting outside, poised to open the limousine door, clad in a badly cut monkey suit and a blue ruffled shirt. He might have blended in at a cocktail lounge on the Jersey Shore but not at the de Lapalisse soirée. Once the car began moving, Emily raised the glass privacy screen so that the driver and Vincent couldn't hear.

"It's idiotic to bring Vincent to the party," she said.

"We can feed him to one of the hungrier females."

"If Alex hasn't tried anything by now…"

"I find it in very poor taste for you to mention that insect by name," Charles said sharply. "I thought we'd settled that. He's capable of anything. And so is Claire."

She hadn't meant to bring Alex up so indelicately. "Couldn't you at least have found Vincent a white shirt?" she deflected, and they fell silent until the limousine pulled up to the awning of the baron's and baroness's apartment building.

Even the lapdogs, she rued on the crowded elevator ride up, were more elegantly dressed than she was. Once inside the apartment, she relinquished her sable coat to a servant. Hearing piano music, she immediately stepped into the living room to see if Claire had a devilish surprise in store. She was relieved, but also disappointed, that the piano player was a wavy-haired silver fox playing an unbelievably white version of Marvin Gaye's "What's Goin' On?"

Taking in the apartment's ostentatious décor with an amused cocked eyebrow, Charles remarked, "Not bad, if you like whorehouses. Don't you agree, my dear?"

"Claire and I appreciate Paris for different reasons," she said, realizing too late that she should have insisted Charles attend the party alone. She had no desire to face Claire's guests, all of them so dressed to kill and primed for prattle. Accompanied by their high-strung lapdogs, they buzzed with a vivacity that normally eluded this set, enlivened by the sheer novelty of the occasion. To fail at bubbling was to be conspicuous, but she was conspicuous anyway, and her body felt too cumbersome to fake it. She glanced around for a straight-backed chair.

Claire, effervescing in sequins and accessorized by poodles, was busily posing for *Women's Wear* and showing off her new apartment. "The baron gave me an unlimited budget, and I exceeded it," she quipped frequently, gliding from guest to guest, dog to dog. The doggie hors d'oeuvres being circulated on silver trays incited some rapacious tussling and growling. Emily found a reasonably sturdy velvet love seat, only to balk when she saw it occupied by a short-haired miniature dachshund, adorned in a pearl necklace and stretched out on its back like a sunbather, pink nipples uppermost. She was about to look elsewhere when Charles unceremoniously shoved the animal to the floor. Emily sat and tried to make amends with the grumpy wiener dog, scratching its head and neck. Vincent milled behind the love seat some ten feet away and tried unsuccessfully to blend in, while Charles snatched two champagne flutes off a passing tray and offered one to her.

"I'm pregnant," she scowled, whereupon Charles guzzled down one flute-full and pranced off with the other to the bar to fetch his wife her usual glass of Evian.

The evening went from merely unpleasant to Kafkaesque when she spotted, to her shock, her father glad-handing his way through the crowd. The Frank Shea she knew would never be caught dead at such a ludicrous occasion. When Oxana emerged from behind a pillar and glided over to his side, she felt outraged, but also embarrassed for him. After spending a lifetime cultivating his reputation, didn't he realize how absurd he looked with a girl a third his age? Did he honestly believe he could pass her off as a business associate? Or that his plastic surgery fooled anyone? Was it hubris, or did this Slavic vulture have her talons deeply into him? Had he not considered the possibility that his pregnant daughter might be present at her friend's party? He was normally discreet at least, if not courteous or kind. Emily watched her father in the Russian's clutches and seethed. Like a schoolgirl with her favorite stuffed animal, Oxana hugged a fluffy white Bichon Frisé against her bosom. If Frank Shea was mortified to stumble across his daughter, he concealed it with the broadest of smiles.

"Emily!" he boomed, striding toward her. "I figured you'd be home tonight, resting up for the big event."

"I'm sure you did," she said, as Oxana traipsed over to join them.

"Oxana loves small dogs, so I thought I'd bring her along," said her father, as if hers was the only presence that required some explanation.

"When are you due?" asked the model in a curt monotone.

"Oh, I'm ready to explode at any moment," Emily said with a withering smile.

With nowhere to go from there, her father and his towering trollop resumed their circuit of the party. Charles returned with her Evian just as the baroness tapped her glass with a spoon to silence the party and then began addressing her guests.

"In this age of world political activism," Claire began in a fake, flute-like voice, causing the head-cocking of some of the tiny canines, "we demand justice for the disenfranchised, the dispossessed, the huddled masses yearning for basic rights. Society is best measured by how it treats its defenseless. And yet in our great beacon of freedom, New York City, we turn our backs on our most defenseless yet most loyal friends: our beloved lapdogs. I know you all agree with me that the banning of lapdogs from New York City restaurants is utterly deplorable and inhumane, not to mention anal. It's a crime against decency." A few random cynics were still murmuring amongst themselves; Claire stared at them like a hawk until they were shamefully subdued. "That is why I say to Mayor Bloomberg: Lift your silly and provincial ban. If our furry friends are welcome in the finest restaurants of Paris and Rome, cities which are the very paragons of culture and sophistication, isn't it our moral and civic duty to follow suit? And if I can give *les petits chiens* the run of my own newly decorated apartment," the baroness gaily told her audience, "then shouldn't Le Cirque, Ciprianis, and La Goulue be just as gracious?"

During Claire's speech, Emily's attentions drifted. Try as she might, she couldn't identify one couple at the party she considered truly happy, or whose relationship she admired. Maybe Claire was right to define love as fleeting, an illusion certain to crumble; and marriage as a business arrangement. Maybe her own expectations for romantic fulfillment were naïve and unrealistic. Wasn't she a spoiled fool not to be grateful for the embarrassment of riches and social status she had with Charles, which so many women coveted? She could find other ways to fulfill her physical and emotional needs: facials, massages, yoga…. Painting would be difficult to sustain; it would forever remind Charles of her erotic period and her drawing of Alex. But he couldn't take away her baby. She would always love her baby, and hopefully raise it with better values.

A newly pressed tuxedo and suave demeanor were all Alex needed to breeze uninvited through the staid Park Avenue lobby and into the elevator. Looking the part had never been his problem. Deep inside his chest, however, like a small, expanding balloon, was a sense of impending doom. In an effort to calm himself, he took several long breaths. The cabin delivered him directly to the gilded foyer of the de Lapalisse apartment, where he slipped into the party unnoticed.

Dozens of wriggling lapdogs, as stylishly adorned and high-strung as their owners, lent a surrealistic quality to the venue. The resemblances between dogs and owners were uncanny: An ivory-skinned woman in a pink bow and diamond choker fed puff pastry to her pale yellow Chihuahua, also sporting a pink bow and diamond choker. A plump dowager gazed lovingly at her equally plump pug, whose snout was buried in a plate of caviar. A gaunt, graying gentleman shared a prawn with his similarly gaunt miniature greyhound.

Claire, bejeweled and bepoodled, was in the throes of a speech, telling her audience that the legal crusade to overturn the city ordinance barring lapdogs from restaurants would require significant funding. The well-groomed guests looked bored but amenable to this unabashed plea for money, as they always did on such occasions. Alex had witnessed similar apathetic acquiescence at gatherings ranging from benefits for beautifying Central Park to fundraisers for cancer research, and oddly enough Claire's lapdog cause seemed to enjoy the same stature as any other. All the usual chic suspects were there, as well as a couple of reporters and a *Women's Wear* photographer, camera flashing.

Peeking around a puffed silk sleeve as if it were a duck blind, he searched among the glittery crowd for Emily. When he caught a glimpse of her sitting down, his heart went haywire, though through the swarm of socialites he couldn't get a good look at her face. What he did see stiffened his spine: Flanking her like sentinels were Charles and the bodyguard. Alex hadn't expected the bodyguard to be present at such an occasion. Apparently Charles wasn't taking any chances. The goon looked like a heavyweight wrestler and was probably packing heat, though Alex was more afraid of what Emily might say or do when she saw him.

Claire ended her speech by proclaiming, "My lapdogs are staying where they belong—on my lap!" After some mild applause and a few forced cheers—along with a couple of doggie yips—she invited the assemblage to the dining room, from which issued the tantalizing aroma of curry and the gleam of silver trays and flickering candles.

Alex watched Charles help his wife to her feet and usher her to the head of the buffet line, followed by their human pit bull. The defenses around her were formidable. He had obviously not thought this through, but he had come too far to retreat and was willing to bet that Charles was too much a slave to appearances to risk a scene. Clearly, he wasn't going to get all the answers he sought, but he was confident that Emily's eyes would reveal something. They couldn't lie to him, even if they tried.

He wove his way in her direction, hoping not to be spotted by anyone he knew. When he glanced across the room and saw Frank Shea and Oxana, standing beside the same settee on which he had kissed the truth out of Claire days ago, his stomach leapt and he remembered the restraining order. Technically he was breaking the law, though right now that was the least of his worries. Darting out of their view and edging through the crowd, he overheard a female guest fervently compliment the baroness on her new apartment ("Sensational, darling, absolutely sensational!"), then shortly thereafter ridicule it behind Claire's plunging bare back ("God, how tacky! Who does she think she is?"). It was true that the place had been overzealously decorated, and as Alex, tiptoeing around a tiny pile of nature's call, got to the dining room, his eyes were treated to the most ostentatious touch of all: gargantuan strawberry taffeta curtains, swooping down from their lofty valances like 1980s haute couture ball gowns.

"Those draperies!" gushed an anorexic dowager, spooning a dollop of curry onto a tiny portion of rice. "They're spectacular!"

"Aren't they?" the hostess preened, unaware of the party crasher in their midst. "They were handmade for me in France. You simply can't get workmanship of that quality over here." She hauled her two poodles to attention and threw a radiant smile at the *Women's Wear* reporter and his cocked camera. "Isn't it fabulous, all this publicity!"

"Fabulous!" echoed the bony guest, as the flash went off.

But the baroness wasn't looking at her; she was looking at *Women's Wear* and saying quotably and rather too loudly, "I believe in picking one cause and really making a difference, instead of spreading myself thin on the charity circuit. What I love about this cause is that it forces us to take a cold, hard look at our own society."

As Alex neared the buffet and finally got an unobstructed look at Emily, he was shocked by the size of her belly. How she had ballooned since his distant sighting of her a month ago! She looked as if she might give birth at any moment. Realizing that any approach tonight would be imperfect, that surprise was the best and only tactic, he did his best to calm his nerves with a deep breath, but that proved futile. With no presence of mind, he stepped into her path just as she was turning to leave the buffet, her plate piled high.

When she saw him, she gasped and went pale; but before either of them could speak, her vigilant husband had snaked one arm around her waist and was shepherding her away. As he went past, Charles tossed Alex one of his iciest smiles. "Your persistence might be amusing were it not so incredibly pathetic," he murmured. The coiled-nerved Alex had a notion to shove him, but before he could, Charles skidded on the same doggie dropping Alex had avoided moments ago and went flying. He managed to catch his balance, but only at the expense of his plate, which flew out of his hand and overturned on the Aubusson rug.

"*Jesus Christ!*" shrieked Claire, completely forgetting herself as lapdogs scrambled for curried lamb. She whirled on Alex. "What the hell are *you* doing here? You weren't invited!"

Charles snapped his fingers, and in a flash his bodyguard had seized Alex's arm and was muscling him away from the buffet. Alex was no match for this neckless brute, and common sense told him to go quietly. But as he was being dragged ingloriously past the wide-eyed Emily, he blindly went for broke, swinging around with his free hand and punching the unsuspecting Vincent squarely in the nose. The crack of cartilage afforded Alex momentary satisfaction as Godzilla howled and released his grip. A second later, Alex ducked a massive fist as it whistled past his ear. He panicked, and with all his pent-up passion tackled his tormenter and slammed him into the silken wall. An enormous Lalique vase filled with white lilies toppled off its pedestal and shattered; a Matisse print was dislodged by the impact and trampled by guests fleeing for safety. Amid the bedlam of crashing bodies and barking dogs, *Women's Wear* flashed pictures.

"*Stop* them! Somebody call the *police!*" screamed the hostess.

Nobody wanted help to come to the rescue more than Alex, whose advantage was already fading. For a split second he glanced around desperately for help, but the onlookers seemed concerned only with the violence wreaked on the décor. Fueled by righteous indignation and terror, he threw a flurry of harmless punches, only to feel his jacket rip as Charles's surrogate heaved him like a rag doll into a mahogany Regency sideboard. This was followed by a savage forearm uppercut that turned Alex completely around and sent him flying face-first into the lavishly laden buffet table. As Alex whipped back around to defend himself, he took a blow to the ribs and felt them crack, but he was too immersed in the fight to feel pain; he was prepared to fight to his dying breath. With a war cry that temporarily paralyzed Vincent, as well as everyone else at the party, he seized a silver tureen and flung its contents into his foe's face, dousing the rug and furniture in the process with a curried goo of carrots, peas, and lamb. The rice bowl was next, followed by the condiments, until Vincent, blinded by buffet, was forced into retreat.

Alex, frothing, spotted Emily in the living room. Her look of distress drew him toward her, until he was yanked backward by his collar. The first punch cracked his cheek, drenching him in pain. Alex threw up his hands, but Vincent's ham-sized fists slammed right through them, battering his face over and over, with the final almighty blow sending him sprawling into strawberry taffeta. As he clawed at the curtains for support, down they came, along with their massive brass rod. The next thing he was aware of was Claire looming over him; the irate baroness delivered the coup de grâce, smashing a champagne flute on his head.

Blanketed in yards of taffeta and bits of shattered crystal, his head aching and his vision blurred, Alex tried to rise, but the heavy curtain rod and a sharp stab in his ribs immobilized him. Blood was pouring from his lower lip and down the front of his pleated shirt. An eye was puffing closed; a tooth wobbled; his face felt distorted beyond recognition, like a Picasso.

The guests closed around him, twittering and clucking in mock concern now that the battle was over. A flash went off in his face.

Charles, having just returned from calling the cops and retrieving Emily's coat, was nudging her toward the elevator. "I think now might be the appropriate time to leave," he said, "before the Mounties arrive."

"You hired a hit man," she cried, "not a bodyguard!"

"Don't be ridiculous. He did his job, and bloody well, too. Halaby attacked me. You never told me he had a violent streak."

"He didn't touch you! You slipped on a dog turd!" Before Emily could make sense of what was happening, she felt a sharp cramp. "Oh, God," she moaned, doubling over as much as a woman in her condition could, "this is it."

"Good grief, Emmy. You about to foal?" As cool as a cucumber at an afternoon tea party, Charles guided his wife in the direction of the elevator, suddenly joined by her father and the rumpled Vincent. Halfway there, the elevator doors opened and out stepped two policemen, a male and a female.

"In the dining room," said Frank Shea, pointing the way.

"That deranged intruder on the floor over there," Charles added, abandoning his laboring wife long enough to escort the cops to the carnage. "He just started wrecking everything. I think he may be on drugs."

"No…" Emily whimpered, but the cops blew right past her, handcuffs out and ready. She took a few reeling steps toward the dining room before her father seized her arm; but by then, someone had commandeered the elevator and they were forced to wait for it, to Frank Shea's supreme irritation. He kept hitting the call button, cursing under his breath.

Seconds later, the crowd in the dining room parted, and the police began dragging Alex in their direction, followed closely by the seething baroness, who suddenly let out a shriek that stopped everyone cold. Heads turned in her direction. Her trembling finger was pointing at a huge wet spot on her Aubusson, directly under Emily's feet.

"Just consider it a Lukes baptism," said Charles brightly, holding his wife's sable up around her shoulders. "All righty everybody, we're off to the hospital," he announced. "Thank goodness I remembered my Cubans tonight!"

"Emily," Alex panted, "don't believe anything…"

He was drowned out as Shea, Charles, and Vincent herded Emily into the elevator. Hemmed in by them, she was too overwhelmed to think. The doors started to close, only to lurch back open as the cops dragged Alex in after them.

"Get him out of here," Shea ordered the cops. When they ignored him, he glared at Alex. "If anything happens to this baby…"

"If anything happens to my baby," Alex panted, spitting blood, "I'll kill you!"

"You hear that?" Shea thundered at the cops. "He threatened to kill me! I want that lunatic locked up!"

"Emily," Alex wheezed, "I never blackmailed…"

"Liar!" bellowed Charles, using his body to block him from her view while the cops tightened their grip on their prisoner. Smothered and confused, Emily couldn't understand why Alex was doing this, burning every possible bridge in Manhattan. Had he completely taken leave of his senses? On the other hand, was this all-out display the act of an underhanded blackmailer? She didn't know what to think as Charles smugly recited to Alex the list of charges that would be leveled against him: "Assault, destruction of property, violating a restraining order. All caught on camera, in front of slews of witnesses. You're finished, asshole."

"Finished," echoed her streetwise father.

The two cops smirked at each other, as if it became abundantly clear, even to them, that they had picked the wrong elevator in which to transport their prisoner. When the door opened onto the lobby, the party people were spilling down the back stairs, led by the *Women's Wear* photographer. They and curious passersby swarmed like locusts as Emily was swept outside by her retinue and hustled toward their idling limousine. Right behind her, New York's finest dragged their manacled captive in the opposite direction toward a flashing police car.

With one leg in the limousine and one leg out, and with Charles pushing her, an unbearable suffocating sensation took possession of Emily. Everything was all wrong. Her baby was about to make its dramatic passage from darkness to light, to embark on the adventure of life, and here she was being pushed around against her will like a dead person! It was not Alex's job to save her; only she could do that. And this would be her last chance for a very long time.

"Charles, stop," she pleaded. He kept right on shoving, so she screamed at the top of her lungs: "*Stop!*" She hauled herself out of the limo and ripped her arm from his grasp, exertions that caused not a little pain. With determination she pushed through the crowd, brushed past her astonished father, and wrapped her arms around Alex. "I'm going with him," she told the police, looping her arm through Alex's cuffed wrists and staging her own sit-in. "Either I have my baby at the hospital or at your police station. It's up to you."

"What the hell's goin' on, ma'am?" asked the baffled male cop.

"He's the father of this baby, and I love him!" she declared, nuzzling Alex. "And I'm in labor—now!" For a moment the entire borough of Manhattan

seemed to go silent. She kissed his puffy eye amid incredulous gasps and a veritable light show of flashes. Through his mauled face, Alex grinned at her as if she
had just handed him the key to paradise.

"Emily, this has gone far enough," came Charles's last-ditch bluff. "I know we
had that little tiff earlier, but isn't this taking things too far?" His attempt at a
smile made his face clownish.

"I'm sorry, *I'm* the guilty one, you did nothing wrong," she announced, making sure the reporters heard her. She was concerned with saving Charles's face,
figuring that that was what mattered most to him; but it also felt cathartic. "You
didn't fail me, I failed you. You're well rid of me."

"You're not getting one thin dime out of me!" Charles warned through clenched
teeth.

"Don't worry, Charles," she said, "I don't want anything from you."

"You little idiot!" Charles exploded, as the baroness materialized at his side in
a show of solidarity. "He's nothing but an out-of-work pantyhose salesman! He
can't support you! He's broke!"

This was one of those unusual occasions when Frank Shea was best served by
shunning the limelight, and whatever ire he may have felt seemed to give way to
pragmatism and damage control. With all the attention squarely on Emily and
Alex, he reached out from his unassuming position in the crowd and dragged
Charles off before he could further embarrass himself. Snatching the sulking
Oxana on the way, he hailed a taxi, stuffed them both inside, and slammed the
door before turning toward Emily. His gaze met his daughter's squarely for a
moment, in a way they never had before, as two formidable presences. Whatever
he was thinking, she didn't care; for the first time in her life she felt completely
free of him. Before she could savor the milestone, her father, like a fresh carcass,
was descended on by a pack of media hyenas.

"Mr. Shea," asked a reporter, shoving a mike into his blinking face and beginning the fusillade of questions, "what about your daughter? Are you disowning
her?"

"How do you feel about her behavior?"

"Do you support her decision?"

He was trapped. Curious as Emily was to see his Houdini act, she and Alex
were suddenly whisked off by the cops to the patrol car. Maneuvering into the
vehicle proved difficult for both of them, with her contractions and his broken
ribs. Once they were inside, the door closed and all went quiet. They gazed at
each other in amazement.

"Which hospital?" barked the policewoman from the front seat.

"Lenox Hill," Emily said. "Please hurry."

As the patrol car pulled away from the curb, Alex murmured, "Guess you're stuck with me now."

Through the rear window, Emily looked back one last time at the crowd of well-dressed people, watching them grow smaller and smaller. Despite the daunting challenges and uncertainty ahead, she couldn't remember ever feeling so free, liberated by her own show of courage. "There's no turning back now," she said, with a fatalistic shrug. They rode for a block in silence. "Where will we live?" she asked.

"We've only been together two minutes," Alex laughed, as piercing pain shot through his ribs. "Please, don't worry, I'll figure something out."

"I know you will," she soothed.

"We're starting out dirt poor," he warned. "My company's going under."

"I know, but I don't care. I love you. It'll be an adventure. We'll do great things, won't we?"

Alex's ringing cell phone preempted the reassuring answer she was seeking. Emily was mystified when he, in obvious pain, thrust his handcuffed wrists toward the female cop riding shotgun and asked for dispensation. Had she hitched her wagon to an incurable cell phone addict? Of all times to answer a call! What could possibly be more important than *this!* Loath to start things off as a nag, however, she stifled herself as the cop unlocked his handcuffs just in time.

"Hello?" Alex huffed into the phone. For the next minute or so he listened attentively, speaking only in occasional punctuations. "Umm hmm … fine … sure … okay … I'll get back to you.…See you later, Dad."

As soon as he hung up, Emily could no longer restrain her displeasure. "You don't see fit to say anything about this to your *father?* How *odd!*"

"That was *your* father."

"*Mine?*"

"Yeah, yours."

"Why did he call? What does he want?"

"To come by the hospital tomorrow and see his grandson."

"No! I don't want him anywhere near me or my baby!"

"Is that any way to treat my new business partner?" said Alex, with a stunned expression.

"What?"

"Your father cried 'Uncle.'"

"What do you mean? What did he say?"

"Something about not wanting the F-word to stand for 'father.' God," Alex giggled, "*my* father won't believe this."

"Do you really want to do business with Frank Shea, after all his lies?"

"I got him right where I want him—thanks to you. Besides, I believe in redemption. If any two people should, it's us, right?"

With a sigh, she nestled her head into his chest, deciding to let everything go for now.

"Think you can stand being married to a pantyhose mogul?" Alex asked, his tone more tongue-in-cheek than irrevocable.

"Christ, I hate pantyhose!" muttered the female cop.

"So duz my wife," her partner threw in. "Hey, remember the bank robber we caught last year who was wearin' one over his head?"

Emily and Alex groaned in unison as the police car rumbled over a pothole.

978-0-595-67631-6
0-595-67631-6

Printed in the United States
56582LVS00003B/179

9 780595 676316